Yours Cheerfully

Also by AJ Pearce

Dear Mrs Bird

AJ PEARCE

PICADOR

First published 2021 by Picador
an imprint of Pan Macmillan
The Smithson, 6 Briset Street, London EC1M 5NR
EU representative: Macmillan Publishers Ireland Ltd, Mallard Lodge, Lansdowne
Village, Dublin 4
Associated companies throughout the world
www.panmacmillan.com

ISBN 978-1-5098-5394-6 HB
ISBN 978-1-5098-5395-3 TPB

The advertisement on page 68, 'War Workers Stay Womanly',
is a slightly modified version of an actual advertisement by the
Ministry of Labour published in *Woman* magazine, 27 September 1941.
The lyrics 'All stick together, birds of a feather' on page 42 are from the song
'We Must All Stick Together' (1939) by Ralph Butler and R. Wallace,
recorded by Billy Cotton and His Band. The song on page 290 is by the author,
to the tune of 'Don't Dilly Dally (My Old Man)' aka 'My Old Man' aka
'My Old Man Said Follow The Van' by Charles Collins / Fred W. Leigh, with
part of the chorus on page 317. The drawing on page 82 is by Elliot Jaffar.

1 3 5 7 9 8 6 4 2

A CIP catalogue record for this book is available from the British Library.

Typeset in Plantin MT Std by
Palimpsest Book Production Ltd, Falkirk, Stirlingshire
Printed and bound by CPI Group (UK) Ltd, Croydon, CR0 4YY

Visit **www.picador.com** to read more about all our books
and to buy them. You will also find features, author interviews and
news of any author events, and you can sign up for e-newsletters
so that you're always first to hear about our new releases.

For my friends.
The heart and soul of Emmy and Bunty.

Congratulations

Letter to *Woman* magazine, 12 September 1942

May I congratulate all married women who are at present doing war work as well as running their own homes?

At present my wife and child are away from home, and every evening on returning from work I face washing, cooking, scrubbing, sweeping, and all the other household jobs which are normally my wife's province. In my splendid isolation I marvel at the spirit of those astonishing women who can do all their household duties week after week, plus war work, and still look fresh and cheerful.

Truly, never has so much been done by so many for so little appreciation. —*J. L. (Sydenham)*

London

Late May 1941

As Mr Collins called a start to the *Woman's Friend* editorial meeting, to anyone watching, it was a perfectly normal Monday morning affair. Kathleen had handed out the agenda, each member of staff had a folder full of their notes, and as usual, Mrs Bussell had brought teas up to the fifth floor despite the stairs playing havoc with her unpredictable leg.

'Might I ask, why are you all staring?' said Mr Collins. He looked down at his waistcoat. 'Do I have something on my tie? I haven't seen a fried egg in weeks.'

The entire *Woman's Friend* team burst into applause.

'Congratulations!' said Kathleen and I at the same time.

'Hurrah!' cried Mr Newton, as if Hitler had just taken a knock.

Mr Collins continued to look baffled. 'Hello?' he said, as if he was struggling with a disappointing telephone connection.

Mrs Mahoney patted his arm, fondly. 'Well done,' she said. 'We're all ever so pleased.'

'Lovely news,' said Mr Brand in his quiet voice.

Mr Collins looked none the wiser.

'About becoming our new Editor,' I prompted.

'Ah, that,' he said, looking embarrassed. 'Well, yes.

3

Thank you, everyone. Bit of a turn up. Didn't think it was my bag.'

'Now you're just being daft,' said Mrs Mahoney. 'With respect,' she added quickly, remembering Mr Collins' new Very Senior Role.

'None needed,' he replied quite happily. 'Nothing will change. Mrs Bird was hardly ever in the office, so you probably won't notice a difference. On the other hand, I hope, perhaps some.'

He paused and gave me A Look. It was only the third day of my probation, after all.

'So far, so good,' he smiled. 'Plenty of time for a catastrophe, of course. Don't worry, Mr Newton, I was only joking.'

Mr Newton, our Advertising Manager, had gone pale. He was very good at his job but did tend to look on the disastrous side of life.

I felt myself flush. My first six months in magazine publishing had not gone entirely to plan, due to what my mother had called Some Unfortunate Hiccups That Couldn't Be Helped. It was very nice of her to put it that way, but not wholly true, as my father had remarked at the time.

'I don't wish to be unkind, Elizabeth,' he'd said to her. 'But I think Mrs Bird could be of the opinion that the Unfortunate Hiccup might actually be Emmy, herself.'

He did have a point.

Mrs Henrietta Bird had been *Woman's Friend*'s longest-serving agony aunt and Acting Editress, and as the new Junior, part of my job had been to open readers' letters so that she could answer their problems. It had sounded straightforward enough, but I had struggled to come to terms with Mrs Bird's approach to giving advice, which was slightly in the manner of Attila the Hun. It didn't matter that since the start of the war many of our readers had been through the most dreadful time; kindness was rarely her first port of call.

It was fair to say that Mrs Bird and I had not exactly got on.

Mr Collins, on the other hand, had been terrifically decent all round, and I was delighted he would now be in charge.

'Thank you for your kind words,' he said. 'While I promise I will do my very best to give the Editor job a good bash, I'm afraid we do have a slight problem now that Mrs Bird has left us to join *Livestock and Pet.*'

The celebratory atmosphere disappeared in a flash. The threat of a blank page was unthinkable. But Mr Collins was reassuringly calm.

'Clearly,' he continued, 'we need a new "Henrietta Helps". I realise it is urgent, but perhaps we should take the opportunity to try to find someone who doesn't actively terrify the readers.'

Everyone nodded their heads.

I said 'Absolutely,' and Kathleen joined in with, 'Too right,' and then Mr Newton used the moment to say, 'There is a war on,' in a grave voice, as if some of us had not yet cottoned on.

'I've looked at trying to take someone from one of the other magazines,' said Mr Collins. 'But frankly, we can't afford them, so I'd like to know who you think could do the job. Perhaps one of our existing contributors? Nurse McClay, for example.'

Nurse McClay was in charge of the *Woman's Friend* 'Mother and Baby Club', and took a similar approach to Mrs Bird, only with a syringe.

'She's awfully busy with her baby advice,' said Kathleen.

'And she puts the fear of God into the mothers,' said Mrs Mahoney, less diplomatically.

Kath nodded. 'That's true,' she said. 'Nurse McClay once told me that after the age of five, people are either quite sensible or absolute idiots. If you haven't sorted them out by then, there's nothing more you can do about it, so you might as well just leave them by the side of a road.'

'Good grief,' said Mr Collins. 'Perhaps *Livestock and Pet* could do with a nurse.'

'Mrs Croft is very nice,' said Mr Brand of our cookery editor. 'Although "What's In The Hotpot?" does take up her time.'

'And her husband's not very well,' said Kath. 'So she's struggling as it is.'

'Well, we certainly don't want to add to that,' said Mr Collins. For someone who always said he understood books far better than people, he was secretly enormously sympathetic at heart.

'I'm sure we can find a new advice lady,' said Mrs Mahoney, who was in charge of Production and known for her practical bent. 'It's not hard if you know what you're doing. A bit of guidance and some sympathy, and most people will cheer up.' She looked around the table. 'You could do it yourself, Mr Collins, except for the fact you're a man.'

'Ah,' said Mr Collins, taking the blow in his stride. 'I do apologise, Mrs Mahoney. It is a failing we must all try to bear.'

Mrs Mahoney gave him an understanding look. 'It's not your fault,' she said generously, and as if there was a possibility it could be. 'Women are just better at being helpful, that's all. Look at Hitler. No help to anyone outside of himself. I'd like to see him raise four daughters all on

6

his own and make sure they're happily married to good sorts. That'd shut him up.'

Mr Collins paused, tapped the end of his pen against his teeth and then smiled at her. At first, I thought it was because Mrs Mahoney had come up with her own plan to stop the world's most obnoxious dictator where so far all of Europe's leaders had failed, but it turned out it had given him an idea.

'As ever, Mrs Mahoney, you are absolutely right. In fact, I don't know why I haven't thought of it myself. The answer is right under our noses.'

Mrs Mahoney frowned.

'There you are, with four daughters, all excellent young women, all happy in their lives, having had the best possible support, growing up. What finer qualification? Your advice would be better than anyone's. How about it? I can see it now: "Mrs Mahoney Helps".'

Mrs Mahoney looked horrified. 'But I'm Production,' she said. 'I don't write. I organise. I like organising. I don't like writing.'

Mr Collins' face fell. 'Not even to help out?' he asked, looking sad.

For all Mrs Mahoney quite worshipping the ground Mr Collins walked on, she was nobody's fool. An experienced and highly respected woman in her fifties, she was as sharp as a pin, and knew a set-up when she saw one. 'Not even if you open your eyes as wide as soup plates and butter me up like a good'n,' she said, as if he wasn't her boss, but a slightly errant son-in-law trying it on.

'I have an idea,' said Kathleen.

'There you are,' said Mrs Mahoney, before Kath could say what it was.

'What about Emmy?' said Kath. 'What if she did the writing? For Mrs Mahoney, I mean,' she added quickly, as everyone looked at her as if she was mad. After all it was my fault Mrs Bird had decided to leave in the first place. In her view, in light of The Unfortunate Hiccups, I should have been sacked.

But Kath was terrifically level-headed and I could see she was being given the benefit of the doubt.

'Emmy could open the letters the way she always did for Mrs Bird, then get Mrs Mahoney's advice on each one and type it up,' Kath continued, turning to the Head of Production, her eyes even bigger than Mr Collins'. 'Honestly, Mrs Mahoney, you wouldn't have to write anything. Just tell Emmy what you'd advise, and then check what she has written to make sure you're happy. It would be smashing. Kindly and cheerful and just like getting a letter back from someone you really trust. A real change from before. We could call it "Yours, Mrs Mahoney".'

My friend had made it sound wonderfully simple. Everyone waited while Mrs Mahoney considered things, and Kath adopted the most hopeful face imaginable. Turning her down would be like thumping a kitten. Mrs Mahoney was not the thumping a kitten type.

'Well,' she said. 'Put like that. But I wouldn't want to have my name or picture on it. I shouldn't want that at all.'

Almost all magazines had a picture of their advice columnist.

Mr Collins leapt in. 'Of course not, not if you don't want to. We can do a silhouette.'

Mrs Mahoney looked doubtful and put her hand to her face.

'And we can call it something different,' he said. 'Whatever you want. We could do it as a trial and if you don't like it, we'll find someone else.'

Mr Collins gave a devil may care shrug for added nonchalance which nearly made me laugh. I could tell he was as keen as anything for her to take the job.

I didn't dare say a word. I loved Kath's idea.

Mrs Mahoney was exactly the sort of person you would turn to if in a fix. And I desperately wanted to be part of the problem page again.

I crossed my fingers tightly under the table. I had seen more than enough letters from readers to know how much help was needed. Although the bombing had recently eased off and our readers were not spending quite so much time in air-raid shelters, life was far from a breeze, in fact for most people it was still downright hard. If Mrs Mahoney were to answer the readers' letters, *Woman's Friend* could really live up to its name.

Mrs Mahoney took a deep breath. 'Well,' she said, slowly, 'if you really think it would help.'

'Enormously,' said Mr Collins, taking this as a Firm Yes. 'Enormously. Thank you very much, Mrs Mahoney. You have made my day, and I should think, everyone else's. Including, if I can presume, Emmy's too?'

He threw me a quizzical look.

'How do you fancy working with Mrs Mahoney on this?' he asked. 'All above board.'

He said it lightly, but I was very much aware it was a chance to prove myself, to show that after my more than wobbly start at *Woman's Friend*, I could really make a go of things. I had mucked up with "Henrietta Helps" but now I had a real chance to redeem myself.

'Yes, please,' I said, and then turned to Mrs Mahoney. 'If you're sure you don't mind?'

Mrs Mahoney gave me an encouraging smile but raised a finger in warning. 'No silly business,' she said. 'Or making up answers all on your own. We shall work together as a team.' She turned to Mr Collins. 'Emmy is already quite busy as it is. If needed, could she work longer hours?'

It was a thoughtful question. I had joined the magazine as a part-time Junior, fitting it in with my voluntary job as a telephonist for the Fire Service, where I was on shifts. I had always worked more than my official hours at *Woman's Friend* as we were a small team and everyone had to muck in. I didn't mind a bit. I wanted to learn.

Writing up Mrs Mahoney's advice, though, rather than just opening the letters as I had done for Mrs Bird, would definitely take up more of my time.

We both looked at Mr Collins.

'A very good point,' he said. 'Can you spare us more time, Emmy? I don't want your Station Captain accusing us of getting in the way of your work for him.'

'I'm sure Captain Davies won't mind,' I said, quickly.

'Excellent,' said Mr Collins. 'Mrs Mahoney, are you happy with everything?'

Mrs Mahoney pursed her lips and thought.

'Yes, Mr Collins,' she said. 'I am. But it mustn't get in the way of my production work. What do you think, Mr Brand?'

Our Art Director, Mr Brand, worked closely with Mrs Mahoney. Always more at home with pictures than words, throughout the meeting he had been quietly sketching, as usual slightly in his own world.

'I'm all for it, Mrs Mahoney,' he said, gently. Then he repeated Kath's words. ' "*Written kindly and cheerfully, like getting a letter from someone you trust.*" But not with your name, of course.' He looked at his sketch book and then held it up for us all to see. 'Just an initial idea, but perhaps something like this might look nice?'

It was the simplest illustration, just a few strokes of his pencil, showing an outline of a woman, clearly Mrs

Mahoney, sitting at a desk reading a letter. Mr Brand had added a title for the page in a large friendly script.

Yours Cheerfully . . .

Woman's Friend is Here to Help

Everyone looked at him and then to Mr Collins.

'It's perfect, Mr Brand,' he said, smiling. 'As ever, you have summed it up beautifully.'

The new Editor looked at Mrs Mahoney and me.

'Here's to our new problem page,' he declared, before Mrs Mahoney could have second thoughts. 'I'm very pleased indeed. In fact, we must celebrate. Could somebody go out and find us some buns?' He put his hand in his pocket and fished out half a crown.

Now we all cheered.

'Well done, everyone,' said Mr Collins, over the noise. ' "Yours Cheerfully" it is.'

London

Four Months Later

CHAPTER ONE

Everyone Must Do Their Bit

It was two minutes to nine on a mild late-September morning and Mr Collins was in danger of being on time. The entire editorial team looked at each other with some astonishment as we heard the doors to the *Woman's Friend* office crash open, and our Editor march down the corridor whistling an upbeat big-band number which took everyone even more by surprise.

'Gracious,' said Mrs Mahoney, looking at her wristwatch.

'That's odd,' said Kathleen.

'Perhaps something bad has happened,' said Mr Newton, looking simultaneously mournful and ecstatic at his dramatic thought.

'Good morning,' said Mr Collins, swinging into the journalists' room as if his being prompt was perfectly normal and happened all the time, or even ever. 'All well, I trust?'

We nodded and managed a collective Good Morning and Yes, Thank You although it came out feebly due to the punctuality shock.

'It's before nine o'clock,' I said. 'Mr Collins, you're never here before nine o'clock.'

Mr Collins laughed, said, 'Slanderous,' and took off his hat and jacket, before sitting at the head of the table.

In the four months he had been in charge, Mr Collins had never managed to join us any earlier than at least a quarter past.

'Lots to get through,' said Mr Collins, happily. 'I say, is that a Peek Frean? Mrs Bussell has excelled herself.'

He helped himself to a broken biscuit.

'Mrs Bussell has a soft spot for you, Mr Collins,' said Mrs Mahoney, which was slightly disloyal to our tea lady, not least as Mrs Mahoney (who would have rather died than admit it) had a soft spot for him all of her own.

'Much appreciated,' said Mr Collins with his mouth full and leaving us unclear as to whether he was referring to the biscuit or the revelation about Mrs Bussell's ardour. 'Where shall we start?'

Kathleen handed him the agenda. It was the same every week.

'Thank you, Miss Knighton. Patterns and Fashion please.'

Kathleen looked eager and started her update, as ever meticulously prepared. Easily the cleverest person I knew although she would fiercely deny it, Kath and I were firm friends and I had been thrilled when Mr Collins promoted her to Chief Sub-Editor. Now she was in charge of all the contributors who sent in patterns and articles, as well as overseeing Hester, our new Junior.

Hester was a good-natured, pasty-faced girl of fifteen, just out of school and prone to uncontrollable giggles. Kath was teaching her, with marginal success, that working at a magazine was not the same as being in a Cary Grant comedy, and instead involved trying to remain calm for almost all of the time.

As a result, Hester was improving, but still alternating between taking things Very Seriously Indeed and shrieking with laughter at the drop of a hat. She was trying hard and as Mrs Mahoney said, it wasn't her fault she had been blessed with Boisterous Lungs.

With Hester taking notes, Kath quickly listed what was coming up on the fashion front in the next couple of issues. Almost everything was now on the ration, and she had become an expert in making coupons go a very long way.

'We have ten ways to update an old hat, and an ever so easy men's pullover where you hardly get out of a basic stitch,' she said, her green eyes earnest. 'Lots of readers wrote in liking the feature on outsize coats, and Mrs Stevens has come up with a marvellous pattern for a knitted brassiere using unrationed yarn. Honestly, Mr Collins, people will be chuffed to bits at that.'

'I see,' said Mr Collins, who tended to be foggy on knits.

'Yes!' said Kath, fervently, thinking he shared her delight. 'That will perk everyone up.'

There was a moment's silence.

'Right,' said Mr Collins.

Mr Newton, who had been staring fixedly into his tea since Kath had said the word 'brassiere', looked pained.

'Nurse McClay has had lots of letters asking how many coupons people need for maternity brassieres,' said Mrs Mahoney, which didn't help. 'I'm just saying in case Mr Newton could get some advertisers in on the subject.'

Mr Newton didn't look as if he would like to in the least, but he nodded weakly.

Hester joined in with a random guffaw.

'Thank you, Mrs Mahoney,' said Mr Collins. 'No need to elaborate, I'm sure Mr Newton is on top of it. Father of three and so on.'

For men who worked on a women's magazine, they were both hopeless about anything to do with what they called That Sort of Thing.

Mrs Mahoney gave a small snort. 'They should be coupon-free in my view. Being a mother during a war isn't exactly beer and skittles. Imagine how you'd feel if Baby needs a feed but you're sitting on a Tube platform in the middle of an air raid.' She looked at the men in the room as if they were wholly responsible.

'Thank you, Mrs Mahoney,' said Mr Collins. 'I'm afraid I can't, but I shall remember it next time I change at King's Cross. Thank you for raising the point. Now then, if we have covered the issue of support garments, shall we move on? The readers, please, Miss Lake?'

'Well,' I said. 'Tons of letters have been coming into "Yours Cheerfully", including lots of people writing to say they were terrifically grateful for the advice about A Difficult Nan. It's getting hard to keep up with all the problems, but that's all right. Although I wondered if we might print some advice leaflets, so that we can help them out that way. It would be quicker than writing to everyone individually.'

'I'm all for it,' said Mrs Mahoney, supportively. 'You gentlemen wouldn't believe the pickles our readers face. Emmy's done a very good list of the questions we get asked the most.'

I smiled gratefully and began to go through my plans. Despite her initial reluctance to take on the problem page, Mrs Mahoney had quickly come to view the entire *Woman's Friend* readership as an extended family to be shepherded through the challenges of growing up, settling down, and tackling middle age, all with the current possibility of death or bereavement at a moment's notice.

Almost as soon as "Yours Cheerfully" had started, her calm, down-to-earth advice had worked. The more letters we answered, the more we received. At the same time, she had been teaching me too. Many of the worries that readers wrote about came up time and time again, and I had learned from her response to each one. Bit by bit I had taken on more of the problem page myself, to a point that now, hundreds of letters later, I was writing much of the advice on my own. Mrs Mahoney had final approval of everything, and I still asked her about the trickiest concerns, but after working on nearly twenty issues together, "Yours Cheerfully" had become almost entirely mine.

'Emmy,' she had said after we had worked together for some weeks, 'you may be young, but you care about the readers. Don't underestimate how important that is. Caring about getting things right is worth its weight in gold.'

It was one of the nicest things anyone had ever said to me, and it struck a chord. I very much *did* care.

When I had dreamt of becoming a Lady War Correspondent, I thought it meant you had to be chasing political stories or reporting on world-changing events. I hadn't considered that there was an equally important job to be done on the Home Front. I may not have been crawling over bombsites or going undercover to get an earth-shattering scoop, but at *Woman's Friend* I was trying to do my bit and knew we were doing something that was worth doing well.

In the past I had been at pains to tell people how I volunteered at the fire station four nights a week and I had rather downplayed working at a magazine. Volunteering with the National Fire Service felt the bigger contribution to the cause. Now, I was proud of what I was doing in my daytime job.

'So that's "Yours Cheerfully",' I finished, pleased that Mr Collins said that if the paper shortage would allow it, my advice leaflets sounded a worthwhile idea.

The discussion then moved on as Mr Collins read out updates from other contributors. Mrs Croft from "What's In The Hotpot?" had received multiple letters following 'Five New Ways With Haddock', while Mr Trevin who did the horoscopes was sadly behind schedule as he had fallen over and broken his wrist.

'I should have thought he would have seen that coming,' said Mr Collins.

Hester giggled and was rewarded with a small smile from our Editor, which I knew would make her entire week.

'I should say,' he continued, 'that things are going very well, apart of course, from the fact that we will be up the spout when Kathleen leaves. I must tell you all I haven't been able to even contemplate recruiting her replacement.'

'I'm bound to be here for ages yet,' piped up Kath, looking awkward. A month ago, she had put her name down to join the Auxiliary Territorial Service. Twenty-two and unmarried, she had tons of potential. None of us wanted her to leave *Woman's Friend*, but the war effort needed her more.

'Kath's right,' I said, backing her up. 'We've had half a dozen letters this week from readers complaining they're having to wait for months before they even get an interview for a job.'

'Hopeless,' said Mr Collins. 'But good news for us. Don't look so horrified, Mr Newton, I'm not being unpatriotic, I just don't want to think about it until we have to. We all know Miss Knighton is irreplaceable.'

Kath looked chuffed, and Mr Newton said, 'Hear, hear,' rather violently, to show he agreed. Unfortunately, this set off Hester, who wasn't at all keen on the thought of losing her mentor, and let out a loud, 'Boo.'

'That'll do, Hester,' said Mrs Mahoney, softly. 'You're not at the circus.'

Hester went puce.

'On to advertising, please, Mr Newton,' said Mr Collins, much to her relief.

The usually congenitally pessimistic Mr Newton reported good news, with revenues up and several new advertisers, including Sta-Blond Shampoo who had paid the full rate for a half-page, and Hartley's Jams who were taking out a series of adverts to tell people there wasn't any.

'Well done, Mr Newton,' said Mr Collins.

'It probably won't last,' said Mr Newton, confidently. 'The National Skin Institute are late paying for their psoriasis series in the Classifieds, and I've had to have a stiff word with Senior's Meat and Fish Pastes about the same thing. I'll get it out of them, don't you worry.'

Mr Collins sympathised, and added he had heard rumours circulating about something big coming up for blancmange.

'Say no more, Mr Collins,' said Mr Newton. 'I'll get on to it at once. We missed out on Custard for Christmas last year and I won't let that happen again.'

With Mr Newton now on a mission, Mrs Mahoney gave a Production update which she managed without any mention of brassieres or feeding babies at all, and by a quarter to ten we had successfully arrived at Any Other Business.

As typically there wasn't any, other than when Mr Newton issued a grim warning about fire hazards in the office (he was an Air Raid Precautions warden and took what he referred to as Lurking Dangers very seriously indeed), we all started to pack away our things in anticipation of the meeting coming to an end.

'Hold your horses, everyone,' said Mr Collins. 'If I could just keep you a moment longer, I wanted to let you know that on Friday I shall be attending a meeting at the Ministry of Information.'

He could not have sounded more casual if he'd tried. Everyone stopped in their tracks. There were a couple of excitable I Says, and Mr Newton said, 'Walls Have Ears,' rather unnecessarily.

'It's all right,' said Mr Collins, 'I haven't joined the War Cabinet, although if any of you turn out to be Fifth Columnists, I shall be sad. And in all seriousness, I would ask you all to keep this to yourselves, if you could.'

Everyone sat up straighter. Mr Collins at the Ministry. This was a turn-up.

'It's a magazine briefing. They're a new thing, and I wanted to say that you should all give yourselves a pat on the back that *Woman's Friend* has been invited. Six months ago, no one would have thought of us, but thanks to a notable team effort we appear to have gained something of a name. It's taken the Ministry two years of war to talk to us all, and that's only because they finally appear to have someone in charge who understands publishing.'

Mr Collins was not an enormous admirer of what he called Establishment Nitwits.

'Anyway, it might be interesting. Or not,' he added, looking sternly at Mr Newton, who had adopted the determined expression of someone about to be parachuted in behind enemy lines. 'They're calling it Doing Your Bit, so we shall see. It'll probably just be a lecture about Digging for Victory, but you never know. By the way, thank you for the onions, Mr Brand, much appreciated in a sandwich.'

Mr Brand looked pleased. 'I shall be planting out the broccoli in my allotment this weekend,' he said in his soft voice. 'And thinking about bulbs.'

'Is that quite patriotic, Mr Brand?' asked Mr Newton, his dander quite unusually up. 'We need to concentrate on food stuffs, not flowers, surely?'

'Ah,' said Mr Brand, mildly. 'And what of morale, Mr Newton? A pot of spring daffodils bringing a little beauty to a world that threatens to have none? I should think that would be a good thing, wouldn't you?'

Mr Newton looked abashed.

'We're going to get last year's bulbs out of the shed,' said Kathleen, keen to support Mr Brand. 'Mum says she's going to plant them in a V for Victory sign in the grass on top of our shelter just to annoy any German bombers.'

'That's the spirit, Kathleen,' said Mr Collins. 'Why don't you mention it to Mrs Fieldwick for "News From the Shed"?' He looked at his wristwatch. 'Right, I think that's about all. I shall report back from the Ministry, of course. Emmy, please put it in your diary, I imagine you'll want to be prepared.'

'What's that?' I said, sounding dim.

'Miss Lake,' he sighed, melodramatically. 'You'll be coming along, too.' He grinned as I stared at him with my mouth open. 'Don't look so astonished, I'm not spending a morning with that bunch all on my own. Yes, you have heard correctly,' he said again, as I felt a rush of blood to my head.

'I have?' I said, as if understanding him was beyond my field of action.

Mr Collins gave me a long-suffering look. 'Emmy,' he said patiently, as my heart began to do flip-flaps. 'I may be regretting this already, but yes, you are coming to the Ministry of Information with me.'

CHAPTER 2

A Meeting with the Ministry

'*The Ministry*,' said Bunty. 'I know I keep saying it, but how exciting! Watch out, this bit of road is awful.'

It was the morning of The Meeting and my best friend and I were on our way to the bus stop just down the street from where we lived in West London. It was the sort of day that had decided to make a real show of itself and throw everyone into the deepest of autumns. There had been heavy rain throughout the night and the pavements were now a bomb-damaged jigsaw of puddles.

'Morning, girls,' called a middle-aged man from deep inside a brown jacket with the collar turned up. 'Don't forget to pick up those cottons I've been keeping for you. Mrs Richards has asked twice if I have any and I'm not one for living a lie.'

'Right you are, Mr Parsons,' replied Bunty as I gave him a wave. Mr Parsons had managed the wool shop until it was bombed out earlier in the year, but after a month at his sister's, he'd returned to London. Now he was running Durton's, the hardware shop, which he'd promised to keep ticking over as Dickie Durton had been called up and his mother said she hadn't the heart.

'Not that there's much to sell,' Mr Parsons had said at the time, which was true. He got hold of whatever he could, including haberdashery which was where his heart really lay. Now he gave us a cheerful wave back and marched off towards the shop, shouting a hello at someone else as his apron flapped about beneath his jacket.

The street was busy with people on their way to work and if you tried awfully hard you might almost, for a moment, pretend that we weren't in the middle of a war. But the swiftest look around would tell you it was all too obvious that we were. Although things had quietened down over the summer and the constant bombing of earlier in the year had eased off, and while everyone had done their best to patch things up, the results of the Blitz were every- where. What had been neat lines of Georgian terraces were now all higgledy-piggledy. There were bits missing from buildings, windows boarded up, railings gone to make munitions, and worst of all, too many gaps where people's homes had been. Now, heaps of rubble sat in their place – disrespectful reminders of what had been lost. It didn't matter how much you stuck your chin up and said that everything would be rebuilt even better after the end of the war, if you weren't careful, you would start thinking about the people who'd been lost with those buildings. It was then that things could sometimes feel a bit much.

Bunty was negotiating her way across the road, which had more than its fair share of craters and holes. I tried not to be over-protective, but she had been through the mill. In March she had been seriously injured in an air raid, and her fiancé, William, had been killed. Bunty was often still in pain, but she said the worst thing was that people treated her differently, either assuming she could shatter in a second, or turning her into some sort of plucky but tragic heroine. Either way, Bunty said, they looked at her with what she called The Face, which she loathed.

'I'm still me,' she would say, always under-cooking

what had happened. 'Just with a gammy leg and some scars.'

She was doing terrifically well in some respects and the same old Bunty was still there, but anyone who knew her could tell she had changed.

It wasn't the fact she walked with a stick, or even the splitting headaches that wouldn't go away. It was when you saw her flinch at a sudden noise in the street, or when the siren went off. Or when she talked about Bill, the fleetest of shadows would cross her face before she smiled at a memory of him.

But as Bunts insisted, tons of people were in the same position, or even worse. With no end to the war in sight, the only thing we could do was to get on with it and try to enjoy what we could, even if some days she did just feel like staying in bed.

Now, Mr Collins' dramatic announcement about the Ministry had given us both a real boost. Bunty, who was always keen on an event, was convinced it was a big step in one of us becoming the first female Prime Minister one day. I thought she was aiming quite high there, but Bunts said I was being defeatist and not to rule anything out.

'It's just a briefing,' I said, trying not to let on that I was hugely excited and apprehensive in equal measures. 'I'll just be sitting quietly at the back. And after all, you go to the War Office every day.'

Bunty scoffed. 'Em,' she said, stepping around a sandbag which had fallen over outside the pub, 'I could sit at my desk stark jolly naked and no one would give me a second glance. You'll be there as an invited guest. It's entirely different.'

'I still think I'll be turned away at the door,' I said, as we arrived at the bus stop. 'That would be awful.'

Bunty shook her head. 'Mr Collins would never let that happen.'

'Well,' I said. 'As long as there isn't a scene or he has to sneak someone five bob to let me in, which we both know he probably would. Anyway, I'm going to try to look serious and mature. Charles said I should practise in the mirror, but I'm not sure I've got it quite right.'

Captain Charles Mayhew and I had met earlier in the year just before he was sent overseas. I had written more letters during that time than I had ever done in my life, and he had written back to them all. When Charles was posted back to England in late summer to work on something he couldn't tell me anything about, we were already in love.

More than anything, I was overjoyed to know that Charles was safe, or at least as safe as anyone in Britain could be.

I knew how tremendously lucky I was. I was also more than aware that I had fallen in love with a man whose brother, or at least half-brother, happened to be my boss.

It had been a little strange at first, but we had all pushed on valiantly, despite not having a clue what the etiquette was in this sort of scenario, and so far, my only problem was remembering to refer to Mr Collins by his first name when I was speaking to Charles. I was getting used to it, but still felt very bohemian every time I managed to splutter out, 'Guy'.

'Gravitas,' declared Bunty. 'That's what you need. Give off the look of someone with hidden depths. By the way, I'm going to try to do the carrot sauce recipe tonight. I know it sounds foul, but they did say it tastes very nearly like chocolate.'

'Worth a go,' I agreed. *Woman's Friend* had recently run an article called 'Novel Ways with Vegetables', which insisted that you could make carrots taste of virtually anything if you put your mind to it.

We continued discussing plans for the rest of the week's dinners and what we might be able to get hold of as the bus arrived, and we got on to ride into central London.

Bunty told me that if in doubt to just sound confident at the meeting, and then we both got a fit of the giggles as I tried this out by speaking slowly in a new, lower-pitched voice.

'You sound as if you've been heavily drugged,' said Bunty, cheerfully. 'Perhaps just nod and look thoughtful, instead?'

As Trafalgar Square came into view, she picked up her bag and stick and prepared to get off at her stop, then paused and gave me a nudge.

'Good luck, old thing,' she said, kindly. 'You'll be fine. Just don't do that demonic voice. It really is quite unsettling.'

With that, she gave me a grin, lugged herself up out of the seat and headed carefully to the back of the bus.

★

An hour later, Mr Collins and I were walking up Montague Street on our way to the Ministry of Information's HQ at Senate House.

I was wearing my best suit and quite a new hat and had three emergency handkerchiefs in my handbag, so felt well turned out and prepared. When I'd told Bunty that you never knew if someone from the Ministry might be about to have a nosebleed, she'd burst out laughing, which hadn't been the response I had hoped for.

'Thank you for letting me come along,' I said to Mr Collins, for the hundredth time. 'Are you sure they won't mind?'

'Well,' he said, lightly. 'For a start, you could be the Chairman for all they know, and for another thing, you've shown terrific get up and go in the last months and deserve to be here. It's been a while since I've been to a publishing do. It might just be horribly dull.'

When I didn't reply, he glanced at me.

'If anyone speaks to you, just remember they probably haven't been here before either. Oh, and try to look about twenty years older. That'll do it.'

'Right you are,' I said, tilting my chin up a bit as I could tell he was trying to put my mind at rest. I was nervous, but it was a good nervous. Whatever the Ministry had to say to us, I was sure it would be exciting and important.

We couldn't say very much more in the street for fear of Careless Talk, so we walked along in silence until Mr Collins motioned to turn left, and a few moments later we came to a halt outside a vast art deco building, its windows blacked out against the white stone.

I felt a flutter of anticipation.

'Ready?' said Mr Collins. 'Come on.'

We made our way past the policemen and into the building where a well-dressed young woman at the reception desk looked at our identification cards, then checked our names on a list and asked us to write our details in a large book. I copied everything Mr Collins did and practised looking blasé as I didn't want to give the impression I was An Hysteric. It wasn't until we got into the lift that I remembered to breathe.

As soon as we arrived at the third floor, it was clear we were in the right place. A dozen or so men and women were standing in something approximating a queue, the women all terrifically smart, the men dapper to a T. Everyone was smoking and they were all a good deal older than me. A small bald man in a dark suit was holding a clipboard and scurrying around making notes and looking serious, when a door opened and a taller, equally serious man in an identical dark suit came out and asked everyone to have their identification ready again and would we all like to come in.

As we shuffled forward, a loud voice behind me boomed, 'I say, Collins, is that you?'

We both turned as a man with an attention-seeking moustache and a limp marched up and walloped Mr Collins on the back.

'I thought you were dead,' he said.

'Not quite,' said Mr Collins. 'Hello, Jarrett. How are you?'

'Clinging on,' said the man. 'Wanted to fight of course but they're picky about having both legs. How about you? Written that book yet?'

Mr Collins gave a short laugh which didn't sound anything like him. 'Rather busy with the day job. This is my colleague Miss Lake. Miss Lake, this is a fellow journalist, Mr Jarrett.'

Mr Jarrett looked me up and down in an off-colour way.

'How do you do?' I said.

'Hmm,' he replied and then nodded at Mr Collins before pushing past us and shouting, 'I say, Thompson, is that you?' at somebody else.

It was an interesting start.

'Sorry about that,' said Mr Collins in a low voice. 'He likes to think he's a character.' He reached into his coat pocket and took out his cigarettes. I began to wish I smoked too, just to fit in.

The queue moved on and finally, we were shown into a large, brown-carpeted room with a number of rather utilitarian metal chairs set out at one end, a small platform

30

at the head, and a long sideboard with cups of tea and an urn at the other.

'Refreshments,' muttered Mr Collins. 'They must be serious.'

Everyone in the room appeared to know everyone else and there was a hubbub of noise as people greeted each other and chatted. I readjusted my handbag on my shoulder and tried not to stare as Mr Collins began quietly explaining who everyone was.

Not only did he know who the other journalists were, it appeared that many of them knew exactly who he was too. There were several nods and smiles in his direction, and to my secret relief, Mr Jarrett seemed to be the rude exception to the rule.

'Guy Collins, is that really you? What a super surprise!' A striking middle-aged woman in a fox-fur jacket glided towards us. 'How many years has it been?' She beamed at him and then kissed him on both cheeks.

It was the most Continental thing I had ever seen.

'Oh, Guy,' she said. 'It's been far too long. Is it true they've finally pinned you down and made you Editor?'

'Hello, Monica, I'm afraid so,' said Mr Collins, not looking remotely surprised by the extravagant greeting. 'It's good to see you. I must say, you never age. Although you're far too thin.'

The woman hooted with laughter, which was another turn-up. She looked far too sophisticated to be a roarer.

'That's absolute rot,' she said, cheerfully. 'Now, introduce me to your colleague.' She turned towards me with the friendliest of smiles.

'Of course. How remiss. This is Miss Emmeline Lake,' said Mr Collins. 'Who has been making a name for herself at *Woman's Friend*. Miss Lake, this is Mrs Edwards, Editor of *Woman Today*.'

Mrs Edwards shook my hand firmly. 'How do you do,' she said. 'Is he an absolute bear to put up with? Actually, don't answer that, you can tell me when he isn't listening.'

She smiled again and then turning to Mr Collins said, 'Word has it you've been working wonders on the dear old *Friend*.' She didn't give Mr Collins a chance to respond to the compliment, but touching him lightly on the arm, added, 'I really am so pleased.'

Then she turned back to me.

'I should explain, Miss Lake, I am embarrassingly sentimental, as *Woman's Friend* commissioned my first ever feature. One never forgets that. I *am* glad it's back. Room for us all and goodness knows people need a bit of cheering up. What I'd do to Hitler if I got my hands on him,' she whispered, conspiratorially. 'Now then, Guy, who have you said hello to? It's so long since any of us saw you.'

I liked Mrs Edwards enormously. I had heard of her of course and was a keen fan of her weekly Editor's Letter in *Woman Today* in which she sometimes expressed a strong view. Last week her column had been a powerfully worded argument for equal pay for women. Now here she was, chatting with Mr Collins as if we were at a cocktail party, and speaking to me as if I was one of the gang.

I was almost disappointed when a very smartly dressed man dinged his fountain pen against a teacup and cleared his throat.

'Ladies and gentlemen,' he announced. 'Would you please take your seats? The Under-Secretary will be here imminently.'

The hubbub of chatter changed to low murmurings as cups and saucers were placed back on the table and the journalists put out cigarettes, took notebooks out of handbags and coat pockets, and settled down in their chairs.

Mrs Edwards made Mr Collins sit next to her and I followed, whipping out my notebook and hoping I looked the part. Mr Jarrett planted himself on the seat beside me, grunting as he sat down and then taking up half of my chair.

A few moments later, four gentlemen entered the room and took their places to be introduced.

'Mr Clough – the Under-Secretary to the Minister, Mr Stratton – Assistant Deputy Director Public Relations, Mr Morton-Stoppard – Controller, and Mr Boe, representing the Ministry of Labour and National Service.'

It was just as well I had good shorthand.

'Good morning, ladies and gentlemen,' said Mr Stratton, taking the stand. 'It goes without saying that everything covered this morning is confidential and any breach of such is subject to prosecution under the 1939 Official Secrets Act.'

He paused momentarily to give a hard stare over the top of his spectacles (as if more of a warning was needed).

I took notes furiously.

'I would therefore ask you not to take notes until I say so,' he said, and my book and pen dropped to the floor with a thud. Mr Jarrett tutted ostentatiously and shoved his notebook back in his pocket.

'Welcome to this briefing specifically for members of the British *women's* press.

Mr Stratton said *women's* as if it was some sort of peculiarity, as if he might have said two-headed sheep just as easily. I glanced at Mrs Edwards who hadn't turned a hair, and taking her lead, I surreptitiously picked up my notebook and put it back in my bag, then sat with my hands in my lap and tried to look as serene.

'Ladies and gentlemen,' continued Mr Stratton, 'I don't need to tell you that the current War Effort requires the labours of not only our military forces, but the full commitment of our men, women and children on the Home Front.'

He paused and looked about the room. Perhaps in his early fifties, immaculately turned out and still enjoying a more than satisfactory head of hair, he sported a look which was very nearly suave.

'To get to the point,' said Mr Stratton. 'Our Services and support services are facing a significant undersupply of manpower. Or, I should say, female manpower. Indeed, many of your publications are benefitting from substantial Government-funded advertising to this effect.'

He stared over his glasses again to press the point home.

'Which is why your collective services are particularly required,' he continued. 'We wish to see an increased commitment in encouraging your readers to take up war work. As you know, the National Service Bill has been much discussed, and female conscription will commence when the Act is shortly passed. Many younger women will join the Services. But we also need older women, married women, mothers, even grandmothers, to volunteer for jobs, especially in munitions production. This, ladies and gentlemen, is where your part is to be played.'

Mr Stratton paused, possibly to ensure everyone was listening.

'Today I am asking you all to inspire your readers. Our need for workers, particularly in the factories, is critical. One million women have joined our vital war industries, but we need at least one million more. Our men fighting need them. The country needs them. And the Government needs you to help us recruit them.'

He leant forward, his hands on the table, and seemed to look at each of us in turn. He may not have been

Winston Churchill, but Mr Stratton certainly knew how to make a speech.

'In summary, ladies and gentlemen,' he said, finally, 'your hour is here.'

The hairs on the back of my neck were standing up.

Until today I had thought we had been doing our best. *Woman's Friend* was full of tips and advice for our readers on all manner of challenges the war had thrown at them. We had even been congratulating ourselves on recent successes.

But this was different. It was a direct call from the Government to help recruit women to the war effort – to *inspire them,* he said. I had always hoped to be a journalist, but I had never dreamt it would involve being part of a campaign like this.

As Mr Stratton began to go into more detail, I was already fully signed up to the call.

After a few more minutes, he asked for questions. Several people put up their hands and made eager enquiries, then, after the most enthusiastic had calmed down, Mrs Edwards raised an elegant hand.

'Mr Stratton,' she said. '*Woman Today* will of course do everything we possibly can to support the Government, but may I ask how long you expect our readers to wait before they are actually given a position? We receive letters daily from women who have volunteered for the Services or factory work but say they haven't heard back in months.'

One or two eyebrows shot up at that, but I leant forward. It was exactly what Kath and I had been saying earlier in the week.

Mr Stratton didn't turn a hair.

'I shall let Mr Boe answer that,' he said.

Mr Boe stood briefly to say something convoluted about the Employment Exchanges doing their best in very difficult times, at which point Mr Stratton interrupted to suggest somewhat coldly that perhaps Mrs Edwards' magazine could highlight the need for more careers advisors.

Mrs Edwards smiled graciously. 'We will, of course,' she said. 'Then perhaps the bottleneck will pass.'

Mr Stratton said that was enough questions for now.

Having made her point and clearly had the last word, Mrs Edwards continued to smile beatifically at him, and I had the distinct impression she knew exactly how to both make her point and get her way in any possible situation. I decided this was a skill I very much needed to learn.

Mr Stratton again handed over to Mr Boe who stood up, only to have to sit down almost immediately when Mr Stratton interrupted again, which gave the impression they were on some sort of seesaw. I watched but could hardly take anything more in.

When I had woken up this morning, I had been anxious about not even being let into the building. Now, here I was at the Ministry of Information, sitting alongside journalists and editors, meeting women who effortlessly held their own in a room full of big-wigs, and more than anything, being told that the Government needed our help.

It was the clearest of calls to arms.

The Government needs you. Your hour is here.

Woman's Friend had been asked to step up to help the war effort.

It was time for me to do so as well.

CHAPTER 3

Trouble in the Lavatory

'LADIES AND GENTLEMEN, that concludes the agenda. Further briefings will be forthcoming. Until then, I remind you to observe the confidentiality outlined. Information should be passed only to key team members. Good morning.'

The journalists left slowly, some turning to their neighbour with muttered remarks, others looking at watches or putting on coats before heading towards the door.

Mr Collins and I filed out from the back of the room, managing to avoid Mr Jarrett, before he could burst my bubble with a cynical prod.

'What did you think?' said Mr Collins. 'Enjoy it?'

I nodded, fiercely. 'I'll say. There'll be loads we can do,' I said. 'We can come up with tons of ideas.'

Mr Collins smiled at me, almost fondly. 'Excellent. I'd bet myself a shilling that's how you'd respond.' He dropped his voice. 'You know, sometimes I fear I'll end up like Jarrett.'

'You never would,' I said, aghast.

'Not with you at my heels, Miss Lake,' said Mr Collins, going all formal. 'First sign of cynicism and you'll bash it out of me.'

I laughed and was about to agree when a thin, greying man I hadn't noticed before came over.

'Ah, Collins,' he said. 'I thought it was you.' He grinned warmly and they shook hands. 'How are you, old man?'

'Hello, Simons,' said Mr Collins. 'It's good to see you. May I introduce my colleague, Miss Lake?'

'How do you do, Miss Lake?' said Mr Simons, shaking my hand. 'I'm so sorry to interrupt, but I wondered if I might have a quick word with you, Guy?'

'How do you do?' I said, in return. 'Mr Collins, shall I meet you downstairs?'

Mr Collins said, 'Yes, thank you, Miss Lake,' and with a Nice To Meet You to Mr Simons, I made my exit.

There was a ladies' lavatory in the corridor and even though I didn't need to use it, I locked myself in one of the cubicles and hung my bag on the hook on the back of the door, sitting down to write up a few thoughts in order to kill time. I was already thinking of features we could run in *Woman's Friend*.

After a moment, I heard some ladies come in. They seemed more interested in chatting about the meeting than using the facilities, so I went back to writing my notes. I planned to stay another couple of minutes and then head downstairs. I certainly wouldn't earwig on their conversation.

'Did you see that *Vogue* came?' one was saying. 'And that coat! So beautiful.'

'Astrakhan,' said the other. 'Pre-war, surely? Gorgeous.'

'I'll say,' said the first one, sighing. 'Do you know, I thought it was quite an exclusive event when I saw her, but then I looked around and they seemed to have invited any old sort. Did you see *Woman's Friend*? I thought it had closed years ago, the poor old thing.'

With that, not earwigging went straight out the window.

'Oh, Freddie, don't,' said her friend. 'I suppose the Ministry wants to get the message out to everyone, including the old ducks. Though Lord knows what war work they'll be able to do. Knitting socks probably.' She laughed, loudly.

I opened my mouth but managed to hold my tongue. Shouting at a stranger from inside a lavatory cubicle would not have been in keeping with the occasion. Even Mr Jarrett, who had thought Mr Collins was dead, probably wouldn't do that. But these women were the absolute limit.

'Honestly, Diane,' replied the other, 'I thought even the old dears had given up on *Woman's Friend*. They can't keep their Editors either. First they dragged Henrietta Bird out of retirement and now apparently they've scraped the bottom of the barrel and given Guy Collins the job.'

At this, I nearly shot out and went for them both. I stood up and shoved my notebook into my bag. Who were these women? Bending down, I looked under the door but all I could see were two pairs of legs, both in high-heeled shoes, one black suede, the other a flamboyant green crocodile.

'Is he still going?' said her friend. 'Good grief.'

'I assume so, if only just. Jarrett was talking about him.'

I heard a powder compact click shut.

'I thought he had some sort of breakdown? Collins, that is.'

I stood stock-still, holding my breath.

'No idea,' said Freddie in a funny voice which I assumed was because she was putting on lipstick. 'He's a has-been either way, so I suppose spot on for the job.' She gave a silly little laugh. 'There, that's better. Heaven only knows what we'll do when Max Factor runs out.'

Heaven only knew what I was going to do if she didn't stop being so awful.

I looked around me and felt ridiculous. Two minutes

ago, I was on top of the world listening to a Ministerial briefing, and now here I was, hiding in a lavatory wanting to punch someone. How the mighty fall.

But I wasn't going to stand for this sort of talk. I pulled the toilet chain forcefully to give them fair warning, and then slammed the lock open on the door.

Trying to exhibit every ounce of cold disdain possible, I went through the charade of washing my hands. The two women were still repairing their make-up and gossiping. They didn't seem to notice me.

I told myself I would not create a scene with them. After all, I was very lucky to come to the meeting in the first place. The women roundly deserved to be ignored. I dried my hands and headed to the door, putting my nose in the air, ready to feel the exhilaration of taking the moral high ground.

But I'd never been a fan of moral high ground.

So, I turned around.

'Hello,' I said, politely. 'Emmeline Lake, *Woman's Friend*. As you seemed to be rather interested, you might like to know that Guy Collins is doing a terrifically good job as Editor. But thank you so much for your concern. Good morning.'

And then I did my first attempt at a Mrs Edwards smile that could shut up a Public Relations man, and left.

As I began to head up the corridor to the lifts, I allowed myself to savour what felt like a small triumph. My point had been made, but in an appropriately dignified way.

Then I realised I had left my bag on the back of the lavatory door.

'Blast,' I said, less appropriately, just as a man I recognised as Mr Boe walked past. He looked appalled, said, 'Really!' and speeded up. Unsurprisingly, swearing wasn't the Ministry's thing. I hung my head, less in shame and more in frustration.

'Excuse me, miss, if you were part of the publishing briefing, might I ask you to move along to the lifts now, please?'

A young man the colour of milk clasped his hands and looked at me dolefully. 'It's just that the meeting is over.'

'I'm so sorry,' I said. 'I've been rather a chump and left my handbag in the ladies' lavatory. Might I just dash in and get it?'

The man wrung his hands but nodded. 'If you see any of your colleagues in there, might you have a word along the same lines?' he asked. 'Security, you do understand.'

'Of course,' I said, now feeling in with the Right Sort. 'Actually, I did notice a couple of ladies still in there. Not lurking or anything worrying,' I added and then I frowned. 'At least I don't *think* so. I'll go and get them out, shall I?'

'Would you?' said my new friend. 'We can't have that. Then I would be grateful if you could make your way to the lift.'

'Of course,' I said. 'Thank you. You've been very kind.'

Feeling bolstered, I took a breath, pushed my shoulders back once again and returned to where my two adversaries were still deep in conversation and now mucking about with their hair.

'The poor thing obviously has the worst crush on Collins,' said the one in the crocodile-skin shoes. 'It really is rather a scream.'

'Oh Freddie, how desperate,' said the other, licking the top of a finger and dabbing it along one of her eyebrows.

'Isn't it? I know there's a war on, but . . .'

They both laughed. It was cheap and uncalled for, and best behaviour promise or not, I wasn't having it.

41

'Really?' I said. 'I'm not sure that you do.'

They both turned, openmouthed. I felt my heart speed up.

'I mean it's hardly the way to speak of a fellow member of the press, is it? "*All stick together, Birds of a feather,*" ' I said, quoting the song as if it was some sort of emergency law.

Freddie recovered herself first. 'Oh silly, I think you must have misheard,' she said, which rather suggested I was deaf. 'We were chatting about a friend. Come along, Diane.'

She picked up her clutch bag from beside the sink and tucked it under her arm.

'I don't think I did,' I said, quietly. 'I distinctly heard you being most unpleasant about *Woman's Friend* and Guy Collins. You know, you can say what you like about me,' I added. 'Even though it isn't true. But please don't be rude about our Editor. He has every right to be here.'

Diane gave her friend a nudge. 'Let's go, Fred, this is dull,' she said.

But her colleague didn't move.

She just tipped her head to one side and looked at me as if I had tried awfully hard but still come last in the Egg and Spoon race. 'Every right to be here? That *would* be a Stop the Press piece of news. You wouldn't be the first secretary to fall into a bout of schoolgirl passion. I assume he is still doing his tortured artist act?' She sniffed. 'You silly girl, I'm afraid it's only fair to tell you that your magazine is seen as quite the joke. And sad old Guy still plugging along on it. Sorry. Just thought you should know.'

Now I nearly laughed. It was an extraordinary display. A grown woman spreading gossip and pushing me around because I was new. It was like being back at school.

'Thank you,' I said, standing my ground. 'It's kind of

you to care, but you really needn't. *Woman's Friend*'s War Effort Recruitment Plan has been in preparation for some time. Mr Collins won't say a word if you ask, but I can tell you that the Ministry is due to receive it soonest. In fact, I assume that was why we were invited today. But I shouldn't be saying a word.'

So, stick that in your pipe and smoke it.

'Excuse me,' I said, sweeping dramatically (as far as I could in a confined space) past them and into the lavatory. Then I grabbed my bag, as if it were quite the done thing to leave it there in the first place, and walked out before either of them had a chance to say another word.

'I'm so sorry, I did try, but they insisted they wouldn't be rushed,' I said to the worried young man who was waiting outside. 'Thank you, again. Good morning.'

And then, as I had no wish to encounter the two women again in the lift, I ran to the doors marked *Stairs* and rushed out as fast as I could.

★

As promised, Mr Collins was waiting outside the building, I could tell he had enjoyed the morning enormously.

'Well, then, Miss Lake,' he said, heartily. 'What did you make of it all? I say, are you all right? You look rather red-faced.'

'I've just run down the stairs,' I said, which was true, although three flights had made no difference at all to the fury I felt over Freddie and Diane.

Mr Collins nodded and didn't enquire about the lavatories as generally no one in their right mind would.

I wanted to put my thoughts in order before telling him about the fracas so that it didn't look as if I had had some sort of over-excited brainstorm, and not only argued with complete strangers but showed off about a lofty plan that didn't actually exist. I had already decided not to mention the nasty jibes the women had made about him.

I shoved the incident to the back of my mind and focused on the meeting itself. Before Freddie and Diane's nastiness had cast a shadow over things, I'd had the time of my life. It was one thing to be doing your bit as a matter of course – everyone in the country was doing that. But it was quite something to sit in a room full of proper journalists and be told we were needed to play a specific part.

We stopped momentarily at a boarded-up newsagent so that Mr Collins could buy a copy of the *Radio Times*. Someone had painted, 'BAD LUCK ADOLF – WE'RE STILL OPEN', in large black letters on the boards.

'If you ever want someone in journalism to look up to,' said Mr Collins, tucking the magazine under his arm and thanking the lady for his change, 'Monica Edwards is one of the best. She can paint an entire picture in one line, never misses a deadline and doesn't shy away from the truth. Ignore the Jarretts of the world, Emmy. Monica is the sort of person to model yourself on.'

I was eager to hear more about the people he had worked with in the past, and as I questioned him further, I tried to forget about Freddie and Diane. I was sure Mr Collins would not be put off by their nastiness, although I did hope he wouldn't be cross with me for taking them on.

When we arrived back at *Woman's Friend*, Hester, who was looking unusually serious, handed Mr Collins a telephone message, at which he frowned but immediately called a meeting to debrief everyone on the morning's events. As I would entirely expect from him, he had taken the directive that information should be passed only to key staff members to mean the entire *Woman's Friend* team. He was clear that we were to keep everything close to our chests, but nevertheless, no one on the team was left out of the shared mission.

'We'll have a proper meeting on Monday,' he said. 'Bring in your ideas on how we can help the effort and we'll speak then. One more thing,' he added, looking thoughtful. 'Don't just think about how we can promote the Ministry's recruitment campaign. Think about the women. They're the ones keeping everything going while the boys are away. Think about the readers. Our job is to help them, just as much as we help the war effort.' He looked at the clock on the wall. 'Now you must excuse me as I will be out of the office for the rest of the day.'

And with that, he had gone. My heart sank. It meant I would have to wait to speak with him about my argument and rashly promised Big Plan. I supposed at least it meant I could organise my thoughts.

I did not read anything dramatic into Mr Collins leaving, but Hester had a different idea and rushed over to me as soon as the meeting dispersed.

'IT'S A PERSONAL THING,' she said in a deafening stage whisper that would have reached the Upper Circle in even the largest theatres of the West End. 'MR COLLINS' FRIEND ISN'T AT ALL WELL.'

'Thank you, Hester,' I said at a normal volume. 'If it's personal then it's a good idea to keep it to ourselves.'

Hester nodded, keenly. 'Yes,' she said. 'The lady calling said it was private, so I've made sure everyone knows.'

'Ah,' I said.

'You know,' whispered Hester. 'Just in case it turns out the person is dead.'

'Hmm,' I said. 'So, telling everyone should avoid any upset?'

45

'That's right,' said Hester looking pleased that I'd managed to catch on. 'Because if someone is dead, we can all pretend we don't know, so there won't be any kind of a scene.'

'Very thoughtful,' I said, thinking that this would be easier if we actually *didn't* know, but it was a bit late for that now. 'Good thinking. In the meantime, why don't we try to come up with some ideas for how we can help win the war?'

'Me as well?' said Hester. 'Do you think Mr Collins will be interested?' She looked at me earnestly, her round face full of enthusiasm. It was impossible not to be charmed, even if she did have the broadcasting range of the BBC.

'Absolutely,' I said. 'We all will. Your ideas are as valid as anyone's.'

Hester looked chuffed, and now that the pressure was off in terms of keeping a confidential message confidential, returned to her usual MO by laughing like a maniac.

'Imagine,' she said, once she had calmed down. 'The Government has asked *us* to help win the war.'

I laughed then as well. Hester may have only been fifteen, but she sounded exactly as I felt.

'I know,' I replied, with more concern than I hoped Hester would grasp. 'And it's really very important that we come up with a plan.'

CHAPTER 4

My Dear Little Pickle

AFTER SPENDING THE rest of the morning thinking up ideas, I decided to put all concerns about *Woman's Friend*'s Entirely Fictional War Effort Recruitment Plan to one side until Monday. Charles had a rare and exciting forty-eight hours' leave and he was coming up to London from his billet the next day.

Or at least that was what we had planned until he phoned the night before.

'I'm so sorry, Em, they've cancelled all leave for at least the next week.' Charles sounded as downcast as I felt.

'Not to worry,' I said, building myself up to a lie. 'Honestly, it doesn't matter a bit.'

'Are you sure, darling?' said Charles. 'I really hate doing this to you, especially so late in the day.'

'Absolutely,' I said, sitting down with a bump on the bottom stair. I had been counting the days to seeing him. 'I wasn't bothered about seeing you, anyway,' I added.

Charles made a good attempt to laugh. 'You know you'll have a far better time with Bunty,' he said.

'You're right.' I hammed it up. 'I really couldn't care less.'

Then I ran out of steam on the chin-up front and neither of us said anything for a moment.

'God, I'm browned off,' said Charles.

He wasn't the only one.

'Bloody war,' I said.

'Bloody war,' he said back.

That cheered us both up, momentarily. Charles would never swear in front of a woman and my parents would have been horrified to hear me swear at all. But this didn't count. It was the way Charles and I checked if the other one was all right, just between ourselves. It had started when we first admitted we were serious about each other and I had said it as a joke in recognition of the fact that if it hadn't been for the war, we'd never have met in the first place. It was the most peculiar thing, that something awful had led to finding someone you couldn't imagine being without.

'I'd better go,' said Charles. 'I'll call you again later, so we can talk properly then. I want to hear about your meeting even though you won't be able to say anything.'

'You're right, I can't,' I said, gratefully. 'But it was awfully exciting. Lots of interesting people. A couple of odd sorts,' I added. 'But I enjoyed myself.'

Neither of us mentioned names, places or specifics.

'I knew you'd do well,' said Charles. 'You'll be in charge of the lot of them before you know it.'

'I'm not sure about that,' I said, pulling a face as I thought about the two women in the lavatory. 'But you'll get told off if I start going on about it now.'

We said our goodbyes and I made a good stab at being hearty as far as I could. Putting down the receiver, though, I sighed heavily.

'Oh well, that's that, then,' I said, in a low way now that I didn't have to pretend otherwise.

When Charles had first been posted back to England, I had been thrilled to bits, and he had said I was by far the best thing about being in a staff job here rather than

48

fighting with the others overseas. But the fact was, the combination of his work and me haring around between *Woman's Friend* and the fire station meant opportunities to see each other were few and far between. Snatched phone calls and long letters had got us through so far and I knew we were lucky to have that. Sending letters overnight was tons better than waiting ages for news from the other side of the world.

As I sat feeling sorry for myself, the front door opened.

'Hello, Em. You'll never guess what,' said Bunty breathlessly, as she fought her way through the black-out curtain, waving a small package and looking as if she'd won the Pools. 'Mr Parsons has managed to get some elastic. I didn't ask how but got a yard and a half. I say, you look a bit blue. Are you all right?'

'Charles's leave has been cancelled,' I said. 'Again.'

Bunty looked sympathetic. 'Oh no, what a stinker,' she said.

I nodded. 'Sorry, I'm being mopey. I'd been looking forward to seeing him, enormously. I'll be all right in a minute. Good news on the elastic.'

'That's rotten luck,' said Bunty, taking off her hat and putting it on the hall table. She crossed her arms and leant against the curled end of the banister. 'He might as well be in Hong Kong or somewhere for all you get to see him. I tell you what, why don't you come with me to Granny's? There's a new litter of puppies at the farm. That can cheer anyone up. I know it's not the same,' she finished.

It might not have been, but it was awfully kind of her to offer. 'It sounds lovely,' I said. 'Thank you, I'd love to come.'

Bunty looked pleased and I slapped my hands on my thighs to gee myself up. The situation couldn't be helped and there was no point being a gloom-bag about it.

'Now,' said Bunty. 'If it won't land you in prison for Loose Talk, I'm dying to hear how it went today at the You Know Where.'

'Ah,' I said, glad to have someone to talk to about it. 'Very well, and then not quite as straightforward.'

'Sounds interesting,' said Bunty, taking off her coat and gloves. 'Are you allowed to tell me?'

'It's all confidential,' I said, fully preparing to ignore that point. 'But to say that I am in a fury is under-egging things to say the least.'

'Oh crikey,' said Bunty. 'That puts my news about the elastic in its place. Come on,' she said. 'This sounds as if it calls for a large cup of tea.'

She looked at me again. I was scowling fiercely. While I was understanding about Charles having his leave cancelled, I could quite happily swing for Freddie and Diane.

'Blow tea,' said Bunty. 'By the sound of it, I think we're going to need some of Granny's gin.'

★

'In my view,' said Bunty the next morning, 'there are women who stick up for each other, and women who don't. You're either one or the other. It's as simple as that.'

We had just arrived at Paddington station to catch the train to Bunty's granny, Mrs Tavistock's, and as ever, the station was busy. Women were herding children in berets and caps onto platforms, holding tightly on to the smallest and optimistically calling out to the biggest to do as they were told and not wander off. A large group of sailors with their huge kit bags smoked cigarettes and stared at the Departures board, while a trio of soldiers bantered with each other as they cut in front of us with some swagger.

Bunty and I were discussing my row at the Ministry in a kind of shorthand, leaving out any identifiable details, but still dissecting the scenario.

'I just want to tell Guy and get it over and done with,' I said, using Mr Collins' first name as it was the weekend. 'I really shouldn't have lost my head like that.'

'You were defending his honour,' said Bunty, staunchly. 'And it's not your fault he had to rush off. Do it first thing on Monday and you'll be fine. Anyway, Freddie Frog and her gormless friend deserved it.'

I grinned. Bunty purposely made them sound like two washouts in the lower fourth at school. Nothing more than an irritant, and certainly not to be seen as a threat.

We joined the queue at the ticket office, behind a handsome young man in uniform, who was arm in arm with an elderly lady in a long coat. In her free hand she was clutching a hankie, but when she looked up at him as he chatted about the weather with almost desperate interest, her face was a picture of determination.

'I used to like railways stations,' I said to Bunty, quietly, as the lad and his grandma reached the window and he asked for a single ticket. 'Just watching people. Now I don't really. There are too many of them saying goodbye.'

Neither of us turned to watch as they walked away. We bought our tickets and after a diversion to buy a copy of *Woman Today* as I wanted to read Mrs Edwards' latest column, Bunts and I headed to the platform and a second-class carriage.

I opened the door and Bunty carefully climbed in first as we joined a young woman in a thin but smart black coat and a green hat that had been knocked slightly to one side by a large, crying baby. The lady was speaking calmly to a very cross little girl, while holding the baby on her knee. She apologised to me as I helped her move several suitcases to one side and the little girl said, 'Hello,' that her name was Ruby, she was four and she wanted to be sick.

'Nonsense, Ruby,' said her mother, cheerily. 'We aren't even moving and anyway, no one is ever sick on a train. Now come and sit nicely with me.'

Ruby looked peeved and hoiked herself up to sit beside me instead, glowering until the train passed through Ealing Broadway, at which point she whispered loudly that she wanted her potty. When reminded that she had Only Just Been, she shuffled herself backwards into the seat and adopted the self-righteous expression of someone thinking, On Your Head Be It.

Bunty, who was sitting opposite, gave Ruby an encouraging smile and valiantly tried to take the small person's mind off things.

'Hello,' she said. 'I'm Bunty.'

'What's that?' asked Ruby, pointing at Bunty's walking stick.

'Ruby,' said her mum. 'Come on now.'

'It's quite all right,' said Bunty. 'This is my stick.'

'Why?' said Ruby.

'It helps me walk,' said Bunty.

'Are you old?' said Ruby, looking unconvinced.

'I'm so sorry,' said her mother, bouncing the enormous baby on her lap. 'Ruby, come and sit next to me.'

'Grandad's old,' said Ruby, unmoved. 'And he's got no hair.'

'I have a bad leg,' said Bunty, helpfully.

Ruby's eyes widened.

'Does it hurt?' she asked.

'Sometimes,' said Bunty.

'Will it fall off?' said Ruby, now agog.

Her mother looked mortified, but Bunty laughed. 'Possibly,' she said. 'You'll have to wait and see.'

'I really am so sorry,' said the young woman again. 'What do we say, Ruby? Curiosity killed the cat.'

Ruby looked concerned, as if this might get in the way of seeing someone's leg fall off, and as she began to ask another question, I offered to hold her little brother to give his mum a break.

'That's so kind of you,' she said. 'As long as you don't mind. He's not even eighteen months yet but he weighs a ton.'

'Fatty,' whispered Ruby.

I ignored her and insisted it would be a pleasure, and she happily handed him over. As we all fell into a chat, I realised his mother had not been exaggerating. The bonny young man was definitely on the cuddly side.

'I'm sorry, we're stopping you reading your magazine,' she said, nodding towards the unopened copy of *Woman Today* that I had put on the opposite seat.

'Not at all,' I said. 'In fact, would you like it?' I could always get another copy later.

The young woman, who introduced herself as Mrs Oliver, looked pleased at the offer.

'That's very kind,' she said. 'Are you sure? A sit-down and a read is such a treat. I don't have time during the day with them both, and as soon as Ruby goes to sleep, Baby Tony usually wakes up.' She took a deep breath. 'We're on our way to my mum's now. I'm starting a new job on Monday.'

I was impressed. Mrs Oliver looked as if she had quite a lot on her plate already.

'Good for you,' I said. 'Are you allowed to say what it is?'

She sat up straighter. 'I think so. It's at an engineering

53

factory. My friend Betty just started there. Mum's going to look after these two while I'm at work.'

Baby Tony gave a loud burp. I stopped bouncing him, just in case.

'That's rude, Mummy,' said Ruby. Tony laughed.

'My poor mother,' said Mrs Oliver. 'It's all right, Ruby, he doesn't realise. Shall I take him from you? No? Well, please have this cloth.' She handed me a large square of muslin. 'Tony, don't be sick. I hope I'm not asking too much. My mother's quite young and Ruby loves her granny, don't you, love?'

'Granny,' said Ruby, a woman of few words.

'I'm sure they'll have loads of fun,' I said to Mrs Oliver. 'Did you work before the war?' I didn't want to pry but was interested to know. She only looked about my age.

'Not for long,' she said. 'I got married when I was eighteen and had Ruby the year after. I know we were young, but Anthony, my husband, was in the army and he said he reckoned that what with Hitler throwing his weight around it was only a matter of time before things got nasty.'

'Daddy,' said Ruby.

'Well done, Ruby,' said Mrs Oliver, beaming at her. 'Yes, "Daddy". Good girl.'

Ruby said Daddy again and put her thumb in her mouth.

Mrs Oliver began to talk about her husband, and as Bunty gave Ruby one of her gloves to play with, I held Baby Tony and listened. It was something I'd learned from Mrs Mahoney. People, she said, like to know someone is listening.

Bunty asked Mrs Oliver how she and her husband had first met, and as our journey dawdled on with the train stopping at random as trains always did these days, Mrs

Oliver chatted happily. They had both been sixteen and he was a cadet, and then they'd got married in 1936, which seemed a very long time ago now. A new calm descended on the carriage as Ruby stroked the fur on Bunty's glove and Baby Tony began to nod off.

'Young missy there was only two when Anthony went to France,' said Mrs Oliver, dropping her voice. 'She doesn't really remember.' She looked at her daughter for a moment and smiled. 'I know she's a pickle,' she said. 'My dear little pickle. Anthony's company was caught at Dunkirk.'

She said it quietly, and then after a glance at Ruby, gave a small, swift shake of her head.

'I had Baby Tony just after we heard. He's been such a good boy, and everyone's been very, very kind.' She smiled at me and then Bunty, proudly this time. 'They're both the spit of their dad.'

'Your husband must have been very handsome,' Bunty said. 'The children are beautiful.'

'Thank you,' said Mrs Oliver, softly. She was very pretty too, with dark eyes and almost black hair, which was un-fussily but immaculately styled.

'Goodness,' she said, brightly. 'I've rattled right on. You must think me awful. I don't know what brought that on.'

'Not at all, Mrs Oliver,' I said. 'It's nice to have a chat.'

'Isn't it?' she replied. 'And please, call me Anne. What about you girls? Do you have beaus?'

It was always difficult for Bunty when someone asked something like this, and as she had made her other glove into a puppet and was now playing with Ruby, I briefly mentioned Charles. I didn't say much, just how we'd met and that I worked for his brother, which I thought would be a good detour to take. I didn't want to say that Charles had also been at Dunkirk but had been lucky enough to come back.

'Is it difficult working with his brother?' asked Anne.

I said not at all, and that he was jolly nice. Then Bunty joined in and mentioned *Woman's Friend.*

'Goodness!' said Anne. 'My mum takes *Woman's Friend* every week. I bought a copy the other day and made the Celery Fingers. How exciting. It must be very glamorous.'

I told her that it really wasn't, but I very much enjoyed it, nevertheless. 'Your new job will be tons more important,' I said. 'Are you looking forward to it?'

We were somewhere near Slough and the train had come to a halt again. Anne took a tiny sandwich out of her bag, unwrapped it, and gave it to Ruby.

'Sort of,' said Anne. 'I've done my Government training course and I got through that all right. Mum managed to keep up with the children so at least she knows what she's letting herself in for. I'll probably just be sitting by a machine, but I am looking forward to it.'

I said I was sure there would be far more to it than that. But as Bunty nodded in agreement, it occurred to me that I didn't have a clue what went on in what I assumed by Anne's saying, *engineering,* was a munitions factory. So much for my claim that *Woman's Friend* had a spectacular plan for supporting women war workers. Other than knowing quite a lot about the Fire Service, and what friends said about their work, I wasn't up to speed in the least. When readers wrote in, all I did was give them the name and address of the relevant Government source of information. It all sounded rather limp now.

I wondered if Mr Collins or any of the others knew.

'Anne,' I said, slightly on a whim, 'once you're settled in, do you think I could ask you a few questions about what it's like? If you were allowed and didn't mind, of course. Perhaps what your friend thinks, too? It might be something our Editor would be interested in.'

Anne thought I was kidding around.

'Would we be in the magazine? Can you imagine? Although the trainers did say we have to be careful who we speak to. I don't mean to be rude, but you could be a spy.'

'Quite right too,' I said. 'We can give you and your bosses lots of proof that *Woman's Friend* is above board.'

Anne told me I was mad, but that it sounded great fun if I really meant it.

'Emmy means it,' said Bunty, loyally. 'She wouldn't say it if she didn't.'

'It's up to my boss, though,' I said. 'I don't want you to think I'm being a Flashy Type or anything. Shall I give you my address so you can have a think about it and then write to me if you really do like the idea?'

Anne happily agreed. I thought it would be nice to keep in touch anyway, as she seemed such a good sort.

Ruby had finished her sandwich. She wanted to know if we were there yet, and wasn't at all impressed when the answer was, Not Quite. I volunteered to take my turn in trying to entertain her, and had a spirited time attempting to answer questions that all started with, 'Why?'

Ruby was a bright button who made me laugh and I hoped we would become friends.

Anne and Bunty chatted, and while I tried to explain to Ruby how clouds were made, I heard Bunty telling Anne about William. As was her way, she spoke briefly of her loss, before turning the conversation to far happier memories. Anne listened and then joined in, understanding Bunty more than most.

As the train trundled on, it was just as well no one joining it made the rash choice of our carriage, as we made a cheerful if noisy group until Ruby declared that Baby Tony Has Done a Smell. With very poor timing, our station came into view, and Bunty and I had to gather up our things and abandon Anne. She was quick to assure me that her mum would be at their stop to get them off the train and they would be perfectly fine.

'Thank you for helping me with these two,' she said as Ruby asked if she could come with Bunty and me because Baby Tony still smelled.

Bunty and I assured Anne that the pleasure really had been all ours, and then stepped down onto the platform.

'BYE, BYE,' shouted Ruby doing her best to wave.

We stopped and turned to wave back. Anne was sitting behind Ruby, smiling widely and making Baby Tony move his pudgy little hand as well. As the train began to pull out of the station, I thought of Mr Collins' words the other day.

Think about the women. They're the ones keeping everything going while the boys are away . . . Our job is still to help them, just as much as we help the war effort.

Anne Oliver was exactly that woman. Keeping going, doing everything for her little family, earning a living and now signing up for war work as well. And all the time with the knowledge that her own boy would not be coming home. We needed to be thinking of Anne and the thousands of women like her, and more than anything, listening to them as well.

Bunty had summed it up. There are women who stick up for each other, and women who don't. It was as simple as that.

Anne had given me pause for thought. I was no longer worried about telling Mr Collins about the argument I had had with Freddie and Diane. Anne was worth a hundred of either of them.

As Bunty and I made our way to the ticket collector, I was already thinking of what *Woman's Friend* could do.

If we did more to actually help our readers when they were signing up for war work, rather than just calling on them to do it, perhaps we really would be doing our bit.

'Anne's such a trooper, isn't she?' I said to Bunty. 'Especially with everything she has on her plate.'

Bunty looked up from where she had been fishing in her coat pocket for her ticket.

'Do you think the Ministry cares what women like Anne have been through?' She said it lightly, but it was the most valid of points.

'I don't know,' I said. 'But I think they'd say that if she works, it's up to her, because she's volunteered. She won't be conscripted because she has young children.'

Bunty made a hmphh noise. 'Have you any idea how much pension war widows get?' she asked. 'Because unless they're married to an officer, or born with a silver spoon in their mouth, they don't have much choice but to go out to work.' She pursed her lips. 'Don't start me,' she said. 'Or I'll get stuck on my soapbox.'

I put my arm through hers. 'I don't mind if you do,' I said. 'I really hope Anne will write to us.'

'Me too,' said Bunty. 'Ruby still has one of my gloves.'

I laughed. Bunty didn't care about her glove. Anne Oliver had struck a chord with us both.

'She'll write,' I said, confidently. 'Ruby will see to that.'

CHAPTER 5

Woman's Friend Goes to War

BUNTY AND I returned to London after a weekend full of cheer, and laden with provisions from the country including a slightly damp cardboard box which held most of a chocolate biscuit cake baked with two real eggs and four tablespoons of caster sugar. We knew the sugar had been saved especially, despite Mrs Tavistock's heated denials, and having each wolfed down an enormous slice, Bunty and I agreed we would happily believe her if it meant we were able to take the rest of it home.

I was grateful to Mrs Tavistock for far more than the cake. The house in Pimlico, where Bunty and I lived, belonged to her, and since before the war the two of us had shared the small flat on the top floor. It had been great fun, but after Bunty had been hurt in the bombing we had moved down to the main house. It was easier for Bunts to manage with fewer stairs, but more than that, it was because the little flat was supposed to become her and William's first home. After Bill died, it wasn't the same. With Mrs Tavistock living permanently in the country, Bunty and I had moved into a couple of the bedrooms and opened up the old kitchen on the lower-ground floor. It was more than roomy, but warmer than the rest of the house, and once Roy and Fred from the fire station had helped move some comfy chairs in from unused rooms, it quickly became our new centre of activity.

Now, it wasn't just the cake that had given me a boost. It had been fun meeting Anne, Ruby and Baby Tony, and workwise, Anne had really got me thinking about speaking to readers who were already doing war work.

As I left for the office on Monday morning, the first post arrived with a letter from Charles, and I read it on the bus, grinning like a loon.

Darling E,

    I'm so sorry to muck up the weekend. Please see the following which I am sure can stand as a binding agreement.

    IOU A DECENT DAY OUT.

    INCL. CAKE.

    NEXT TIME I WON'T LET YOU DOWN.

    PROMISE.

    SIGNED: CAPT. C.H. MAYHEW

    Actually, it's more like heaps of days.

    I miss you, Em.

    All my love. Always.

    C xxx

    PS: Excuse haste – trying to catch the post.

    PPS: Bloody war.

He'd written the IOU in mad, swirly writing and drawn a square round it.

'Idiot,' I said, and buried my face in the paper. Then I put it in my pocket to re-read later, which as it turned out was in about five minutes.

I had tons I wanted to tell him, but while I had written to him at the end of both days of the weekend, it was never the same as just being able to chat.

As the bus stopped to let on two smart young women

in uniform, I turned my thoughts to work. This morning would be my first opportunity to talk to Mr Collins about my rashly promised Big Plan, and I was keen to get things out in the open.

By half-past eight, everyone other than Mr Collins was in the office and all speaking at once. Inspired by his news from the Ministry on Friday, we all wanted to share our thoughts now we were safely back at work and could speak openly about what was already being referred to as You Know What.

'I must admit I jotted down some ideas in a rather rudimentary code, just in case,' said Mr Brand. 'I haven't done that sort of thing for quite some time, but it was a wonder how swiftly it came back.'

He looked quietly pleased. In his early sixties and always spotlessly turned out, Mr Brand seemed to live in another world behind his little round spectacles, but I always had an inkling there was more to him than met the eye. That he would effortlessly remember writing in code struck me as a clue to possible adventures in his past. But he was giving nothing away and quickly retreated to sketching a cartoon.

'Well,' said Mr Newton, looking around as if he was about to give out Goebbels' address. 'I said to Mrs Newton, "I can't say why, but As A Matter of National Security, I'm going to sit in the cellar and think." It's quieter there, you see,' he added for clarity. 'Then she said, "Larry, I couldn't be prouder." And she wouldn't let me go down without a flask of tea and two squares of Bristol Plain Chocolate which were meant for the children.'

Mr Newton's eyes were shining, and I nodded keenly in support, partly because I liked him very much, but also because I was struggling with the image of him sitting in the coal cellar in the pitch dark, and I couldn't think of quite what to say.

'I've put together all the ideas from the editorial contributors that might be useful,' Kathleen said, producing a great wodge of notes. 'I don't know why I haven't done it before now.'

Everyone looked at their own efforts which now came across as a bit thin.

'Honestly,' said Kath. 'I've done nothing, really, it's everyone else's work. Although I did come up with some thoughts on how to make your whole wardrobe for the year.' She held up a page that looked like advanced mathematics. 'I've worked out the coupons, but I'm still looking at the cost. It's at ten pounds at the moment,' she said, frowning.

'Ten pounds,' said Hester, glassy-eyed. 'Imagine.'

'It is a lot of money,' I said, sympathetically.

'Do you know,' said Kath, 'last month, *Vogue* said to buy a basic black dress and ring the changes with accessories. The one they suggested cost eight guineas. Eight guineas. For a *basic* frock.'

Hester's eyes nearly fell out.

'It's another world,' said Mrs Mahoney. 'I treated myself to a new settee from the Army and Navy just before war started, and that only cost nine pounds t   's very well sprung, as well.'

'You could buy a nice little greenhouse for eight guineas,' said Mr Brand.

'Or go to Paris,' I said, getting carried away and despite the fact that I didn't have a clue how muc'   vould cost. 'If there wasn't the war.'

'I'd go to America,' said Hester. 'If I won the Pools.'

'I wouldn't spend eight guineas on a frock if I had it,' I said, feeling socialistic.

'Anyway,' said Kath, hauling us back   .e subject. 'Between Mrs Pye on fashion and me on knits, we can

63

come up with some patterns that are almost exactly the same.'

'Well done,' said Mr Brand, who was now drawing a greenhouse.

'Hear, hear,' said Mrs Mahoney. 'We can't have our readers feeling they can't be as smart as they'd like just because they weren't born with a silver spoon.'

I grinned. The *Woman's Friend* office was hardly a hotbed of radicalism, but the idea of an eight-guinea dress as A Basic had fired everyone up.

There was a knock at the open door and Mr Collins put his head in.

'Morning all,' he said. 'What's going on? I thought I was early, but you're already storming the Bastille.'

'We're doing no such thing,' said Mrs Mahoney who was a keen royalist and still felt let down by the last king.

'We're thinking of new ideas,' I said, before Mr Collins had a chance to say anything even more inflammatory. 'We've got loads.'

'Excellent,' said Mr Collins. He was looking quite chipper, which I took as a sign that his friend must have taken an upward turn over the weekend. 'I knew I could count on you all.'

He put his gas mask on the table and took off his coat, throwing it over the back of a chair and plonking his hat on top of it before sitting down. Mrs Mahoney frowned.

'It's already creased,' said Mr Collins amiably. 'I've been fire-watching. My God, it was cold. Now then, following on from our brief meeting on Friday, Kathleen, why don't you carry on?'

Kath began to talk through her thoughts properly. Everyone listened intently, even though a phone began to ring in Mr Collins' office next door.

Hester started to get up to answer it, but Mr Collins

shook his head. 'Thank you, Hester, but just ignore it. I trust you asked Switchboard not to put any calls through for the next hour? Thank you. Carry on, Kathleen.'

Hester said, 'Yes, Mr Collins,' and looked at him sympathetically, which I guessed was just in case The Worst had happened and he was putting on a brave front.

Kathleen ran through everything she had on file from the *Woman's Friend* contributors. Mrs Pye who did Fashion had suggested a new column on how to look on top form at work. It was called "On Duty for Beauty (Pamela Pye Reporting To Help)" and everyone agreed would be good for morale. Mrs Croft from "What's In The Hotpot?" had sent in some smashing ideas for dinners that took no time at all after a day at work, and after Mr Newton shared the results of his afternoon in the cellar, when Mr Collins turned to Mr Brand for his thoughts, things began to really motor.

'I've had some thoughts about our covers,' he said, reaching into his leather portfolio bag. 'I thought this sort of thing might help us set out our stall.'

We all leant forward to look, as Mr Brand laid out his ideas.

There was a collective, 'Oh I say,' all round.

The pictures Mr Brand had created showed happy, confident women, but instead of wearing a cardigan or a nice frock, they were in uniform. One in khaki was wearing a tin hat, holding binoculars and looking up into the sky, while another who was clearly in the Women's Auxiliary Air Force was discussing something inspiring with a dashing-looking chap. You couldn't see much of the man – the focus was entirely on the woman.

The last cover, though, really caught my eye. Under the large *Woman's Friend* heading was a blue-eyed woman with her hair poking out from under a scarf tied around her head. She was wearing dungarees and holding a large tin mug. Even though she had perfectly plucked eyebrows and slightly more lipstick than I would wear for a night out on the town, it was clear she was at work, and no doubt in a factory at that.

Mr Brand sat quietly, waiting to see what we all thought.

'Well,' said Mr Collins as everyone crowded round to look more closely. 'Mr Brand, you've created a triumph. These are spot on.'

I couldn't have agreed more.

'That one looks like my Gwen,' said Mrs Mahoney, with a catch in her voice.

'I wouldn't mind being like them,' said Hester shyly, from the back of the room.

'Need I say more?' said Mr Collins. 'Has anyone seen other magazines with covers like this?'

We all shook our heads.

'There we are then,' said Mr Collins. 'Thank you, again, Mr Brand. Now we just need to make sure the inside of the magazine lives up to your work.'

He looked over at me with an amused glint in his eye. 'Emmy?'

I opened my notebook, took a deep breath and dived in. 'The obvious thing,' I said, 'is a series with information on each of the Services and civilian war work, but other magazines have already done that. So, I thought we could give our readers a different approach – something more helpful.'

Everyone was listening so I ploughed on. I had decided to mention Anne Oliver at the end, once I'd tried to get everyone keen on the idea.

'The careers articles never tell you what it's really like to be a radio operator or a welder, or to be in digs with lots of strangers. From all the letters we get, tons of our readers don't know what to expect. So, I thought we could give them proper practical advice about what the life is really like, not just what they say in the adverts.'

Mrs Mahoney agreed. 'Some of the youngsters are as keen as mustard, but not in the least bit prepared.'

'Exactly,' I said. 'Listen to this. Hester, don't write these down as they're private.'

I rifled through a pile of letters that I had brought with me, until I got to one that was carefully written in a very neat, rather schoolgirl hand.

'*Dear Yours Cheerfully,*' I read out.

I am nineteen years old and about to join the Women's Royal Naval Service. I do so want to do a good job but as the work I have done before has just been with other girls, I am worried because I don't know how to treat the men I will work with. I don't have any brothers and my father died when I was small, so I don't know who to ask.

I'm sure I might put my foot in it by doing or saying the wrong thing. Please could you help?

Yours,

Worried About Men

'Bless her,' said Mrs Mahoney. 'It makes you want to go along on her first day and tell them all to be kind, doesn't it?'

'Exactly,' I said. 'Then there are the ones who think it's all one big jamboree. Last week some Bing Crosby fans wrote in to complain that their factory was boring and could we find them some soldier pen pals to liven things up. Preferably Australian,' I added.

Mrs Mahoney looked weary. 'I'm all for romance,' she said. 'But we've enough on as it is.'

'The readers are already keen to step up,' I said, turning

to Mr Collins. 'What they really need is practical advice. Look at this.'

I opened our current issue. There on the inside front cover was a striking advert by the Ministry of Labour and National Service. It had a headline that said, '*War Workers Stay Womanly*', and included several drawings of women supposedly doing something vital involving heavy engineering. But the pictures just showed a girl drying her hands for no obvious reason and another one standing around with her hands in her pockets not doing anything at all. The only one doing any work was poking vaguely at a bit of pipe as if it might bite her.

'*You will probably be given dungarees, which women of all ages say suit them, whatever their figure!*' I read out.

'I very much doubt it,' said Mrs Mahoney. 'I'd look like the back end of a bus.'

'No, you wouldn't,' said Kath.

'Not in the least,' I agreed.

The three men in the room joined in with a series of well-intentioned but uncertain noises. It was clear that none of them were sure if voicing an opinion on the trousers of an esteemed lady member of staff was quite The Done Thing.

I could have sworn I saw Mrs Mahoney roll her eyes. 'The point is,' she said, 'Emmy is right. If our readers think they'll be wafting around a factory looking like Greta Garbo in slacks, they're going to have the shock of their lives.'

'Exactly,' I said, grateful for her support. 'And this is where I think we might help. I've met someone who is about to start working in Munitions herself. She's called Mrs Anne Oliver and I don't think she'll mind being interviewed for *Woman's Friend*.'

'Go on,' said Mr Collins, looking interested.

'Well, I thought we could ask her what war work is really like. The news magazines do it all the time. *Picture Post* did rat-catchers last month. It's a horrible job but ever so important. They interviewed the men who do it and by the end of the article, you were cheering them on. We could do the same sort of thing, only with women doing war work. Women like Anne.' I finally paused for breath.

Mr Collins leant back in his chair. When he didn't say anything, I pushed on again.

'Anne's a *Woman's Friend* reader and that's the best part. Instead of us just telling them things from the Government, we can get the readers to tell each other instead. I thought we could call it "Woman's Friend at Work".'

Mr Collins narrowed his eyes and ruminated. 'Good name,' he said at last. 'And I like the idea. Mrs Mahoney – your thoughts?'

'Very good,' said Mrs Mahoney. 'If you ask me, most readers just want to know what they're getting into and that they'll be in it together with some other good sorts.'

'*In it together*,' repeated Mr Collins, more to himself than anyone. 'That's good too. Thank you, Mrs Mahoney. We could have a column with news on how women are working in areas that make a difference to the war. "A reader from Stafford is bolting ten thousand rivets a day", that sort of thing. "In It Together". Kathleen, can you look at this with Hester? Put that beside Emmy's "Woman's Friend at Work", add Mrs Pye's "On Duty for Beauty" and I think we have something. Mr Newton, could you sell advertising from this?'

Mr Newton nodded vigorously as Hester raced to write everything down.

While the whole team seemed very geed up, I was more

relieved than anything. Without any of them realising, they had come through with what could be the Big Plan I had shown off about in the lavatories. Not that I deserved it, but my colleagues might have got me out of rather a jam.

There was just one problem.

'Right,' said Mr Collins. 'Kathleen, can we kick it off with a small announcement in the next issue asking readers to write in with what they've been doing?'

Kathleen said calmly, 'Yes of course,' while Hester looked overwhelmed to be involved in a Ministerial project, but recovered herself after a hiccuppy swallow and a low-level guffaw.

'So, that leaves you, Emmy. Can you do a proper outline for "Woman's Friend at Work" by tomorrow? We'll need a horrendous amount of Ministry permissions to go anywhere near a war worker, but we can sort that out as long as your friend is still keen. Perhaps follow her progress, meet her workmates, see how she settles in? If we drop enough Ministry names the factory will jump at it. I like this,' he said finally. 'It could run as a series.' He stopped himself. 'What's the matter?'

I was staring at him and not writing anything down. My idea was getting bigger by the second, and from what I could make out, he was telling me to run the whole thing.

Mr Collins didn't wait for me to reply. 'It's about time we had you out and about being a journalist.' He looked at his watch. 'Thank you very much everyone, excellent work.'

He thought for a moment. Then instead of calling the meeting to a close, he continued.

'You know, this is our chance to do even more than our bit. I've absolutely no doubt that we'll be in the running to show both the Ministry and all our publishing peers that *Woman's Friend* is on form. But don't think about that.' He looked around the room at each of us. 'I know I mentioned this on Friday, but as we put plans together, I want you to focus on the readers. The country needs them to volunteer for war work, but what do *they* need? What do our readers want – and come to that, deserve? As we ask them to step up, how can we help? Those of you who lived through the first war know how hard war work really is.'

He glanced at Mrs Mahoney and they shared a moment of mutual acknowledgement before Mr Collins went on. 'Let's show the Ministry what our readers can do, and let's look after our readers while they're doing it.'

I had never heard Mr Collins speak like this before. He usually operated in an understated way, but today it was as if going to the meeting at the Ministry had reminded him he used to be a member of the first eleven and not just on the substitutes' bench. He could not have been more different from the man the two awful women in the lavatory had been discussing so rudely.

'And that,' he said, looking at everyone with almost a twinkle in his eye, 'is the closest you'll ever hear me attempt to be stirring. It won't happen again. Everyone all right? Then I think that is all.'

We all replied with exclamations of Absolutely and I Should Say So, together with heartfelt promises of working as hard as we possibly could. Mr Newton nearly broke into applause but thankfully for Mr Collins' blushes, Mrs Mahoney quietly put her hand on his arm, and he had second thoughts.

Inspired to the last man, everyone started speaking over each other with ideas on how everything could be done.

But I sat quietly. Mr Collins' words had hit home.

Let's show the Ministry what our readers can do, and let's look after our readers while they're doing it.

If this wasn't inspiring enough on its own, it was a throwaway comment that had left me unable to speak.

It's about time we had you out and about being a journalist.

Ever since school I had dreamed of this, and now it was happening. While it had been my idea to speak with Anne, I had not for a moment thought I would be running a feature series to be done with approval from the Ministry.

I was thrilled that Mr Collins thought I could manage. I hoped Anne would still be keen on the idea.

Just under a year ago, Mr Collins had been the person to give me a job at *Woman's Friend*. Now he was giving me the chance to take my first steps to becoming a reporter.

I wouldn't let him down, or the Ministry, of course. As I began to collect the readers' letters and carefully put them back in my file, I thought of all the women who had written in wanting to help the war effort. So many of them had been waiting months for an official reply or been told they were too old or too young or were simply worried about doing the right thing.

This was our chance to help them.

And it was time for me to step up.

CHAPTER 6

Stitched Up Like a Kipper

'THERE'LL BE A bit of juggling on this one,' said Mr
Collins. 'Just to keep everyone happy.'

I was sitting in his office after the meeting and he was
thinking out loud. After the excitement of coming up with
the new plans, there was a huge amount to sort out. We
would have to make sure Anne was on board for the
articles, persuade her employers it was worth their while,
and above all, ensure we had all the official approvals in
place that would give us access to a Government Supplier.

None of which had crossed my mind when I volunteered the idea.

Mr Collins, however, seemed quite happy with the
scenario and didn't appear to think there was anything
insurmountable.

'I'll get onto the permissions, and Emmy, you contact
your friend. If she's still interested, find out who runs the
place and draft a letter to them. Write it from me but say
I have directed our Careers Editor to take charge of this
very important Ministerial project.' He smiled. 'You'll find
people can be insufferable snobs about titles, so do you
mind going along with that? It's ridiculous, but all part
of the game. We should get you some cards printed up.'

Careers Editor! Cards! I tried not to look as giddy as
I felt. But I did wish Mr Collins might pause for breath.

It was more than time that I told him about my disagreement in the ladies'.

'Don't look so concerned, Emmy, I've every faith in you,' he said, misunderstanding my reticence. 'Just be honest, don't mess people about, and never make anything up, because despite what you may hear about being a reporter, the best ones don't. Happy with everything?'

'Ah,' I said, wondering if the rule about Never Make Anything Up could start from today rather than including last Friday. 'Yes. Very much so. Thank you. Careers Editor is quite a lot to take in, even if it is made up.'

'Hmm,' said Mr Collins. 'I realise I've just broken one of my own rules.' He rolled his eyes at himself. 'Emmy, do try not to follow my terrible example.'

This was making my secret worse.

'There was just one thing,' I said, uneasily.

'Fire away.' Mr Collins leant back in his seat and reached for an empty packet of cigarettes on his perennially messy desk. A slightly uncertain knock heralded Hester, who poked a flushed face around the half-open door.

'Mr Collins,' she gasped. 'I'm sorry but there's a lady on the telephone. From an office. For you.'

'Thank you, Hester,' said Mr Collins, patiently. 'Please take a message and I'll call her back.'

Hester looked pained. 'She says could you do that quite urgently, please? She says she's already called once, and Mr Clough has to go into a meeting in a minute and he very much wishes to speak.'

'The Under-Secretary?' I said, now feeling warm, myself. 'The man from the Ministry.'

It came out dramatically. Mr Collins looked unconcerned.

Hester nodded vigorously. 'That's right. From the Ministry.'

'Ah yes,' said Mr Collins, as if it was the butcher calling to say he'd saved him a chop. 'Thank you, Hester. Is that the number in your hand? I will return her call after Emmy and I have finished.'

Hester offered to ring the secretary and put Mr Collins through.

'No need,' said Mr Collins. 'I can manage myself. Now, Emmy, I believe you were about to say something?'

As Hester retreated into the corridor, Mr Collins looked expectantly at me and I attempted to pick up my line of thought. It was safe to say that Hester was not the only one who had been unnerved. The secretary of an actual Under-Secretary to a Government Minister had called our office. This was not an everyday thing, even if Mr Collins was taking it in his stride.

My mind darted about as I thought of possible reasons. Perhaps the Ministry men were calling all the Editors as a sort of follow-up to the meeting. Or perhaps Mr Collins knew Mr Clough personally. Then my mind wandered off track as minds do when you have behaved perfectly above board, other than just one small thing that perhaps hadn't gone quite entirely to plan.

I found myself gripped by a sudden and particularly ferocious bout of paranoia.

What if someone had noticed me loitering outside the lavatories well after the Ministry briefing had finished? I had absolutely belted downstairs too, which must have looked shifty. Not to mention implying to the man by the lift that the two journalists in the lavatories were refusing to leave.

'EMMY,' said Mr Collins, loudly. 'Are you still with me? I really should phone Clough back.'

He began to look under a pile of papers for a new packet of cigarettes.

'About that,' I said. 'You know, when we were at Senate House?'

'Ah ha,' he said, now opening a drawer and rummaging around.

'Well, there were these journalists – ladies – in the lavatories.'

'Ah ha.' He found a new packet and began to open it.

'And they were being rather unkind.'

Mr Collins took out a cigarette.

'About *Woman's Friend*. In fact, rather rude. Very rude really.'

'Ah,' he said, with no Ha.

He put the unlit cigarette down, paused, and then rubbed his hand across his chin. 'I thought you looked flushed when we met up. At this point, may I interrupt with a wild guess?'

I nodded.

'Did you by any chance put them right on this point?'

In the last months, Mr Collins had come to know me well, and as he had previously bailed me out of a sticky situation when I had taken some matters into my own hands, it seemed likely he would presume I had gone off the straight and narrow again.

'Yes,' I confirmed.

Mr Collins now put the cigarette in his mouth, took a match out of a small silver box on his desk, struck it and lit up. He took a long drag and then, as he blew out the smoke, began to smile.

'I knew I shouldn't have left you on your own,' he said. 'Come on, let's be having you. This is bound to be good.'

*

It took me some time to give Mr Collins a blow-by-blow account of my argument with Freddie and Diane. I left out the really nasty personal things they said about him, but didn't hold back on how low an opinion they had of our magazine. I also told him how I had shown off about *Woman's Friend*'s tremendous War Effort Recruitment Plan that didn't actually exist.

'I'm really, very sorry,' I said. 'Have I dropped a terrible brick? Also, I told someone they were loitering and refusing to leave. Do you think that's why Mr Clough has called?'

I held my breath, wondering if my temporary title of Careers Editor was about to be withdrawn. Even if it was purely for show, it would have been ever so nice.

'Well, Emmy,' said Mr Collins. 'Somehow I don't think the Under-Secretary would be trying to track you down himself. He'd probably have just sent the Military Police. THAT WAS A JOKE. Oh God, you look as if you're about to be ill. I do apologise. Here, have a cigarette. Damn, I forgot you don't smoke.'

He looked at me with an expression of exasperation. I was still fighting off the possibility of actually being sick. The Military Police. The horror surged over me like a wave.

'Emmy, it's absolutely fine. Really. You should have told me straight away. I hope you haven't been concerned. They sound ghastly. Well done for keeping your end up.'

I nodded weakly, feeling foolish. Mr Collins sighed. 'You know, I'd like to think the publishing lot rub along with each other pretty well most of the time, but it's like any industry, you get the good ones like Monica or Simons, and you get the idiots, like these two or Jarrett. Don't give it another thought. And certainly not regarding the Ministry's call. Speaking of which, I'd better see what he wanted.'

I thanked him, delighted not to have made a complete howler. I was about to take my leave when Mr Collins' phone rang again. He gave me a grin and motioned me to stay where I was. 'Could be him,' he said and picked up the phone.

'Collins . . . Ah, Hester. Yes, yes, of course.' He paused as I assumed Hester put Mr Clough through. However, it was somebody else.

'Miss Jackson,' said Mr Collins. 'Good morning. Yes, thank you.' He paused again, cleared his throat and stubbed out his cigarette. 'Lord Overton. Good morning, sir.'

It wasn't the Ministry at all, but the owner of Launceston Press himself.

I sat very straight in my chair. I had only met Lord Overton once, in a quite terrifying encounter I would never forget, but the portrait of him in the reception area downstairs greeted me every day when I arrived at work, and I always silently wished it a respectful Good Day. I had admired Lord Overton from a distance before I joined *Woman's Friend*, and since meeting him respected him more than ever. His generosity, along with Mr Collins', was the reason I had any sort of a career.

'I see,' Mr Collins was saying. 'Very nice to hear and decent of him to call. Of course. Mr Clough. Excellent chap. Yes. I'm about to speak to him now. Ha. Yes indeed – perhaps a little premature. We're still working on the details, but I think they should go down well. Of course, sir. As soon as we can. Yes, wasn't it? Great pleasure. And to Lady Overton as well. Thank you, sir. Goodbye, now.'

Mr Collins put the phone down and looked at me, thoughtfully. 'Tell me, you didn't by any chance get the names of those women, did you?'

'Not entirely,' I said. 'Just Freddie and Diane.'

Mr Collins raised his eyebrows for just a second. 'Of

course,' he said, almost to himself. 'Freddie Baring. *Ladies' Week*. I thought I saw her. Ah, the joy.'

'Do you know Mrs Baring?' I asked.

'A little,' said Mr Collins. 'I imagine you may have gleaned that she and I are not tremendously good friends.'

I kept quiet and Mr Collins grinned. 'I won't ask if she said anything about me,' he said. 'I can hazard a pretty good guess if she did. We've clashed swords now and then over the years. Baring's her pen name. She's Freda Clough by birth.'

I gaped at him. It was the same name as the Under-Secretary to the Minister of Information.

'And I'd wager she has very kindly told her brother all about the big plan he is now expecting from *Woman's Friend*. Well, it's certainly grabbed the Ministry's attention. You could probably make out that he hasn't only been on the telephone to me.'

Now I really did feel the blood run from my face.

'Don't worry. Lord Overton sounded quite happy. He's a sporting man and enjoys the thrill of the chase. He won't have missed a thing.'

For a moment, Mr Collins sat and thought, staring into mid-distance as he mulled it all over. Then, and to my complete surprise, he let out a huge laugh. 'You know this is actually quite fine,' he said. 'Freddie B has tried to stitch us up like a kipper. No matter!' he said, standing up and thumping both hands down on his desk. 'We can handle it. Emmeline Lake, whether you meant to or not, you have put *Woman's Friend* onto the Ministry's map. Now we just have to make sure that's where we stay.'

'Really?' I said. 'And is that all right?'

Mr Collins stared at me. 'Of course,' he said, becoming serious. 'Emmy, don't waste a moment thinking about what happened last week. I'm afraid Mrs Baring can be quite a piece of work, and I'm sorry she tried to bully you. But actually, she has done us a favour. This is a real opportunity for *Woman's Friend* to make its mark with both the Ministry and Lord Overton. I have every faith we will rise to the challenge. Emmy, I have every faith in *you*.' He leant forward over his desk. 'You leave the Ministry to me and now, if you don't mind, can I suggest you go and write that letter to your friend?'

★

With the knowledge that Mr Collins had faith in me, and no small amount of relief that he found Freddie Baring a silliness rather than a threat, I was eager to write to Anne and get things moving. To my delight, she was quick to agree to the idea.

Dear Emmy,

Thank you so much for your letter which arrived today. We thought Ruby had mumps but she was just over-tired. Of course, she thinks she has and is now telling everyone that she has Monks!

I can't believe Woman's Friend would really like to interview us about our work! Are you sure? As I've only just started, I don't know how helpful I'll be, but the other girls will have more to tell you. Betty can't wait, but as you said, we're keeping it a secret.

So far, I like it here. It's a long day but the girls are friendly, and the canteen is good — three-course meals for a shilling, and more greens than you can fit on your plate.

Mum is enjoying looking after the children although Mrs Bagley next door told me Tony screams for the first hour after I've left the house in the morning. Mum says it's not nearly that long, and I hope so, as I have to leave at a quarter past five. I'm a bit tired, but Betty says I'll get used to it.

The factory's director is called Mr Terry. I've not met him, but Betty thinks he would be the one to write to. She reckons he'll jump at the chance because it will make him look good! Don't say that though if you meet him. I hope it was all right to put his name in a letter. I haven't put my address or anything in case this letter gets lost.

I'd better go as Ruby should have been asleep hours ago. She really is a one.

Hope you are all right. Do say hello to Bunty from us all.

Yours,

    Anne

Dear Anne

Thank you so much for your letter. I am so pleased you're settling in and things are going well. I've told Mr C who is very pleased. He'll sort things here and then if all is well will write to the person at your end and agree details.

More from me later and hope to see you soon!

Yours,

    Emmy

    PS: Do Ruby and Baby Tony like Beatrix Potter?

Dear Emmy

Please excuse the postcard, I always seem to be in a rush. Thank you for your letter. Goodness, it's really happening.

Ruby loves B.Potter but is scared of the frog!

Your friend,

    Anne

Dear Emmy

LOVE RUBY
X X X

Dear Ruby

Thank you for your lovely letter! We were thinking of you and thought you might like these books to read with Mummy or Granny. Don't worry as Jeremy Fisher (the frog you don't like) is not in any of these books.

Please tell Mummy that everything she talked about with Emmy on the phone is going to plan and definitely happening this Thursday!

Love from,
Mummy's friends, Emmy and Bunty
Xxx

CHAPTER 7

We Always Welcome Ladies

IT SEEMED AN absolute age before the Ministry finally gave the go-ahead for me to interview Anne and her friends, even if it was only just over three weeks. I was raring to go and began to grumble unpatriotically that everyone involved was just too slow to catch cold.

But that, as Mr Collins said, Was The Civil Service For You, and in his view, getting approval for interviewing workers at a munitions factory in such a short period of time was like watching Jesse Owens do the hundred-yard dash.

In the meantime, I had more than enough to be getting on with. I was working two half-days and three full days at *Woman's Friend* and managing to fit my fire-station shifts around them as well. My friend Thelma at the station said I must be mad, but as she had two jobs and three children, she had to agree that I was hardly alone. As Thel said, everyone we knew was pushing themselves as far as they could.

In the office, all the ideas the team had come up with for our grandly named War Effort Recruitment Plan were put into a fancy presentation and sent to Mr Clough as well as the Ministry of Supply, the Ministry of Labour and National Service, and Lord Overton himself. The morning Hester took them down to the post room, Kath and I waved her off as if we were sending her across the Atlantic.

'There's no going back now,' said Kath, cheerful in a fancy-neck knit.

'You've just made my stomach go again,' I said, feeling it flip. 'Talk about people in high places. I'm surprised we're not sending a copy to the King.'

'His is in the next post,' said Kath. She gave me a gentle nudge. 'Don't worry, Emmy. Think of how good it will feel when it's all gone to plan.'

She had made a good point. As long as we delivered on what we had promised, our magazine would be able to hold her head up high. I had to admit to giving a thought to rotten Freddie Baring and her friend. So much for *Woman's Friend* not being up to the mark. Already our plan felt far bigger than anything I could have imagined.

By the time everything was set up for the interview, Anne had been at the factory for nearly a month, which was perfect timing to ask her about both her initial reaction to a job in munitions and how she was getting on now that she had settled in.

When the day of the visit finally came, however, while I was very much looking forward to seeing Anne and meeting her friends, I had to admit to a forceful bout of first night nerves.

As much as I had tried to play it down both at work and with Bunty and Charles, the enormity of my very first journalistic assignment had been giving me butterflies for days.

At a quarter to six o'clock in the morning, I lay in bed looking forward to what felt like a mixture of Christmas Day and the biggest exam of my life. I had read and re-read a Highly Confidential document sent from the factory's Public Relations Manager and now repeated parts of it out loud in the dark.

'"Chandlers is a large engineering organisation reporting to the Ministry of Supply and making parts for guns," I recited. 'Production is on a twenty-four-hour basis with three shifts per day. It employs over fifteen hundred women and aims to recruit at least double that figure." It takes over an hour to get there on the bus, and on Thursdays the canteen always does sponge with a sauce.'

Anne had told me about the bus and the sponge.

'Come on, Lake,' I said. 'You've been dreaming of this since you were twelve.'

Lolling in bed talking to myself was not going to get anything done.

My clothes and bag were ready and hanging up outside the huge Edwardian wardrobe that dominated my bedroom. I wanted to give the Factory Director an impression of maturity while also looking approachable to Anne's friends, so had enlisted Bunty to help choose what I should wear. I even ran through my decision with Charles when he phoned to wish me good luck, although he hadn't the slightest idea about clothes.

'Well, Em,' he said brightly, 'that sounds top drawer. I had no idea that adding a square pocket to a jacket tells people you are both professional and friendly at the same time. I must say, it's like some sort of code.'

'It is,' I said. 'I am only sorry you didn't realise it before. You have been missing vital information for months.'

'I couldn't be more ashamed,' said Charles. 'You're going out with a dud.'

Then he had wished me good luck and told me that I already sounded like a journalist of the highest order and everyone would be enormously impressed.

I dressed quickly and checked my bag to make sure I had everything I needed. The brown leather case held a letter of introduction from Mr Collins, approvals in writing from two different Ministries and another set referring to the man from the Photographic News Agencies who was coming to take photographs after I had had lunch with Anne and her friends.

By far the best of all were the cards I had been given by Mrs Mahoney the previous day.

Miss E. Lake
Careers Editor

WOMAN'S FRIEND MAGAZINE

Launceston Press Ltd,
Launceston House, London EC4.
Telephone Central 6271

Even though I knew the job title wasn't true, it didn't matter. I usually stood five foot four inches high. With these I felt at least six foot two.

I also had my reporter's notebook including a long list of questions, a spare notebook, two pens, three pencils, and two hankies. I was fully prepared and ready, but at the last minute after a stern look in the mirror, I quickly took off my earrings, wiped away the precious lipstick I had applied and switched my perfectly acceptable and smart brown felt hat for a sort of flowerpot thing that did me no favours at all.

Bunty was already up and in the kitchen when I rushed downstairs to make a sandwich to eat on the train.

'Morning,' she said, then did a double-take when she saw me. 'Good grief. I don't wish to be unkind, but what on earth's that?'

'Do I look awful?' I asked. 'I was trying for gravitas.'

'That's one way of putting it,' said Bunty. 'I love you dearly, Em, but if you turn up in that, they'll lock you up. Go and get rid of that terrifying hat, and I'll make you a sandwich. AND PUT ON SOME LIPSTICK,' she shouted as I thanked her and belted back up to my room.

Three hours later, and looking slightly more acceptable again, I had arrived in Berkshire and was waiting outside the railway station for my lift to the factory. The rain was hurling itself down in the sort of way which makes you feel it is bearing a personal grudge, and I began to wonder if it would have been easier to try to find a bus. Unlike Anne who had a twenty-minute walk and then an hour's ride to work, I had been told that Mr Terry, the Factory Director, would come to collect me himself.

Twenty minutes after the agreed time, finally, a shiny black Austin 16 drew up to the kerb. It was just the sort of impressive car one would imagine a man in charge of a large factory to own, not least as he must be getting special permission to have the petrol to run it.

As the windscreen wipers clunked their way back and forth, I could just make out a large, dark-haired man. He looked out of the window and stared straight past me.

Turning the collar of my coat up against the rain, I strode up to the car and knocked on the window. It didn't feel the most dignified start to my reporting career, but it was either that or wave frantically and risk looking slightly mad.

The window rolled down an inch.

'Yes?' said the gentleman, clearly unused to lunatics accosting him in his car.

'Mr Terry?' I shouted, aiming to be heard above the wind which was whipping itself up into a state.

'Mmm?'

'I'm Miss Lake. From *Woman's Friend* magazine. For the interviews?'

'Oh!' he said and wound up the window. Then, just as I thought he was going to drive away, he got out and ran around to open the passenger door for me.

'In you go,' he shouted, slamming the door behind me and just missing my foot. Then he ran back and got in again on his side.

'How do you do?' I said, wriggling round to face him.

'Terry,' he answered, shaking my hand, or rather, just holding it for several moments. 'Factory Director,' he said, still holding on. 'Thought a chap was coming. Our Public Relations Manager mentioned a Mr Collie?'

'Mr Collins,' I said. 'Our Editor. He has instructed me to write the feature. It should have been in the confirmation letter from the Ministry.'

'Shame. Thought he'd like a ride in the jalopy. You won't like cars of course, but we always welcome ladies.'

Then he smiled with lots of teeth and started the car, and before I could say anything we hurtled away from the station as if we were on the run from the police.

Mr Terry had the air of a man who was used to attention. He was perhaps fifty and although slightly going to fat, looked like the sort of man who would wallop himself in the stomach and say, 'See that? All muscle,' to someone who hadn't really wanted to know.

As we drove at breakneck speed and Mr Terry narrowly avoided hitting a delivery boy on a bicycle and then a rag and bone man's horse, he gave me his own version of the history of the factory, helpfully explaining that since he had joined the operation, it had started doing tremendously well.

'I'm not surprised the Ministry is interested,' he said. 'The results speak for themselves – or would if the Censors let us. Ha! And our ladies couldn't be happier. Good pay, good hours. They'll all say it. Mr Rice will tell you what you need to know. He's one of the Works Managers.'

Mr Terry spoke in the same manner as he drove, with the result that listening to him was like being verbally run over. I told myself not to go with my first impression. The journey took us just over fifteen minutes and Mr Terry didn't bother with brakes until the very last moment when the car had to stop at the security gates to the factory.

'Morning boys,' he said, saluting the guard as if he was their Commanding Officer. 'I have Miss Lake here from the press.'

The security guard looked at me and asked me to get out of the car. I did as I was told and passed him my identification documents together with the folder of introductory letters.

'She'll just be in Shed Twelve,' said Mr Terry. 'And the canteen.'

The guard pursed his lips, checking everything as I stood by the car being looked at by one of his colleagues until he gave me back the folder together with a piece of paper with my details, a stamp with the date and BLUE SHIFT DAY PASS ONLY. Then he handed me a large badge that read VISITOR and TO BE ACCOMPANIED AT ALL TIMES, and said that under no circumstances was I to go anywhere on my own. Finally, he looked through my bag, which I didn't mind though I was self-conscious about the remains of my sandwich.

With the OK to continue, I rushed back to the car and Mr Terry made the engine roar before we took off again. As we drove along a wide road with numerous others leading off it to vast camouflaged buildings, all with blacked-out windows or no windows at all, we passed a long line of lorries on their way to the exit. The whole place was bigger than the village I had grown up in.

'Can you tell me about some of these buildings?' I asked.

'You'll like the canteen,' said Mr Terry. 'I don't eat there.'

He drove to the front door of a huge two-storey building, stopping just before we hit a brass sign with his name on it.

I opened the door and climbed out of the car, pausing for a moment to straighten my jacket and compose myself after the dare-devil ride.

Mr Terry stood by the entrance to the building, waiting for my full attention. Looking very much like the cat who got the cream and was then offered a second helping, he opened his arms.

'This is it, young lady,' he said, loudly. 'Welcome to Chandlers.'

CHAPTER 8

They're Better Than a Lot of the Men

AFTER HIS FANFARE, Mr Terry ushered me through an unremarkable set of steel doors and into a small foyer with three wooden chairs and a low metal table with copies of *The Motor* magazine on it. A receptionist sat behind a small hatch with a grille on it which made the room look rather like a railway station ticket office. Also there, to my great delight, was Anne, who was standing to attention and looking very professional in dark trousers and a brown coat, her hair sensibly tied back and half hidden under a blue knitted snood. She was smiling broadly, and I very much wished I could say hello properly and give her a hug.

Next to her stood a stocky, balding gentleman whose face did not exactly say, 'Welcoming Committee.' No wonder Anne looked as if she was on parade.

'Ah hah,' said Mr Terry. 'Mr Rice. And, um . . .'

'Mrs Oliver,' I said, before it became too obvious that he either didn't know or had forgotten Anne's name.

'How do you do, Mr Rice?' I said, realising I had just blotted my copybook by saying hello to Anne first. 'Miss Emmeline Lake. I'm very pleased to meet you. Launceston Press is most indebted to you for your help.'

'Mmm,' said Mr Rice. I stretched out my hand, daring him not to shake it. 'How d'you do,' he continued, looking cross.

Mr Terry appeared to have lost interest. He looked over to the receptionist and shouted, 'Noreen,' at her, to which she diligently replied, 'Good morning, Mr Terry,' and he seemed to cheer up.

'Miss Lake,' he said. 'I will leave you in the capable hands of Mr Rice and your friend. Good day.'

And without mentioning when I might be able to interview him properly about women recruits, he strode off through a door marked PRIVATE and was gone.

The three of us stood in silence for a moment. Anne surreptitiously raised her eyebrows at me.

'It was very good of Mr Terry to come to the station,' I said, to fill the lull.

'If I had that car and his petrol, so should I,' said Mr Rice. 'Miss Lake, this is a very busy factory. Where are you from, again, and how long will this take?'

Anne frowned, but after Mr Terry's non-stop gushing, I found myself preferring Mr Rice's straightforward approach.

'I'm from *Woman's Friend* magazine,' I said. 'I'm here to write an article on women war workers. It's part of the Government's recruitment drive.'

'That explains it,' snorted Mr Rice. 'If there isn't a knighthood handed out here by the end of the war, I'll watch a pig fly past in a Spitfire.'

Anne stared innocently at the ceiling for all the world looking as if she didn't know who he meant. I wondered whether I was supposed to laugh or not. Mr Rice looked at me.

'I've worked at Chandlers most of my adult life,' he said as if it told me everything I needed to know. He turned to the receptionist, his tone less stern. 'Mrs Noakes, I'm assuming you know about Miss Lake's visit? Thank you. Come on, Miss Lake, I'll give you a tour. Mrs Oliver, you know the way.'

As Mrs Noreen Noakes nodded and gave a friendly smile, Anne opened a door and led us down a long corridor. Even before we left the reception area, I could hear the rumble of machinery.

'This is Shed Twelve,' said Mr Rice, walking beside me. 'It's one of the biggest. You'll see that Management are upstairs and if they care to, they can watch what everyone is doing. It's not the same for all the sheds, so you can decide for yourself if Mrs Oliver is lucky or not to be in this one.'

We stopped at a pair of heavy double doors. Mr Rice looked at me, as if inspecting a machine.

'Your shoes are all right, but Mrs Oliver, can you please give Miss Lake a scarf for her hair. You'll be fine with those earrings. There's nothing likely to go "Bang" in here. Watch your step as it can get greasy. Stay close, and don't put your hands or face near anything noisy or moving.'

'You don't really need this,' whispered Anne as she showed me how to twist the scarf into a sort of turban over my hair. 'That's it, tuck in the ends. Don't worry about the bang thing. He just means there's no explosives.'

I nodded and tried not to look relieved. Anne mentioned explosives as a casual aside. The last time I saw her she had been gently handing bread and jam to her daughter. I was very impressed.

As Mr Rice opened the doors and motioned me to follow, I entered an entirely different world. A small army of women were working at benches or standing at thumping great pieces of machinery, pulling levers, pushing through unidentifiable chunks of metal or deftly changing parts that were being cut or hammered into shape. Kitted out in the same uniform of brown overalls or coats as Anne, they all had their hair tied back in a wide variety of different coloured scarves, as if to remind you that they were individuals and not just additional cogs in the factory machine.

A few men with clipboards were walking around looking over the women's shoulders and occasionally speaking to them, although I couldn't imagine how anyone could hear a word. The rumbling I heard before had now become an almost deafening roar from the hundreds of drilling, cutting and pounding machines.

Mr Rice gave an unexpected wink. 'You'll get used to it,' he shouted, not unkindly.

'Right you are,' I shouted back. There was no point trying to pretend I had seen anything like this before. The noise was overwhelming, as if every bus in the country had stopped outside your house with its engine running, while people took it in turns to whack it with huge iron bars and scrape nails along the sides.

For a moment I was embarrassed that it was a shock to me, as if I was just on a day out from my little office in London. But after months of the Blitz and night after night of planes and guns and the falling of bombs, I felt I'd earned the right to look Mr Rice in the eye. I had no need to apologise that being in a factory was new to me.

More than anything, I wanted to understand what the women were working on. I watched as some yelled information at each other, while others pored over their work, deep in concentration. A few were even managing to chat. One or two nodded at Anne. Everyone knew exactly what they were doing and as if they had been working there all their lives. It was one of the most striking things I had ever seen.

'I'm on one of the capstans,' yelled Anne, as we went over to a woman deftly switching instruments over to set them drilling like mad. 'Watch out, there's swarf all over the place. I'll go and find Sally. She'll clear it up.'

94

'It's part of the barrel,' bellowed Mr Rice. 'After here they go onto Fourteen for the next stage.' He paused for a moment and then fixed me with a stare. 'Miss Lake, if you want to know about women workers, I can tell you that this lot are all right. Some of them talk too much,' he nodded at a group nearby, 'but they're doing good work.'

'Are they all new recruits?' I shouted, as we moved on and a fearsome piece of kit smacked down on some metal, squashing it flat and threatening to burst my eardrums.

'Most of them.' Mr Rice warmed to his subject. 'They're better than a lot of the men I've dealt with over the years.' He gave a quick, unexpected grin. 'That's surprised you, hasn't it? I bet you reckoned I think women can't do the job.'

I denied the thought as we moved away from the production line to where it was very slightly quieter. 'Why is it the women make such good workers?' I asked, partly to see if he was just humouring me, and partly because if he had a good answer, it could work perfectly in the article I wanted to write.

'Miss Lake,' said Mr Rice. 'Have you a brother, or a sweetheart who's joined up?'

'Yes, both,' I said. 'RAF and Artillery.'

'Good lads,' said Mr Rice. 'And the main thing you care about is that they'll be safe and come home in one piece?'

'Of course. That and winning the war.'

'Well, in my view that's why the women work well. They've a personal interest in knowing full care has gone into every single weapon or piece of metal that comes out of this factory.'

I understood what he was saying. There was a strange comfort in seeing the power of the munitions factory for myself. In peacetime I would perhaps have felt differently. In the middle of a world war, I wanted to know that Charles, or my brother Jack, or any other man who was risking his life, would have every possible chance to defend himself.

'Of course, they're also good at the detail work. It's the smaller fingers.' He held up a sausagey hand. 'They're better equipped for the fiddly bits. Now, what else do you want to know?'

I wanted to say, 'Everything.' What guns were the women making? How many hours did they work? What were they paid? And was it as hard as it looked?

Most of all, I wanted to talk to the women themselves, to find out how they felt about their jobs and being part of such an enormous team effort. Politicians said, 'We're In It Together,' endlessly but I wanted to see if Chandlers' women workers felt the same way. Did they really feel they were doing their bit for their boys, or was Mr Rice just being fanciful?

'When can I speak with the women?' I shouted as a screeching noise threatened to drown me out.

As Anne re-joined us, Mr Rice looked at his watch. 'Not long, now. And Mr Terry definitely said he was happy about this?' he said, which I thought enigmatic. Then his face changed completely.

'Hold up,' he snapped. 'What the hell's that?'

I followed his stare. To my astonishment, two young children were sitting cross-legged on the floor by the wall. They couldn't have been more than twenty feet from one of the lathes.

'Take Miss Lake to the canteen,' Mr Rice barked at Anne. 'TO THE CANTEEN, MRS OLIVER,' he shouted, as Anne made a move towards the children instead.

'Blast it,' she said, as women at their benches began

96

to look round and I tried to see what was happening. 'Come on, Emmy. It'll make it worse if we stay. He's going to hit the roof.'

Looking over my shoulder, I saw that one of the men with clipboards had rushed over to Mr Rice and the two of them were now having a very animated discussion. Mr Rice had his hands on his hips and looked absolutely livid.

'Anne,' I said as she dragged me out. 'What on earth are children doing in a munitions factory?'

'Ssssh,' said Anne, even though with the noise of the factory there was no chance we could have been overheard.

She hustled me out of a side door and into the damp air where she finally let go of my arm.

I asked again. 'Why would anyone in their right mind bring their children here? This is the last place in the world they should be.'

Anne's face had been a picture of concern, but now a look of anger flashed across it. 'Don't be so quick to judge,' she said, hotly. 'Their mum Irene is one of my friends. She hasn't a choice. They've nowhere else to go.'

*

As Anne and I made our way to the canteen in the building next door, she began to fill me in on what was happening in the factory.

'I'm sorry to shout at you. This is the third time Irene's been caught since I've been here,' she said in a low voice as we walked through an empty corridor. 'The chargehands usually turn a blind eye because there's nothing Irene can do, but now that Mr Rice has seen them, it's another matter. Honestly, Emmy,' she stressed, 'it's not her fault.'

She pushed open the door to the canteen. 'We're not supposed to be in here for another ten minutes but let's try to bagsie a table. The other girls are due at half past.

97

I hope you don't mind eating so early. Our shift started at six.'

I wasn't at all interested in food or drink. I was still shocked at seeing children in such a dangerous place.

'It's pretty grim though, isn't it?' I said, after Anne had told one of the dinner-ladies that we'd been sent by Mr Rice, so she let us sit at one of the long wooden tables. 'What if one of the children gets hurt?'

'Of course it's grim,' said Anne, who I could see was trying not to be short with me. 'But her husband's in the navy and she hasn't any family locally. Sheila – she's seven – is at school mostly, but if a neighbour can't look after Enid then she's up a gum tree. So Irene's managed to sneak the girls in here. Sheila looks after Enid and stops her running around.'

A seven-year-old looking after her younger sister in a factory. No wonder Mr Rice had seen red.

'Sorry to be snappy,' said Anne, again. 'I was on the same section as Irene when I first started. She was very kind to me, and we've become friendly. My mum had the girls once, but Irene lives on the other side of town, and Mum has her hands full with my two as it is.'

Anne leant her elbows on the table. She looked worried and tired.

'What about you, Anne?' I asked. 'How are you settling in?'

Anne took a deep breath and smiled, immediately changing to a cheerier look. 'Oh, I'm fine thanks,' she said. 'The girls are a good lot and I enjoy the work. If I was single, like Betty, I wouldn't have a care in the world. But it's a twelve-hour day including the bus, so I go home, help Mum with the kids and the house and by then, I'm almost dead on my feet.'

She laughed, slightly unconvincingly. 'Do you know, I

98

can sleep at any time of the day, now? Crash, I'm asleep! Although if I've been on the nightshift the children think I'm there to play with them all day. I'm not complaining, Emmy. I miss them ever so much when I'm here. But I'm flipping lucky to have my mum.'

'Do you have to work such long hours?' I asked. 'Could you share a shift with someone else? And please tell me if I'm being too nosy.'

'It's all right,' said Anne. She put her head slightly to one side and stared at me for a moment. 'I don't mind telling you. I need to work full-time,' she said. 'When Anthony was alive, because he was off fighting, I got twenty-eight shillings a week Married Woman's allowance, and twelve and six for each of the children. With the money he sent out of his wages it added up nicely if I took care. But if your boy dies, you lose his wages of course, and they stop the twenty-eight shillings because they say you're not a Married Woman anymore. So then, you have to pay single woman's tax on your wages and the pension, too. It makes a big difference.' She paused. 'I'm sorry. I know it's poor form to talk about money.'

For the first time today, Anne's face lost its stoicism. She looked utterly defeated. Then her brown eyes narrowed, and she raised her eyes to meet my gaze.

'You know, Emmy, you don't just lose *them*,' she said quietly. 'Even if no one ever wants to talk about it, the fact is, loads of us have lost almost everything.'

CHAPTER 9

It's the Same Everywhere

I SEARCHED FOR something to say. We'd had letters to "Yours Cheerfully" from war widows, women who were struggling with the unspeakable pain of loss, and some who were now struggling in very different circumstances, but no one had ever spelt it out so starkly. And there was me blithely suggesting Anne could just go and work part-time.

'I'm the one who should say sorry, Anne,' I said. 'That was stupid of me.'

'Don't worry,' Anne said, leaning forward and patting my hand. 'You can't know everything.'

'Well, I jolly well should know *these* things,' I said. 'I work for a women's problem page, for goodness' sake.'

Anne shrugged. 'Chandlers doesn't have part-time workers anyway. But let's not talk about me. I'm more worried about Irene finding someone to look after the girls, or at least a nursery for Enid. But she hasn't a chance. Nurseries don't fit in with our hours.'

Before I could find out more, Anne stood up and looked for the friends she had arranged to come and talk to me during their break. Spotting them, she waved vigorously, and a small group of women hurried across the canteen.

'Here they come,' she said. 'Now then, I'll let you have a good chat before I mention Irene. I want you to get a decent view of this place, but if we start off by talking about her being in trouble, you'll end up thinking we all hate it, which wouldn't be fair. And you wouldn't have much to write in your article either,' she said, now smiling. 'We can't have that.'

I quickly agreed and thought how lucky I had been to meet Anne. She was one of the most generous people I knew.

While we had been talking, the room had begun to fill up. Large groups of women in their brown work coats and overalls streamed in for their lunch break. The huge canteen was now a hubbub of noise as women put bags on chairs or tables and then grabbed trays and joined the queues for a hot dinner, standing in line and stretching their arms and moving their shoulders after working in the same position for hours.

'Girls, this is Miss Emmeline Lake, from *Woman's Friend*,' said Anne, becoming rather formal. 'Emmeline, this is Betty who I've mentioned, and these are my friends Violet and Maeve. We all work together.'

'Hello,' I said, as we shook hands. 'Do call me Emmy. Has Anne volunteered you all for this? It's not too late to back out.' I gave them what I hoped was a reassuring smile.

'Oh, no,' said Betty. With her brown hair and dark eyes, she could have been Anne's sister. 'We don't mind at all. We've never been in a magazine before.'

'I hope I won't say the wrong thing,' said Violet.

'You always say the wrong thing,' said Maeve, and the girls laughed.

'It's all right, Violet,' I said. 'So do I.'

Everyone laughed again and with the ice broken, we went off to get some food.

As we queued up, Maeve gave a running commentary of the ups and downs of the menu.

'Avoid the Scotch Broth,' she said, pulling a face. 'The greens are nice enough, but if there's sprouts, they'll be like bullets. They do a good steak and kidney pud and you get loads of potatoes if you ask nicely.'

I hadn't had kidneys in ages, and at three courses for a shilling it was nice to see something to be cheerful about after my conversation with Anne. I glanced at the posters that lined the walls, advertising lunchtime concerts in the canteen.

'We had Arthur Askey last week,' said Betty, noticing me looking. 'He's even smaller than you'd think. But he did make us laugh. I wish we could get Gracie Fields though.'

'Or Ambrose and his Orchestra,' said Maeve.

'You'd never fit them all in,' said Violet. 'Remember when we had those jugglers? One of them kept falling off the side of the stage. They had to pretend it was part of the act.'

The conversation turned to our favourite performers and within minutes we had started on our loaded-up trays and were chatting, with any nervousness now gone. *Workers' Playtime* started playing out of some loudspeakers and the tunes added to the feeling of not having to do or say anything 'the right way'.

I had out my notebook although everyone seemed keener to ask questions about *Woman's Friend*.

'We've all started reading it since we met Anne,' said Violet.

'Viyyye,' interrupted Anne. 'What did we say?'

'Oh, bother,' said Violet. 'I told you it would be me. Sorry, Emmy, we promised to tell you we'd all been reading it for ages.'

Violet was clearly the youngest of the friends and seemed quite happy in her role as scatterbrain.

'Not at all,' I said. 'I don't want you to think you have to.'

'Oh no,' said Vi, poking an errant curl back under her yellow headscarf. 'We really enjoy it. It's not half as. old-fashioned as I'd thought.'

Anne shook her head in dismay.

'We are proper readers, honestly,' said Maeve, looking at me sincerely through her glasses. 'Are you allowed to tell us about the problem page? We're all dying to know about it.'

'I'll say,' said Vi. 'Do people ever write back? I'd like to know what happened to the girl who was having the lodger's baby.'

'Or the woman whose husband went off with her friend?'

Now they were all firing questions at me. Half the time, they said, they were convinced that the letters printed in "Yours Cheerfully" had been sent in by people they knew.

'I'm ever so pleased you like it,' I said. 'But honestly, I want to talk about you.' I looked up at the big clock on the wall by the window. 'Tell me anything you like. What made you choose working here?'

Encouraged by Anne, the four women began to tell me their stories.

They had all started their jobs in the last few months and agreed that it felt wrong if you weren't doing some-thing as part of the war effort. Maeve had fancied joining the ATS, but didn't want to leave home, so as she had three brothers in the army, munitions work was the least she could do. Betty said she was bored of working in an office so had decided to apply to Chandlers rather than wait to be called up and run the risk of getting sent to the back of beyond. Violet wanted to work and save up for when her husband came home. She was nineteen and they had got married last year. Now her husband was somewhere near Singapore. Violet carried a letter from him in her handbag, in which he'd said how proud of her he was for pulling her weight.

'I don't mind the long hours,' Violet said. 'But I wish I didn't spend three hours a day on the bus.'

'Especially when Betty starts going on about politics,' added Maeve, giving Betty a nudge with her elbow.

Betty grinned. 'I was only saying I thought it was about time Mr Churchill had a lady MP in the War Cabinet and this old bloke in front got all funny and told me to be quiet.'

She looked entirely undaunted.

'I don't think it helped when you said, "Put a sock in it, Grandad," ' said Maeve, deadpan. 'But I agree with Violet. It is a long day.'

I noted it down.

'Is there anything else that's hard, apart from the work itself of course?' I asked. It was a leading question, but I was interested to know if everything was quite as wonderful as Mr Terry had made out. 'I won't put it in the article.'

There was a pause as the women glanced at each other. Then Betty spoke first.

'I'll tell you what makes me peeved,' she said. 'And that's the men getting paid more than us for doing the same work. I don't think that's fair.'

'They don't have to do all the shopping and cooking at home either,' said Maeve, scraping the last bit of sponge out of her bowl. 'But that's never going to change. Personally, I'd rather not work at weekends because of the kids, but as my husband said in one of his letters, they don't get weekends off in Libya either.' She looked philosophical. 'So that's what I tell the children. "If your dad's got to work weekends to win the war, then so do

I to make sure he's got enough guns to kill all the baddies." '

The Ministry of Labour didn't mention this in their adverts.

'We aren't moaning,' said Maeve, quickly, as she noticed me listening intently. 'It has to be done.'

'Of course,' I said.

'I can't really complain,' said Betty. 'I'm single and live in digs, so I don't have to do much. The others have to fit in loads more than me.'

'And old Rice Pudding is all right, really,' said Violet, meaning Mr Rice.

'Don't say that to Irene Barker,' said Anne, who had been quiet up until now. 'We were with him just now when he spotted the children.'

Everyone looked at her with concern. Clearly word hadn't reached the whole of Shed Twelve yet.

'Why didn't you say?' said Violet.

'Poor Irene,' said Maeve. 'What happened?'

To a chorus of sympathy, Anne told them the little that we had seen.

'It's just not fair,' said Betty. 'She's been so unlucky to get caught.'

'Do other people do it too?' I said, perhaps a little too quickly.

There was a moment's hesitation.

'It's nobody's fault,' said Maeve, firmly. 'If you can't get someone to look after them, what can you do? I'm lucky mine are old enough to fend for themselves. Not,' she added, 'that I like leaving a thirteen-year-old in charge all the time.'

'Isn't there a Women's Welfare Officer?' I asked. 'One who might understand? Irene can't be the only one here struggling like this.'

'You're joking,' said Maeve. 'I don't think the management realise that we have different lives to men. I don't mean to be rude. As Vi says, Mr Rice is decent enough when he's not in a grump, but Mr Terry's the one who decides, and everyone knows he prefers to have girls here who don't have kids.'

'Not that we ever see him,' said Betty. 'Him and his big car. Flash Harry.' Then, as if she'd noticed the others looking downcast, she began singing to a George Formby tune.

'He thinks we're impressed
He's bursting out his vest,
Mr Terry, Rich from Jerry.
That's Mr Terry.'

Violet joined in with the last line and everyone laughed, before looking round to make sure no one important had heard. I glanced over at Betty with renewed respect. I had the feeling she played up her role as the single girl with few responsibilities while actually trying to keep the others' morale up.

The women were a good bunch all round, but it bothered me that if anything went wrong, Anne or Maeve might find themselves in the same jam as Irene Barker.

'What about nurseries?' I asked, following up on Anne's earlier comment. 'Not the normal ones, but the Government ones. We're doing an article on them next week as they're crying out for people to work for them.'

'There's your answer,' said Maeve. 'Everyone wants us to come into munitions, but they haven't thought it through. It took a petition to get mirrors in the Ladies' and when they put them in, you'd have thought they'd given us each a gold clock. Blimey,' she added, 'Emmy, you must think we're a right bunch of whiners.'

'Not at all,' I said. 'It's really interesting.'

'I don't know about that,' said Maeve. 'But we're not the only ones. My cousin works in munitions up past Birmingham and it's the same there. As I say, they just haven't thought things through.'

'Mind you,' said Anne, 'I'm not sure a Government Nursery is ready for my Ruby. Unless it's run by the police.'

Everyone laughed, although no one actually disputed it, and I took the opportunity to ask how the children were. Anne had been right about not mentioning Irene Barker until I had got to know the others a little. The tone of our discussion had certainly changed.

Perhaps Anne was aware of this as she began to say how Ruby was keen on next door's rabbits and now wanted one of her own. Conversation became lighter again and with more than enough food for thought on my part, I stopped asking questions and joined in with the chat.

As *Workers' Playtime* came to an end with a song and then a cheering message from Vera Lynn, a piercing whistle sounded which was the sign for everyone to go back to their work. Perfectly on cue, Mr Rice appeared in the canteen. He was looking less apoplectic than when we had left him, although Anne and her friends stopped talking as soon as he came over.

'Well, ladies,' he said. 'I hope you've given Miss Lake the information she needs.'

'Oh, yes. Everyone has been enormously helpful,' I said, beaming at him. 'They are an absolute credit. Mr Terry must be very proud of such a committed workforce.'

Betty who was sitting next to me, innocently smiled at Mr Rice and started humming 'Our Mr Terry' under her breath. The rest of us tried to ignore her although Violet looked as if she was going to burst.

'Indeed,' said Mr Rice, in quite the most neutral voice

I had ever heard. He took his fob watch out. 'Isn't your photographer supposed to be here soon?'

I said that he was due any minute now, as my new friends took the hint and began to gather up their trays. I knew they all wanted to find out about Irene.

I thanked them all profusely for their help. I had much to be grateful for. Anne and her friends had given me the sort of honest views I would never get from official information.

My challenge now was what to do with it.

As Anne and her friends left the canteen Mr Rice said he would show me back to reception to wait for the photographer.

'Mr Rice,' I said, as we walked back down the corridor, 'what is your view on children in the factory?'

Mr Rice looked at my notepad as my hand hovered over it, ready to write. 'Are you from a women's magazine, or the *Daily Herald*?' he said, shortly.

I softened my approach. 'It's just that shift work and all the travelling looks quite hard if you have a family?'

'That's why conscription is for unmarried women,' said Mr Rice, which was rich, seeing as Chandlers must have had hundreds of mothers working right under his nose.

'But it's not just about conscription, Mr Rice, is it? A lot of married women have to work, don't they? Especially if their husband has gone.' I thought of Anne. 'And you've said yourself that they are really pulling their weight.'

I waited, hoping I hadn't pushed my luck. I now knew full well that Mr Terry had allowed my visit as he thought it would make Chandlers – and him – look good. I hadn't been allowed in to ask difficult questions. More to the point, I didn't want Mr Rice thinking that Anne and her friends had been trying to use my interview to make any sort of demands. I thought quickly. 'I don't wish to speak out of turn,' I said, before he could answer. 'I'm just concerned about the children I saw.'

Mr Rice sucked his teeth. Finally, he spoke. 'Miss Lake,' he said, evenly, 'all you need to tell your readers is that our sole aim is to do everything we can to help win the war, and that that is what we will do if more of them work for us and the other munitions factories. Now, after your photographer has finished, what time is your train?'

He hadn't gone red and didn't even sound cross, in fact he was peculiarly mild, considering the fury he'd been in earlier.

Then the penny dropped. This may have been my very first assignment, but I'd bet a week's wages Mr Rice had been speaking to Mr Terry's Public Relations Manager. Mr Rice may not have been Mr Terry's biggest fan, but when it came to it, he was very much a company man. I felt like a rather green young boxer who had ambled into a ring unprepared.

Luckily, he hadn't quite knocked me straight out. There would be lots more rounds to go.

'They're every hour,' I said, pleasantly. 'But Mr Terry said we would speak again.'

Mr Rice looked at me as if I had said that the Factory Director had offered to buy me a pony.

'I think you've had your chance there,' he said. 'He's a very busy man.'

So much for Mr Terry's big show this morning.

'I quite understand,' I said, smoothly. 'You and the ladies have been more helpful than I can say.'

A phone rang which was answered by Mrs Noakes, who then informed Mr Rice that Security at the main gate needed him to come and sort out a funny-looking chap with a camera.

Mr Rice made one of his Hmmf noises and told me

to come with him, so I dutifully followed as he began to talk about tool shops. My mind, however, had already turned to the article I was planning to write. What if Maeve was right and the women of Chandlers weren't the only munition workers feeling the strain? I thought of "Yours Cheerfully". There had certainly been letters about war work, but had I taken them seriously enough, or had I been concentrating too much on the lovelorn and romantically baffled?

Who exactly was I trying to help? The Ministry I was so desperate to impress, or the readers I had promised to do everything I could to support?

'Do you have what you need for your magazine now?' asked Mr Rice.

'Very much so,' I said. 'I have lots to be getting on with for now, thank you.'

I gave him my best professional, yet approachable smile and said nothing more.

I was thinking what to do with the information I was sure the Ministry would want me to leave out.

CHAPTER 10

Actually, I Don't Want You To Shut Up

'Darling,' said my mother, 'I'll put a penny to a pound that nothing has changed since factories in the last war. Thousands of perfectly capable women being managed by a lot of silly old men without an ounce of sense between them. Don't start me.'

Father gave Bunty a look as if to say, 'Too Late', and she stifled a smile. It was the weekend after my visit to Chandlers, and Bunts and I were visiting my parents in Hampshire, as it was my mother's birthday. As was always the case, we had been greeted with open arms. My parents had known Bunty since she was tiny, and she was as much a part of the family as my brother and me.

'The problem is,' continued Mother, sitting on the sofa in a new cardigan and hardly giving the impression of leading a workers' revolt, 'that most men haven't the faintest idea how to cope with women in an industrial setting.'

She glanced at my father. 'Alfred, you're making a face.'

'My face can't help it,' said Father, fondly.

My mother turned to Bunty.

'When I was working in the first war, I gave the men in charge some suggestions on how I thought things could be done a little better. They weren't enormously keen.'

'What was wrong with them?' said Bunty. 'Idiots.'

'Thank you,' said my mother, squeezing Bunty's hand. 'I knew you'd understand.'

'And the moral of the story,' said my father, grinning, and gesticulating with his pipe in a learned way, 'is that this is where Emmy gets her somewhat direct approach from. Chip off the old block.'

'Hurrah!' I said.

'Hear, hear,' added Bunty.

Mother smiled at us all. She knew Father worshipped the ground she walked on.

'I'm so glad you've come,' she said, changing the subject. 'It's the best present I could have had.'

'It can't be,' I said. 'We've brought proper ones.' I handed over a small package. 'These are from me. I made them.'

'You shouldn't have, darling,' said Mother, untying the string as I watched with anticipation. I had worked on them all week. 'Thank you very much. You've knitted something splendid. I love them.' She looked up at me. 'What are they?'

'Mother, they're mittens,' I said, trying not to look crestfallen. Knitting was not my forte.

'Of course they are!' cried Mother. 'Now I can see it. Thank you. Look, Alfred. Mittens. Just what I wanted. I shall wear them to church. Which hand is which?'

She started to try them on. Even though I had unpicked them both several times, one was still considerably larger than the other.

'I've done a matching hat,' said Bunty, giving my mother her present. Bunty could knit in her sleep. 'Emmy did the pompom,' she added, loyally.

'Yikes,' said Father.

'Alfred, stop teasing,' said Mother happily. She held out her mittened hands, one of which was now the size of a hot-water bottle. 'I love them. And we know Emmy is awful at knitting, so it makes them all the more special.'

'Thank you,' I said, unsure exactly as to why.

'Now,' said Mother. 'What's the time?'

'Ten past eleven,' I said. It was the third time she had asked in an hour. 'Are you expecting someone?'

'Absolutely not,' she replied.

There was a loud knock on the front door.

'That can't be for me,' said Mother. 'Emmy, would you go and see who it is, please?'

'It's probably a patient for Daddy,' I said, getting up.

'I'll be there right away,' said my father, not moving an inch from his armchair.

I made my way out of the living room and down the hall. Even though it was a Saturday, my father, a doctor, would always see people if they needed him. It was probably someone with a colicky baby, or a grateful patient with something from their vegetable garden as a thank you.

Tucking a stray piece of hair behind my ear, I opened the heavy front door, thinking how nice it would be to be greeted by a bunch of parsnips.

But it was something even better than parsnips.

'Hello, Em,' said the man on the doorstep, taking off his army cap.

'CHARLES!' I shouted. I hadn't a clue what he was doing here. I threw myself into his arms. We hadn't seen each other in weeks.

'Am I interrupting?' he asked as he kissed me and then hugged me into his chest. 'I heard there was a birthday.'

'You rat,' I said, taking his hand and dragging him into the house. 'You kept this quiet.'

Charles laughed as we went into the living room and everyone got up to greet him. Bunty was as surprised as me to see him, but my father shook his hand warmly and Mother admitted they had known all along.

'Many happy returns, Mrs Lake,' said Charles, handing her a pot of jam. 'My landlady said I couldn't come empty-handed. It's plum. I hope that's all right.'

'It's my favourite,' said Mother, which I was fairly sure wasn't true, but I knew how much she liked him. 'Thank you.'

'How long do you have off?' I asked Charles, still in a delight at seeing him.

'Just this afternoon, I'm afraid,' he said. 'It was late notice and as I knew you were visiting your parents, I phoned up and they very kindly said I could call in.'

'It's my best present so far,' said Mother. 'Other than the mittens. We must make the most of your time. Why don't you and Emmy go for a walk? I need to call into next door to thank them for the piccalilli.'

'Wouldn't you like a cup of tea first?' I said to Charles. He hadn't even sat down.

'Of course not,' said Mother. 'Charles can have tea later. You two don't get any time together – go and make the most of it.'

I looked at Bunty.

'I'm going to sit here and have another biscuit,' she said.

'So am I,' said my father. 'And I want to bore Bunty about my chickens. Go on, Emmy. If you have to pretend you're not about to go pop at seeing Charles for much longer, I'll be treating you for an embolism when I should be enjoying an oatmeal button.'

I needed no encouragement at all. 'Let's walk down to the canal,' I said. 'We can easily get there and back in time for Mother's birthday lunch.'

Charles was quick to agree and a few minutes later I

was wrapped up in my coat and we were walking along the lane arm in arm.

'This is the best ever surprise,' I said. 'I really hadn't a clue.'

'Ha,' said Charles, not giving anything away. 'I must say I am chuffed to see you.'

Even though he and I had only been together a few months, as my friend Thelma had once said to me, time worked quite differently during war, and it already felt as if Charles and I knew each other enormously well. He was intelligent and kind, quieter than me and more measured, but he could make me laugh with almost no effort at all. We were quite different in some ways, particularly as I had a tendency to charge into situations without thinking things through first, but I could make him laugh even more than he did me, and modesty aside, I wasn't a dimwit. We could hold our own with each other and I liked that very much. Falling in love with him had been the easiest thing in the world.

'I can't quite believe it,' I said. 'Although you're looking at me in an odd way. Is it my new beret?'

Charles broke into a smile. 'Not at all. It's delightful! Very red.'

He ran out of steam.

'You're hopeless,' I said.

'Thank you. I always think it must be such a relief living in Russia where everyone seems to wear the same thing.'

'Communist,' I said and a man walking past gave me a look as if he was about to call the police.

Charles rolled his eyes. 'Only sartorially,' he said. 'Now then, we need to get cracking.'

He began to pick up some speed, which as I was half a foot shorter than him, threatened to turn my part of the walk into a jog.

'It's all right,' I said, pulling him back. 'We've lots of time. We could be late for lunch and no one would mind. Let's just wander for a bit and pretend we're two normal people who see each other all the time.'

Charles stopped and for a moment looked at me, his blue eyes quite serious. Then he broke into a smile. 'You're right. I'm gabbling on and being a twit. I'm just glad to be spending some time with the girl that I love. That's you by the way,' he added, taking my hand.

'That's a relief,' I said, smiling back.

'It's only because of that hat. I can't resist a girl in a beret,' he said. Then he kissed me.

'Bloody war,' I said, and holding tightly on to the beret with one hand, I kissed him back.

★

We walked on, past the church where Reverend Wiffle shot by us on his bicycle with a wobbly wave, and then down to the towpath by the canal. In the weak winter sun, it was the loveliest walk. There had been little rain, so the ground was more than dry enough without a galosh. A small flock of swans, along with one rather bossy goose, patrolled down the centre of the water and if it hadn't been for the occasional plane flying overhead it would have been almost possible to pretend everything was right with the world. As much as I loved living in a city, I always enjoyed coming home to the countryside. You could never forget the war in London. Here, sometimes, you could forget almost anything apart from being together.

Despite the letters and phone calls, whenever we saw each other it always felt as if there was tons to catch up on.

Charles knew about the Ministry, of course, and how much I wanted to make a good fist of things for *Woman's*

Friend. I'd told him about Freddie and Diane, and while he had assured me not to worry about Guy, as he said that beneath the writerly exterior his brother was used to this sort of pettiness, it was quite clear that Charles was as eager as I was to put them smartly back in their place.

'I've written my first war work article,' I told him, trying not to sound too proud of myself. 'I did it after I got back from the factory, so everything was still fresh. Guy said he'll read it this weekend. I hope he thinks it's all right.'

'Have faith,' said Charles. 'He wouldn't have sent you if he hadn't thought you could do it. How was the place?'

'Well,' I said. 'Interesting.'

We were quite alone as we continued to walk along the towpath, and I was able to tell him about Chandlers without being overheard. Charles listened quietly, occasionally asking questions, but letting me get my thoughts off my chest.

'I told my parents about it just now,' I said, dropping my voice as we followed the canal under a brick-arch bridge with 1802 written on it. 'Not where it is or what they do or anything of course,' I whispered, as my words echoed slightly. 'Just about Irene and what Anne's friends had said. Mother says men don't know what to do with women.'

Charles laughed.

'I'm not saying a word,' he said, stopping to hold up a branch which was overhanging the path by the bridge. 'I say, is this near the ruins you've mentioned?'

'It is,' I said. 'I thought you might like to see them.'

We walked a few yards and then turned off from the canal and through a kissing gate onto a narrow path next to a field that then turned into woodland. Although Charles had been to my parents' house once before, we hadn't been down here together, and I was eager for him to see where I had spent some of the very happiest times of my childhood. We stopped talking about work and the war, and turned to simpler times as I pointed out where my father had first taught me and my brother Jack how to pitch a tent, during what had become the grand adventure of sleeping outside for a whole night.

'That's where Bunty tried to get on a cow,' I said, pointing across the field. 'She was about eight and convinced it was the same as riding a pony.'

'And was it?' asked Charles.

'Not at all,' I laughed. 'The cow was quite clear about it.'

We walked on as Charles told a funny story about a friend, and I updated him on the state of some hardy annuals Bunty and I had found at the back of the garden shed.

They were light, meaningless topics filled with gentle exaggerations and self-deprecation to make each other laugh.

As we made our way through the woods and along to the ruined house where as children we had pretended to be King Arthur and the Knights of the Round Table, I embarked on a long and, I thought, funny story involving Kathleen's cousin and a pair of curtains that nearly caught fire. The build up to the punchline took some time, but it had made Bunty laugh like anything when I'd told her earlier, so I felt confident Charles would find it hilarious as well. Admittedly it was a very long story and after a while I realised he had gone quiet, but when I got to the end it was rather a blow when Charles didn't seem to get the punchline at all.

'Blimey, Phyllis, you're not saying they used to be my slippers?' I said and then roared at my own joke. 'Do you get it? Slippers?' I repeated, proving that I would make a hopeless comedian by bashing the point home whether it was funny or not.

'Oh yes,' said Charles. 'Slippers. Sorry. Yes. Ha.'

He clearly hadn't been listening. I laughed a bit more to prove he'd missed a belter and then said, 'Ahhhh dear,' in the way people do to make a laugh carry on if there's an unfortunate hush.

'Ha!' said Charles again, trying to make up. 'Yes.'

'Kath said they all laughed for ages,' I said, and then gave him a slight shove with my shoulder. 'You are a swine,' I said. 'You stopped listening. I'd been saving that one especially.'

Charles nudged me back and sighed.

'Only you, Emmy Lake, would wallop a poor hard-working serviceman for not laughing at your joke. Whatever happened to romantic silences, long gazes and batting your eyelashes?'

I looked into his eyes and tried to bat my eyelashes.

'It's no good,' I said. 'I bet it just looks as if I'm getting a stye.'

Charles shook his head.

'I give up,' he said, not looking as if he did in the least.

We walked over to the old building. What was left of the little house sat bravely holding itself together, while the sun eased its way through windows that were no longer there. The path from the wood went back to the canal, and years ago it must have been the nicest place to live. I'd taken off my beret as we'd walked, and a slight breeze blew through my hair.

'Isn't it lovely?' I said, forgiving him for not laughing at my joke.

'Utterly,' said Charles. 'It's almost as if we've escaped from everything. Do you know, ever since you first told me about this place, I've wanted to come here with you.'

'To enjoy the silence?' I said, aware that I hadn't given him a chance on that front.

'Something like that,' he smiled. 'It's all right though. I don't know if you noticed but I slowed down to a crawl so you could finish the thing about the curtains.'

I tucked my arm into his. 'That was kind,' I said. 'You should have told me to shut up.'

'Not at all,' said Charles. 'That's the thing, Em. Actually, I don't want you to shut up.'

He turned to face me.

'In fact, I'd rather like it if you would tell me bewilderingly complicated stories forever.' He paused and I didn't interrupt. 'You see, Emmy, I love you. And I want us to tell each other ridiculous jokes and make each other laugh, and to let each other know about things that bother us and sometimes, somehow even manage to forget the rest of this entire nonsensical world altogether. As if it's just us two.'

He took hold of my hand. 'My darling, darling, Em,' he said as he got down on one knee. 'Would you do me the honour of being my wife?'

I gazed at him with astonishment and he very gently spelt it out all over again.

'Emmeline Lake,' said Charles. 'Will you marry me?'

*

Of course I said yes.

The two of us looked at each other rather incredulously for a second, and then Charles stood up and we kissed and hugged each other for ages and I for one got a bit watery, which I think was allowable under the circumstances.

While I was sniffing, Charles said, 'Thank God you didn't say no,' and, 'That was the longest walk I've ever been on.'

The sun seemed to get brighter even though it probably didn't, and the sky even seemed bluer which it definitely wasn't, and it was just us on our own, laughing and being amazed at how wonderful this was and how incredibly lucky we were.

'Oh, grief. I nearly forgot,' said Charles. 'I'm so sorry, I'm really not very good at this.' He reached into his pocket. 'I wondered if I might give you this? Only if you like it of course. It was my grandmother's. On my mother's side.'

I opened the little red velvet box to find the most beautiful engagement ring, Victorian in design, a dark sapphire with a diamond on each side. When I tried it on, it fitted perfectly.

'Oh, Charles,' I said. 'I love it.'

I put out my hand and we both admired it as if it had magically appeared without anyone doing anything.

'I say, darling,' said Charles, very cheerfully indeed. 'Looks like we're engaged.'

Even looking down at my hand, it felt hard to believe. I loved Charles more than anything, and now we were going to be married. I felt overwhelmed.

'Does anyone know?' I asked.

Charles grinned. 'Your father gave me the all-clear. I came to see him last week. I have to say I was almost as nervy as just now, but he was very good about the whole thing and said yes, straight away.'

'He was probably relieved,' I laughed.

'That's what he said,' said Charles, warmly. 'Actually, he was awfully kind. Your mother is pleased too I think.'

'I can't believe you've all been in on the secret,' I said. 'No wonder Mother virtually marched us out of the house.' Then I paused. 'Um . . .'

Charles waited, and when I didn't continue, said, 'I

talked with Bunty. I hope you don't mind. I asked her what she thought of the idea of you and me making a go of things. She was jolly good about it and said I have to tell you that she's as pleased as Punch. Actually, she told me I should hurry up and get on with asking you. Oh, and if I mess you around in the slightest, she will track me down and happily swing for me.'

He raised an eyebrow. 'I would like you to know that consequently I most solemnly swear that I will not mess you around.'

Charles smiled the tiniest bit. 'I love you, Em, and I think we could be happy. Once this wretched war's over, there's no end to the adventures we can have.'

If I hadn't thought I was the luckiest person alive already, now I knew I most certainly was. Here was a man who loved me and had asked me to marry him, but who knew that my best friend's feelings would be uppermost in my mind. I wondered how many men would understand that. It might have sounded strange, but that he had thought to talk to Bunty meant more than anything to me. It was little more than seven months since she had been the one getting engaged. Sometimes it felt like no time at all.

Charles and I sat quietly on what was left of a wall of the old house. I wanted to marry him with all my heart, and I was still almost breathless that he had asked, but there was no doubting that for all our joy, there was a bitter sweetness to it all. This was the year my best friend should have been married. This was supposed to be Bunty and William's year.

Since Charles and I had become closer, Bunts had been the most enormous brick about things. Not once had she begrudged my happiness, and even though I had tried to play it down, she had been adamant that I shouldn't. As she trudged through the agony of bereavement, forcing on a brave face when I knew that even getting up was often a trial, she always, *always* wanted me to be happy.

Bunty was the most extraordinary of best friends, and to his eternal credit, the man who wanted to marry me knew it.

'I'll speak with Bunty of course,' I said. 'But it sounds as if the two of you have pretty much sorted everything out.'

'That was the plan,' said Charles. 'Now then, might I suggest we head back? If you'd like to speak with her before we say anything, I can wait in the front garden if that helps.'

'Thank you,' I said. 'But the fact Bunty has threatened you with murder has put my mind at rest. She wouldn't do that unless she was taking you seriously.' I looked up at him and felt the happiest I had ever been. 'Darling Charles,' I said. 'Let's go and tell everyone we need to start planning a wedding.'

CHAPTER 11

You'd Better Crack On

As we made our way back to the house, Charles and I decided that we wanted to get married as soon as possible. We were both terrifically keen to be together, and not least because no one knew what might be around the corner, there was no reason to delay. Engagements these days were a matter of weeks, and sometimes less.

We walked hand in hand, both grinning like loons, looking at the ring on my finger and marvelling slightly at what had just happened. I was certain my family and friends would want to celebrate and muster up a wedding party at short notice, although on Charles's side, numbers weren't quite so robust.

'How do you feel about your ghastly old boss being best man?' he asked, meaning his brother. 'Although if you don't want him to, it will take half the army to stop him.'

'I'd love it,' I said. 'If it wasn't for Guy, I wouldn't have met you. And Charles, do you think we might get married in London? It feels the right place to do it.'

I didn't have to say that the little church we had walked past was where Bunty had been supposed to have her wedding.

Charles readily agreed to London. 'I'll put in for leave as soon as we have a date,' he said. 'It may only be forty-eight hours, but it will be enough for us to say, "I do" and perhaps have a night away. I'm sorry that's probably as close as we'll get to any sort of honeymoon.'

'I don't mind a bit,' I said. 'Anyway, it would feel unpatriotic to go gallivanting off.'

As we arrived back in Glebe Lane and came to a stop outside my parents' house, I turned to face Charles.

'Now then, Captain Mayhew,' I said. 'This is your last chance to back out. Once we go in, I can't be responsible for the levels of excitement which will make it almost impossible for you to change your mind. Your goose will be well and truly cooked.'

I grinned up at him, trying to make sure he knew I was kidding around, which I almost entirely was, but I had to admit to butterflies. I had been engaged once before and it hadn't turned out awfully well.

'My goose is very happy to be cooked,' said Charles, wrapping his arms round me. 'And anyway, it's already too late. You've said, "Yes", and I'm not letting you get out of it.' He looked at me quite seriously. 'Em, I've never been more sure of anything in my life. I promise. Now let's go and tell them all. You can speak with Bunty, and I must say I wouldn't mind giving Guy a call if your parents don't object.'

We crunched our way across the gravel carriage-drive outside the house and as I knew the front door would not be locked, we went straight in.

'Hello?' I called as I took off my coat and put my hat on the stand in the hall, stretching out the last moments of keeping the news just between Charles and me.

'We're in here,' I heard my mother call in an unusually high voice, and with one last smile at each other, we went through.

The living room was usually cosy and very informal,

a place where piles of books wobbled slightly beside elderly but much-loved chairs, and people lounged around chatting or left the newspaper half read on the sofa. Now it was exactly that, apart from the fact that three of the dearest people in my life were all sitting bolt upright in various overly studied casual positions, all of which looked uncomfortable. Mother was holding a teacup with hardly any tea in it, Bunty was being interested in a napkin, and Father was holding a book on embroidery I had left on the arm of his chair earlier on. None of them said a word. They just stared at us, rather like deer getting a sniff of something important.

'Hello,' I said again, as I saw Bunty shoot Charles a violently quizzical look.

Charles looked at his shoes and pretended he hadn't seen.

'All well?' I said, enjoying myself.

'All well,' confirmed my mother.

'Yes,' said Bunty at the same time.

'That's right,' said Father. 'I've, er, I've been reading this book. Sewing and that sort of thing. Quite an eye-opener.'

My mother and Bunty looked at him.

'So, darling,' said Mother, 'did you have a nice walk? With Charles? Was it, um, very, er . . .'

It was no good. Bunty broke first.

'OH, COME ON!' she boomed, getting up from the sofa. 'THIS IS TORTURE. FOR GOODNESS' SAKE WILL ONE OF YOU JUST PUT US OUT OF OUR MISERY?'

Charles stopped looking at his feet. Father threw the book on the floor.

'Yes,' I said. 'I said, "Yes."'

Then, as they still stared, I said it out loud for the first time, possibly to make it clear to me as much as anyone else.

'Charles and I are going to get married.'

Now everyone was on their feet. With the speed of a leopard, Mother was out of her chair and hugging me, Father was shaking Charles's hand and saying, 'Well done, old chap,' and then Mother grabbed Bunty and the three of us were hugging each other at the same time.

'This calls for sherry,' announced Father, as Mother denied she was crying and turned to kiss Charles and tell him how thrilled she was.

Bunty had another go at squeezing the last bit of breath out of me. 'Oh, Emmy,' she said, 'WELL DONE,' as if I had got into the Olympics or come first in a particularly difficult subject at school. 'I'm so pleased,' she whispered. 'Honestly, Em, I am *just so* pleased for you *both*. I really couldn't be happier.' Her eyes were brimming with tears. I knew she meant every word.

'You'll make me cry,' I said, already beginning to sniff.

'Quite right,' said Bunty, blinking hard. 'It's all too lovely. And it's been SO hard not saying anything.'

'I did hear you were in on it,' I said, looking at Charles, who came over to Bunty.

'I'm afraid I had to let the cat out of the bag that you knew,' he said. 'I wasn't sure she was going to say, "Yes", if I didn't.'

'Don't be daft,' said Bunts, looking tremendously pleased.

Charles gave her a kiss on the cheek. 'Thank you,' he said, quietly.

My father brandished a very dusty bottle of Harvey's Bristol Cream and having poured everyone a drink, raised his glass. 'To Emmy and Charles,' he said. 'The very greatest of happiness.'

Mother and Bunty joined in to all say it and then the toasts began to flow. Charles thanked Father and said, To us all, and then Mother said, To a Long Peaceful Life Together, and Bunty joined in with, The King, and I said, To Peace, and then Father had to top everyone's glass up and Mother said she would get giddy, but didn't stop him.

There was a moment of silence after that, until Bunty cried, 'The oven!' which took everyone by surprise. 'I'm doing Fat Rascals as a celebration,' she wailed, 'and I can smell burning.'

She put her glass down on an occasional table and headed for the door.

'I'll help,' I said, picking it up and following her to the kitchen, noting that Bunty could move quite quickly these days.

'Just in time,' she said, pulling the cakes out of the oven and setting the tray down on an iron plate stand.

'Ooh, thank you,' I said, as I liked Fat Rascals very much. 'Don't forget your sherry.' I pulled out a chair and sat down at the old oak kitchen table. 'This is all quite mad, isn't it?'

'Absolutely not,' said Bunty, wiping her hands on a cloth and looking for a knife. 'Em, it's wonderful.'

'So,' I said, narrowing my eyes. 'Exactly how long have you known he was going to ask me?'

Bunty went red and poked a cake to see if it was done. 'I have no idea what you mean.'

My best friend was one of the cleverest people I knew. However, along with being asked to leave the Little Whitfield Junior Wind Band for her ear-piercing failure on Third Clarinet, her inability to lie dominated a very small list of weaknesses. Or perhaps it was a strength. Either way, keeping even the smallest of secrets could bring her out in a rash and make her garble like an idiot. I decided to let her off the hook.

'It's all right, Bunts,' I said. 'Charles told me everything. I don't think he'd have asked me if you'd said that he shouldn't.'

'Rubbish,' said Bunty, looking relieved. 'Wild horses couldn't stop him. But he was awfully thoughtful.' She smiled. 'He's perfect for you, Em. And you know I'd say if I thought he wasn't up to scratch.'

'You would,' I said, raising my glass. 'You have very good taste in chaps.'

Bunty raised her glass in return.

'Thank you,' she said. 'And jolly well done, you.'

'Absolute fluke,' I said. 'Hopefully we can get married before he comes to his senses.'

'Stop it, he's lucky to have you,' said Bunty, taking a decent sip of the sherry. 'How are you getting on with the wedding plans?'

Bunty was a very good organiser and never happier than when she was drawing up some sort of a list. When we were fourteen she had come to Cornwall with my family, and the first morning produced a clipboard with a list of things to tick off during the trip. It scared the life out of us Lakes, but we all had our postcards written, posted and out of the way by eleven o'clock and everyone agreed they had never seen Bunty happier.

'Funny you should mention plans,' I said. 'I wondered if you might have some ideas?'

'Really?' said Bunty. She put down her glass. 'Are you sure? I did start to have a little think. But honestly, not if it's going to interfere.'

'Oh, Bunts,' I said, moving round to sit next to her. 'I can't imagine even trying to do this without you. As long as you want to, of course.'

Bunty looked at me, her blue eyes serious. 'I absolutely do, Em,' she said. 'I can't think of anything nicer than helping you, and Charles too of course.' She paused and took hold of my hand. 'And you know Bill would be cock-a-hoop for you too. He really would.'

I squeezed her hand and nodded, a lump in my throat making saying anything quite impossible.

For a minute we sat together in the quiet of the kitchen. I could hear laughter coming from the others and at that moment I'd have given anything in the world for Bill to still be here, even if it meant Bunty was the one getting married and not me.

'Cock-a-hoop,' said Bunty again, almost to herself. Then she gave me a big smile, cleared her throat and said, 'Now then, there's not a moment to lose. Where's my list?'

She rooted around in her skirt pocket and pulled out a pencil and small green notebook. Licking the end of the pencil as if she was about to take down an order for a week's fruit and veg, she fixed me with a keen stare.

'So,' she said. 'Do you have a wedding date in mind? Where are you thinking of having it? Do you want a big Do, or a quiet one?'

She turned to a page which appeared to have a large number of headings.

'Goodness,' I interrupted. 'You're fast out of the traps.'

'Just a few initial questions,' said Bunty, sounding like a police detective intent on solving an exciting new murder case. 'Honestly, Em, you might as well crack on.'

Bunty of course knew this better than anyone. But I entirely agreed. Anything could happen at any moment. If you loved someone you needed to get on with it.

'It depends on when Charles can get leave,' I said. 'But January might be rather nice. It's always rather a duff time, isn't it? This might cheer things up.'

'Perfect,' said Bunty. 'It will be the loveliest start to the New Year, and it gives us two months to organise.'

I swallowed. That didn't sound very long.

'Which is tons,' said Bunty.

She wrote down, 'NEED ACTUAL DATE' in capitals and then, 'URGENT,' which she underlined twice.

'In terms of a spread, we'll have some pretty stiff work on the coupon side to be able to come up with very much,' I said, frowning. I knew my family and friends would want to celebrate, but I couldn't imagine how we were going to cater for a party.

'Don't worry,' said Bunty, briskly. 'Everyone will pitch in. People will find all sorts of things they've put by.'

She gave a conspiratorial wink which made me snort. It sounded as if she was actively involved in the black market.

'Crikey, Bunts,' I said. 'Do you have questionable contacts that I don't know about, or will under-the-counter petty crime be a new venture for you?'

'Lies, all lies,' said Bunty, calmly. 'I just mean that almost everyone is bound to have something stored for a special occasion and with Christmas coming up, it's terrifically good timing.'

Then I really did laugh. Clearly, Bunty was planning to filch seasonal fare wherever she could find it.

'You won't even know there's a war on,' she finished triumphantly, adding, 'ALL MUST HELP WITH SPREAD' to her list. 'Moving on. The venue?'

'London. Somewhere.'

'Hmm,' muttered Bunty, looking down the page. Then she wrote, 'London', followed by, 'MUST NARROW DOWN' in large, impatient capitals.

'What else?' she asked looking at me with a keen expression.

I was beginning to feel I should have come more prepared. After all it had been a whole hour since Charles had proposed.

Bunty went back to her notes, wrote, 'URGENT' again at the top, drew a big ring around it and then started tapping the end of the pencil on the kitchen table.

'I don't know,' I said. 'I'm still in shock that he asked. Although there was one thing we did talk about.'

'Oh good,' said Bunty, looking expectant and flipping over a new page.

'Well,' I said. 'It's rather crucial actually.'

Bunty nodded vigorously.

'I just wanted to ask if you would be my chief bridesmaid?'

Bunty put her pencil down. A huge smile spread across her face.

'Oh, Em,' she said. 'Really?'

I nodded. 'Of course! But only if you'd like to, that is.'

Bunty looked down at her hands. For a moment she didn't say anything. When she finally looked up at me, her eyes were full of tears.

'I would love to, Em,' she said. 'There's nothing I would like more. Thank you. It's going to be the best day ever, you know.' She dabbed at her eye with her finger. 'I'm sorry, I'm being a weed.'

Then, picking up the pencil, she turned back to her notebook, and where she had put 'BRIDESMAIDS' as one of her headings, she very carefully added beside it, ME.

CHAPTER 12

Dear Yours Cheerfully

ONE OF THE nicest things about getting engaged, other than of course getting to marry Charles, was how happy everyone was when I told them the news.

The day after the engagement, once Bunty and I had returned to London, a double shift at the fire station turned into uproar as I broke the news to B Watch who all decided the celebrations should begin straight away.

Somehow we all still managed to answer the calls when they came in, but it was pure luck as when I made my announcement, Mary burst into tears, Joan nearly put out a hip when she leapt up from her chair, and Thelma shouted, 'I BLOODY KNEW IT!'

Then she got told off by Captain Davies for swearing while in uniform even though she tried to persuade him that when someone got engaged, rules like that shouldn't really count.

Roy and Fred and the boys were even louder, and as soon as the pubs opened for lunchtime, Fred secretly dispatched Big David to see if he could get some bottles from the King's Arms, particularly as the girl who served in the public bar was soft on him. Drinking while on shift was understandably even less acceptable than swearing, and it was fair to say that B Watch trod a very fine but celebratory line throughout the entire shift.

Someone was smiling on us as it was an uneventful Sunday, and when Roy and Fred and a couple of the others had half a weak shandy each, Captain Davies sent the other lads out on a call. Nothing was said, but there had been many, many shifts when celebrations had been the last thought in any of our minds. An excuse to cheer and sing and look to the future was more than deserved for every last member of the Watch.

On Monday morning and still walking on air, I arrived early at *Woman's Friend*, eager to share the news with the whole office. I had spoken briefly to my future brother-in-law and current boss when Charles had phoned him from my parents' house, but I was still looking forward to seeing him when I arrived at work.

Mr Collins was in his office when I arrived, which was unusual, but I wanted to see Kath first so that I could tell her before the others got in.

'Morning, Emmy,' she called, already at her desk and typing at nineteen to the dozen. 'Good weekend?'

'Morning, Kath,' I said. 'Marvellous, thanks. How was yours?'

'I made Mum a very nice skirt.' She looked up from her typewriter. 'I say, what's happened? You look very much in the pink.'

My plan to be cool as a cucumber disintegrated on the spot. 'I'm engaged,' I said. 'To Charles,' I added, just to be clear.

Kath catapulted up from her desk. 'Oh, my goodness, Emmy!' she cried. 'That's wonderful. Tell me everything. When did he ask? What did he say? Was it awfully romantic?'

I couldn't answer any of her questions as she was hugging the breath out of me.

'Did somebody mention an engagement?' said a voice at the door. It was Mr Collins, beaming like a lighthouse.

'Oh, Mr Collins!' said Kath. 'Isn't it lovely?'

'It certainly is,' said Mr Collins. 'I'm getting a sister-in-law.'

He looked really very pleased indeed, which was ever so nice, but I felt suddenly shy. What was the etiquette in this situation? We were, after all, at a place of work. I didn't know whether we should share a firm handshake, or perhaps I should just shout, 'Hurrah!' Hopelessly unsure, I did nothing and looked gormless.

'I'm delighted for you both,' said Mr Collins, formally.

I grinned, not all the ticket. Kath was no help as she just stood there as well.

'Oh, for God's sake,' said Mr Collins. 'Kathleen, avert your eyes. I am going to have to kiss Miss Lake.'

Kath giggled and put her face in her hands, as Mr Collins, or Guy, or whatever I was now supposed to call him, strode over, and holding me by the shoulders, kissed me on the cheek.

'Well done,' he said.

'AAAAAGHHHHH!' A horrified Hester arrived and let out an ear-splitting scream, dropping a huge pile of buff folders all over the floor. 'MR COLLINS!' she bellowed.

'It's all right, Hester,' I said as I hurried over to her. 'I've just got engaged to Mr Collins' brother. Honestly, everything's fine. Look,' I said, putting my arm round her and showing her my left hand. 'I have a ring and everything. Mr Collins was just being nice.'

Poor Hester remained unconvinced and continued to look daggers at him for stepping so terribly out of line.

'What's going on here?' Mrs Mahoney walked into the room, still in her overcoat and hat, and with an expression that suggested she was ready to knock heads together should it be required. It was all too much for Hester who promptly started having an embarrassed cry.

'Oh, God,' said Mr Collins. 'This has gone well.'

It wasn't quite how I had imagined sharing the news.

Amid the commotion I found Hester a clean hankie and Kath began to explain to Mrs Mahoney that there was actually some very good news, despite appearances suggesting someone had let themselves down.

'Well now,' said Mrs Mahoney. 'That's smashing and just what we all need. Now come on, Hester, let's stop all these tears. Many congratulations, Emmy. And to your husband to be.'

Hester managed a wobbly smile and blew her nose loudly, which elicited a kindly 'Well done,' from Mrs Mahoney, and everyone got back on track with saying how pleased they all were.

Soon, Mr Brand and Mr Newton arrived, and within ten minutes word appeared to have got around the building and Mrs Bussell came in with a hitherto secret box of what she said were Seventh Floor Biscuits. Even Clarence the post boy called in to very properly offer me his congratulations, before venturing to tell Kathleen that she'd 'be next'. For someone who had only recently got over the most debilitating crush on Kath, Clarence managed well, until he became over-confident and attempted a slightly rakish wink. When he didn't quite pull it off, he reverted to his old less senior self and backed out of the office, glowing a spectacular red.

It was the loveliest start to the day, and I only wished that Charles could have been there.

'You're all invited to the wedding, of course,' I said. 'It won't be a big event, but I would love you to come.'

That went down very well, and I thought of Bunty as everyone immediately started volunteering various foods. Mrs Mahoney and Kath said it was about time they gave up sugar so I could have their rations, Mr Newton was confident Mrs Newton had a tin of fine ham put away, and Mr Brand revealed he had a range of home-made pickles that wouldn't look out of place in Fortnum & Mason. Mrs Bussell said she would be pleased to see what she could do on the sweet front and when someone brought up the issue of alcohol, Mr Collins nodded sagely and said to leave it to him.

As everyone reluctantly realised they had to go and do some work as we had deadlines to meet, Hester shyly sidled up to me. 'I'm sorry I made a scene and spoilt things,' she said as I assured her it was a misunderstanding anyone could have had. 'Thank you ever so much for saying I can come to the wedding. I don't think Mum's got much in the way of party food, but I thought if you needed someone, I was a waitress in a café last summer, so perhaps I could help out?'

It was the nicest offer of them all and the straw that broke the camel's back. Failing entirely to hold back the tears, I gave her a great big hug. This year had been a steep business to get through and now I felt overcome by the happiness getting engaged had brought.

'Come on, soppy dates,' said Mrs Mahoney. 'Hester, I'm sure those folders need re-sorting, and Emmy, you and I have "Yours Cheerfully" to look after.'

I let go of Hester, who returned to form with a shy giggle and diligently took her folders away. I pulled myself together and began to gather my files before joining Mrs Mahoney for our weekly meeting about the problem page.

Mr Collins had stayed behind. 'Are you all right?' he asked.

'Absolutely,' I said. 'Sorry – I went a bit watery there.'

'Understandable,' he said, sitting back against one of the desks. 'I do want to thank you, Emmy. I can't tell you what it means to me to see my brother so enormously happy.'

'I'm blissfully happy, too,' I said. 'And I should be the one thanking you. I'd never have met Charles if Bunty and I hadn't bumped into you at the tea house.'

'Kismet,' smiled Mr Collins. He looked at his watch. 'Damn, I'm late for a meeting. Oh, one other thing. Your factory article is excellent. Really very good indeed. Two tiny changes from me, but nothing important. I'll get Hester to send it to Clough and Stratton, and the censorship chaps today, and we can put it in the next issue.'

I managed to stammer a Thank You. He thought my article about Anne and her friends was good!

'It wasn't too . . . positive?' I asked.

When I had returned from the factory trip, I had told Mr Collins everything, including what Anne and the others had said. He had listened sympathetically, especially about Irene and her daughters, but he was quietly clear about the article he expected me to write. Britain needed war workers and the Ministry had invited us to help find them.

'But we're here to help our readers, as well,' I'd said. 'You said that yourself.'

'I did, and I meant it,' said Mr Collins. 'But if we don't defeat Hitler, the very worst of anyone's problems will pale into insignificance.'

'Of course we'll defeat Hitler,' I said, patriotically.

'Not if we don't have enough kit we won't.'

It had been a sobering conversation, but I knew he was right, so I had gone away and written as cheery a piece as I could. Now at least I knew he was pleased.

'For someone whose very first article is going to be checked by the Government,' Mr Collins said, 'you've done a first-rate job. Look, Emmy, I know you're concerned about your friends, but one step at a time. You're doing well. Keep at it. Now I really must go, and I expect you to do very little but talk to the others about weddings today. That's an order.'

And with that, he left.

★

In all the excitement of Charles proposing, it had been easy to put my visit to Chandlers to the back of my mind for the last couple of days. Sometimes your own happiness insists on being selfish. Now that Mr Collins had approved what I had written, Anne and her friends shot right back to the front of the frame.

I had sent a letter to Mr Terry to thank him for his hospitality, and to praise both Mr Rice and the staff for their help with the article. I didn't want to be too much of a toady, but some professional flattery was required. Several mentions of how impressed I was by his staff, together with what a fine example his organisation was, would, I was sure, go down well.

I hadn't taken to Mr Terry in the least, but I wanted to go back to the factory for more articles in our series, and he was the person who could say yes or no. When I was growing up, my mother always said to be nice to the people you like, and nicer to the ones you don't. It had bewildered me when I was young, but now I was beginning to understand. As I wanted to find out if more could be done to make life a little easier for Anne and her friends, there was every reason to have the Factory Director on my side.

There was another reason as well. Meeting Mrs Edwards at the Ministry had inspired me. She was intelligent and charming and not afraid to say what she thought. I had the feeling this was the reason behind her success, and while it might have sounded quite lunatic on my part, I quietly aspired to be in the same vein.

And now an article that I had written was about to be sent to His Majesty's Government's Censors. Everything had become rather real.

WOMAN'S FRIEND AT WORK

In the first of our new series, EMMELINE LAKE joins recent women recruits at one of Britain's vital Munitions Factories.

They're working long hours of course, but the girls are proud to be pulling their weight and supporting our boys overseas. 'Productivity is high,' says the man in charge, as the nimble-fingered women make short work of the most intricate jobs . . . New recruit, widow and mother of two, Anne, has been quick to find her feet – as well as a grand bunch of new friends!

I had made the article informative and upbeat, and everything I had written was true. I just hadn't mentioned any of the bad parts.

This would be the first time I had ever had my name in a proper magazine, and I wanted to savour, and even celebrate, the moment. As Mrs Edwards had said, you never forgot your first commission. I just wished I had been able to report the full story, even if that wasn't the aim. I had to remember that my job was to encourage readers to volunteer for war work. If Anne and her friends were doing *their* duty, then in writing this I was doing mine.

Nevertheless, it was hard to feel entirely proud about writing *'every woman is doing her bit'* when I'd just seen a seven-year-old, babysitting her sister in the middle of a gun factory.

Struggling to take my mind off that image, I picked up my "Yours Cheerfully" file.

I wrote the "Woman's Friend at Work" articles to help the Ministry's plans. The aim of "Yours Cheerfully", however, was to help the readers as much as I could.

Tucking the file under my arm, I strode off to see Mrs Mahoney. Perhaps that was where Anne's friends could be helped.

★

Dear Yours Cheerfully,

   I am eighteen years old and my mother told me the facts of life when I was young. Now though, my friends have been talking about this and I am worried I have misunderstood. Please could you clarify the things on this list as some of them sound awful.

   Yours,

    Wrong End of the Stick

Mrs Mahoney ran her eyes down the attached sheet of paper. 'Oh dear,' she said. 'I don't think the poor girl quite knows one end of the stick from the other. And this list is no help either. I'm all for each to their own, but some of it is rather exotic. Let's put her in the pile for a personal reply and an informative leaflet.'

Mrs Mahoney tutted to herself quite happily as I scribbled down notes. It was such a pleasure to work with someone who wanted to help everyone and didn't shy away from some of the more colourful queries. When Mrs Bird was in charge, you only had to mention the opposite sex and she went into a blue fit.

'There seems to be some confusion in this one as well,' I said, handing Mrs Mahoney a letter written in a wild, spidery hand by a worried teenage reader. 'There's no name or return address though.'

Dear Yours Cheerfully

I'm fifteen and haven't had my monthly period. My friend Pearl says she bets I'm going to have a baby because I used the public toilets when we went on a day trip to Hull. I think that's rubbish, but Pearl says you can and she's older than me. Please help as I'm ever so worried.

I can't give you my name, but I live in Sheffield.

Mrs Mahoney read it and frowned.

'That rotten girl's pulling her leg,' she said. 'Although she could be pregnant from the conventional route so let's put, "To Worried From Sheffield" in the next issue and say it's very unlikely from that source, but to see her doctor about her health in general.' She sighed and took her glasses off to give them a clean with her hankie.

'It's a funny old job, this,' she said. 'As far as sex goes, sometimes I think half of them don't know even the basics, and the other half know far too much. No wonder they get so confused, poor loves. Who's next?'

'A lot of affairs still,' I said, going through my shortlist of letters that I thought should go in the magazine. 'Husbands going off, wives finding themselves new loves as well. It does put you off getting a lodger. But we've featured so many recently. This one is a bit different, though. It made me quite cross and I think we should put it in the next issue.'

I began to read.

Dear Yours Cheerfully,

I'm in the WAAF and had a day off yesterday so I decided to treat myself to a film. None of the other girls were free so I went on my own. The cinema was full, and I ended up next to a man who couldn't keep

142

his hands to himself. I told him three times to stop it,
but in the end I had to give up and leave.

I feel angry with myself that I didn't do something
more. I'm not feeble but all I wanted was a nice
afternoon to myself. I went home feeling quite humili-
ated. What should I have done?
Yours
L. Hayward (Corporal)

'Horrible behaviour,' said Mrs Mahoney, with contempt. 'I wish Corporal Hayward had reported him, but I know that's not as easy as it sounds. That sort of third rate wants you to feel embarrassed. If it was one of my girls, I'd march her straight back to the picture house and demand they put the lights up and find him.' She paused, thoughtfully. 'Of course, she could always do what my Milly did to a sad article who bothered her on the top of a bus.'

'What was that?' I asked.

'Lighted cigarette,' said Mrs Mahoney, mildly. 'She *accidentally* burnt his leg. Milly said he ran off so fast, he fell down the stairs.'

'Good for her,' I said. 'No one should have to put up with that.'

Mrs Mahoney nodded.

'That's what I say,' she said.

I looked at Corporal Hayward's letter again.

'It's not on,' I said. 'Here we are doing this big campaign to get the readers to sign up and work themselves silly for the war effort, and they can't even go to the cinema without being manhandled.'

'Let's definitely print the Corporal's letter,' said Mrs Mahoney. 'Say that she had every right to complain to the cinema and that we've heard of a way she can fend off unwelcome attention. That will answer her letter and it might help some other readers as well.'

'Thank you,' I said. 'We haven't put anything like this in "Yours Cheerfully" before.'

'Well,' said Mrs Mahoney, 'perhaps you and I are getting into our stride now we've been doing it for a while. The readers have enough on their plates without being bothered by this sort of behaviour.'

For the hundredth time I thought how lucky I was to be learning from Mrs Mahoney. Her confidence and experience couldn't help but rub off.

'Can I ask your opinion, please?' I said and began to tell her about the factory visit, and Irene and her girls. 'I know they're desperate for workers and as Mr Collins says, it's the only way we'll win the war. But how can I encourage our readers to go into munitions when if anything goes wrong, or they have problems at home, no one is interested, or worse, they might even be given the sack?'

We were sitting in the Production Office and the notice boards were plastered with the front covers Mr Brand was working on for future issues. Our new styling made a colourful and even stirring display where women, often in uniform, looked positive and optimistic, and cover lines announced, *How to Find the Right War Work for You* and *We Answer Your War Work Questions*, alongside the usual *Three Woollies for Winter* and *Is Baby Teething? How to Tell It's A Yes!*

Were we really answering the questions that mattered?

Whether it was Wrong End of the Stick, or Corporal Hayward, or the women whose lives were falling apart because of errant husbands or because they had fallen in love with the wrong man, we always tried our hardest to help as well as we could.

I turned back to Mrs Mahoney. 'What would we say to Irene Barker if she wrote in?' I asked, starting to make up a letter.

'Dear Yours Cheerfully,' I said. 'I have two young daughters (aged seven and four) and I work in munitions. My husband is in the navy and I have no family nearby to help out. None of the local nurseries can fit in with my shifts and there are only so many times the neighbours can help out. I've had to take the girls into the factory with me, but I hate having to do it, and I'm worried I'll lose my job if I'm caught doing it again.'

'What would we say?' I finished, turning to Mrs Mahoney.

'She needs to find proper, reliable help,' said Mrs Mahoney, straight away. 'Someone to have the children if she can afford it, or a nursery that fits in with her shifts. And she should have a word with her manager too, rather than trying to avoid him. That never works.'

Mrs Mahoney's solid, practical response made perfect sense.

'But what if she's tried all of those?' I said, pretty sure that from what Anne had said, Irene had.

'Then we'll have to come up with some other ideas, won't we?' said Mrs Mahoney, looking me squarely in the eye. 'I can't imagine that Mrs Barker is the only one. Emmy, we can't fix the whole world in twenty-four pages a week, but if this is a problem you think affects other readers as well, then it's our job to try to sort something out.'

Mrs Mahoney had a wonderfully comforting ability to make you feel that there was always an answer if you looked hard enough.

'I'd like to,' I said. 'I don't want to let down the Ministry or *Woman's Friend*, but I worry that we're not doing enough to help our readers if they sign up to do what we ask.'

I must have looked as concerned as I felt.

'I don't know what is going on inside that one-hundred-mile-a-minute mind of yours,' said Mrs Mahoney, gently, 'but don't go getting yourself in a muddle. We will come up with something.'

She smiled at me warmly. 'Now, can I suggest we go through the rest of this pile so you can start drafting some replies?'

'Yes, of course. Thank you, Mrs Mahoney,' I said, my mind racing straight past the one-hundred-mile-a-minute mark. 'Would you mind awfully if I write one other letter before I start on the drafts?' I smiled to myself as I began to think of a plan. 'I know we can't go trying to change the world just like that, but all the same, there's a Factory Director I would very much like to meet up with for a bit of a chat.'

CHAPTER 13

Stick to Stories for Your Ladies

WHOEVER SAID THAT flattery gets you nowhere had not met Mr Terry. Keeping my fingers tightly crossed that my first article about Chandlers would go down well with both the censors and the Ministry, I wrote to Mr Terry again, this time taking the opportunity to say what a mark his factory had made.

> *. . . I understand the Ministry has been most pleased with the article, which I fully credit to the help Woman's Friend received from the Chandlers' staff. Perhaps I might send you a copy of the issue for your interest? Might it be possible to gain a short meeting? A quotation from you in the next article would very much inspire our readers . . .*

I was beginning to sound like a modern-day Uriah Heep.

But it worked. Two days after the letter had been sent, Mr Terry's secretary called. Mr Terry would be away for the rest of this week but could see me for fifteen minutes at some point during the next.

It had been remarkably easy. Even Mr Collins was impressed. 'I thought you said he wouldn't recognise you again in the street,' he said. 'It sounds like you made an impression.'

'I buttered him up,' I admitted. 'I thought it was the sort of thing Mrs Edwards might do.'

Mr Collins laughed. 'Quite possibly,' he said. 'But be careful. He sounds a tricky sort. Are you sure you don't want my help?'

'I'll be fine, thank you,' I said. 'I really am just going to get a quote for another article and ask him one or two things about female workers, like part-time work and nurseries. I'm going to talk to Anne Oliver before I see him, so I don't put my foot in it.'

As well as writing to Mr Terry, I had sent a letter to Anne at the same time, filling her in and asking for her opinion. The last thing she and her friends needed was me rushing in like a bull in a china shop and saying the wrong thing. Anne wrote back quickly, saying she'd spoken with Betty and the girls and they reckoned it was worth a go. She suggested meeting her in town before my appointment.

At ten o'clock on the day of the interview, I once again caught the train out to Berkshire, and this time, following her directions, walked out of the railway station and headed up to the high street where we had arranged to meet.

I easily spotted her, standing near a very long queue that was going into the fishmonger's. She was wearing her green coat and work trousers, with a shopping basket hooked over one arm and Baby Tony very much taking up the other. Ruby, dressed in a dapper tweed coat, was showing Anne how high she could jump off the pavement.

'Emmy!' cried Anne, putting down her basket and giving me a wave. 'Ruby, look who it is.'

I ran over to greet them, swinging Ruby round in a circle which made her scream and, understandably, ask that I do it again. Once she and I were both thoroughly dizzy, the four of us headed to a very small tea shop, where an appropriately very small lady called Mrs Phillips welcomed us in out of the cold.

'It's so lovely to see you,' said Anne as we settled down in our seats. 'And congratulations! I want to hear all about the wedding plans. I do hope I don't smell out the place, I've just got a nice piece of haddock.' She spoke quietly. 'Mr Andrews, the fishmonger, is very kind. His daughter works at You Know Where and he knows we do funny hours, so he makes sure there's always something when we come in. Nothing under the counter or anything, but it does help.'

'Where's the lady with the stick?' asked Ruby. 'She was pretty.'

'Do you mean Bunty?' I asked. 'She couldn't come, I'm afraid.'

Ruby thought for a moment. 'I'm getting a rabbit,' she said, recovering well, which was rather crushing for poor Bunts.

Anne grimaced. 'Ruby, we're only thinking about it at the moment, aren't we?'

'It's called Bun Bun,' confirmed Ruby. 'And it's going to have babies.'

'I hope not,' said Anne under her breath.

She helped Ruby take off her coat. 'I made this from Anthony's jacket,' she said in passing. 'I'm quite pleased with it.'

The little coat was tailored beautifully and looked as if it could have come from a grand department store. Anne folded it carefully and put it on the seat next to her. She looked tired, which was no surprise as she had been working all night.

'How was the night shift?' I asked, sympathetically. 'They really turn your clock upside-down, don't they? It took me ages to get the hang of them at the fire station.'

'They're wretched, aren't they?' agreed Anne. 'But it does mean I can get things done during the day and give Mum a break from these cheeky monkeys.'

'I'm not a cheeky monkey,' said Ruby.

Anne and I looked at her.

'I think you probably are,' I said. 'Would you like a bun? A special one that only monkeys can have?'

'I'm a cheeky monkey,' said Ruby, now able to clarify things.

As Ruby concentrated on her Monkey Bun and Baby Tony gnawed contentedly on a crust, Anne and I continued to chat, mostly in code, partly as she wasn't supposed to talk about work and partly so that Ruby, who had the hearing of a bat, wouldn't understand.

'I'm interested in what Mr . . . ahem . . . thinks about some of the things we spoke about when we last met,' I said in a low voice. 'But are you happy for me to ask about specifics? I won't ask if you're worried.'

'We've talked about it,' whispered Anne back. 'Me and the others, and we think if you're quite casual about it, and perhaps talk generally about other places, you might get a response. Some of the girls have said things but not got anywhere.' She glanced at Ruby, who I assumed was not strong on confidentiality. 'B.E.T.T.Y. asked the U.N.I.O.N. but there's no interest from them. The factory is short-staffed so I can't see them allowing P.A.R.T. time.' She paused to have a sip of tea. 'I hope I don't sound flat, Emmy, but productivity is the key thing, so I'm not holding my breath.'

I said of course she didn't sound flat, but actually, Anne did.

'Is everything all right?' I mouthed.

Ruby was a picture of happy concentration and not interested in her mother and me in the least.

'Yes, thanks,' said Anne. 'Although my M.U.M. is being run ragged, I think. But she insists that she's fine.' She shook her head. 'I hope so. She may just have forgotten what hard work M.O.N.K.E.Y.S. are. Ah, Ruby, I see you've finished. Do you think you could go and ask Mrs Phillips to give your hands a wipe with her cloth? Good girl.'

Ruby, slightly surprisingly, did what she was told and pottered off to see Mrs Phillips. Anne leant towards me. 'There is one thing,' she said, looking around and lowering her voice again. 'I'm really not supposed to say anything, but it's about Irene and it makes everything even worse.' She hesitated. 'This is really secret. Seriously.'

'I won't say a thing. I promise.'

Anne pursed her lips and then seemed to make her mind up to tell me. 'Her husband's ship is missing,' she said in a whisper. 'No one else knows except me. Not that she should have told me, but she thought I might know what to do, you know, because of losing Anthony.'

'Anne, I'm so sorry,' I said. 'And I assume Mr Rice has no idea?'

'Gosh, no. Honestly, you're absolutely not allowed to say anything until it's confirmed one way or the other.' She looked worried. 'I really shouldn't have told you. But I feel so awful for her. Irene's having such a difficult time with the children. She's on her final warning. If she brings them to the factory again, she'll be sacked, and she just can't lose her job now she's the only one earning.'

'But she'll get his pay, until, well, as usual?'

Anne shook her head.

'Irene gets her allowance, but as he's missing, they stop his pay, and she won't get anything else as he might not be dead. I've told her not to give up hope, because you can't, but obviously Irene's been knocked for six.'

'What can we do to help?' I said, without thinking. I didn't even live in this town.

'People would rally round, but as she can't tell anyone, no one knows how badly she's struggling. I'd get her to bring the girls to ours, but Mum's up to her neck as it is.'

'Well, that settles it, doesn't it?' I said. 'I know I mentioned it last time I was here, but I'm going to ask You Know Who about a Government Nursery. There aren't many yet, but they do exist. That would make things easier, surely? They're supposed to be very reasonable.'

'If they could fit in with the shifts, yes,' said Anne. She ran her hand through her hair. 'Although Irene needs help now. Betty was ever so fed up with the response from the union.'

'What did they say, exactly?'

'Men only. I mean, she knew that, but she wanted to push them. They wouldn't even discuss it.'

'They won't be any help then,' I said, noticing that Ruby was now on her way back, proudly holding a tiny teacup and saucer. 'Has anyone asked about nurseries before?'

'I know Irene said something to one of the foremen once, but didn't get anywhere.' She turned to the cherubic figure wobbling towards her. 'Hello, Ruby Oliver, you're looking very grown up.'

As Ruby announced that her cup belonged to an elf, Anne clapped her hand over her mouth and started apologising like mad as we hadn't talked about Charles and the wedding.

'I've a brain like a sieve,' she said. 'Please tell us all about it. I could do with chatting about something exciting and fun.'

For the next hour we did exactly that. Anne was genuinely keen, and we both enjoyed playing up the frivolous side of things and talking about plans. I asked Anne if I might send an invitation to her and the children once we knew the date and then she really did perk up.

When it was time for me to head back to the station, where I had been told to wait for someone from Chandlers to pick me up, Anne and I parted fondly.

'Good luck with him,' she said as we hugged goodbye.

'I won't let you down,' I said. 'I'm going to make jolly sure he knows how good you all are.'

'Thank you for trying to help,' said Anne.

'I'm just being a nosy journalist,' I said, laughing. 'Anyway, I'm the one that should say thank you. If it wasn't for you, I wouldn't have been given my very first assignment.'

'Rubbish!' said Anne.

'I'm serious,' I said. 'The least I can do is to try to find out the lay of the land with his nibs, and report back.'

'Just be careful,' said Anne.

'I'll be fine,' I said. Then I kissed Baby Tony, gave Ruby one last hysterics-inducing spin, and with a final Goodbye, headed off to face the factory's boss.

★

Mr Terry was, I was reliably informed, a very busy man, with quite a short memory.

'I'm a very busy man,' he said. 'What was it you wanted?'

I explained that I had written to him the previous week about the articles I was writing.

'Your women workers?' I prompted.

'Ah, that,' he said.

I smiled brightly, a hopefully winning effort that I had practised on Bunty at home. It was a tricky thing to pull off. I needed to be taken seriously, while pandering to the ego of a middle-aged showy type and strictly avoiding looking flirtatious or giving the impression of being in awe.

As Bunty had said, it would be far easier if I could just hit him over the head with a brick and then forge his signature on whatever it was I wanted him to do for Anne and her friends. However, as this was real life and not a Laurel and Hardy picture, I found myself sitting very stiffly on an uncomfortable leather chair in front of Mr Terry's large but neat desk.

For all his fast car and fast life appearance, the Factory Director's office steered clear of ostentation. The furniture, while of good quality, was functional rather than pretentious, and the overall appearance was of a recently formed gentlemen's club where the focus was on business rather than pleasure. There was a musky smell explained by the walnut cigar box on his desk, and the only thing that gave a nod to personal interest was a large marbled Bakelite ashtray with 'Rolls-Royce' printed on it. I wondered if visitors were supposed to assume Mr Terry was a proud owner. Either way it had the air of sales department Christmas gift.

'Mr Terry,' I said. 'Everyone is delighted with the first article about your women workers. It is exactly the sort of thing they think will encourage more women to go into munitions.'

'Ah hah,' he said.

'Led of course,' I added, not letting my smile slip, 'by the Ministry.'

Mr Terry looked rather more interested. 'Yes, of course,' he said. 'We very much welcome lady workers.'

'Excellent. Consequently, I thought it would be helpful to include something from you in one of our next features. A quote perhaps on why you value the women working here? We wouldn't mention you by name of course as a security issue, but a word from the very top could really inspire.'

I opened my eyes slightly wider and looked expectant.

Mr Terry came across as if I'd asked him to remember a particular brick in a wall. There were so many, and they all looked the same.

'What do you think women contribute to the factory?' I prompted.

'They're not bad,' said Mr Terry. 'Some of them can't manage it. I don't know what they expect. It's a factory. But overall, they'll do.'

Saying they would 'do' didn't strike me as inspiring anyone. I pressed on.

'What would you say to women thinking about going into munitions? Would you say it is their patriotic duty?'

'Definitely. But productivity is the key,' he said, finally warming up. 'We only want the good ones, who get their heads down. If they're young and willing to put in the hours, it's a great life. I don't mind if they're old, either, as long as they get on with the job.'

'That's a super point about Patriotic Duty,' I said, writing it down as if he had come up with it on his own. 'Thank you. And "women of any age" is very encouraging as well. Does it make a difference if they're married, or have children?'

I looked at him with what I hoped was a blank-faced interest, for all the world, hanging on his every word.

'What do you mean?'

'Many of our readers are in that position. They're very keen to make a contribution.'

'They're all welcome,' he said. 'As long as they don't go making a fuss.'

I watched Mr Terry closely. Sitting in his office he was

more guarded than when he had driven me in his car. More careful, perhaps, of what he was saying.

'What sort of fuss?' I asked. My smile was beginning to make my face ache.

Mr Terry shifted in his chair and stared at me. 'Do you really want my opinion?' he said.

'Of course.'

'Will you print it?'

'Only if you want me to.'

There was a soft tap on the door. It was Mr Terry's secretary, Mrs Cleeve, who I had met earlier, a large woman with a no-nonsense stare.

'Your next meeting, Mr Terry,' she began.

'Five minutes, Mrs Cleeve,' he replied, and she backed out of the room. When the door was shut Mr Terry lit a cigarette from a case he took from his jacket. He did not offer me one, but gave me a long stare. I smiled back, as pleasant as the day was long.

'Here's what I think about women workers, Miss Lake,' he said, inhaling deeply. 'If they work hard and produce as much as the men, and to the same standard, that's fine. If your readers want to do their bit, earn good money and help the boys, I'm all for them. The problem I have is when they expect special treatment. Asking for different shifts, or time off because Little Jimmy has a runny nose, or the butcher's had a delivery and they want to leave early as they don't want to miss out.' He sniffed. 'You don't have those problems with men. There'll be the odd one who comes on shift drunk and you just sack him, but with the females, half of them have personal problems they bother my foremen with. Quite frankly there are far more important things to be getting on with.'

'I see. Perhaps if you had a Women's Welfare Officer?'

I said. 'Or a Women's Union? The Government is keen for all workers to be looked after.'

Mr Terry stubbed out his cigarette, grinding it into the Rolls-Royce ashtray. 'The Government wants to win the war, that's what it wants. That's what we should all want. You do realise that, don't you?'

It was the second time in a matter of days that a man had told me how important winning the war was, as if I hadn't a clue. It was beginning to grate. 'I certainly do, Mr Terry,' I said calmly. 'And my understanding is that that is why they are recruiting more women to the Employment Agencies and as Welfare Officers. And of course, starting nurseries for women workers' children. In fact on that point, I just wanted to ask . . .'

Mr Terry snorted so loudly he drowned out what I was trying to say. 'Don't start on that,' he snapped. 'We're making armaments, not running a babysitting service.'

'But wouldn't it help the women stop making a fuss, as you put it?' I said.

'We're very good to our lady workers,' said Mr Terry. 'We've just put mirrors in all their lavatories.'

'And I believe they were thrilled,' I said.

'A year ago, we didn't even have ladies' lavatories,' said Mr Terry, defensively.

'But a Government Nursery wouldn't cost you anything,' I said. 'The Ministry of Labour and your Local Authority would sort it all out, if you told them you needed it.'

It came out in a rush, but I had done my homework. Mr Terry did not appear impressed.

'What are you driving at, Miss Lake?' he said, sharply. 'I've agreed to see you to give you a quote, not to get the third degree. Has someone complained?'

I was still smiling, but my heart had sped up. 'No one

at all,' I said, realising it would be wise to pull back. 'Mr Terry, the women I've spoken to have had nothing but praise for their managers and the factory facilities. I also had several comments on the quality of the canteen, not to mention the fact they had been treated to Arthur Askey for free. No complaints whatsoever.' I put my notebook down on my lap. Even a gentle questioning of the factory amounted to criticising him.

'I only mentioned the Government Nurseries as we are working on an article about them.' I smiled. 'They sound rather helpful.'

Mr Terry grunted. 'It's nothing to do with me. If ladies' other commitments mean they can't do the job, then they shouldn't apply.'

'But wouldn't that mean the country missing out on thousands of excellent workers?' I said, failing to back down.

Mr Terry's argument didn't make sense and I was pretty sure he knew it. He didn't look happy at all. I thought of my promise to Anne that I wouldn't let her down.

'Mr Terry,' I chirruped, 'your factory and your women workers are an inspiration. Thank you very much indeed for seeing me today. I have some lovely words that I know our readers will find most stirring.'

Mr Terry bit his lip thoughtfully as I put my things in my bag and stood up, smiling as confidently as I could while hoping I hadn't pushed him too far. I extended my hand to shake his, and he slowly stood too. He was considerably taller and far bigger than me, but I kept my shoulders back and my chin up, and I didn't move my arm until he somewhat reluctantly took my hand.

He didn't quite shake it though, but just held it firmly.

'I look forward to your next article, Miss Lake,' he said. 'As I am sure the Ministry will. I have many contacts within the various Governmental departments. It will be interesting to hear their views on whether the ladies' magazines actually help. Mrs Cleeve will arrange for you to be escorted back to the station.'

'That's very kind,' I said. 'Thank you so much. I hope you will be happy with our next article.'

Mr Terry nodded, finally letting go of my hand, which was a relief, and walking me towards the door.

'Stick to writing stories for your ladies, Miss Lake. And leave me to run my factory.'

I thanked him again and wished him a good morning. My smile didn't drop until I was well outside his office door.

At least now I knew.

Stick to writing stories for your ladies.

My foot, I would.

No wonder Maeve had said that nothing would change. Mr Terry hadn't the faintest interest in helping his female workers.

It was time to come up with a new plan.

CHAPTER 14

Unmistakably Like a Bride

'IF YOU DON'T stand still, I'm going to stab you and then we'll get blood on the dress.'

I was standing in my bedroom with my arms out while Bunty pinned the bodice of what, if the pattern was to be believed, would be Every Bride's Dream Dress.

'The thing is,' I said, trying not to wriggle, 'I underestimated him and that was a mistake.'

'It'll be an even bigger mistake if I get this wrong and it looks like a sack,' said Bunty, through a mouthful of pins. 'Don't be so hard on yourself. He sounds a difficult character to deal with, and this is your first big project. Now move round a tiny bit.'

She deftly added the last of the pins and stood back to look at her work. 'Not bad,' she said. 'Now then, don't move. I'm going to turn the record over and then you can look in the mirror and tell me what you think.'

It was Saturday afternoon, the day after I had met Mr Terry, and all talk of work was supposed to have been banned. With the wedding confirmed for the second Saturday in January, I had a wedding dress to make, and Bunty was keen to update me as she and my mother had been plotting reception ideas on the phone.

Charles was coming up to take me out for the evening but wasn't due to arrive for several hours, and despite my misgivings over the meeting the previous day, there was a definite feel of giddiness in the air.

Bunty leant over to the gramophone, turned the record over and put up the volume so that when 'Sing Sing Sing' started, it filled the room.

'DON'T DANCE,' commanded Bunty as I started jigging about. 'This fabric is precious.'

When Charles and I had got engaged, my plan had been to make myself something new out of whatever fabric I could get my hands on, ideally a nice day dress that I could easily wear again and again.

This plan had changed however, when two days after the engagement, my younger brother Jack, who was a pilot, turned up at the house in Pimlico on the back of his friend Chaser's motorbike, wielding a large paper package. As Chaser waited on the bike, Jack ran up the steps to the house, rapped on the door, and after a brief kiss hello, shoved the package into my arms, and said, 'There you are, Sis. Call it an early wedding present.'

I had forced them both to come in for a moment so that I could open the parcel, which turned out to contain a good five yards of parachute silk. It was ripped down one side, but Jack said not to worry as no one had died in it and it had just been mucked up in a training session by an idiot none of the squadron liked. As Chase helpfully pointed out, there wasn't even a grass stain on it, let alone any blood.

Jack said it was a shame to let it go to waste, although should anyone ask, if I could deny any knowledge of where it had come from it would probably be for the best.

It was lovely of him and I had to admit, it was smashing fabric by anyone's standards. Before I could entertain any idea of getting the material dyed, Bunty had declared the training mishap an act of God (which seemed a bit of a stretch, even if we did all love the RAF) and talked me into making a proper white wedding dress.

'You can dye it afterwards and use it for informal evening events,' she said, which rather suggested she had been reading fashion magazines. 'Then you'll get two outfits out of the one.'

Going the whole bridal hog with a traditional long dress didn't feel quite my thing, so I found a very nice pattern for a three-quarter-length frock with rather elegant panels at the front and long sleeves that would be ideal for a winter wedding.

'Do you think it's a bit tight,' I said, breathing out as far as I could. 'I want to be able to fit in that vest you knitted.'

Bunty looked horrified. 'The one I've just made?' she said. 'Why on earth would you do that?'

'Bunts, it's going to be January. I don't want to freeze.'

'You can't go wearing a long-sleeved vest on your wedding day.' Bunty was aghast. 'It's the most romantic day of your life.'

'It won't be if I get pneumonia,' I said.

'What's Charles going to say?'

'I can't imagine he'll mind in the least,' I said. 'He's very practical.'

'Of course he'll mind,' said Bunty. 'Have you actually met a man before? You do realise a long-sleeved vest probably isn't what he's expecting on your wedding day, don't you? You're supposed to be a lovely young bride, wearing lovely things and looking, um, lovely.'

'That's three lovelies,' I said. 'I won't be able to manage that many in one go, not even for Charles.'

Bunty was shaking her head, so I sought a compromise.

'How about if it's cold I'll wear the vest to the church and for the standing outside afterwards, and then when we come back here, I'll sneak away and take it off.'

'Then the dress will be too big,' said Bunty, standing her ground.

'No, it won't. And anyway, you and Mother and the girls from the station are planning so much food that after the buffet I'll be lucky if the buttons don't fly off during the first dance. I have no idea how many people you've coerced into contributing.'

Bunty surveyed her pinning work. 'A decent list,' she said. 'Everyone's looking forward to a good do. How about making a little jacket? That'll keep you nice and warm. I bet there's enough fabric left.' She stood back from me with her hands on her hips.

I smiled at her. Not because of the dress or the vest or any of that, but because I realised that she had been standing without her walking stick for the last five minutes. Her left hand was definitely better than it had been as well. I didn't want to make a big deal of it, but I was thrilled to see Bunty getting better. I knew how much it meant to her to get back, as far as she could, to her old self.

'Absolutely,' I said, happy now to agree. 'A jacket is a super idea. I'll go through my patterns to see what I can find.'

'That's the ticket,' said Bunty, pleased to have won the vest debate. 'Now then, have a look and tell me what you think.'

I waddled over to the long mirror, aware that a dozen pins were threatening to poke me should I make a wrong move. My hair was all over the place as I hadn't done anything with it that day, and I hadn't a scrap of make-up on. I was also wearing thick socks and a pair of beige shoes that were too big but we thought the right height for the dress. All in all, I was not exactly making an effort.

But despite all of that, and I supposed because normally

I would never wear white, I realised I looked unmistakably like a bride. Bunty's handiwork had made a huge difference and now that it was more fitted, the dress was beginning to hang as it should. The sleeves were just pinned in and everything needed finishing properly, but there was no doubt what it was going to be.

'Gosh,' I said and then ran out of steam.

Bunty had sat down on my bed and was looking at the mirror so she could see the expression on my face. I turned round to look at her. Neither of us said anything, but we both had tears in our eyes.

'I don't know,' I said. 'I think maybe it's a bit much? What if I did dye it, a pale blue perhaps? I like blue.'

I looked too bridal.

I pushed off the shoes and stood awkwardly in my socks. I wanted to go and sit with my best friend, but the pins meant I had to stay standing.

Bunts got up from the bed, still managing without her stick, and came over to stand in front of me. Then she took both my hands.

'It's perfect,' she said. 'Honestly, I promise. You're going to look beautiful, Em. On your day, just as you should. As you deserve to. I know you're worried about me, but please keep the dress white. I really want you to.'

'It shouldn't be like this, Bunts,' I said. 'It's not fair.'

It was supposed to be Bunty and Bill.

'Now then,' said Bunty and her voice shook. There was a tear running down her face and I knew I was about to follow suit. 'We are both going to talk about it and probably cry, and then you have to promise me that from now on, you will only be happy about this wedding.' She wiped the back of her hand across her eyes and then went back to holding my hand. 'Em, you deserve all of this. And you have to be happy. For all of us. Please say you will.'

I took a breath and nodded. I would be happy. I was already. My grandmother always said, wishing was good time wasted, but I couldn't help wishing more than anything that Bunty and William could be together. They should have had the happiness I'd been so lucky to find.

'All right,' I said slowly. 'I promise.'

And even though hugging someone when you are dressed as a gigantic pincushion is a quite lunatic thing to do, that, very carefully, was exactly what Bunty and I did.

★

With the pinning all done and both of us having managed not to inflict mortal damage by harpooning each other, Bunty and I spent a happy afternoon tacking and measuring and then getting me to try the dress on again to make sure it would fit. Bunts and I were singing along to the gramophone, so neither of us heard the front doorbell ring. We also didn't hear when Charles let himself in, followed the sound of 'Beat Me Daddy, Eight to the Bar' up to my room and even though the door was open, was chivalrous enough to knock on it loudly.

'Anyone in?' he called. 'Everyone decent?'

We were. I was. But I was still wearing the wedding dress, albeit now with only one arm in which wasn't quite the look I was hoping for.

'NO,' I shouted at the top of my voice and then added, 'DON'T,' which made no sense but was all I could come up with.

'GET DOWN,' shouted Bunty wildly at me. 'CROUCH.'

As Charles didn't have the benefit of being able to see her, it was understandable if he was in need of some clarification.

'Do you mean me?' he asked from behind the door.

'NO,' shouted Bunty again. 'STAY THERE. SHE'S IN THE DRESS.'

'Ah,' said Charles, laughing. 'Can I see?'

'NO,' shouted Bunty and I together, although you couldn't hear me that well as I was on my knees hiding beside the bed as if someone had just located an incendiary.

'Shame. I'll sit on the stairs then,' said Charles, cheerfully. 'Can I just mention that it has taken me three hours to get here?'

'Can you help me out? I can't undo the back,' I whispered to Bunty, as if speaking at the proper volume would give something away. 'WE'RE COMING,' I added, beginning to feel a little bad about the reception poor Charles was getting.

'Are you all right?' said Charles. 'You sound muffled. Are you going to marry me in some sort of hood?'

'Shut up,' said Bunty as I started to giggle which didn't help, as actually I was rather stuck. 'Both of you.'

'Nearly there,' I said, as Bunty finally managed to extract me from the fabric. 'Well at least we've found the neck's a bit tight.'

'Ssshhhh,' said Bunty. 'Don't listen, Charles.'

I could hear him chuckle as I heaved on my skirt and shoved a jumper over my head.

'You can come in now,' I called. 'No, hold up, we need to hide the . . . wait . . . I'M COMING OUT.'

I raced out of my room and onto the landing. Charles was sitting on the stairs opposite, his head bowed, with one hand covering his eyes and the other holding a bunch of flowers.

'I do hope that's you, darling,' he said, standing up but not moving his hand from his eyes. 'Or there's an embarrassing danger I'm about to kiss your best friend. Mind you, Miss Tavistock is a very attractive woman.'

'I heard that,' called Bunty. 'I'm staying in here.'

'I saw you first,' I said as Bunty put on 'Song of the Volga Boatmen' at full blast. Laughing, I kissed him until I was confident he had made the right choice.

'Never in doubt,' said Charles, eventually. 'Never in doubt.'

It would have been the most romantic moment, apart from the fact that Charles then remembered he had just seen Mr Parsons outside Durton's, who wanted him to pass on some very important news.

'He said to tell you that the time has come for Pauline,' said Charles. 'And that he'll bring round some sausages next week.'

'Poor old Pauline,' I said. 'She's a lovely pig.'

'Mr Parsons says it's what she would want,' said Charles, philosophically.

'I must dress,' I announced, slightly as if I was Louis XV.

'Watch out for pins,' said Bunty, coming out of my bedroom. 'There may be some on the floor. CHARLES, DON'T EVEN LISTEN.'

'You've used PINS?' he said. 'Good God, you've virtually given away the whole frock.'

'She can still change her mind, you know,' said Bunty, as he gave her a kiss. 'Come on, I'll make you a drink while you wait.'

I slipped back into my bedroom to find my decent going-out frock. Bunty had hung up the half-finished wedding dress on the wardrobe door, hidden again beneath the sheet we had been using to protect it from dust. Now on my own, I sneaked another look. The dress was definitely starting to look the part. I needed to do lots more work on it before it was ready, but for the first time I could see myself wearing it, standing next to Charles at St Gabriel's and taking our vows.

From downstairs I could hear chatting and laughter, as Charles and Bunty headed for the kitchen.

With one last glance at the wedding dress, I carefully put the sheet back over the top. The dress would be lovely, but when it came to it, I didn't really mind what it looked like. It was the man downstairs that mattered.

In just a few weeks' time we would be married. As I began to change for the evening, I put on another record and began to sing along. It couldn't come fast enough for me.

CHAPTER 15

An Army Man and All That

AN HOUR LATER, Charles and I made our way to the restaurant in the West End that he had booked for dinner. We had been here together before and were fond of it as it was slightly off the beaten track and at this time of the evening, quiet and low-key. Later, of course, it would jazz up, with the post-midnight crowd queuing to get in for a very late supper and some music and cabaret on the tiny space they used as a dance floor. Now though, as it was unfashionably early, it would be far easier to talk and we wouldn't have to shout over any sort of a din.

As it was in the basement, the restaurant was always dark, lit only by small art deco lamps which sat on the white cloth-covered tables. Tonight the waiter showed us to one of the nicest tables, in the corner, not far from where the band would squash themselves in later. Although the smart set had probably not even begun to think about going out or were having pre-theatre drinks somewhere more chic, many of the tables were already taken. Almost all the men were in uniform, and many of the women too. A party of good-natured Canadians were telling the waiter they were lining their stomachs for the evening, which he took very well and continued to go through the menu even though the boys didn't seem to mind what they ate. A very good-looking Polish officer was having an intense conversation with an equally beautiful English woman, while two young Wrens were being wined and dined by a pair of very cheery naval officers. I almost wished I had worn my NFS uniform, but it was nice to put on a dress and go out with Charles as if things were normal, even if normal meant him in a uniform of course. In the months since we had met, I had almost never seen him in civvies.

'You've worked out everyone's story, haven't you?' said Charles, as we sat down. He was used to me watching people as a matter of course. 'I saw you as we came in,' he smiled. 'Some people walk through a room expecting everyone to turn round to see who they are. You walk through a room and don't expect anyone to look at you, but you always notice everyone else.'

'I sound like a secret agent,' I said in a stage whisper, feeling rather pleased. 'How exciting.'

Charles laughed. 'You're too honest,' he said. 'You'd last about two minutes under interrogation. Of course, you'd be brave to a point of madness, and before they realised it you'd be asking questions and getting them to talk about themselves. Actually, I retract my comment. You'd be a top-drawer secret agent.'

'Thank you,' I said, modestly. 'We should be careful, or the other diners will think you're here to recruit me. I should imagine this is how it's done. You know, asking one out to dinner and then saying, "you'd be a top-drawer secret agent" quite loudly in public.'

We both laughed. I liked talking nonsense like this with him.

'But I think you're hiding your own interrogational light under a bushel,' I continued. 'As soon as I met you, I didn't stop talking. It's a wonder you wanted to see me again. Anyway, I'm always lying. I don't say that with any pride,' I added as the waiter appeared with a wine menu that defied any suggestion there was a war on. 'Goodness,' I said, when he had gone. 'I hope the food menu is as good. I shall have fourteen eggs and a very large steak. They don't appear to have cut back one bit.'

'What do you mean you're always lying?' asked Charles. 'Don't tell me you're about to reveal you're a twice married divorcée with a terrible dependency on gin?'

He said it lightly, but I could see he was puzzled. It had been an odd thing for me to say.

'Oh, nothing like that,' I said. 'At least not the gin.' I tried not to sound too serious. 'It's just having to say the right thing at work when you don't always agree with it. A letter where a reader is fed up to the back teeth and wishes the war would just end, and you entirely agree with her but have to reply, "we understand but we must all keep going." That sort of thing. And now, writing articles but leaving out anything contentious. Especially with you know who.'

Charles understood I meant the Ministry. 'I thought it was going well on that front?'

'It is,' I said. 'Very.'

I quietly began to tell him what had happened with Mr Terry.

'And I feel as if whatever I do, I will let somebody down,' I finished, glad that the wine had now come and I could take a large sip. I didn't want to burden Charles with my worries, but it felt better that he knew.

'Have you spoken to Guy?' he asked.

'He knows how I feel. Everyone is very happy with what we're doing, and I don't want to make waves. And after those women at the Ministry were so rude about everything, it makes for a sweet revenge. I don't want to mess anything up, but I wish we could help Anne's friend. If my meeting is anything to go by, they're unlikely to get any help from the Factory Director, that's for sure. Let's not talk about it.' I smiled at Charles. 'I don't want to spoil our evening. I can't believe you nearly walked in on seeing the dress. Hideously poor wedding form.'

'Wasn't it? You know I wouldn't care if you turned up in Churchill's old siren suit, but it will be lovely to see you dressed up to the nines. I hope this will be all right,' he said, looking down at his uniform. 'I'm told it's really quite "In".'

'I was thinking of that just now,' I said. 'Can you believe that after the war we'll just be a normal married couple? I won't have to make clothes out of parachutes, and you can spend your life in a pullover if you want. None of it will matter. Restaurants won't be full of uniforms and we won't be feeling awful about eating food that really should be on the ration.'

I looked around pensively. I hoped I sounded optimistic rather than maudlin, and I didn't feel entirely bad about looking at a menu with more food than I had seen in the last month.

'It's going to be idyllic,' I said.

Charles smiled, his eyes as wistful as I felt. 'Won't it?' he said. 'The thought does keep one going. Although I'm an army man and all that, so you may have to put up with me in uniform for a while after we've won. I'll probably still be in for a few more years, if they want me and I'm still in one piece.'

He was so matter of fact about it, but 'if I'm still in one piece' was a horrible thing to hear.

'Darling, please don't put it like that,' I said. 'Of course you'll be in one piece.' I paused as something frightening occurred to me. 'You are happy being back in England, aren't you?'

'Oh yes!' he said, too quickly.

I looked him directly in the eye.

Charles held my gaze. 'I'm not going anywhere,' he said, gently. 'Not if you don't want me to. I haven't applied or volunteered for anything.'

He didn't say 'yet' but I waited. Ever since he had been back from overseas, I'd known I had him on borrowed time.

'There are always opportunities, as they put it, but you know, someone has to do the desk job.'

I could tell he was trying, but even the way he said 'desk job' showed how little he cared for it.

If he wanted to go off to fight again, it had to be his decision, not mine. I would happily have chained Charles to the table to stop him going into danger, but it was not up to me and it should not be my responsibility either.

'It's not about what I want you to do,' I said softly. 'Charles . . . darling, I'm not the sort of woman who tries to make her husband do what she wants, and you aren't the sort of man who exists only to make his wife happy. I wouldn't love you if you were.'

I leant across the table and took his hand. 'I don't want you to go away. I don't want you to fight. I want you to have a nice safe job here where I can talk to you on the phone and when you get twelve hours' leave you can rush into town and we can go to nice places like this and pretend nothing awful is happening. I want you to stay with me and live forever and do crosswords when you're ninety. Or thirty, or whenever you like. But I also want you to be happy. I want you to look back on this stupid, horrible war and know you did what you were best at, and not regret anything.'

Charles began to interrupt, but I stopped him.

'Please let me say this and then I promise I'll shut up and listen to you – properly.' I took a breath and tried to

173

find the right words. 'Your brother once said to me, *find out what you're good at and then get better at it*, and I agree, but I also think, if you're really, really lucky, you get to find out what you *love* to do. And then you should cherish every moment you get to do it.' I paused before saying what I had dreaded. 'Is being at a desk what you love to do?'

Charles was silent, but his expression gave him away. It was one of enormous sadness. 'I love *you*,' he said. 'More than anything. *Anything.* But no, I don't love my job. I don't even like it. I'm not doing what I'm best at. I hate the fact that my friends are halfway across the world having a stiff time, while I've been picked out to stay here. I'm not saying that the chaps in the safe jobs aren't doing important work and doing their bit. It's just it's not what I ever wanted to do. There's been talk batted around of a promotion and I can't tell you how bad that makes me feel.'

'Charles, you work all the hours God sends,' I said, forgetting I had said I would shut up. 'You've hardly had more than an evening off for the last month, in fact since you came back. And they wouldn't have asked you if they didn't think you would do a good job.'

'Ach,' he said, refusing the compliment. 'I'm good on details, that's all. My lot like that sort of thing. Damn it, Em, this evening was supposed to be a treat. We should be talking about the wedding.' He lifted my hand and kissed it. 'I'm sorry, darling, I don't mean to spoil it.'

'Don't be silly,' I said. 'The wedding is out of our hands. Bunty and Thelma and my mother are desperate to organise it.'

It raised a smile from us both, as the waiter had arrived with the soufflés.

'Where on earth did they get the eggs?' I asked when the waiter had gone away.

'It's probably just one each, very fluffed up,' said Charles looking at the concoction. 'Even so.'

'Under the counter,' we whispered at the same time and then really did laugh. It wasn't very funny, but we were both desperate not to be sad.

'Bloody war,' I said, enjoying the chance to swear.

'Bloody war,' said Charles.

He looked around. The table with the Wrens was having the gayest of times and one of the men had let out a hearty guffaw.

'I just feel I could be of more use,' said Charles. 'Leaving you would be unbearable. I can't even think of it. But yes. If I answer honestly, and I very much want to do that, then yes, my darling Em, I do think I should go.'

We had ordered a meal that was supposed to be eaten within seconds of arriving. Neither of us had so much as poked a fork into the probably illegal fluffy eggs.

Instead, we ignored them completely and held hands over the table, both of us glassy eyed.

'We're very lucky we've been able to discuss it,' I said, which took about as much strength as I could manage. 'Most women's chaps just get sent. I didn't think I could get much prouder of you, Captain Mayhew, but tonight I just have. I am utterly behind you, whatever you decide you should do. Then when we've won this awful thing, you and I will wear pullovers which I will knit while you are away so they will be dreadful, but you will have to say that you love them. And I'll keep things going here and do my bit at the magazine and the station, and I'll write so many letters to you, you won't be able to keep up and will have to ask me to stop. And everything will be absolutely fine.'

Even though I had never felt surer of anything in my life, or prouder that I was marrying this man, I wasn't sure I could keep my voice steady for much longer.

'Should we order more wine?' I managed to squeak out. We had hardly touched the first bottle, but now I picked up my glass and took a very large gulp.

Charles still held my hand. We didn't break eye contact, but he nodded, and reached for his glass.

We didn't order another bottle. Neither of us were what you could call heavy drinkers and after two glasses I felt heady enough. We ate little, which was a waste of the menu, and instead talked, not about Charles going back overseas, but about getting married and what life was going to be like when we were together, after the war.

The peculiar thing was that the evening was lovely, which one probably wouldn't have put money on considering the gravity of the conversation we had just had, but that was how it turned out. I was pleased Charles had been honest and told me how he felt about things. He hadn't sloped off to volunteer for something, or pretended he'd been cornered by someone important and had no choice but to go, and that was something to put on a list of things to be cheerful about. It wasn't a long list, but it was something.

I took several deep breaths and Charles ordered a large whisky, and then we talked about where we might like to live and how it should probably be near London as by then, Charles said, I would be a very established journalist and he, I said, would be in enormous demand for some sort of high-ranking job with the War Office. We wondered whether Guildford would be too expensive or perhaps somewhere near Reading instead, and then I wanted to know if Charles might be keen on getting a dog, which he was but then we worried that if we were both working it might be sad being alone all day so we might have to get another one as well.

Then one of us mentioned children and we both said

two would be lovely, or more if it happened, and I would absolutely still work, probably writing articles in the study at home. I was very much looking forward to that and it also meant we realised we were going to need rather a large house what with the children and the dogs and the garden and the study, and also a garage as Charles wanted to keep his motorbike somewhere. Then we laughed and I said at this rate we'd be unrecognisably dull and doing everything purely to keep up with the Joneses.

'From the sound of it, *we'll* be the Joneses,' said Charles. 'I can't see us as that. Come on, let's go for a walk and come up with a more bohemian plan.'

We had gone out for dinner early as Charles had to get the train back to his billet for something operational and important at seven the next morning, Sunday or not. Neither of us though was in any mood for the evening to end. After we left the restaurant, we walked to Waterloo through the blackout, our arms around each other, purposely extending the journey by not hailing cabs and passing each bus stop without either of us suggesting we stop.

London was busy now, a typical Saturday night, or at least the typical it had become. Groups of people, lovers or friends, all hurrying along trying not to bang into someone in the dark, determined to enjoy themselves however they could. We were just another couple in the middle of the hubbub, but later I would think of how that night I felt as if I had more in common with everyone else than ever before. We were all in the same boat, and we just had to do whatever it took to make sure it didn't go down.

As Charles and I walked across Hungerford Bridge, the wind whipped up from the river, making the night air bitter.

'Do you know,' said Charles, 'when all this is over, one of the first things I want to do is to walk across this bridge with you when all the lights are back on.'

'That's a lovely idea,' I said. 'We could go to one of those restaurants on a boat. The ones that have lanterns hung up everywhere. And I want to go back to Piccadilly just to look at the advertisements lit up again.'

'And in our enormous nouveau riche house we shall keep the lights on for a week,' said Charles. 'With no blackout, and all the curtains open.'

'Damn the expense,' I cried. 'We'll never switch them off!'

Charles hugged me tighter.

'Isn't it mad that leaving curtains open has become a great ambition?'

I sighed. 'I shall make soufflés as if they are going out of fashion. Omelettes for breakfast and enough bacon to feed an army.'

'You know, Em,' said Charles, 'it is going to be all right. The army that is. I'll come back and we'll do all these things, and thousands more. Everything you've ever thought of even for a moment, we'll do it.' He stopped walking and as we stood together in the dark, he wrapped his arms around me. 'My darling Em, I promise you with every fibre of my body, I will come back. Never forget that. Nothing will stop me being with you.'

'I know,' I said, as I buried my head into his coat and held on to him as tightly as I could. 'I know.'

I believed him. The whole world was full of people killing each other and destroying everything they had loved, but I believed him.

Because when it came to it, what else was I to do?

CHAPTER 16

Miss Lake, Is It My Fault?

I WAS GLAD to have the taxi ride home to gather my thoughts, and I sat quietly, replaying the evening and everything Charles had said. No one in their right mind would want the person they loved to tell them they wanted to go off to fight, but as we drove through the dark streets towards Pimlico, odd though it may have sounded, I understood what he meant.

The simple fact was that Charles was an army man and had been for years prior to meeting me. He hadn't been conscripted, he hadn't volunteered, and he had always known that if a second war came, it was his job to go. As much as it made me shudder to think of him going into danger, it had been my choice to love him and agree to be his wife. It was up to me to have the strength of character to live this way.

I asked the taxi driver to stop a couple of streets away from the house, so that I could have a few more moments to think. I dug my chin into my scarf and used my dull little torch to help find my way home.

'Right then,' I said to myself. Along with hundreds of thousands of other women all over the world, I would have to get on with it. I felt a renewed surge of what was already ingrained hostility towards the enemy. 'We'll have you for breakfast,' I muttered.

When I got back to the house, Bunty was still up and eager to hear how my romantic evening had gone. It must have been quite a surprise when I marched into the house with a look of fierce resolve on my face, rather than a dreamy smile.

'It might be ages before he's sent somewhere,' I said, leaning on the banister at the foot of the stairs as we talked. 'And that could have happened at any time, anyway. We just need to hurry up and win.'

'I'll say,' said Bunty firmly, as if the two of us were about to sort it all out by ourselves. 'First things first, we'd better crack on with the plans for your wedding. Can't have Charles sloping off before he's become the luckiest man in the world.'

'I'll have his guts for garters if he does,' I said, not remotely worried.

Bunty grinned and suggested we have a full operational update over breakfast.

As the bongs of the hallway's grandfather clock suggested it was time to call it a day, we headed upstairs to our rooms. When we got to the landing, Bunty gave me a hug.

'Night, Em. If you need me, you will just call, won't you?'

'Thanks, Bunts,' I said. 'Honestly, I really am fine.'

From that night on, determination would become the heart of everything I wanted to do. I would marry Charles, I would know that he was going to be safe, and I would get on with everything back here in London, so that when he returned, we would properly start our life together.

Charles did not have a firm idea about what job or regiment he might move to, but now that we had talked about it, I knew he would be on the lookout for a posting. It made for a feeling of uncertainty all round. He could be in England for some time, or, as I rather feared, picked up for something quickly. I decided not to badger him for updates, but to carry on as usual and focus on my work. In short, do what I always did when things felt as if they were going off on the wonk.

Luckily, there was no shortage of things to be getting on with. Plans for the wedding picked up some necessary steam. I finished making my dress and was well on the way with a rather pretty one for Bunty. Invitations had been put in the post and somehow we were planning to cater for thirty people. Almost everyone had said yes, with the notable exception of Charles's parents. I knew he wasn't close to them, but I was still concerned when they said his elderly father could not manage the journey and his mother would not leave him on his own. Charles had expected as much, so as he did not seem disappointed, neither would I.

The wedding plans, I knew, would be fine. It was work that was far more of a quandary. I had written another article on the munitions industry, telling the *Woman's Friend* readers about the different jobs they might do in a factory. Once again, I had been gung-ho (*'Women excel at the most intricate details,' says the Works Manager, with pride.*) and left out anything controversial, while trying to give a realistic view (*It's hot work, but the welders can take it!*). I'd even included a quote from Mr Terry, which I'd made up and attributed to him, *the Factory Director, who reports that productivity is at a high, and tells us, 'Our female workers show that patriotism wins!'*

Mr Collins didn't change a word of my draft and the Ministry approved. We even received some letters from readers who said that after they'd read "Woman's Friend at Work" they had decided munitions work was the job for them. One asked us what sort of food to expect. Another was hoping she'd make friends like the nice girls we'd written about.

The letters didn't come by the sackful, but the plan we had promised the Ministry appeared to be starting to work. I was pleased of course, but my nagging doubts about being too rose-coloured about things, if anything, became worse.

Mr Collins was sympathetic. He was well aware that I worried I wasn't giving a realistic picture.

'Emmy,' he said, 'this is all very good. I realise you have your concerns, but you are helping the war effort. You know that for every person who writes in, there are another fifty feeling the same way.'

It was a generous thing to say, and I knew he meant it. I was pleased too. My first attempt at writing articles for *Woman's Friend* was getting noticed. I knew how important the work was, I wasn't telling lies, I wasn't even over-egging anything. I just wasn't mentioning some of the things I thought were unfair.

Never mind, ladies! You may worry about who will look after your children! The local nurseries can't fit in with your hours! You can't join the union and you won't get paid the same as the men!

Of course I would never write something like that, but I found it frustrating to write encouraging articles while knowing my friends weren't being listened to in real life. Even my mild query to Mr Terry about a Government Nursery had been met with a wall of disinterest. I wondered what hope women like Irene had. I wondered what hope the readers I was writing for would have too.

As I had clearly irked him in our meeting, it was a surprise when I heard that my next visit to the factory remained unchanged. Even if he was unimpressed with my questions, Mr Terry was at least allowing the articles to continue. I assumed that he saw me as an irritant rather than any real problem, and I was happy with that if it meant I could carry on.

Two weeks after my last meeting with him, I was on my way back for my third visit. ENSA, the Entertainments National Service Association, were putting on a lunchtime concert for the workers in the canteen, and it was the perfect opportunity for a cheery piece I was writing, called 'The Social Side of Factory Work'.

This time, however, Bunty came with me. Anne's mum was going away for a couple of days to check on her elderly mother-in-law in Chippenham, and Bunts had volunteered to look after Ruby and Tony so that Anne could still go to work. I would have to go back to London on my own first thing the next day.

Bunty hadn't seen Anne and the children since we had first met on the train, so it was the perfect excuse for a trip out of London. As we found our way to Anne's house, the two of us were in a chipper frame of mind. I was relieved I hadn't entirely blotted my copybook with Mr Terry and was looking forward to seeing the ENSA show.

'If you see him, just put on your best smile,' teased Bunty as we followed Anne's directions and turned into Wilton Street, the small Victorian terrace where she lived. 'Otherwise he'll have you escorted off the premises and you won't be able to do the article.'

'I don't think he'll be there,' I said. 'I've been handed over to their Public Relations Manager. Apparently a Mr Adams will look after me.'

'Does *look after* mean not let you out of his sight?' said Bunty.

'Without a shadow of a doubt,' I answered. 'And don't worry, I shall be an utter delight. I've promised our Editor, so I have to be.'

We were both smiling as we came to a stop outside number thirty-two and knocked on the red front door. There was an immediate and unmistakable roar from inside, and as the door opened, Ruby fought her way out before Anne even appeared.

'They're here!' shouted Ruby as she flung herself at me. 'Do roundabouts, Aunty Emmy!'

'Please,' said Anne from the doorway, which Ruby dutifully repeated in an ear-splitting shriek.

As I swung the chubby thunderbolt round and wondered how she could have grown in the last fortnight, Bunty and Anne said hello, and then, oddly, Anne didn't ask us to come in. I put Ruby down and gave Anne a hug, noticing she looked both tired and unusually serious.

'It's lovely to see you both,' she said. 'Thank you so much for looking after the children, Bunty. Ruby, be a good girl and go in and find your teddy, please.'

Ruby nodded obediently, and after she had trundled off, Anne closed the door behind her and stayed outside. She ran a hand through her hair and looked at Bunty and me.

'Just to tell you,' she said in a low voice. 'Absolutely rotten news. Irene's been sacked. She's inside with the girls.'

'Oh, Anne,' I started to say.

'I know. I'm sorry to land this on you, but do you mind looking after her two for an hour as well as mine? I said I'd go with her to the Labour Exchange and if we go now, I'll be back in time to come in with you for the ENSA show.'

'How is she?' I asked.

'Crushed,' said Anne. 'But she's putting on a brave face.' She paused. 'Have you told Bunty about . . .?'

I nodded, assuming she meant Irene's husband.

184

'I'm sorry, I know it's a secret,' I said.

'I haven't told a soul,' said Bunty, deadly serious. 'Is there any news?'

Anne shook her head. 'Nothing.'

A small hammering started from behind the door and Anne turned to open it, before picking up Ruby and asking us to come in. Bunty and I followed her inside and down the narrow hallway to an immaculate kitchen where a slight woman in her early thirties was sitting at a small table. She had Baby Tony on her lap, and her two girls were playing pat-a-cake while Irene got Tony to clap his hands.

'Irene, these are my friends Emmy and Bunty I told you about,' said Anne as Irene got up to hand her Tony. Although she smiled, Irene looked shattered, with huge dark rings under her eyes as if she hadn't slept for a week, which I imagined was not far from the truth.

As we all said hello, Irene began to apologise.

'I'm sorry I've pushed in on your visit,' she said, then turned to look at Anne. 'Honestly, Anne, I can go to the Exchange on my own.'

'Don't be daft,' said Anne. 'The girls don't mind, do you?'

'It's no trouble at all,' said Bunty. 'We'll just be playing so two more will add to the fun.'

'Hello, girls,' I said, being overly cheerful, when what I really wanted to do was to tell Irene how very sorry I was about everything.

'These are Sheila and Enid,' said Irene. 'They're seven and four. Girls, say hello to Miss Lake and Miss . . . oh I'm sorry, I don't know your surname.'

'Tavistock,' said Bunty, smiling at the girls. 'It's a bit of a mouthful, isn't it?'

'That's all right, Miss Tavistock,' said Sheila, in a shy voice.

'Ruby calls me Aunty Emmy,' I said. 'Don't you, Monster?'

'Aunty Emmy,' confirmed Ruby. She stopped, stared at Bunty and said, 'You're Aunty Bunty.'

Despite the situation, 'Aunty Bunty' sounded ridiculous, and Bunty snorted.

'Bunty Aunty,' declared Ruby.

'Bunty Bunty,' said Enid, looking pleased with herself.

'BUNTY BUNTY,' shouted Ruby, in delight.

Good-natured as ever, Bunty laughed, and looking at the grown-ups, said, 'This is going to stick, isn't it? No, please don't tell them off, I rather like it.'

Everyone had a little laugh, grateful for something to take away the awkwardness of meeting in such very difficult circumstances.

Anne looked at her wristwatch. 'We'd better get going,' she said.

'Are you sure you don't mind?' said Irene to Bunty and me.

'We'll have a lovely time,' I assured her. 'Won't we, girls? We've brought comics and sweets and we know tons of games, so if they're happy to stay with us, we'll have lots of fun.'

Sheila nodded shyly, and Enid didn't seem to mind as she was now whispering, 'Bunty Bunty,' with Ruby and jumping up and down at the same time.

I took off my hat and shooed the women out of the kitchen, hoping Anne didn't mind me making myself so at home.

'We'll be fine,' I said once again as Anne and Irene said goodbye to the children and made their way to their coats, which were hanging up in the hall. Irene wrapped a flowery scarf around her neck, but then hesitated again.

'Good luck,' I said firmly. 'We'll see you later.'

I gave a small wave as the two women left, and once the front door was shut, let my smile drop.

Irene Barker: two daughters, a missing husband and now without a job, and I was sure, with no reference.

It just wasn't fair. Something had to be done.

★

With their mums off to the Labour Exchange, I quickly announced buns all round in case anyone felt wobbly lipped about being left behind. The children, though, were good as gold. Ruby and Tony were happy with us, and Enid was keen to be best friends with Ruby, so they were no trouble at all. Sheila was quieter but joined in with the buns, and a shambolic version of Hide and Seek. The younger girls were happily awful at it, which was just as well as Bunty and I hadn't a clue where anything was.

I couldn't help but notice that Sheila watched over Enid rather than enjoying things for herself, and when to the amazement of the other children Bunty revealed her ability to make chains of little animals out of sheets of newspaper, I asked Sheila if she would like to make a cardboard dress-up dolly with me instead.

Baby Tony was happy to sit at Bunty's feet and rip up the rest of the news, so Sheila and I retreated to the front room with an empty packet of Corn Flakes and some scissors. As we sat together on the sofa and thumbed through some magazines for ideas about clothes for the doll, Sheila became chattier.

'Can we do frocks, Miss Lake?' she said. 'I've been learning to sew on Mum's machine and I'm making a skirt on my own. Mum watches but I haven't gone wrong,' she added proudly.

'Gosh, you're very clever,' I said. 'Well done you. Shall we make a paper version of it so that you match?'

187

Sheila was keen on the idea and began to tell me about all the clothes she planned to make one day when she was older and you didn't need coupons.

'I want to be a dressmaker when I grow up,' she said, shyly.

'What a great idea,' I said. 'You'll be so good at it.'

Sheila looked pleased, but then her face clouded over. 'Mummy's got to find a new job,' she said. 'Will she get one?'

'I'm sure she will,' I said. 'I don't know how long it will take to find one she likes, but I bet she'll get something just right.'

Sheila sat for a moment looking down at the magazine. Finally, she spoke, but didn't look up. 'Miss Lake?' she said. 'Was it my fault?'

'About what, love?' I asked.

'Mum getting the sack. Was it because I couldn't make Enid sit still? She did try, but she's only young.'

I put on what I hoped was a kind and encouraging smile, but my heart could have wept.

'Oh, Sheila, of course not,' I said, gently. 'Nothing is your fault. You've been such a good girl and the very best big sister to Enid. Mrs Oliver told me you look after her *ever so* well.'

'Mum said that,' said Sheila. 'But then she kept crying.'

I put down the card I was holding and moved to sit closer to her. It was one of the saddest conversations I had ever had.

'Shall I tell you a secret?' I said. 'Sometimes grown-ups cry. I do sometimes, if I'm a bit tired – and I'm twenty-three so absolutely ancient.'

'Do you really?' said Sheila, now looking up.

'I do,' I nodded. 'And afterwards I feel a bit better

about things. That's why people talk about having A Good Cry. Does that make me sound a bit silly?'

Sheila shook her head. 'Not really.'

'That's good,' I said. 'And do you know, I even feel better now I've told you. The main thing is, you mustn't worry if you hear a grown-up having a cry. And never feel you have to fix things, because you don't. That's our job. The grown-ups.'

'So it isn't my fault?' Sheila looked at me hopefully.

'No, my lovely,' I said, smoothing back a strand of her hair that had fallen across her eyes. Then I put my hand over my heart. 'Sheila, I promise that absolutely none of this is your fault.'

I didn't know how far Sheila believed me, but it was the easiest thing I had ever sworn to. I thought of Mrs Mahoney saying that I couldn't change the world overnight. All Irene was trying to do was keep Sheila and Enid's world going. I wondered how many thousands of other mothers were doing the same thing across Britain.

Woman's Friend might have been doing our bit on the recruitment front, but we had to do so much more to offer these women support. There had to be more that "Yours Cheerfully" could do.

As Sheila began to cut out pictures again, I made a promise to her that we would.

CHAPTER 17

Comrade Baby Tony

WHEN ANNE AND Irene returned from the Labour Exchange they had very little good news. As expected, it didn't matter how much workers were needed, a woman who had just lost her job for bringing children into a factory was not at the top of the list. The Female Vacancies Supervisor had asked Irene how she planned to look after her children if she did get a new job. It was a fair question she could not answer.

Irene was doing her best to put on a brave face, especially for Sheila, so Anne suggested that they all stay for the rest of the day. The children were having a lovely time and it would be a shame to break up the party. While Bunty ordered Irene to put her feet up, Anne and I headed off to Chandlers for what now felt an inappropriately cheery concert.

I was beginning to feel like an old hand as we arrived at the canteen and I was met by Mr Adams, a tall, talkative and not unpleasant Public Relations Manager. He stuck to me like glue and kept up an impressive running commentary about how wonderful everything was.

The ENSA concert had drawn a packed crowd, and as we watched a knock-about routine by a hardworking comic with very clicky false teeth, Mr Adams nudged me with his elbow and pointed out how much everyone was enjoying themselves.

'We're going all out to get Tommy Trinder next,' said Mr Adams. 'Only the best for the Chandlers staff.'

His commitment to the factory's propaganda effort was impressive but exhausting. I feigned a need for the lavatory to escape the enthusiastic prods and was just using the famous mirrors when Anne's friend Betty sidled up.

'Anne says to ask if you don't mind staying up late tonight?' she said in a whisper as if Mr Adams had infiltrated the ladies' conveniences. 'She said you want to help do something about Irene, so we thought we'd come round. It'll be really late as our shift ends at ten.'

'Of course,' I said.

'But don't bring your new boyfriend,' added Betty.

I rolled my eyes. 'Tragically, he only has eyes for his work,' I said. 'And he's probably waiting outside as we speak.'

I wasn't wrong about that.

Twelve hours later, with Baby Tony safely tucked up in his cot, and all three girls somehow top and tailing in Ruby's small bed, Anne arrived home with Betty, Violet and Maeve. I stood back, waiting to introduce Bunty as they met Irene with an outpouring of sympathy and angry exclamations of how badly she had been treated.

As Irene put on one of the bravest fronts I'd ever seen, I felt uncomfortable. Betty, Maeve and Vi still didn't know that Irene's husband was missing. Anne had said she probably shouldn't have told me, and I knew I shouldn't have told Bunts. It was easy to see how something confidential could suddenly become anything but.

It certainly was late, and they all looked tired after an eight-hour shift. I'd written two articles and drafted some replies for "Yours Cheerfully", but had spent the evening playing with the children.

With everyone now crammed into the front room, where they were tucking into savoury sandwiches, Betty was giving us her own news from Chandlers.

'What exactly do they want you to do?' asked Maeve as Betty declined a square of dark chocolate.

'Well, this afternoon, Mr Rice told me that Mr Adams wants Chandlers to do a recruitment parade. I've been asked if I want to take part.'

'A *what* parade?' asked Maeve.

'Like on the newsreels?' said Anne. 'We saw one the other day when I took Ruby to see *Dumbo*. There was this big procession in Birmingham with women sitting on the back of lorries pretending to work on bits of Spitfires, with big signs saying things like, "Help Us Help Our Boys".'

'That's almost word for word what he said,' nodded Betty. 'Apart from the part about *Dumbo*, which must have been where he got the idea. I told them it would be a good start if they didn't go around getting rid of the workers they already had.' She looked at Irene. 'I'm sorry, Irene. We came round to talk about you, not go on about me.'

'It's all right,' said Irene. 'It's given me a boost just being here. And I'm interested in what they've come up with. Honestly, Betty, go on.'

Maeve licked a bit of potted meat off her finger. 'But why *did* they ask you? And are you going to do it?'

'I don't know why they picked me,' said Betty. 'Diane Philpott was asked. And Marjorie and Jane Watson.'

Anne, Violet and Maeve looked at one another.

'What is it?' I asked.

Maeve pushed her spectacles up on the bridge of her nose. 'They're all young and really pretty,' she said. 'Even Betty.'

Betty said, 'Oi,' at her, but looked quite pleased.

'They'll look lovely on a carnival float,' said Anne. 'You should have seen the girls in the newsreel.'

'That's guff,' said Betty. 'They could have picked any of us.'

'Not me,' said Maeve, cheerfully. 'I'm a right old four-eyes.'

'No, you're not,' said Vi, loyally. 'And you could always take your specs off once you were on the lorry. I'd get dizzy and fall off.'

'Rot!' said Anne and Betty at the same time, and the friends began to defend each other. It was exactly the sort of argument I would have with Bunty or Thelma and the girls at the fire station, with everyone refusing to let the other do themselves down.

Finally, and when they had convinced each other they should all have been asked to take part, I turned to Betty. 'Have you decided if you'll do it?' I asked.

'I don't know,' said Betty, sighing. 'Everyone knows we need more workers. And I'll look awful and unpatriotic if I don't. It's just . . .' She puffed out her cheeks and looked unimpressed.

'They've just sacked our friend,' said Anne.

'Exactly,' said Betty. 'Irene's looking for work and I'll be lording it around in a parade.'

No one said anything. I could hear it raining outside.

Finally, Irene spoke. 'You mustn't feel bad, Betty,' she said. 'We know they need the workers.'

It was the most generous thing she could have said.

'Well, they'd better give us all signs saying, "But not if you've got children," then,' said Betty, hotly. 'It sticks in my craw.'

'You're right,' said Maeve. 'We're always expected to work harder or faster when they need us to, and do weekends as a matter of course, but they don't give a fig about the fact we still have to run homes, look after children and all the rest. I notice they haven't asked any of the women with kids to do the parade. No offence, Bet.'

'None taken,' said Betty. 'You can't go anywhere without being reminded the Government needs everyone to pitch in, and then look what's happened to poor old Irene. I'm not going to just smile and wave and become a walking advert for factory work without telling the truth.'

I winced. I knew Betty hadn't aimed her comments at me, but they stung.

While I had sympathised with the women workers, and worried about the articles I had written, I had still got on with it. Betty, on the other hand, had the courage of her convictions and wasn't afraid to make her point known.

I thought of the photographs we had run of them smiling at their machines. '*After only four weeks, Betty is an old hand at the lathe! Nineteen-year-old Violet says, "I'm doing this for my husband and the boys."* '

If that wasn't turning them into adverts, what was?

I wondered if other women felt the same way as Betty? Did readers see articles like mine and think, She Doesn't Know The Half of It?

The others continued to talk as I stared at the fire, thinking furiously. I had been so thrilled to be there when the Ministry of Information asked us to help with a crucial campaign, and I still felt proud to be part of that. But where were the calls for women to get better facilities so that they could do what was asked? The women sitting with me weren't asking for special favours. They all wanted or needed to work.

How long would it be before the next person got into the same fix as Irene? Would it be Maeve or Anne or one of the other women on their shifts?

I thought of my own job. Everyone was doing their best to make the magazine helpful, entertaining, and even inspiring. Despite all our hard work, currently it didn't feel as if we really were 'Woman's Friend'.

Betty saw the thoughtful look on my face.

'Oh crikey, I'm sorry, Emmy,' she said. 'That came out wrong. I don't mean the magazine. I loved having my picture in *Woman's Friend*. My mum's cut it out and put it in a frame, she's that proud.'

'Don't worry, Betty,' I said. 'You're right. I bowled in here, asking you all to put on a good front and be part of a campaign, but I haven't been any help in return.'

'You tried to speak with Mr Terry,' said Anne.

'I just made him cross,' I said. 'And anyway, one of you would have found a way to him in the end. Is there anything I can do to properly help?'

'That's very kind, Emmy, but I can't see how,' said Anne. She sounded exhausted. 'What we really want is for them to give Irene her job back.'

Irene gave her a brave smile. 'There's no point if I can't find someone to look after the girls. That's where I need the help.'

'We can all keep asking round,' said Vi. 'See if anyone who can't do factory work could help?'

'That's what the woman at the Employment Exchange said,' replied Anne. 'She said they wanted older women to step up.'

I listened closely. I'd read a Ministry press release saying exactly the same thing.

'That's all very well,' said Maeve. 'But are they going to take them in at five in the morning, or have them until this time of the night?'

'One of our neighbours already complains that I wake them up when I leave for work,' said Anne. She gave a hollow laugh. 'Not everyone wants a job looking after babies.'

'Have you asked Mr Rice about any of this?' I asked.

'Yes. I did ask him about getting a nursery,' said Irene. 'But he said there weren't any plans. And I asked about sharing shifts, not that that's ideal, money-wise. But he said not to fix what wasn't broken.'

'I asked my National Service Officer, just to see what she thought,' said Betty. 'She said things were being done as fast as they could, and people would just have to wait.'

'Mr Terry isn't bothered about families,' said Anne. 'I expect they're all used to having men working there who can leave everything to their wives.'

'Surely,' I said, concerned at the emptiness in her voice, 'as Chandlers is an official Government supplier, there's a strong case for getting a proper nursery set up.'

'But if Mr Terry doesn't think so,' began Maeve.

'Sucks to Mr Terry,' I said, rudely. 'Let's find a way to do it without him. You aren't alone in wanting help. There was an article in *Picture Post* last month about needing more Government Nurseries. I'll try to find it when I get home. Irene, could you ask the Female Vacancies Supervisor if she knows who to speak to in your Local Authority?'

Irene nodded, but I noticed she was beginning to look overwhelmed. The strain she was under must have been unbearable.

'Well, I'll happily write to anyone if it will help,' said Anne. 'Hold on, I can hear crying. Is that Enid?'

'Yes, it is,' said Irene. 'She's probably woken up and doesn't remember where she is.'

'We could ask around at work,' said Violet, as Irene hurried out of the room. 'To see who else might be interested in getting a nursery. I heard that Evelyn Bryant in the assembly shop has resigned. She said when she heard about Irene, she decided she'd rather jump than be pushed. The more of us involved, the better.'

Betty sat up straighter. 'I might write to our MP,' she said. 'He's about a hundred and ten, but you never know. At least I'd feel as if I was doing something.'

'I can do that too,' said Violet.

'I'll ask around at work to see if anyone knows people in the Labour or Health Ministries,' said Bunty. 'You never know. Emmy, can you get Mr Collins to ask some of the bigwigs he speaks to?'

It was easy to say yes to that as I felt sure he would be happy to help, and I was keen for him to know about tonight's meeting so that I was keeping everything above board. I wasn't trying to start a revolution, but I wanted him to know what I was doing.

As I looked around the room, I saw that the mood had changed. With us all together and everyone chipping in ideas, it was as if we were a team. I felt my spirits rise, even when Maeve brought up a reluctant point of practicality.

'I hate to be a damp squib,' she said, lowering her voice, 'but how is this going to help Irene? She's still unemployed with no wages. I suppose she can't even tell her husband. He's at sea, isn't he?'

I held my breath, but Anne didn't turn a hair. 'He is,' she said, firmly. 'And that makes it even harder for her. The main thing is we show her she isn't on her own. Emmy said Sheila thinks it's her fault Irene got the sack.'

'Oh, that's awful,' said Betty.

'Poor love,' said Maeve.

'We'll all pitch in,' said Violet, hotly. 'See if anyone knows of work. Ask around if there's anything part-time.'

'You'll be lucky,' said Maeve. 'Thank goodness she's got his pay.'

Anne gave a tighter smile to that. 'So, you're going to tell them no, about the parade, then, Betty?' she said, changing the subject abruptly.

'I don't want to do it,' said Betty. 'But I don't want to be unpatriotic either. They're doing it in January as they want it to be a New Year thing.'

'You could always hold that sign,' said Maeve. 'Ask them for one that says, "Help us help our boys" and get out your lipstick and write, "And help my friends get a blooming factory nursery, too," on the back!'

It raised a laugh.

Maeve looked at the small silver clock on the mantelpiece.

'I really should go,' she said. 'I've got my niece with the children and she'll think I've skipped the country if I don't get back soon.'

But I had one more idea.

'You could always have your own parade,' I said.

They all looked at me.

'If you had some sort of march, you could write your own "Help Us Help Our Boys" signs. Then Betty wouldn't have to waste her best lipstick.'

I tried to sound jokey in case the others thought I was going too far. But they didn't. Maeve sat back down.

'Are you serious?' said Anne.

'Why didn't I think of that?' said Betty.

'Is it legal?' said Violet. 'I don't want to get arrested.'

'I think so,' I said.

'Definitely,' said Bunty. 'As long as it's not un-patriotic, which it wouldn't be because you're actually saying you want to do more. People are still allowed to say what they think. Em and I went to a rally in Trafalgar Square about equal injury compensation for women. Dr Summerskill, the MP, did a speech. It was ever so good.' Bunty smiled. 'Don't worry, Anne, you haven't left the children with A Radical.'

'Although Ruby now calls Baby Tony, "Comrade",' I grinned.

'Shush, you two,' said Anne. She was perched on a kitchen stool and while she still looked awfully tired, now her eyes were bright as a button. 'I think it's a wonderful idea. We'll try all the other ideas as well, but if we did a parade, we might get more people on our side. We could walk around the marketplace. What do you think?'

'I think we'd all get the sack,' said Maeve.

'No, we won't,' said Betty, up for a challenge. 'We'll be ever so nice and not angry or anything. It'll just be a group of women on a walk.'

'You'd need to make sure that people see you're trying to help, not be un-patriotic. That's really important,' I added, feeling responsible for the idea. 'It needs to be clear that you are doing this for the right reasons.'

'Can we ask other friends to come too?' said Maeve. 'My cousin has a baby and she's finding it hard. She's at a different factory though.'

'The more the merrier, I reckon,' said Betty.

'Mr Terry or Mr Rice might see us,' said Violet, not yet convinced. 'We'd get in trouble.'

'Not if we're nice about it,' said Anne. 'And anyway, Emmy will get us into the papers saying we just want to work to help the war effort. It would make Mr Terry look awful. You could do that, couldn't you, Emmy?'

Anne's faith in me was lovely, if over-confident, but the last thing I wanted to do was to dampen the enthusiasm.

'I'll give it a good go,' I said. 'No one knows who I am, but I'll try to get an article printed somewhere.'

The women all looked at me with interest. I wasn't being modest. I really didn't know if I would be able to.

Certainly not in *Woman's Friend*. But I could try one of the more political magazines, where they encouraged discussions like this.

'Would you do that?' asked Anne. 'You wouldn't get into trouble at work?'

'Of course I'll do it,' I said. 'I need to make sure my boss knows, but I think he'll understand. He might even know who I could send it to.'

'If you're willing to do that for us,' said Anne, lifting her chin up, 'then if you need to put real people in it, you can use my full name.'

'And mine,' said Betty.

Violet and Maeve looked at each other, then nodded and agreed. It was a brave move.

No one had looked at Irene since she came back from checking on Enid. She had enough on her plate. But Irene thought differently. 'Can I come?' she said, quietly. 'Even though I'm not at Chandlers now, I'd like to join in. I'd like to try to make people listen.'

Anne reached over and took her hand. 'You don't need to ask, Rene,' she said, gently. 'You do whatever you want to do. Whatever is best for you.'

Irene smiled. 'I'll come,' she said.

'Thank you, everyone,' I said. 'Now, the last thing I want is to get any of you into trouble, so perhaps before definitely having a parade, you should try Mr Terry one more time. Just to make sure he can't be convinced.'

'We could write him a letter,' said Anne. 'Put down all the arguments. We could copy in the Labour Exchange and the Council too, so they see we're trying to do things properly.'

The others nodded in agreement.

'Hang on,' said Maeve. 'We should be making notes on all this.' She reached into her handbag and brought out a pencil and shopping list pad. 'I was a flipping good secretary before I got married.'

'Just one thing,' said Anne. 'Are you sure you're all happy to make this about the children? There are lots of other things we could be asking about. Betty, you wanted to join the union. And then there was the point about us not getting paid as much as the men. And not all of you need nurseries.'

Maeve spoke first.

'In my view,' she said, 'we can't fight for everything at once. We've seen what happened to Irene and it could be you or me next.'

Anne went pale. 'Oh, Maeve, don't,' she said.

'I'm sorry,' said Maeve. 'I'm sure it won't be, but if we get somewhere on this, it would be a big step forward.'

'I agree,' said Violet. 'It could be any of us. If my Cyril ever gets leave, I could be in the queue next.'

'Show-off,' said Maeve.

'Get you, Mae West,' said Betty, laughing.

Violet went red.

'We know what you meant, Vi,' said Anne. 'And you're absolutely right. If we could do this it will make life easier for lots of us.' She stifled a yawn. 'Now then, shall we call it a night? Comrade Tony will wake up in about four hours and I really must get some sleep.'

The others readily agreed, but it was a different group of friends who parted now. With Maeve's shorthand notes in her knitted bag, it felt as if there was a plan of attack. As the girls put on their coats, turning up collars and wrapping brightly coloured scarves around their necks, Betty started whistling a socialist song and had to be told to stop before Anne opened the door because of the neighbours.

After whispered Goodbyes, Anne and Irene began gently arguing over who should sleep on the sofa as it was now far too late to go home. When Irene went to check on the children, and Anne showed Bunty and me to her mum's room which we were going to share, she thanked us for the hundredth time.

'Honestly, we haven't done anything,' I said. 'I just feel horrible for Irene. I didn't want to say it in front of the others, but Sheila rather shook me today.'

'There but for the grace of God,' said Anne, seriously. She shuddered.

'If you're ever in a fix, please do say,' said Bunty. 'I don't want to be too forward, but if Irene gets into problems, there's space with us at my granny's house. Any of you can always come and stay. I know that doesn't solve anything,' she added, looking self-conscious. 'And you might not want to bring children into town.'

Bunty hated sounding like she was trying to be grand or showy, but I knew it was from the heart. The big old house was half-empty.

'Thank you,' said Anne. 'That's the kindest thing ever. But we'll be all right. You mustn't worry about us. Everything is going to be fine.'

CHAPTER 18

Just Go Without Me

WITH BUNTY STAYING on to babysit for one more day, I raced back to London on the first available train the next morning and headed straight to work, nearly crashing into Clarence as I ran up the stairs to the *Woman's Friend* offices.

'Sorry, Clarence,' I yelled, as I swerved past him, unbuttoning my coat as I went. 'All well?'

'A full post-bag today, Miss Lake,' he called back. '"Yours Cheerfully" is getting popular.'

I thanked him and rushed on. Mr Collins was very understanding about the hours I worked and about me fitting things in around volunteering at the fire station, but I didn't want to muck him about. Strolling in two and a half hours late after a night at a friend's was rather pushing it.

'Morning, Kath,' I said as I finally arrived. Clarence had not exaggerated as Kath was half hidden behind a huge pile of letters stacked up on her desk.

'Morning, Emmy,' she said. 'I thought I'd sort these as Mrs M has taken Hester to the printers. How was your trip?'

'Very good, thanks,' I said. I hung up my coat and hat and gas mask, and pulled a chair over to her desk so that I could give her a hand.

'Is Mr Collins in?' I asked. 'I'll take his post into him if you like. I need to see him about the factory.'

'I think he's about to go out,' said Kath. 'So I'll get a move on. Those are his so far.' She pointed to a small pile of letters that looked more official than most of the others. They were next to the biggest heap. 'Those are for "Yours Cheerfully", and this pile is for you.'

I took the letters with interest. Since starting to write the "Woman's Friend at Work" articles, I had begun to receive letters asking for careers advice, and more often from readers writing to say they had put in to do munitions work or had just started their training. I always replied with whatever information I could find, or sent a letter wishing them the very best of luck with their new job. It was still new to me to receive letters by name and one of my favourite parts of the job.

'I'd better tackle the problems first,' I said. 'They're becoming a small mountain.'

Kath continued the sorting, and I began to open the letters to "Yours Cheerfully", now organising them by subject. It was a far cry from when she and I had first worked together, when a tiny trickle of letters had been very much the norm.

'Goodness, another one about marrying a cousin,' I said.

'I wouldn't want to marry any of mine,' said Kath, without malice.

'Hmm. My father tells his patients it isn't exactly ideal.'

I carried on, making a new pile from women whose husbands were having affairs. It was one of the topics we had the most letters about. Some of them were horribly sad and we could easily have put a letter in every issue on the same subject. I frowned as I read one from a lady in Lincolnshire who was being badly bullied by her husband. She hadn't given an address as she couldn't risk us writing to her. I put the letter into a file marked URGENT and made a note to recommend to Mrs

Mahoney that we put it into the very next issue. It didn't feel nearly enough, but it was the only thing we could do.

The next letter was more unusual, from a lady who had told her fiancé she didn't want to give up work once they were married.

I wondered what Kath would think and began to read it out loud.

Dear Yours Cheerfully,

I am twenty-eight and engaged. However, my fiancé is unhappy that I want to continue with my work after we marry. He has said I may until the war is over and then I must stop.

He is a good man and I do love him very much, but I also love my job (I work in analytical chemistry) and don't see why I should give it up. He is a travelling salesman and truth be told, I earn more than him and mine is the steadier job.

Do you think I am marrying the right man?
Yours
Frances Gage (Miss)

'I'm not sure that she is,' I said.

'Perhaps he'll come round,' said Kath. 'I don't even know what Analytical Chemistry is, do you?'

'No idea. But can you imagine how hard that must be to get into?' I shook my head at the thought. Science had not been my best subject at school. 'You could do it though, Kath. You're tons cleverer than me.'

'Rubbish,' said Kath. 'I say, is that the Affairs Pile? It seems to get bigger every week.'

I nodded. 'It's not just the men. We're getting them from women who have got themselves involved with someone else too.'

'Does it ever make you feel down?' asked Kath. 'Now that we get lots of letters? There are so many people having such a horrible time.'

I put down the letter opener. It was a good question. 'Mrs Mahoney says you have to try to keep a distance or it will catch up on you,' I said. 'But some of them *are* horrible.' I thought of the letter I had just read. 'Sometimes I just want to hare round to their house and stick up for them.'

'You're doing your best,' said Kath, a bit glumly. She twisted one of her curls around her finger.

'Mrs Mahoney says that too. She says we have to try not to worry, because if we do, we'll end up as miserable as the people we're trying to help. It's not all bad,' I said, as Kath still looked rather down. 'Some of them are quite fun. This reader wants to know if you can become a vegetarian if you don't like vegetables.'

'Why does she want to do that?' asked Kath.

'She doesn't say. But my Aunt Pat tried it once. She came for lunch and refused to eat anything. Then Father asked about her fur stole, and she said it had already been murdered by the time she liberated it from the shop.'

'Did she stick to it?' asked Kath.

'No. She had a beef Wellington the next week and admitted defeat. The next time we saw her she'd nearly been arrested for punching a Blackshirt in the face.'

'Good for her,' said Kathleen.

'I know. We all said she should be given some sort of award. She was a rotten vegetarian but spot on when it comes to walloping Nazis.'

'Your family's quite um, exciting isn't it?' said Kath.

'I hope you still say that after the wedding,' I replied, laughing. 'Do you think that's all for Mr Collins? I'll go in before he disappears.'

Kath handed me his post and I took it to his office, knocking softly, in case he was in the middle of writing a story.

'Come in. Emmy, hello. Hold on, let me just get this down. Have a seat.'

He went back to writing rather wildly as I sat down on the chair opposite his desk. As ever, his room was a rubbish tip of disorder, with books and magazines stacked into haphazard piles. His Anglepoise lamp had its head bent right down as if it was about to snatch a piece of paper off the desk and eat it. The shelves on the walls were overloaded, as were the three in-trays which all of us tried to keep under control for him. No one was ever allowed to move anything.

For anyone who didn't know Mr Collins, it was the room of an intellectual or an eccentric, the sort of person who worked all night, slept all day and had only the slightest grasp on reality. But I had learnt that he was nothing like this. Creative of course, and a little unpredictable at times, but behind the office wilderness, Mr Collins missed little and cared far more than he let on.

Finally, he came to the end of his notes, looked at the paper with contempt and muttered, 'Awful.' Then he put it to one side and looked up. 'Terrible piece of writing,' he said. 'I should retire immediately. Hello. How can I help?'

'Just your post,' I said. 'And I wanted to update you about the factory.'

He looked at me vaguely.

'But it can wait, if you'd rather?'

'No, no, go ahead. Apologies. My head is elsewhere.'

I began to tell him about the previous day, saying that I'd written the next article, and then giving brief details about Irene and the concerns of Anne and her friends.

'So I just wondered if I could ask someone at next week's Ministry meeting if they have any contacts I could approach in the Labour or Health Ministries?' I said. 'To see if factory workers might petition them directly. I'd really like to help the women. I thought I might even do an article about them and try to get it placed somewhere?'

Mr Collins didn't reply and seemed to just look through me. I wondered if he had been listening.

'Would that be appropriate?' I prompted.

'Sorry. You just want to ask for a contact?'

'From the Ministry, yes. And you can always stamp on my foot or something if I say the wrong thing.' I waited for a droll reply, but it didn't come.

'Oh God, the meeting,' he groaned. 'When is it?'

'Monday. Mr Collins, do you mind me asking, are you all right?'

He didn't appear all right in the least. Usually, he was sharp as a knife.

'I'm fine. Thank you. Yes. Ask your question. It sounds very appropriate, so, er, well done. I'm not sure when I'll be back.'

'What?'

'I'm taking a few days off.'

Mr Collins never took time off.

'An old army friend isn't doing too well, I'm afraid. A couple of us are trying to rally round.'

'I'm terribly sorry,' I said, assuming it must be the same person he had been to see a few weeks ago. 'I hope they'll get better soon.'

'Unfortunately, I think probably not. Here we are doing our bit to win this war, when too many people are still fighting the last.' He looked contemptuous. 'It never just ends when they say it does.'

'Is there anything we can do here while you're away?' I said, wishing I could be of more use.

'That's very kind, Emmy,' he said. 'Just keep up the

good work. Mrs Mahoney will be in charge, but I have complete faith in you all.'

He stood up from his desk and began putting some papers into a case.

'Of course,' I said. 'And don't worry, I'll let the Ministry know we won't be at the meeting.'

Mr Collins stopped, peered at me and said, 'No need. Just go without me.'

'To the Ministry of Information? On my own?'

He smiled just a little. 'Emmy, you're a journalist now. You've been marching off to interview an egotistical munitions tsar without turning a hair, and Mrs Mahoney says you pretty much run "Yours Cheerfully" on your own. You aren't the well-intentioned, if obvious lunatic I interviewed a year ago.'

'It's just that I find it hard to forget that it's only six months since I was nearly sacked,' I said.

'Never disclose your weaknesses,' said Mr Collins, trying to be his usual self. 'You'll be fine, I promise. I have every faith that you'll represent *Woman's Friend* perfectly. Now I must go, or I'll miss the train. I'll see you soon.'

He nodded and began to walk out of the office, but then paused in the doorway and turned round. 'Don't start any fights,' he said. 'And just to be sure, perhaps use the lavatory here before you go.'

Then he gave me a brief, kindly smile and was gone.

I sat for a moment in the empty room.

Yesterday I had been organising a factory workers' protest march. Today I had been told to perfectly represent *Woman's Friend* on my own.

For the second time in twenty-four hours, I could hear the same words.

Everything was going to be fine.

CHAPTER 19

Stick To It and You Won't
Let Them Down

I WAS NERVOUS about going to the next Ministry meeting on my own, but more concerned about Mr Collins. He was usually utterly unflappable, always had an answer to a problem and, I realised, since becoming Editor had become pivotal to everything the whole team did.

None of us had any idea how long he might be away, but as Mrs Mahoney said, we all knew what we were doing and had more than enough of it to be getting on with.

'And that includes you, Hester Wilson,' she said sternly, as on the news of Mr Collins' sudden departure, Hester had taken to pulling dramatic faces and muttering about fatalities. 'For someone so giggly, you have a very strange fascination with the Grim Reaper.'

Hester looked pained but like the rest of us, made a concerted effort to keep the *Woman's Friend* ship on its course.

'It is rough,' said Charles when we spoke on the phone. 'Some of the chaps he was with in France haven't had a terribly easy time. The others try to help out. He'll be pleased if you all carry on as normal.'

It was very much Charles' way to downplay things and remain calm. I knew I could learn from both him and his brother, and particularly as I was representing *Woman's*

Friend on my own, I was determined to do my best to put on a good show of things.

The morning of the meeting, I was wearing a very smart dark suit that belonged to Bunty, and a blouse I had run up with some off-cuts of Jack's parachute dyed a rather decent blush pink. I did have some nerves, but this time I knew where I was going and what to expect. There was a decent chance I would be something of a wallflower, but I didn't mind. I would look confident and hope for the best. My only jittery moments were when I thought about what I might do if I came face to face with Freddie Baring and her friend. My plan was to stick my nose in the air and ignore them, even if that hadn't exactly worked the last time.

Striding up the steps and into Senate House, I felt quite the old hand as I was signed in and made my way to the third floor, trying not to feel intimidated by its imposing stairs and endless corridors.

Once again, mingling appeared to be a key part of the event for most of the journalists, and I surreptitiously looked around to see if I recognised anyone from the last time.

I tried not to think of Freddie and Diane. I had more than enough on my mind and since I was confident that *Woman's Friend*'s efforts had been decent so far, in general they had slipped from my concern. Now that I was back in Senate House, however, I felt on the defensive, but I was more than aware that Mr Collins' jovial remark about not picking fights was his way of reminding me to act in the appropriate manner.

As I walked into the meeting room, the entire British women's press seemed to be deep in conversation with one another. Either they knew exactly what was going on with everyone else's publication or were pretending not to know a thing, but their conversations were lit up with expressions of surprise, exclamations of interest and a fair amount of good-natured repartee.

I was relieved not to see Freddie and Diane, but not necessarily delighted at the first person I recognised.

'Billings! Is that you? I thought you were dead.' Mr Jarrett had not updated his routine.

For a horrid moment, I thought I might be unlucky enough to be in his eyeline, but to my huge relief and delight, a familiar voice called my name.

'Miss Lake, how nice to see you again,' said Mrs Edwards, appearing from nowhere. Impeccably turned out in a grey suit and pearls, she shook my hand warmly. 'Shall we move over here?' she added, smoothly steering me out of Mr Jarrett's orbit and making me wonder if I would ever operate with such élan. The answer was almost certainly No.

'I should imagine your ears have been burning,' she said. 'I've been hearing some very good things about your magazine from all sorts of places. And quite right too. Is Guy with you today?'

'I'm afraid not,' I replied. 'He has been called away for a few days, but I understand he will be back soon.'

Mrs Edwards' smile did not fade, but an interested look very fleetingly crossed her face.

'I do hope he is not unwell?'

'Oh no, he is quite well,' I said. I didn't know just how friendly Mrs Edwards and Mr Collins were, so felt I should err on the side of reserve.

'Monica! How are you?'

I was saved from having to decide by the arrival of another of Mr Collins' acquaintances, Mr Simons.

Mrs Edwards greeted him as she had Mr Collins, kissing him on both cheeks, which I was now entirely sure

I would never get used to unless I moved to Paris for at least the next thirty years.

'Miss Lake,' acknowledged Mr Simons, and I managed to say hello, thankful that no one volunteered any cosmopolitan kissing as I didn't feel quite ready for all that.

'Have you seen Guy?' said Mrs Edwards. 'Miss Lake tells me he has been called away.'

To my surprise, Mr Simons nodded. 'Do you remember Robbie Forrester? I'm afraid he's not doing so well.'

Mrs Edwards did remember and said how very sorry she was. Then she turned to me. 'Since your Editor has come out of hiding, several of us have been catching up,' she said. 'Old friends. It's rather nice. Now as you're here on your own, shall we stick together? Perhaps we should find somewhere to sit.'

Mrs Edwards led me to a row of three chairs which were neither too keenly near the front, nor hiding away at the back. Mr Simons came with us, and as we sat down, I had the distinct feeling I was being taken under her wing. Mrs Edwards could have chummed up with anyone. It was more than kind of her to invite me to sit with her, not least because everyone else in the room knew who she was. To my eternal shame, I couldn't help hoping Freddie and her unpleasant friend were here to see.

Before I had much more of a chance to become entirely full of myself, there was some clearing of throats and shushing, and the panel from the Ministry arrived. Mr Clough was absent, but once again Mr Stratton took the helm, introducing Mr Morton-Stoppard, and then Mr Boe from the Ministry of Labour. This time, a lone woman had joined them; Miss Eggerton, an imposing figure with neat greying hair which had been effectively permed.

'As you know,' said Mr Stratton, 'we have recently

asked you to increase the amount of support in terms of female recruitment, particularly in light of the second National Service Act which will be passed imminently. Indeed, Miss Eggerton, Mr Boe's colleague from the Ministry of Labour, is with us today to go into more detail on this point.'

He bowed slightly in her direction and she gave an impassive nod in response. Mr Stratton cleared his throat and continued. 'Before I hand over to Miss Eggerton, I have been asked to pass on the Ministry's appreciation of your collective efforts over the last two months. In particular, Mr Clough, the Under-Secretary to the Minister, has himself asked me to mention a most instructive series of articles on munition recruits, in, I believe . . .' He consulted his notes. 'The *Woman's Friend* magazine.' He looked up briefly. 'Very good. Now, I have several updates I will go through.'

Mr Stratton continued with the agenda, hardly drawing breath or sounding remotely excited about the commendation he had just made. But as far as I was concerned, it was as if he had made the announcement while riding around the room on an elephant, accompanied by the Band of the Coldstream Guards.

A most instructive series of articles on munition recruits . . . Woman's Friend *magazine.*

Mr Clough, the actual Under-Secretary to the Minister, had specifically picked out *our magazine* for praise. I could hardly believe my ears.

I almost wanted to call out at Mr Stratton and ask him to say it again, just to ensure it was true.

Instead, I sat dead still, feeling my face burning as I stared at my hands which I had clasped together so tightly the knuckles had gone white.

'Brava, Miss Lake,' said Mrs Edwards, just loudly

enough for the people immediately surrounding us to hear. I smiled a thank you and wished I wasn't so red, as several of them casually looked round.

Put that in your pipe and smoke it, Freddie and Diane!

'Good for you,' whispered Mr Simons, who looked as if he was enjoying the moment immensely.

As I pretended to listen to Mr Stratton, now I didn't hear a word he was saying. All I could keep thinking was that *Woman's Friend* had Been Mentioned. It had been the quickest acknowledgement, but my goodness, it had been the only one by name, and as I sat among all the journalists and magazine editors and Ministry people, for the first time I actually felt as if I deserved to be here.

I just wished that Mr Collins and the rest of the team could have heard it as well. Mr Collins would have hated the attention, of course, but how lovely it would have been to see him publicly triumph as *Woman's Friend*'s Editor. I had no doubt that Mrs Edwards would have kissed him all over again.

With my mind wandering, I took several careful deep breaths and tried to focus on Mr Stratton again, before my head grew to the size of a balloon.

'Ladies and gentlemen,' he was saying, 'even with conscription coming, every single one of you is needed to pull his weight to reach every last one of your readers. We still need to recruit hundreds of thousands of women. They must play their part.'

Although I had heard Mr Stratton say it before, as I managed to pull myself together and listen properly, it was impossible not to feel as if I was being personally asked to do more.

I certainly didn't care about Freddie and Diane and their rudeness now. More fool them if the two of them preferred gossip and pettiness when so much was at stake.

After Mr Stratton's call to arms, Miss Eggerton stood to run through recruitment areas needing significant support.

Barely referring to notes, she spoke well, although without emotion, of the need to encourage more women to step up, especially in the factories – munitions, armaments and planes. Unsurprisingly, she was cagey about details, giving, I was to realise later, hardly any information of substance, but at the time, perhaps because I was giddy in the moment, she might have been speaking for the Prime Minister himself.

'The fight will be won,' she said. 'But we must add to the workforce, free up more men to go to war, and take on their jobs until we have peace. All women must play their part, whether conscripted or not.'

As I listened, I thought of Anne and Irene and the others. I wondered if Miss Eggerton, a female in the Ministry of Labour and National Service, might understand what women were going through, how hard they were working and what a strain it could be. Perhaps she would be on our side.

Each member of the panel took their turn to speak, and when they had all finished, Mr Morton-Stoppard nudged Mr Stratton and whispered something to him. Mr Stratton stood, thanked everyone and said that with regret there was no time for questions, but he and some of his colleagues would stay for another ten minutes to speak directly with those who required their attention.

Other than one journalist who said loudly, 'I wanted to ask about carrots,' everyone else began standing up, stretching, picking up bags and putting on coats.

Mrs Edwards and Mr Simons launched into a discussion about today's speeches, in which I was kindly involved, and several people came over to interrupt and say hello.

When she introduced me, Mrs Edwards made sure they knew which magazine I was from.

After several minutes I noticed that Miss Eggerton was standing quite near us and was in the process of shaking hands and saying goodbye to a serious, rather whiskery older journalist. I whispered a quick Excuse Me to Mrs Edwards and approached Miss Eggerton before it was too late.

'Miss Eggerton,' I said, planting myself between her and any possible exit route. 'How do you do? Emmeline Lake, *Woman's Friend*. I just wanted to say how much I admired your speech today. Especially what you were saying about women making all the difference.'

I said '*Woman's Friend*' slightly louder than I had meant. I told myself to calm down.

Miss Eggerton did not come across as the warmest person, but as none of the Ministry men did either, there was no reason why she should.

'How do you do, Miss Lake,' she said. 'Are you connected with the munitions workers articles?'

That was interesting. They really were keeping an eye on us all.

'That's right,' I said. 'I've been to a munitions factory several times now.'

'And you have been impressed.'

I didn't know if it was a question or a statement, but I knew the expected answer.

'Enormously. The women are hard-working, utterly committed, and their senior managers speak highly of them all.'

'Good,' said Miss Eggerton. While she hadn't cut me dead, she did not appear to want to chat to any great degree.

I kept talking, hoping she wouldn't walk away.

'I've been particularly impressed with how they manage to work and maintain their roles as wives and mothers, what with such long hours and difficulties in finding care for their children,' I said in a rush. 'Although we have heard from readers who are struggling in this area.'

I decided on the spot not to mention Chandlers so I wouldn't get anyone into trouble.

'Your point being?' Miss Eggerton asked.

Her deadpan expression was hard to read. I had no idea if her interest was based on sympathy or disapproval, so I adopted what I hoped was an impartial tone.

'I believe,' I said, 'that readers have queried how they might work full time and still care for their children should they be on shift-work. I also understand that some women who have been widowed find things a stretch on their pensions.'

'Did your magazine answer them?' asked Miss Eggerton. 'I take it you do advise them about the Government Nurseries?'

'Indeed,' I said. 'Although many areas do not have the Government facilities. I understand the factories them-selves have to request them. At least so our readers report,' I added, attempting to sound objective.

'Your readers are most open,' said Miss Eggerton. 'I hope they are as patriotic as they are verbose.'

'They see us as someone to turn to,' I said. 'And there is no doubt they are as fiercely patriotic as anyone. Many have husbands, brothers or sons in the forces. They have more reason than anyone to want us to win. But it is hard for some.'

'Miss Lake, we are at war. It is hard for everyone.'

'I wondered if you could advise me on who women workers might apply to directly,' I said. 'For nursery facil-ities.'

'I'm afraid this is between the factory management and their local authority,' said Miss Eggerton. 'Then of course the Ministry of Health needs to be involved, as well as the Ministry of Labour, in the decision.'

It all sounded interminable.

'But if the factory management does not see the need, then in all probability, there isn't one,' she finished.

'Miss Eggerton,' I said, 'I'm afraid we know from our readers that there is.'

She had begun to look unimpressed. 'A handful at most?' she said.

'I believe they could be the tip of the iceberg,' I said. 'You've just said in your speech that *all* women are needed to play their part, including the ones who won't be conscripted, which must include women who have children. What are they to do when working nights, or when they have to leave home before five in the morning for a six o'clock shift? Surely, more of them need help?'

If Miss Eggerton came across as a hard nut, she did not appear to like it in somebody else. 'Miss Lake,' she said, becoming tart, 'you take my words too literally. It is highly unlikely we will need every single mother of young children to work. And should they be required, then utilising older women to care for their children is an obvious solution. I think we all agree that mothers' true places are in their homes with their families, as of course they will return to when the war has been won.'

I wasn't sure quite where to start in response.

Had Miss Eggerton ever been to a factory? Did she even know any women in real life? It didn't seem to occur to her that some mothers needed to work, or might even actually *want* to.

Before I could say anything, I felt someone move to my side.

'Miss Eggerton. Monica Edwards, *Woman Today*. How do you do? I wonder if I might join you both? I was just remarking to my colleagues how well-deserved Mr Clough's praise for *Woman's Friend* was today. And how very informative your speech was. You have inspired many of us through your words this morning.'

It was the work of a prima ballerina crossed with one of the army's most relentless of tanks. Mrs Edwards smiled throughout, not even pausing for breath. She might just as well have had gills.

Miss Eggerton hesitated, perhaps weighing up whether to be charmed or annoyed. Mrs Edwards gave her no time to decide. 'I must apologise but would you mind terribly if I steal Miss Lake away from you? I wanted to ask her advice on a feature I'm planning.'

Miss Eggerton nodded and said, 'Of course.'

'Miss Eggerton,' I said, knowing that Mrs Edwards had stepped in to save me from getting into hot water, 'thank you for listening to my query. I hoped you might find it an interesting point. Most of all, thank you for your briefing. I agree wholeheartedly with Mrs Edwards. It was very inspiring indeed.'

Miss Eggerton's eyes glinted. Not, I would bet, because she was taken in by flattery, but because she recognised a capitulation when she saw one. 'Miss Lake,' she said. 'A piece of advice. Please remember that we work with the women's press so that they can inform their readers and support rather than question Government policy, or indeed, feature their readers questioning Government policy. I would advise to leave that to the more Trotskyite members of the press.'

'Of course,' I said, smoothly. I was beginning to learn how this worked. 'I do hope that is not how my words might have appeared.'

Miss Eggerton let me off. 'Not to me, Miss Lake,' she said. 'But others might take a rather different view.'

I extended my hand and she shook it. 'Thank you, Miss Eggerton,' I said. 'I look forward to continuing our support to the highest degree.'

'As do I,' said Miss Eggerton. She turned to Mrs Edwards, shook her hand and said, 'Thank you for your timely arrival.'

Then she walked briskly out of the room.

That, I thought, could have gone better.

'Thank you for saving me,' I said to Mrs Edwards. 'Mr Collins did tell me not to start fights.'

Mrs Edwards touched my arm lightly. 'Don't worry,' she said. 'He used to do it all the time. But he didn't back off like you very sensibly did. Well done. You knew when to step back.'

She smiled and put her arm through mine. 'Shall we go?' she said. 'I've just heard a rumour you're about to become part of the family, and I am embarrassingly keen to know if it's true.'

I nodded and said it was.

'How wonderful,' said Mrs Edwards. 'You must tell me more. Oh, and Miss Lake, whatever it was that Miss Eggerton was avoiding answering, you don't have to let it drop. It's a fine line to tread, but whoever you are trying to help, I could see you feel passionately about them.'

'I do,' I said. 'Very much.'

Mrs Edwards nodded. 'Then keep going,' she said. 'You may need to find a different route to take, but stick to it and I promise, you won't let them down.'

CHAPTER 20

It's a Good Thing Isn't It?

I WAS BOTH buoyed and perturbed by the meeting, my head thoroughly stuffed with things to consider. I was thrilled to bits of course about *Woman's Friend* being commended by Mr Clough, which went down marvellously on my return to the office, but more than dismayed with Miss Eggerton and her lack of inclination to be of much help.

There are women who stick up for each other, and women who don't.

Miss Eggerton was one of the Don'ts. In fact, she didn't even seem to think that women should *be* at work once they had children. I knew what my own mother would say in response, and it would probably start with, 'Granny didn't chain herself to railings so that . . .'

I wondered what the point of Miss Eggerton being a spokeswoman for the Ministry of Labour and National Service was when she seemed to think that going to work was a matter of choice.

After all, it might have been *highly unlikely* that the Government would need *every mother of young children to work*, but she didn't appear to realise that it wasn't just about what the Government needed. What about the women themselves?

Miss Eggerton was letting them down.

As Anne and the women began organising a parade, it was time to redouble my efforts in terms of what I might be able to do. Mrs Edwards had been right. I needed to take a different route.

While Anne and Betty tried again to get a response from the factory managers, as well as writing to their local authorities and making enquiries at the Labour Exchange, over the next week, Bunty and I made a list of anyone on a national level that might be able to help. Then we spent every minute we could writing letters and asking for advice.

With Mr Collins away, I wrote to the Ministry of Health for information about the Government's nurseries scheme as we were planning a feature. This was entirely true. I also wrote to all the news magazines asking if they were interested in an article about a women workers' Patriotic Parade. This was above board as well, but I wrote to them from myself and not *Woman's Friend*.

Bunty and I contacted our MP, and Bunts sent an impassioned letter to Dr Summerskill, asking for her help. I wanted to write to Mr Bevin, the Minister of Labour and National Service, himself, but Bunty said she would do that as I'd just given Miss Eggerton the right pip and you never knew if my name was now on some sort of list.

We weren't naive enough to think any of these people would actually have time to read our letters, but we carried on, nevertheless.

Everyone kept each other updated whether we had made headway or not. All of us had to go out and buy extra stamps.

Dear Anne,

Saturday 20th December sounds perfect for a parade. Bunty and I will come of course. Bunty is bringing her camera.

I spoke with someone at the 'M' and I'm afraid they weren't very helpful, but don't worry, I shall find someone who is. Bunty is going to write to Mr Bevin himself! If Betty doesn't get any joy from writing to the union, perhaps she should too?

I'll write more asap.

Love

Emmy x

Dear Emmy and Bunty

The children are finally asleep, so I have five minutes to write. Thank you for your letters. We are all THRILLED you can come to the parade! As it is so close to Christmas, we hope the town will be busy (not that there's anything to buy) and we've been told there will be a tree in the square, so that gives us something to march around. We have been trying to quietly spread the word and there's been quite a good take-up by some of the other girls. We've asked everyone to keep it secret. I don't trust you know who.

Some bad news. Mr T refused to even meet us. Mr R says it's out of his hands and we reckon T has told everyone to close ranks. It's just too mean of them all. I'm pleased we're planning the other things.

The children are well but running rings around Mum – Ruby ran away again today. She only got as far as the next street when someone found her, but Mum was in bits.

Better go. I think Tony's back teeth are finally coming through, poor love.

With love to you both,

Anne x

Dear Anne

That's rotten about Mr T. I'm not enormously surprised, but still. Horrible.

But the plans for the 20th are wonderful. I have sent out letters about writing an article but have not put the specific details in yet. Do you think your local newspaper will be interested? I think leave it to very near the date to ask them, just in case.

Love,

   E x

WOMAN'S FRIEND AT WORK
They're Old Hands Now!

In the last of our series about women munitions workers, EMMELINE LAKE finds out how our New Recruits are doing after two months in the job.

We first met our friends several weeks ago when they were the new girls on the team. They were freshly trained and hard at work, but if that impressed you, you should see them all now! . . .

```
MESSAGE - URGENT
To: Mrs Mahoney & Miss Lake
From: Miss Hester Wilson
   A quarter to eleven: The lady from The M
called for Mr Collins and said Mr S would
like to speak to him URGENTLY. I said would
Miss Lake do, but she said it has to be Mr
Collins. I didn't say we don't know where
he is.


MESSAGE - URGENT
To: Miss Lake
From: Miss Wilson
   Half past two: Miss Jackson from Lord
Overton's office asked if Mr Collins is back
```

yet. I said thank you very much but no he
isn't, and she asked when he might be as
Lord Overton would like to speak to him (Mr
Collins). I did ask but like the other lady,
she didn't want you either.

Darling

*Thank you for your letter. It so cheered me up. You'd
think I was in Timbuktu for the amount of time we get
together.*

*I'm angling for a meeting in London so that I can try to
see you, but let's try to speak on the phone until then.*

Not long till we're married. I am counting the days!

All my love.

Cxxx

Dear E&B

*Some good news: we think there may be up to twenty of
us on the 20th! That's good, isn't it? And Betty has written
to Mrs Churchill because, Betty says, she is such a good sort
and might listen. Ruby wanted her to ask Winston why
barrage balloons don't have faces drawn on as they'd look
funnier if they did. Betty told her she put it in as a PS!*

*Other things: Irene's found a bit of cleaning work so that
has helped. She still hasn't had any news.*

*Mum has a dicky tummy which she can't shake off, but
the rest of us are all right so that's a relief.*

See you soon.

Anne x

It was good to feel we were all trying to do something
that might help. Then two things happened which changed
everything.

The first didn't really affect anyone much, or at least

no one outside of a small group of people, to whom it mattered more than anything. The second affected the whole world.

Both stopped us in our tracks.

As letters flowed between us all and out to the people we thought might have a sympathetic ear about helping women working in war work, news arrived from Anne. I supposed Bunty and I had half expected it, but it was no less awful when it came.

Dear Emmy and Bunty

Irene has had the worst news about her husband, Douglas.

She is being very brave. We're all trying to help.

She has taken the girls to Maeve's. Enid doesn't under-stand but poor Sheila very much does.

I suppose at least now it is out in the open, but it's shaken us all. Another one of our precious boys.

I hate this stupid, horrible war.

Anne xx

PS: Sorry — I should have called, but it's just so dreadful and sad, and I didn't want to cry on the phone.

Bunty and I sat in silence for ages after we'd read the letter. We hadn't even met Douglas, and we'd only met Irene the once. But if anyone knew how she felt, it was Bunty. And if anyone knew how Irene's friends felt, I had to say it was me.

As the war had gone on, I had found that sometimes concentrating on your own little part of the world could make things easier. I had always been an avid follower of the news, as we all were these days, and reading letters as part of my job meant I could never entirely ignore what was going on, even if I'd wanted to. But now and then, when it all felt as if everything was inch by inch getting too much, I would stop reading the newspapers for a couple of days, avoid the radio, and steer clear of discussing what was increasingly grim.

Perhaps I had thrown myself into concentrating on plans and letters about the parade partly to block out the news, especially if it was probable that Charles would go overseas at some point. Now it was right on our doorsteps again.

Bunty and I of course wrote to Irene, sending our sympathy and love, and telling her that if she could think of anything we could help with, to just say. We didn't know her well enough to be much good, but we wanted her to know that we cared.

The second thing that happened could hardly have been further away from us. On Sunday 7th December, the Japanese bombed an American naval base in Hawaii. It was the most awful attack and there was no question of wanting to avoid the news now. We were all glued to our radios as soon as we heard.

By Monday morning, the headline was the same on every front page. Japan had declared war on America and Britain. Now the whole world really was at war.

Charles hardly ever talked about what was said in the papers, and certainly nothing to do with his work, but now I was desperate to hear what he thought.

I rushed home from work, hoping he would call. When the phone rang, I snatched it up so quickly I nearly dropped it.

'Hello, darling,' said Charles, from a phone box. 'How are you?'

'I'm very well,' I said, over heartily. 'Quite busy. How are you?'

'Jolly well, too,' said Charles, sounding even more hale

228

than me. 'What's the latest? I read your letter and I'm so sorry about Anne's friend. How is she?'

'Anne says she is coping. It's wretched, though.'

'I'm sorry,' said Charles again. 'Tell me about work. How are things with Guy away?'

I didn't really want to natter on about work when the world seemed to be getting more dangerous by the minute, but I went along with him, for form's sake.

'Absolutely fine. I'm a bit worried that both the people we can't mention and Lord O are trying to get hold of Guy. I keep thinking Miss E may have complained. Other than that, nothing to report. I've finished writing the series on the factory. Bunty's well and we're writing letters to everyone we can think of.'

Everything tumbled out incoherently. It had been over a week since we last spoke and Charles listened kindly as I whittered on.

'So, goodness, yes, that's it,' I finished. 'Have you frozen to death in the phone box while I've gone on?'

'Snug as a bug,' said Charles staunchly, which was probably untrue. 'It's what I'm here for, although I do wish I could be of some help. Do you really need to contact Guy?'

'Not for me, no, but I am rather worried about the important people. I wish he'd left a forwarding address or a number.'

'I'll track him down,' said Charles. 'Sorry if that sounds rather clandestine. He's terrifically loyal to the chaps he was with in the army, but hardly talks about it. Things must be bleak, though, if he hasn't been in touch. Leave it with me.'

I thanked him and Charles said it was a pleasure. Then, and unusually, there was a silence between us.

'Ooh,' I said, brightly. 'Nicer news – the vicar has confirmed that the choir can definitely do the wedding, which is lovely. And Mr Bone says he knows a florist who can do some nice arrangements if we can supply the greenery. Bunty thinks if she and I can't manage to go down ourselves to pick it all, her granny will find a way to get some sent up. Isn't that kind of her?'

'Yes,' said Charles. He didn't sound very excited by it. Then again, floristry possibly wasn't his thing.

'And Roy and Fred from the station want to bring some sort of speaker and look after the music so everyone can dance afterwards.'

That was more up Charles' street.

'Very good,' he said.

His voice was flat as a pancake. I waited while there was another lull in the conversation.

'The thing is,' said Charles. 'I'm so sorry, Em, but I think we may need to bring the wedding forward. I mean obviously I'm not sorry about getting married sooner. It's just . . .'

The receiver felt heavy in my hand. I screwed up my eyes and waited.

'I think there'll be a position for me overseas.'

If everything had seemed better two minutes ago, now it felt anything but. 'Ah,' I said, playing for time so that I could get my voice in order before speaking. 'Right-oh,' I managed. 'That's all right. What with the news and everything I had rather thought . . .'

'I'm so sorry, darling,' said Charles, sounding as wretched as I felt. 'I've no idea what or where, yet. It may have nothing to do with all that.'

I took a very deep breath and mustered every bit of miserable fortitude I could. 'Not at all,' I said, as if someone had just apologised for taking the last seat on the bus. 'So, you can't really tell me very much?'

'A bit,' said Charles. 'Several of the medium gun chaps

need people and they seem to think I might be the right sort. Possibly lining up to become a BC. It was rattling around before Hirohito's lot did their party piece, so things may now have changed.' He went quiet. 'Damn it, E, I'm so sorry. This has happened a lot faster than I thought.'

He sounded awful, but he should have been thrilled. He had hoped to become a Battery Commander at some point, and he'd always said that he loved being out in the field. This sounded like his chance.

It was my time to step up. I was marrying a career officer. He had been training for this since he was eighteen.

'Em, are you still there?' His concern was obvious.

I cleared my throat and answered. 'Of course, darling,' I said. 'It sounds very exciting. Just your sort of thing which really is awfully good.'

My knuckles were white as I gripped the telephone. When he answered, it sounded as if he knew it.

'It should be all right,' he said gently. 'They're all good bunches of men.'

'Of course,' I said again. I couldn't stop saying, Of Bloody Course. 'As if the Gunners would be anything else.' I tried to make a little joke of it, even managing to do a small laugh. 'So you don't know where you'll be off to?'

'Off to' made it sound as if it would be quite the cheerful day out.

'I can't say anything at the moment.' Silly question. 'But I think it'll be soon.'

He didn't say when, but soon was enough for me.

'Will there be enough time?' I asked. 'For the wedding.'

'We'll make sure there is,' said Charles. 'I'm not leaving until we're married.'

It was one thing to keep hold of.

'But, darling, if you're up for it, I think we should try

to get married as soon as we possibly can. I'll get on to the church and sort out a new date. Would that be all right, do you think?'

'I think that would be lovely,' I said. 'And it's a good thing, isn't it? We've both been counting the days.'

I knew I didn't sound anything like my usual self, but I was doing the best that I could, and Charles knew it.

'Bloody hell, I wish I wasn't doing this on the phone,' he said. 'You're being terribly good about it.'

'I'm a lovely person,' I said, going for a spot of humour.

Tears were rolling down my cheeks. I hoped he couldn't hear them in my voice.

'That I know,' said Charles. He sounded awful. 'I'll contact Reverend Lovell and see if he can change the date. I'll sort a special licence if we need one and put in for emergency leave. I will make this work. I promise.'

There was no way I would let him hear me cry.

'Thank you.' I didn't know whether I wanted to stay on the phone for ever or just get up and run. 'That would be super.'

'I love you, E.'

I couldn't bear this.

'I love you too,' I said.

The pips started going at the end of the line.

Everything was just getting worse every day.

'I love you too,' I said again. Then as I knew Charles would be putting more pennies into the slot, I put down the receiver and sobbed.

CHAPTER 21

Smile and Look Innocent

CHARLES CALLED BACK later in the evening and we spoke for longer. I tried hard to be chipper and felt slightly better about playing my part. We would crack on with the wedding plans and then Charles would go off and do a very good and important job and I would do mine back here, and that was all there was to it, which in wartime was perfectly fine.

If I said that enough times, perhaps it would be true. Still, I wanted to curl into a ball and wait for the war to just go away.

This would not help anyone.

Bunty was out, so I went to bed early which gave me a whole night to sort myself out.

I hated the idea of Charles going, but for now he was still here, alive, in Britain and I would get to marry him. That was a lot more than many people had. Of course I thought of Irene and Bunty and Anne. I was damn lucky. It was as simple as that.

I wrote to Charles in the middle of the night, to say properly how proud I was of him. Even though I had told him a dozen times when we had talked, I wanted him to have it in black and white.

He wrote to me at exactly the same time. He wanted to thank me for being such a brick. Even though he had said it a dozen times when we had talked. Most of all, he said, I had to know that he loved me more than anything else in the world.

I kept the letter in my bag and read it over and over again.

Two nights later, Bunty, Thelma and I were sitting in the kitchen, which Bunty had just re-named the Wedding Office, eating pickled cucumbers for our tea. In her self-appointed role as Bunty's deputy in charge of wedding plans, Thelma had called round before our shift at the fire station so she could go through Bunts' frighteningly efficient lists to see how far a change of date might mess things about.

I knew that the two of them had decided to make things as cheery as they could, and I was more than keen to join in.

'I always think that keeping your chin up isn't that hard,' Bunty had said, when I first told her about the change of plan. 'You just need to lift your face. It's your heart that takes the effort. When it falls over it can be so stubborn about getting back up.'

'I've decided just to think about the wedding,' I said. 'That's the lovely bit and it would be such a shame to spoil it.'

Bunty had taken up the challenge with gusto. 'If we refer to List A,' she now said, authoritatively, 'which as you know covers outfits, then whatever date Charles manages to get, you are definitely prepared.'

Thelma diligently consulted the list while I loudly bit into a cucumber and Bunty threw me one of her Looks.

'Sorry,' I mumbled, with my mouth full. 'List A. Lovely.'

'I'll move on. List B: Guests,' said Bunty.

'List B,' said Thelma, heartily. 'I'm there.' She looked across the kitchen table at me. 'Keep up, Lake.'

I tried not to laugh but succeeded only in choking slightly.

Bunty rolled her eyes. 'It all depends on whether it's a weekend, but I think we should plan for a party in the evening either way,' she said. 'Does that sound sensible?'

'Absolutely,' I said. 'Corporal Thelma?'

'Oh yes,' agreed Thel. 'Although can't I be an officer as I'm Second in Command?'

We both looked at Bunty. 'No,' she said. 'List C: Food.'

'Crikey, Bunty,' said Thelma. 'If you were in the War Cabinet, you'd sort them all out and this whole business would be over by Christmas.'

Bunty smiled and leant back in her chair. 'Can you imagine?' she said, almost dreamily. 'Over by Christmas. What a lovely thought.'

For a moment no one said anything.

'Come on,' I said, before the mood could become too contemplative. 'List C: Provisions. Tricky one. If we don't have champagne and caviar by the bucket load, I'm calling the whole thing off.'

'Quite right too,' said Thelma.

'I'll say,' said Bunty. 'And bananas and pineapples for pudding.'

'Covered in toffee and ice cream,' said Thel.

'Which we'll eat until we are sick,' I said, happily bringing down the tone.

'And then have some more,' said Bunty, revoltingly. 'Hold on, there's the telephone. I'll go.'

I was pleased to see Bunty get up almost easily and march off to the stairs. Her injured leg was getting stronger, and I could see her finding it easier to get around, often without using her stick.

I sat back and began to crunch my way through another cucumber, thinking how nice it would be with a big lump of mature Cheddar and some newly baked bread covered with fresh butter. Then I heard Bunty shout for me from the floor above.

Her voice sounded urgent, so I put down my fresh-bread-less pickle and hurried upstairs, wondering if it might be Charles again.

'I see,' she was saying. She put her hand over the receiver. 'It's Anne,' she whispered. 'Or rather, it's Betty calling about Anne.'

'Emmy's here now,' said Bunty as we put our heads together in order to listen.

'Hello, Emmy,' said Betty. She was breathless as if she had been running. 'I don't know how to put this. Anne's been sacked from Chandlers.'

'What?' said Bunty and I at the same time.

'I know. It's a long story, but her mum's been out of sorts again. Anne thinks it's her nerves. Anyway, Anne managed to get a neighbour to have Tony, but she ended up having to take Ruby to work.'

Bunty and I looked at each other over the phone.

'Is she all right?' asked Bunty.

'Yes, yes, they're both fine. But Ruby wouldn't sit still. You can guess what happened.'

'Why on earth did Anne take her in?' I said, cross with the worry. 'We all know what Ruby's like.'

'I would say she probably had no flaming choice,' said Betty, hotly. 'You know the situation.'

'I'm sorry,' I said. 'That was unfair of me. Where are they now?'

'They were sent home,' said Betty. 'Mr Rice said he's not giving out second chances any more. There's another thing. The march is off,' she finished. 'Someone told Mr Terry.'

'No!' said Bunty.

'He's announced that he'll sack anyone who joins in. If you ask me, they've used Ruby as an excuse to play rough and get rid of Anne. Terry hauled her up about the letter asking for a meeting to discuss a nursery and then he heard about the parade. It was perfect for him. Old Ricicle isn't a bad sort. I reckon Terry's the one playing at Jimmy Cagney and being the tough guy. I don't know what else to say.'

Betty sounded thoroughly defeated.

'This is awful,' I said. 'Asking him outright wasn't even Anne's idea. It was mine. Betty, this isn't fair. If he should pick on anyone, it should be me.'

'Don't worry,' said Betty. I heard her light a cigarette. 'You tried. We all tried.'

'Why don't I talk to him?' I said. 'I'll explain that everything was my idea. That I talked everyone into it. If I'm the troublemaker, maybe he won't make Anne leave. Let me try to see him.'

It had been very easy to come up with suggestions, but the nearest thing I had done to putting myself in any risk was to have a mild row with Miss Eggerton, and then I'd quickly backed down at the first sign of a fuss.

'I don't know,' said Betty. 'Maybe. Would he agree to a meeting, though?'

Bunty looked at me and shrugged.

'Do you want to speak with Anne first, Betty?' I asked. 'If she'd rather I keep out, then I will. If not, I'll come tomorrow on the first train. Please tell her we will make this right.'

'OK,' said Betty. 'I'd better go. I'll call back when I can.'

We said hurried goodbyes and then Bunty put the phone down.

'You'll make this right?' she said, not unkindly. 'How

are you going to do that? He sounds just as vile as you said.'

'I've no idea,' I said, as Thelma appeared from downstairs, looking concerned. 'But it's my fault and I can't just sit here and do nothing. Maybe if I appeal to his better nature – make him be the hero of it all. Sorry, Thel, we've just heard our friend Anne's been given the sack.'

'Flipping heck,' said Thelma. 'That's horrible.'

'It wasn't just you, Emmy,' said Bunty. 'I was there too.' She looked at the grandfather clock. Even its tick tocks sounded gloomy. 'You and Thel need to go to your shift. I'm going to think of who I can write to next. You're right, we can't just let it go.'

'And I'll think of what I can do about Mr Terry,' I said. 'What on earth is Anne going to do now?'

★

I slept badly that night, tossing and turning as I tried to think of how to help my friend. Writing letters to politicians was all very well, but it wasn't going to do Anne any good.

Somehow, Mr Terry had to be convinced to give her back her job, and somehow I was going to have to find a way to talk him into it. I knew he wouldn't agree to another meeting. This time I would try a surprise visit.

I took the first train out of London the next morning.

'None of this is your fault,' said Anne as she gave me a hug at the railway station, where she had been waiting for over an hour as my train was delayed. 'It really isn't. Mum has been struggling to cope with the kids. That's why I ended up taking Ruby in, not because of you. And more to the point, shouldn't you be at work?'

She was probably right, but I didn't say anything.

Anne rubbed her hands together in her bright red

238

woollen gloves. They matched her scarf and hat and made her look for all the world as if she was getting ready for the festive season to start.

'How are you feeling?' I asked. She looked terrible.

'I must admit I've been better,' she said. 'Honestly, I don't know what I was thinking. I should have got someone to say I was sick, although I have done that twice before. Poor Ruby, she didn't know what was going on. Shall we sit down?'

The railway station had a small tea and waiting room, and mainly to try to get Anne warm, I agreed. Betty had called back later last night and said that Anne would meet me if I really did want to come. It was good to see her, but her bloodshot eyes gave her away.

'What did Mr Rice, say exactly?' I asked, as we chose from a doleful selection of stale-looking baked goods.

'He just said bringing in children had to stop. Apparently, it's happened in other parts of the factory and Mr Terry has had enough.'

'And he said that was it, right on the spot?'

'Yes. He said to get my cards and go, so I did. Ruby was howling by then and I just wanted to leave.'

I paid the lady at the counter, and said, 'My treat,' which was entirely wrong under the circumstances. Then I followed Anne to a table.

'Look at this,' said Anne. 'Betty took it off the wall and hid it down her shirt to smuggle it out.'

She passed me a handbill. On it was printed a short announcement.

It has been brought to the attention of the Chandler Management that a number of employees are planning to stage a protest march regarding facilities in the factory.

We would like to remind all employees that this is against both company and security rules. Any personnel taking part in protests will be subject to disciplinary action, including dismissal and legal proceedings.

Signed.

MT Terry

Factory Director

'That's when I knew I was done for,' said Anne. 'I'm such an idiot. I don't know what I'm going to do. I've left the children with Maeve as she's on nights. Mum's a worrier so I've just told her they're changing our shifts. The thing is, she can't cope with Ruby and Tony for twelve hours a day.'

Anne took off her gloves and leant her elbows on the table, putting her head in her hands. I knew the girls had to scrub them like mad every day to get the oil and the dirt out, and they were red raw and cracked. Anne was looking a shadow of the woman I had first met.

'Eat that scone,' I ordered, as if it would make a difference. 'I'm going to try to see Mr Terry and tell him it's down to me. I'm sure if you hadn't been in *Woman's Friend* you'd be less noticeable, and you'd probably have gone about the nursery request more quietly if I hadn't made that stupid comment about a parade.'

'I don't know about that,' said Anne, cutting a scone in half which I knew she would share with Ruby later. 'It's lovely of you to try. But I'm the one that took Rubes into work.'

'I'll tell him I let you down on babysitting,' I said. 'And if I say all the stuff about trying to get better facilities was my idea and I put you all up to it, then he might relent. But I'll only go if you are happy for me to try it.'

Anne hesitated. 'I've got no job, I'm lying to my mum and everything we've all tried so far hasn't worked,' she

240

said. 'I don't think things could be much worse. I didn't expect Mr Terry to talk to us when we wrote to him, but he didn't even get one of the Welfare Managers to listen to what we had to say. If you can find a way to get to him, you tell him from me, there's a factory full of women trying their best, but we can't do everything. Whether he's interested or not, we're trying to look after our families and homes too. Not to mention hoping to God our boys come back in one piece,' she finished, her face now flushed with anger.

If I had wanted to appeal to Mr Terry before, now I felt that nothing would stop me.

'I don't know if I'll even get as far as his office,' I said. 'But I'll do everything I can. I promise.'

'Well, I've flipping failed,' said Anne. 'I keep thinking what Anthony would say and I know he'd be telling me not to let him push us around.'

She was holding my hand tightly. 'I don't want to get you into trouble, Emmy,' she said. 'And how are you going to get in to see him?'

Now I smiled. 'You won't. Do you see that van?'

Anne looked through the window. A nondescript goods van had parked outside the station and a man in a dark jacket and cap was taking some boxes from a porter.

'That's Mr Noakes,' I said, beginning to pick up my things. 'Do you know him? His wife's Mrs Noakes, on reception. He's given me a lift to and from Chandlers twice now and is awfully friendly and kind.' I gave Anne what I hoped was an encouraging grin. 'Also, he does a daily pick-up from the train that comes in just about now.'

Anne's face lifted. 'You crafty old thing,' she said.

'It may not work,' I replied. 'But I must catch him before he leaves, so please eat up, and would you mind taking mine for Ruby if she'd like it?'

Anne said, 'Thank you and good luck,' then handed me a piece of paper with an address on it. 'I'll be at Maeve's,' she said. 'Will you come as soon as you've seen him?'

I nodded a yes, and tucking the note into my pocket, headed off to Mr Noakes.

'Don't take any old nonsense,' called Anne. 'And give him what for!'

*

Outside the station, Wilfred Noakes was putting the last of his boxes into the van and I quickly walked over, calling out a Hello.

'Miss Lake!' he said, his breath showing how cold it was. 'We can't keep you away.'

'Good morning, Mr Noakes,' I said. 'How are you and Mrs Noakes?'

'Very well, thank you,' he said. 'Should I be giving you a lift?'

I looked around in case of being overheard. 'Probably not,' I said, unwilling to lie to him. 'Unless you want to be part of what is probably A Very Bad Idea.'

Mr Noakes laughed heartily. 'Best offer I've had all day,' he said. 'Come on. Get in.'

Wilf Noakes was as thoroughly decent as I had thought. He was slightly built and had lovely brown eyes. He and his wife Noreen made a handsome couple. I decided to tell him what was going on, so he could make me get out if he thought he might get into trouble. To my surprise however, he seemed to know at least as much as I did.

'That Mr Terry's such a . . . well I won't say the word, but I've no time for him,' he said. 'He's only been in charge a year and he's upset more people than the canteen's made hot dinners.'

This was news to me. From the way he spoke, I had assumed that Mr Terry had been part of the factory's success for ages.

'He's just sacked two of my friends,' I said, abruptly.

'Mrs Barker?' said Wilf.

'And now Mrs Oliver too,' I said.

Wilf snorted. 'I heard it from Noreen. And this is why you want to see him?'

I nodded. As we drove out of the town and towards the factory, I made another confession. 'Mr Noakes, I haven't any papers for the security guards,' I said.

'Now there's a turn-up,' said Mr Noakes, quite calmly. 'And call me Wilf, although probably not in front of the guards.'

'Thank you, Wilf, and please call me Emmy.'

Wilf nodded and was silent for a moment.

'Emmy,' he said, thoughtfully. 'When we get to the gates, tell me if you recognise any of the lads. It could be helpful.'

We were nearly at Chandlers, and I was beginning to feel nervous.

'This isn't going to get you or Mrs Noakes into trouble, is it?' I asked.

Wilf shook his head as he expertly drove the van around a tight bend. 'Don't worry,' he said, 'I can always say I assumed you were back for an official meeting. Noreen will be fine. To be honest,' he added, 'we're leaving anyway. She doesn't like the way Terry looks at her, and neither do I. You see, everyone has their secrets. Right, are you ready?'

We had drawn up to Chandlers' main gates. I looked closely as two security guards walked up to the van.

'The one on the right has seen me before,' I said.

'Good. Now smile and look innocent and leave this to me.'

Wilf rolled down the window of his van and leant out.

'Frozen to death yet?' he called, handing over a sheet of paper. 'It's all on the list. Here's the key to the back, and I've picked up Miss Lake again for the chief.'

If I'd thought Wilf was hatching a complicated cover story, it was clear he was more of a Look Confident and Tell the Truth sort of man. Handing over my identity card, I tried to look innocent, or failing that, unthreatening at least. I had nothing to prove I should be there.

Before the guard could question it, Wilf turned up his chatter. 'Somebody here's made quite an impression on the boss,' he said, giving me an unsavoury wink. 'I think this one has an open invitation.'

'Hmm,' said the guard. 'Stay there until I get you a pass.'

I almost gasped. Wilf might just have done it.

'You could look a bit less shocked,' he said through his teeth, trying not to laugh. 'Thanks, mate,' he added as the guard returned and handed him my pass.

As soon as we drove away, Wilf let out a guffaw and thumped the steering wheel. 'I'm sorry,' he said. 'Noreen would have a right old go at me for that. Although you're going to have to work on your Mata Hari impression if you want a career in spying. Your face!'

'*I think this one has an open invitation?* Wilf, I'm engaged!' I said, in mock-protest, then beginning to laugh, 'And as for the wink.'

Wilf roared. 'You're a good sport,' he said, wiping his eyes. 'I couldn't think of how else to get you in. Never mind, at least it worked.'

A few moments later he brought the van to a stop at Shed Twelve. 'I can wait just down here if you like,' he said. 'In for a penny and all that.'

'Thanks, Wilf,' I said, getting out. 'I won't be long.'

'Be careful,' he said. 'Try to tell Nore that I know what's going on.'

I nodded a thank you and walked the short way to Shed Twelve. A large, shiny black Austin 16 was parked at an angle outside.

Mr Terry was here.

Noreen Noakes was sitting in her little booth. We exchanged Hellos, and now, feeling slightly dry-mouthed, I told her I was here to see Mr Terry. I didn't say I had an appointment.

'Thank you, Miss Lake,' she said. 'I'll call up for someone to come and get you.'

'No,' I said, in a stage whisper. 'Please don't.'

Mrs Noakes looked at me with surprise.

'I've come about Anne Oliver,' I said, speaking urgently and hoping she would get my drift. 'And Irene Barker. I saw Mr Noakes at the station, and he kindly gave me a lift. He said to tell you I've told him why I'm here.'

Despite my lack of coherence, Mrs Noakes cottoned on. 'It's a poor business,' she said quietly. Then as if everything was perfectly normal, she said, 'Just sign your name here. If Mr Terry said to go straight up, then please take the doors on your right. You know your way of course.'

'Thank you,' I said, and had never meant it more.

As I made my way up the stairs to the offices, I wondered how many other people at Chandlers were less than fans of the Factory Director. The thought gave me a small boost of confidence. Perhaps other people would stand up on Anne's side?

There was no time to think about it. A middle-aged man in a suit came out of the doors on the first floor, so I smiled and thanked him which meant he held them open for me. I was just another young woman in a suit. Now

I needed to get past Mr Terry's secretary, Mrs Cleeve. There was no way my luck was going to stretch this far.

Her desk was directly outside his office, like a sentry who had been to the perfume counter at Boots. I couldn't risk a row, so I didn't dare stop.

'Excuse me?' she said as I walked past, rudely ignoring her. 'Is that Miss Lake? Do you have an appointment?'

Mr Terry's office was within touching distance. The door had his name on it, on a sign above the sort of glass that you couldn't see through.

'Miss Lake,' demanded his secretary, loudly. 'I must insist.'

I thought of Anne. And so must I, I thought to myself.

Then I reached for the handle, opened the door, and went in.

CHAPTER 22

*I Don't Like People Who
Pick On My Friends*

As I HAD feared, my arrival did not go down well.

'What the hell is this?' barked Mr Terry, rising out of his seat. He had been at his desk, talking to a man who I recognised as Mr Adams, the Public Relations Manager.

'Good morning, Mr Terry,' I said. 'Mr Adams. I apologise for the interruption.'

'I should damn well think so,' said Mr Terry. 'Who let you in?'

Mrs Cleeve had followed me into his office and was looking more than perturbed. 'Mr Terry,' she said, 'I have no idea how this young woman got through security.'

'Then I should get her out,' said Mr Terry, rudely.

'Please!' I said. 'I have come to apologise. And to offer you an explanation. I believe you have heard Mrs Anne Oliver brought her daughter into work. This is entirely my fault. I'm afraid I let her down over babysitting and left her no choice.'

'Mrs Oliver?' said Mr Terry.

Mr Adams muttered something to him.

'Oh, her. One of the troublemakers protesting.'

'No, they're not,' I said, almost forgetting my plan to be as pleasant as possible. 'There's no protest, sir. There was going to be a Patriotic Parade, but that was about

247

recruiting more women if there were the facilities to help them.'

It wasn't an untruth.

'But it has been cancelled,' I continued. 'And Mr Terry, please know that the parade idea was entirely down to me as well, not Mrs Oliver.'

I moved further into the room in case Mrs Cleeve felt the need to try and bundle me out.

'Really?' said Mr Terry, sarcastically. 'Why aren't I surprised? The last time you were here, under the pretence of interviewing me, I was harangued about employees' childcare. Then your friends started sending me demanding letters and arranging anti-patriotic demonstrations. And now here you are, having found your way into a high-security munitions supplier to the Government. It's all somewhat rum, don't you think?'

'That was no pretence, sir,' I said. I quickly unlocked my briefcase and brought out a copy of the latest issue of *Woman's Friend*. 'I hope you will see that I have quoted you – not by name of course, but as Factory Director, quite extensively.' I put it on his desk with the page open. 'There. Just under the picture of all the women enjoying the entertainments. I hope you'll see the article is fulsome in its praise.'

Mr Adams craned his neck to study the magazine, but Mr Terry just continued to look furious and increasingly unattractive.

'Mr Terry,' I said. 'I am so very sorry if I have caused trouble. The articles in our magazine have all been terrifically positive, but perhaps personally, I had become over-enthusiastic about the Government's excellent initiative of providing nurseries for war workers. Please do not penalise the women. Especially Mrs Oliver. I understand she is a very effective employee, and I know she is thoroughly committed to her job.'

While I was finding my own words quite sickeningly obsequious, I tried hard to make my voice calm, keeping the pitch low and even attempting to be slightly charming. Flattery had worked with him previously, and I knew Mr Adams had no axe to grind with me. I tried to catch his eye, but he was staring fixedly at his hands.

I thought of how I had managed to back down in the face of Miss Eggerton's crossness, and of how Mrs Edwards would have managed my current situation.

She would have glided in, enraptured the two men and got them to sign an agreement on a veritable chain of nurseries, decent working hours, equal pay and wall to wall lavatory mirrors within minutes.

But I was no Mrs Edwards.

Mr Terry sat back down in his large chair and crossed his arms.

'Mr Terry, should I escort Miss Lake out?' asked Mrs Cleeve.

'I can handle this,' said Mr Terry, testily. 'You can go.'

I wondered how Mrs Cleeve put up with him.

'Miss Lake,' said Mr Terry. 'You must be aware that anti-patriotic dissent is a matter for the police.'

'It isn't anti-patriotic, Mr Terry,' I said, as sweetly as I could. 'They just want to be able to work. That's what the Government's recruitment campaign is for: getting more women into war work. It's just that they can't easily do that when the shifts make caring for their children impossible. That's not a criticism,' I added.

'And what does the Ministry of Information make of your views?' said Mr Terry.

I hesitated. 'They are fully committed to recruiting more war workers,' I said. 'Just last week, my magazine was praised by the Under-Secretary to the Minister, for the articles about your factory. I am not here to be troublesome.'

By now I was almost pleading. I hated myself for doing it, but it was worth a shot. If I could make Mr Terry feel like the big man, perhaps he would be a little better disposed.

I was wrong.

'Miss Lake, as you appear to be quite the name with the MOI, I am sure my friends at the Ministry of Labour will be delighted to hear all about you and your magazine, and the way you have infiltrated and influenced my workers. Protests and marches and whatever else you've been stirring up don't quite fit with your little articles.'

I opened my mouth to defend myself, but Mr Terry had had enough.

'MRS CLEEVE,' he shouted.

Mrs Cleeve hurried back into the room. She must have been standing right outside the door and was looking even more severe than ever.

'Please ensure Miss Lake is removed from the premises,' he said.

'Yes, Mr Terry,' said Mrs Cleeve. 'I've arranged transport. Many of the workers are on their way to early lunch so I thought it best not to make a fuss.'

Mr Terry nodded, curtly.

But I hadn't had my say, and far more importantly, Anne hadn't had hers.

'What about Mrs Oliver?' I asked. 'Will you give her her job back? She will not bring her child in again.'

Mr Terry shrugged. It was written all over his substantial face. He didn't give a fig.

Mr Terry. Rich from Jerry.

That's Mr Terry.

'You know, sir,' I said, speaking quietly now, 'the women I've met who work in your factory really do care about what they do here. They may never earn your kind of salary, or drive a big car like yours, or have a Rolls-Royce ashtray.' I looked at the one on his desk with contempt. 'And neither will I. But they'll give everything they possibly can, including the men they love, to help win this war.'

I thought of Anne and Anthony, of Irene and her husband, Douglas. Of Bunty and William, and of my brother Jack flying across the Channel in the dead of night. And as my heart lurched, I thought of Charles, my darling boy who I loved more than anything.

We all wanted factories like Chandlers to produce munitions and armaments and every single other thing needed for the war effort, because then the boys just might come back alive. But it didn't mean a woman doing her best for them should be treated as if she was just another spare part.

The only way we were going to get through this war was to help carry each other along. If it took him a hundred years, Mr Terry would never understand.

'Mr Terry, I'd put my hat on it that if these women were in your position, they wouldn't bully people or ignore polite requests for some help to which they are perfectly entitled. They'd do everything they could for the war effort, only they would understand that it's not about money and Government contracts and friends in high places.' I held eye contact until he looked away. 'It's about doing your bit and helping to win this war for all of us.'

Then I turned on my heels, and followed closely by Mrs Cleeve, I walked out.

★

I may have managed to get the last word, but I was under no illusion that I had won. With my heart in my boots, I waited for Mrs Cleeve to call for Security to escort me off the premises.

'Miss Lake,' she said, forcefully. 'Time for you to leave.'

She took me by the arm and guided me out of the managerial offices in no uncertain manner.

'Through there,' she said, half pushing me out of the doors towards the stairs as a man in a brown overall who I judged might be a foreman stood and stared.

She led me downstairs, where to my surprise Noreen Noakes was standing outside her booth looking anxious.

'Miss Lake,' said Noreen. 'What happened? Mrs Cleeve called to say Mr Terry is in an absolute fury.'

'Did you manage to find Mr Noakes?' asked Mrs Cleeve, grimly.

'He's outside in the van,' said Noreen.

I nodded. I didn't have the foggiest idea what was going on.

'I should get a move on, Miss Lake,' said Mrs Cleeve. 'You've been a silly little fool today and probably just made things worse for your friends. Thank you, Mrs Noakes. Good day to you.'

As Mrs Cleeve marched solidly back to Mr Terry, Noreen Noakes ushered me out of the building.

'Make sure you tell Wilf everything,' she said. 'Then he can tell me. Go on, before she changes her mind and calls Security. And don't worry. I don't know what you've just done, but I bet it's not half as bad as she says.'

They were kind sentiments and I thanked Mrs Noakes profusely, but Mrs Cleeve's words rang in my ears. I was still seething over Mr Terry, but what if I had been a fool? More to the point, what if I had made things even worse for my friends?

*

Wilf Noakes didn't just escort me off the premises, but all the way to Maeve's flat. As I had promised his wife, I told him what had happened, although swearing him and

252

Mrs Noakes to secrecy. I didn't want either of them to get mixed up in my row with the head of the entire Chandlers operation.

Wilf listened intently as I tried not to overdramatise what had just taken place.

'I admire your gumption,' he said, as he wound his way to Maeve's address without looking at a map. 'Noreen and me live two streets away,' he explained as he stopped the van outside Maeve's and put the handbrake on with a crunch.

'That explains it,' I smiled. 'Wilf, do you think I went too far? And are you sure you won't be in trouble?'

'I think you said what was right,' said Wilf. 'And sometimes that has to be done. Don't worry about me, I think old Terry will want to keep all of this quiet. Good luck to you, Emmy. Take care of yourself.'

I thanked him again and got out, waving goodbye as he drove off. I was hugely grateful for his help but more than aware he hadn't answered my question. I waited for a moment before ringing the doorbell. The peculiar euphoria of giving Mr Terry a piece of my mind was beginning to wear off. Now I had to confess that I had failed.

Maeve answered the door. 'Blimey,' she said, 'you look awful. Come on in. My girls are playing with Ruby and Tony in the bedroom, so we won't be disturbed.'

We climbed the stairs and went straight into the front room, where, to my surprise, as well as Anne, Betty and Violet were there too.

It was a small but cosy room with framed family photographs covering the wallpapered walls, and a bookcase laden with paperback books. A large ginger cat sat on the back of the sofa, and Violet was leaning forward so that she didn't get in his way.

'Let me take your coat, Emmy,' said Maeve, bustling about. 'Marmalade, get off there. Emmy, sit on that chair.'

Marmalade didn't move.

'Hello, everyone,' I said, failing to put on a very good smile.

'How was it?' asked Anne. The four women waited anxiously.

I sat down on the chair with a bump. 'He wouldn't move an inch,' I said, feeling worse by the minute. 'It's quite clear that he doesn't care. It's an inconvenience to him. I'm really sorry I got you into all this.'

A chorus of denials came in response.

'Don't be soft,' said Violet.

Maeve patted my shoulder.

'He's foul,' said Betty. 'Tell us everything.'

Taking a deep breath, I recounted the entire episode. At the second time of telling, it sounded even more desperate, like a goldfish trying to take on a shark.

'He ended up by saying we were un-patriotic and that what he called a "protest" could be a matter for the police. I told him it was a Patriotic Parade but thank goodness you called it off. He's nasty with it.'

Finally, I came to what I really wanted to say.

'I'm so sorry, Anne. You said not to take any of his nonsense, but he wouldn't listen. I've really let you down. All the talk about letters and marches. It was easy for me to say. I shouldn't have let you risk so much. I'll do everything I can to help you get another job.'

Anne was sitting bolt upright in an armchair at the other end of the room. I could hardly look her in the eye.

'That man is a pig,' she said. She was as pale as ever, but her cheeks were highly coloured and red blotches had appeared on her neck. She looked even angrier than she had earlier this morning.

'How dare he?' she said, her voice shaking slightly. 'Don't you dare apologise, Emmy. You aren't the one who took her little girl into a factory. That is entirely on my head. You could have just written your articles and taken all the praise from the Ministry people, but you didn't. You've shown more interest in our welfare in the last few weeks than Mr Terry ever will.'

'That's true,' agreed Betty.

'Well, damn Mr Terry,' said Anne, which took everyone by surprise. 'And his bullying.' She looked around the room, her face set and her eyes almost black. 'I'm going to bloody well march anyway.'

She stood up, as if she wanted to start right there and then.

'All I wanted was to go to work. Look after the children and Mum, do my bit and pay my way. And I'm going to write it on a flipping sign and walk to the town hall, just as we had planned. I'll leave the kids with Mum. She won't need to know.'

I looked at the others.

'Then I'm coming with you,' said Betty. 'You're not doing it on your own.'

'He'll sack you, Bet,' said Anne.

'Not if I've resigned first.'

Marmalade had jumped onto Violet's lap. She stood up, holding him to her chest.

'I'll be there,' she said. 'I'll walk with you, too.'

I watched on. Betty was holding Anne's hand.

Marmalade wriggled and leapt out of Violet's arms, landing on the floor and arching his back. He strutted past Maeve and out of the room.

Maeve watched him, her lips pursed. Of everyone, she was the one with the most to lose. I could hear the children laughing in the other room.

'No, Maeve,' said Anne. 'It's too much of a risk. He will sack you too if you come.'

Maeve gave a little smile. 'Can we all stay at Bunty's if he does?' she said, looking at me.

'Every single one,' I said, without a shadow of a doubt.

'I'm only joking,' said Maeve.

'I'm not,' I said. 'If you don't mind it being a bit of a squeeze.'

'Count me in, then,' said Maeve. 'I don't like people who pick on my friends.'

'You lot are mad,' said Anne. Her eyes were full of tears. 'Let's do it then. Not just for me. Let's do it for Irene as well.'

There were Hear Hears all round to that.

'If it's on the twentieth as planned, would it be all right if Bunty and I still come?' I said. 'We'll stand with you or cheer you on. Whatever you want.'

'Absolutely,' said Anne. 'If you're sure.'

'I wouldn't miss it for the world,' I said.

'You can be the press,' said Betty, looking inspired. 'Take notes and interview us when we stand there, so people can see. That'll make it look more impressive.'

'Although we're going to need someone to look after the children,' said Maeve. 'Would your mum do it, Anne?'

'You could bring them with you,' I suggested. 'We said last time it's really important you don't look as if you're trying to bring down the Government. What could be less threatening than a group of women with children and prams? Unless you think they'd be frightened or upset by it of course.' I screwed up my face.

'Mine will be fine,' said Maeve. 'They like a parade. We'll tell them it's a jolly to help get somewhere for them to play while we're at work – bingo!'

'Ruby loves a parade too,' said Anne. 'She did May

Day this year and wore her little paper flower crown for days afterwards until it fell to bits.' She stopped and thought for a moment. 'Why don't we do that? Make paper flowers for them to wear. It'll be more of a carnival. We can wear them too and carry signs. No one will think we're a group of troublemakers then.'

'Anne, it's perfect,' I said. 'If it's all about being able to help the men win the war, and you have the children with you, no one will have any doubt about what you're marching for.'

'There's nothing more patriotic than a kiddie in a flowery crown,' laughed Betty. 'We'll have to take it in turns to carry Tony, though.'

'I know, he's a lump,' grinned Anne. 'He can come in his pram.'

As Maeve went to check on the children and the other women sat down again to re-start their plans, I watched quietly, joining in a little, but mostly deep in thought.

Often at work, when I opened letters to "Yours Cheerfully", the readers referred to something a friend of theirs had said. They weren't always complimentary, but invariably you knew that their friends were a central part of their world, especially with so many men now away. Whether it was Anne and the girls, or me with Bunty or Kath or Thelma, we were just the same. Sticking with each other through the best bits and the worst in the war, without even thinking – it was just what we did.

'That's sorted, then,' said Anne. 'Full steam ahead for the twentieth.'

There was a whoop from the bedroom and moments later, Ruby galloped into the front room.

'Aunty Emmy,' she cried. 'Why are you here? It's not our house.'

She bundled herself onto my lap.

'I've just called in to say hello,' I said, giving her a hug. 'How are you, Monster?'

'We're getting a bun bun,' said Ruby.

I looked at Anne.

'I'm still not sure about that,' she said. 'But I've got the very next best thing.'

'Is it biscuits?' Ruby shrieked.

'Better even than that,' said Anne. 'How would you like me to make you your very own crown?'

CHAPTER 23

A Surprise That Goes Wrong

THE JOURNEY HOME was long, with another extended wait due to a problem on the line, and not a sandwich to be had anywhere. By the time I got on the Tube to go down to *Woman's Friend*, several nights of very little sleep together with the high emotions of the morning were beginning to have their effect. I wearily trudged into the office and began to put some work into my bag so that I could spend the evening catching up on my day spent playing truant.

Kathleen told me I looked as if I needed a decent rest, which I couldn't disagree with, and I promised her I would be on far better form the next day. For now, I just wanted to go home, have a warm bath if there was any hot water, and then sit on the sofa and try not to nod off while I worked. I was also rather hoping Bunty might be cooking dinner.

By the time I got back to Pimlico, I was fit for nothing. It was well after blackout as I pushed open the front door and fumbled my way through the heavy curtain into the darkness of the hall.

To my surprise, music was coming from the drawing room. That was odd as it was a rather grand room and never used, mainly because it was far too big and always very cold. Billy Cotton and His Band were playing, and I could hear Bunty hooting with laughter, with what sounded like Thelma. They were joined by a man, whose voice I recognised at once as Charles'.

I'd had no idea he was coming. It was a smashing surprise at the end of a long couple of days and an immediate pick-me-up. I found the light switch, flicked it on and rushed down the hall, flinging open the drawing room door to greet them. The door though, didn't fling, but walloped into the back of Bunty.

'Ooof,' she cried as she nearly went flying. 'Oh, Emmy, it's you.' She sounded a little flustered.

'Sorry, Bunts,' I said. 'Did I whack you? Hello, darling, what a lovely treat. Hello, Thelma. Goodness, what are you all doing?'

I looked round the room to see that some of the furniture had been pushed to the sides and several of the dust sheets removed. A gramophone had been set up on a side table and several empty glasses sat beside it. To my travel-weary eyes, quite a party appeared to be taking place.

'I popped in to talk about food,' said Thelma.

'Darling!' said Charles very brightly. 'I was just leaving,' which was a peculiar greeting. 'I had a meeting in town so called in as a surprise. I'm so sorry I've missed you.'

He came over and kissed me.

'The trains were up the spout,' I said.

'Charles helped us move the furniture,' said Bunty. 'So we could see if it will work for your reception.' She was flushed. 'I may have overdone it,' she added and then laughed.

I couldn't quite see the joke. 'Right ho,' I said. Entirely unreasonably, I felt cross that I hadn't been there, and then I realised I was being petty and felt even crosser at myself for that. 'Well, it looks as if it will. Work, that is,' I managed, flatly.

'How did it go?' asked Charles. 'Shall I get you a drink? Come and sit down, darling, you look worn out.'

He was being quite lovely. Interested in my work, concerned that I was tired. But I wasn't in the mood for drinking, and the last time we had spoken it had been to talk about him going off to war. A cheery greeting and Shall I Get You a Drink, as if I had turned up late to a cocktail party, didn't sit agreeably with me.

'I wish I'd known you were coming,' I said, churlishly. 'It's a shame it had to be today. Still, you've had a jolly time, I see.'

I was trying to say that I was disappointed I hadn't been able to see him, but instead I sounded like a spoilt brat. Bunty and Thelma looked slightly awkward. Charles didn't say anything.

'Well,' I said. 'Charles, did you say you have to leave?'

He looked at his watch. 'I really should,' he said. 'I'm so sorry, darling. I rather hoped you might be here.'

'No, I was being shouted at by a Factory Director who wanted to call the police,' I said.

Anyone nice, or possibly less tired, would have been pleased to see him having fun with their friends. But I didn't feel nice.

'Sorry,' I managed.

'Actually,' said Charles, 'I've got some good news. That's why I wanted to see you. I rather hope you'll like it.'

He had the broadest smile and was looking both chuffed and excited at the same time. My grumpy heart melted.

'Thel, shall I put the kettle on in the kitchen?' said Bunty, diplomatically.

'You might want to hear it as well,' said Charles.

'It must be good,' I said, feeling much cheerier. 'But I really have to sit.' I pulled a dust sheet off a fancy antique chair and plonked myself down.

'Well,' said Charles, 'I won't drag it out any longer. I've just been over to St Gabriel's and managed to see

261

Reverend Lovell. This is the good part. He said if I can get us a licence, he can marry us before Christmas.'

Charles was absolutely right. It *was* the very best news. The last remains of my crossness disappeared entirely.

'Darling, that's wonderful. Thank you!' I cried, throwing myself into his arms and kissing him. Now I knew why he looked as if he had just won the Derby.

Bunty and Thelma, meanwhile, were cheering loudly.

'When?' I asked. 'We need to tell everyone. What's the actual date?'

'It's the last Saturday before Christmas,' said Charles. 'A festive wedding and with a bit of luck, people will still be able to come. What's the matter?'

'Saturday the twentieth?' I said.

'That's right. Two o'clock. And I've managed to get a seventy-two-hour pass so we can even have a honeymoon of sorts. That's not by the book at all, but the CO has been terrifically decent.'

I didn't know what to say. He looked so very happy.

But there was no way to dress things up.

'That's the day of the march,' I said.

Charles's face fell.

'But it was cancelled,' said Bunts.

I shook my head. 'Not now. They're going ahead. I've just promised Anne I'll be there as a reporter.'

'It didn't enter my head,' Charles said. 'That's rotten luck. I'm afraid Reverend Lovell said that was the only time we could possibly have.' He looked at his watch. 'Em, I'm so sorry but I really do have to go.'

Rotten luck?

That did get my goat.

'Right,' I said. 'I'll see you out.'

'I'll tidy up,' said Bunty, who seemed far more aware of the enormity of the situation than my fiancé.

'I'll help,' said Thelma quickly. 'Cheerio, Charles.'

He said Cheerio back and followed me out, shutting the drawing-room door behind him.

When I handed him his coat from where he had hung it up in the hall, he didn't put it on, but instead, tucked it under his arm and fixed me with a stare.

'You are going to come?' he said. 'To our wedding.'

'Of course, I am,' I said, crossly. 'That's a silly thing to say. Anyway, I don't have much choice. I've just missed a fleeting chance to see you and I don't know how many I'm likely to get. So if a wedding is the only way to make sure we get more than five minutes together, I suppose that'll have to do.'

I winced as I said it. Even if it was the truth, I sounded bitter. It wasn't an attractive trait.

Charles took it on the chin but didn't rise to it. Instead, he tried to be placatory. 'I know it's not easy,' he said. 'My job never is.'

I wondered if I was being slow on the uptake. He was so pleased about managing to bring the date forward and I knew I should have been thrilled about it as well. I tried not to be unreasonable, but I couldn't help but think of the morning's events.

'Well, at least you have a job,' I said. 'I've just come back from a group of people who probably haven't.'

I was already wondering how I was going to tell Anne about not being at the march.

I'd promised them, '*I wouldn't miss it for the world.*'

I closed my eyes. I couldn't miss my own wedding.

'Em, I'm really sorry about the date,' said Charles. 'Truly. But now that the Americans are involved, and the Japanese are causing chaos, everyone's plans have gone wild. I'm pretty sure we'll ship out before the New Year. Darling, I could be gone in two weeks.'

That was a punch in the gut.

'So, if we can't do the wedding on that date . . .' he began.

'Of course we will,' I snapped. It came out angrily which wasn't how I had meant to say it at all. *Gone in two weeks.* It made me feel sick.

Charles sighed heavily. 'Look, I can't believe I'm suggesting this, but could you go to the march first?'

It was a decent enough thought, but impossible. 'I'll never get back in time,' I said. 'It's taken me nearly three hours today, and that's on a weekday. Don't worry. I'll tell them I won't be there. They'll be fine.'

It wasn't true and he knew it.

If anyone had ever sounded less enthusiastic about setting a wedding date, I was yet to hear of them. I hated myself for that. But I hated myself almost as much for letting Anne down.

'I'd better go,' said Charles, dully. 'If I miss this train I'll be put on report and then I won't be going anywhere.'

I didn't dare say a word.

He shoved his arms into his greatcoat and shrugged it on. Then he stopped and we stood staring at each other until I sighed and shook my head.

'Thank you for trying,' I said. 'Don't miss your train.'

Charles nodded. He couldn't look less like a man who was marrying someone he loved.

'I'm sorry the surprise hasn't been what I hoped,' he said.

I didn't know how to answer that, so I didn't say anything.

Charles picked up his cap from the hall table and gave me the briefest of kisses on my cheek.

Then, as I didn't say goodbye back, he walked to the door and was gone.

★

I had watched Charles carefully pull the blackout curtain behind him and then listened as he shut the front door, wishing all the time that I could somehow find the will to raise my voice and call out, 'Goodbye.' But it just wouldn't come.

I walked slowly back to the drawing room and tried to gather my thoughts. Just a few hours before, I had raged at Mr Terry, in part inspired by the thought of my boy going off to war. And now, when that same boy had made a lovely effort to surprise me with a new date for our wedding, I had hardly managed to agree to turn up. I couldn't blame that on just being tired.

Bunty had turned off the gramophone and was now smoothing a dust sheet over a chair. She turned round as I came in.

Thelma had put her coat on. 'I'll get going, love,' she said. 'I'm so sorry about tonight.'

'It's OK, Thel,' I said. 'Sorry you got dragged into it.'

'See you soon,' she said, giving me a concerned squeeze on the arm. 'Bye, Bunty. I'll see myself out.'

As Thelma left, I sat down, put my hands over my face and shook my head.

'I'm sorry, Em,' said Bunty. 'It must have looked as if we were having a beano while you were having an utterly rotten day.'

It was her way of excusing me for being so off.

'It wasn't that,' I said.

I looked around the room, trying to find the right words. With its tall Georgian windows permanently curtained and all the furniture in shrouds, it wouldn't have been out of place if Miss Havisham had been sitting in the corner next to a mouldy old wedding cake. Despite that, I knew the room would soon be transformed. A ton of elbow grease would bring it up to scratch and it was easy to imagine it filled with festive trimmings and even more festive family and friends celebrating Charles and me getting married. I should have been the happiest girl in the world.

'I just wish he'd checked,' I said, finally. 'Am I being horrible, Bunts? Oh, it's not just the fact it's now an awful clash with the march, although that's bad enough.' I grappled with how to explain. 'Now that Charles has sorted a new date he'll go back to his billet, back to planning how to head off with the chaps to goodness knows where, while you and I will re-arrange everything so that the day is still lovely and then he will leave and all I get to do is wait here and hope that one day I might be lucky enough to see him again.'

I paused to draw breath.

'Are you sure you don't want a drink?' said Bunty.

'No, thanks.' I looked up at her. 'I'm being vile, aren't I? Bunts, I love Charles. I really, *really*, love him. And now I've just ruined his big surprise.' I groaned. 'I'm rubbish at this.'

Bunty frowned. 'At what?'

'I don't know – romance. I had one fiancé who dumped me and now I've just had a scene with a lovely one who wants to get married as soon as we possibly can.'

'The last one doesn't count, because he was a stupid, boring fool,' said Bunty, matter-of-factly. 'You are right though, this one is lovely. And if you want my view, you aren't being vile at all.' She got up from the chair and came and sat next to me. 'Look, you've only just heard that Charles is being posted. On top of that you have two jobs and you're trying to help Anne. That's tons on your mind.'

She smiled kindly. 'Don't be so hard on yourself, Em. At least you two have now had your first lovers' tiff. It is the first, isn't it? Please tell me you haven't been secretly rowing for weeks?'

She said it with a twinkle in her eye.

'Never,' I admitted.

'Thank goodness for that. So, what are you going to do?'

'I'm going to marry him.'

'And the march?'

I chewed my lip for a second. 'I can't let them down, Bunts. There may only be the four of them there. Betty said she'd resign if she had to, but they won't let Anne do it alone. But I haven't enough time.'

Bunty and I sat quietly for a moment. I knew she was thinking about Anne and the girls too.

'Right then,' she said, breaking the silence. 'You're on.'

'What do you mean?'

My best friend smiled. 'What kind of a chief bridesmaid would let the bride go off on her own on her wedding day?' Bunty looked resolute. 'We both know full well that you're going to try to get to the march, and I'm pretty sure you told them I would be with you.'

She knew me too well.

'I did think you'd want to.'

'Of course I do,' spluttered Bunty. 'I've no intention of letting them down either.' She looked at me sternly. 'I'm getting you a drink whether you like it or not. Having to organise a wedding and a round trip to the back of beyond is going to take us some time.'

Bunty got up.

'Get your thinking cap on, Emmeline Lake,' she said. 'We're going to work out how you can do both.'

CHAPTER 24

It Gives Me Nearly
Four Hours

THE MARCH WAS to start at ten o'clock on the Saturday morning. Our wedding was at two. There *was* time, but it was going to be horribly close.

Bunty and I went down to the kitchen and pored over the train timetable, which in peacetime would have made perfect sense. Now though, everyone knew that it made little or none.

'When it comes down to it,' said Bunty, 'it's a gamble. Everything on the winner, no hedging your bets.' She blew out her cheeks. 'It's going to be awfully tight.'

'I know,' I said. 'But I promised. Oh, Bunts, you should have seen Anne this morning. This means everything to her and I won't let her down now. I'm going to go as a reporter. I haven't heard back from all the magazines yet, so I may still get someone to take the story. And anyway, doing their own event was my idea.'

'Then you have to go,' said Bunty.

'But what if I can't get back?'

'Then don't,' said Bunty, who was playing devil's advocate far too well for my liking.

I grimaced.

'This is horrible,' I said. 'If I don't support the girls it goes against everything I believe in, and if I can't get back

268

to London in time, I'll miss my one chance to marry the man I really do love.'

I got up and wandered around the kitchen.

'I need to speak with Charles,' I said. 'We didn't even say goodbye properly. I hate that with anyone, let alone him. In fact, I'll send a telegram tomorrow morning. I'll write a proper letter as well, but I can't spend all weekend wondering about things. I'll go mad.'

'What will you say?' said Bunty.

'No idea,' I said. 'Something like, *I'm sorry I was cross, and I do want to marry you more than anything, it's just that I wish you'd said before you'd gone ahead and sorted things without talking to me.* You know, something like that.'

Bunty was counting on her fingers.

'I don't want to be unkind, but you do know it's a penny a word after the first sixpence, don't you?' she said, smiling. 'How about you just ask him to give you a call. Then you can talk it through properly.'

'Bunty Tavistock,' I said, pretending to scold, 'my entire future is hanging by a thread and you're telling me to watch the pennies so the pounds will look after themselves?'

Bunty shook her head.

'No, you chump,' she replied. 'I'm telling you to talk to him so he can help us come up with a plan.'

POST OFFICE TELEGRAM

AM SO SORRY EM MY DARLING COULD NOT FEEL

WORSE WILL CALL REV LOVELL RE TIME MAY

OFFER HIM BRIBE WE WILL SORT THIS CALL

YOU ASAP = ALL MY LOVE C.

POST OFFICE TELEGRAM

DARLING CHARLES I FEEL TERRIBLE WILL

WRITE PROPERLY BUT WOULD LOVE TO TALK =

ALL MY LOVE E PS DO YOU THINK REV

LOVELL COULD BE PAID OFF

POST OFFICE TELEGRAM

DEAREST EM SO GLAD WE SPOKE DARLING THE

REV HAS WORKED MIRACLE AND CAN DO 3PM IS

THIS ANY GOOD? = ALL MY LOVE C XXX

POST OFFICE TELEGRAM

YOU ARE BEST BOYFRIEND IN WORLD GIVES ME

4 HOURS MUST BE ENOUGH THANK YOU FOR

UNDERSTANDING I LOVE YOU I WILL BE THERE

ON SAT I PROMISE PHONE ME XXX

CHAPTER 25

Mr Collins Returns

CHARLES HAD MANAGED to get us a precious hour more.
It had to be enough. War on or not, Christmas was
Reverend Lovell's busiest time, he told Charles, and if the
church collection box had a pound note for everyone who
wanted to get married before the New Year, they would
be halfway to buying a new roof.

It wasn't so much the additional hour that meant the
most to me. It was that Charles understood how I felt
about my commitment to Anne.

Bunty and I worked out the finer details and we felt
confident that if we went for the start of the march around
the market square, took tons of pictures, and interviewed
the girls outside the town hall, we could leave by eleven
with double the amount of time that it took when the
trains ran to plan. The Reverend's Hour, as we had started
to call it, gave us the cushion we needed.

Meanwhile, Charles would come to Guy's flat in
London by lunchtime and the two of them would make
their way to the church for three o'clock.

If I had any second thoughts about trying to fit both
a trip to Berkshire and a wedding in Pimlico into one day,
the decision was made for me the next morning when I
received a letter from *Pictorial Week*. They would consider
a short piece about a women's march if I could provide

photographs of a decent quality and one hundred words of prose. I hastily sent a reply, and as I sat on the bus on the way to work, scrawled a postcard to Anne. She would be thrilled.

★

On the Monday before the wedding, I pushed open the double doors and made my way down the *Woman's Friend* corridor, passing the familiar lines of artwork which decorated the walls. Some months ago, Mr Collins had declared that Mr Brand's illustrations for the weekly stories were too lovely to be thrown away after the magazine went to print, so we had arranged to have our favourites framed. Now dramatic scenes were proudly displayed – an ice-skating accident and a romantic clinch, a young woman looking determined in a field, and just outside the office I shared with Kath and Hester, the most beautiful illustration of a bride being walked up the aisle by her father. She was serenity itself.

'Let's hope so,' I said, under my breath.

I intended to work a long day to make up for being out of the office at Anne's and I was looking forward to focusing on something other than myself. Now that letters were coming in thick and fast, Mrs Mahoney and I had resumed discussing ideas for a series of helpful "Yours Cheerfully" advice leaflets on popular subjects. This morning I planned to bury myself in writing a draft of "Making Friends", a leaflet to help readers settle in if they had to live away from home for the first time. We were getting a lot of letters about that now.

It was a dark morning, another dull day in what had been a mild and murky December so far, and a light was coming from the open door to Mr Collins' office.

I quietly continued to my desk, took off my coat,

hat and gloves and paused for a moment. In all the hoo-hah with Charles over the weekend, I hadn't asked him if he had spoken with Guy. Clearly his brother had returned to work, but I had no idea how he might be. With the office not yet busy, it was a good time to find out.

A normal enough, 'Come in,' answered my gentle tap on the Editor's door.

'Hello, Emmy,' said Mr Collins, putting down his pen and looking up from his desk. He had lost weight and needed a haircut even more than usual.

'Hello,' I said, just managing not to add, 'You look awful,' and instead, asking him how he was.

'I'm fine thank you. Do I look grim?' he answered.

'You do a bit. A go with some scissors wouldn't do any harm.'

It was the most British of ways to tell him I was concerned.

'Point taken,' he said. 'Has everything been all right here? I hope I didn't leave everyone in the lurch.'

'Not at all,' I said. 'It's been fine.'

Other than urgent calls from the owner of Launceston Press and a Government department.

'Lord Overton called and so did Mr Clough,' I said, lightly. 'But we got a commendation at the Ministry meeting,' I added, more brightly. 'By name. No one else was mentioned at all. Mrs Edwards said, Brava, and people looked round. I do so wish you'd been there.'

It made Mr Collins smile. 'Well done,' he said. 'I hope you had buns?' He seemed keen to talk about work rather than himself, which was entirely understandable, so I continued.

'We wanted to wait until you were back. Mrs Edwards and Mr Simons were both terribly nice. They missed you.

Mrs Edwards said you used to get into arguments with people when you were young.'

'A contentious allegation,' said Mr Collins, 'and something I would hotly deny. Come and sit down and tell me everything that's been happening. Between you and me, I've had a rough couple of weeks and hearing what you lot have been up to will be music to my ears.'

He leant back, wearily. I had never heard him admit to difficulty with anything before. Even though he was the same age as my parents, I rather wanted to put him on a train and send him to my mother so she could look after him for a bit.

'I would offer you a tot of brandy if it wasn't nine o'clock in the morning,' said Mr Collins, attempting levity. 'Don't look alarmed, I'm joking. I never touch the stuff. That bottle I have seen you pretending not to notice for the last year is purely a souvenir.'

I glanced at the half-empty bottle on one of his bookshelves. He was right, I had sneaked the odd look.

'I did notice the level never goes down,' I admitted.

'There you are. Now, start with the Ministry. Possibly with why the subject of getting into arguments came up.'

For the next half an hour I updated Mr Collins on everything that had gone on, at least in terms of work, rather than concerning his brother. He listened closely, occasionally asking a question, but mostly taking it all in.

I saved the latest about Chandlers and Mr Terry for the end.

'What a delightful piece of work he is,' he said, as I described our last meeting. 'There's no sensible reason for Terry to be so obstreperous about the idea of nursery facilities. They won't cost him anything if Chandlers apply to the Government.' He rubbed his chin. 'I would put money on it being something of a chest-beating performance on his part. Do you know what the women will do?'

I hesitated. 'They're still doing their march,' I said.

'Good for them. That takes some guts.'

'And I'm going too. With Bunty. She's going to take photographs and I'm going to interview them. One of the weekly news pictorials says they may run it if it's good enough. They won't use my name.'

I had wanted to say it calmly, rather than blurting it out like a guilty secret. I looked at the bookcase behind him, with sudden interest.

Mr Collins gave nothing away.

'I don't even know if we can make it look newsworthy,' I said. 'Mr Terry has had notices put up that say people will get the sack if they join in. He's also said he has friends in the Labour Ministry. I think he's trying to scare me.'

'I'm sure he is,' said Mr Collins. 'Are we running the last piece in the factory series?'

'As long as it passes the Censors,' I said. 'Which I think it will.'

'Good. That should placate everyone. And you're sure you think it wise that you go to the march?'

I blanched at that. 'Yes. I think it's right that I do,' I said. 'They're aiming to make it more of a parade than anything contentious.'

'Are you going as a friend, or as a journalist from *Woman's Friend*? In the light of your discussion with this Miss Eggerton.'

'Anne is my friend,' I said. 'And so are the others. And no, it probably isn't as a journalist from *Woman's Friend*, which is why I have tried to get interest from the news magazines. I know we wouldn't print something like that.'

'That's true,' he said. 'Go on.'

'But I think there's a good argument that we should.

Not necessarily this particular event, but I do think we should be sticking up for the readers on something like this.'

I shifted in the chair, bit at one of my fingernails, and when Mr Collins said nothing, I decided to plough on. 'The thing is,' I said, 'we've been doing all this stuff in our Big Ministry Plan, and it's gone down frightfully well with important people, at least, so far and we are rightly all ever so proud of it. I don't want us to get in any trouble or undo any of that. But if you ask me, we're not quite doing what we've always said we would. When the Ministry first asked all the magazines to come up with ideas, you said it was our chance to do *more* than do our bit.'

I quoted his own words back to him.

'You said to think about what our readers wanted, what they deserved. And how could we help them. You said we had to look after them.'

I realised I had gone hot in the face.

'If Anne and her friends aren't those readers,' I said, 'then exactly who is?'

I shut up. I hadn't been rude, but I had spoken from the heart. More than that, I didn't have a clear answer to that question. I had struggled with it for weeks now and there was no point saying to not get involved. I for one couldn't separate my job from my life.

Mr Collins nodded, thoughtfully. 'I agree,' he said. 'The Chandlers women deserve to be heard. Go to the march. See if you can place a piece on it. Do what you can.'

I broke into an enormous smile. 'Thank you,' I said. 'What about Lord Overton and Mr Clough?'

'I'll call them,' he said calmly. 'There is of course, the off-chance that they may not be asking for me in order to complain about you. World spinning on its own axis and all th'

I blushed. It was a good point. 'There's just one other thing,' I said. 'About the march.'

'Yes?'

'It's on the day of the wedding.'

At this, Mr Collins momentarily lost a hold of his usual composure.

'In Berkshire,' I added.

'Ah.' He raised one eyebrow slightly. 'Emmy, do you remember about half an hour ago when I suggested that hearing what you'd been up to during my absence might cheer me up?'

'Yes.'

'Could you just confirm that this is still part of it?'

'Don't worry,' I said brightly. 'It's going to be fine.'

'Oh, good,' he said. 'Does Charles know?'

'Yes.'

'What did he say?'

'He wasn't entirely sure to start off,' I said, at which point Mr Collins made a funny noise that sounded like he was beginning to choke. 'But Bunty and I are coming up with a plan.'

'Dear God,' said Mr Collins.

'Yes,' I said.

He stood up, ran his hand through his hair and then sat down again.

'Honestly,' I said. 'Speak to Charles. I know he's been trying to get hold of you to tell you. You know, Guy,' I added, 'I really wouldn't do it if I didn't think I would be back in time.' I had never called him Guy at work, but now I was speaking to him as a future sister-in-law, not an employee.

'I promise I won't mess it up for Charles.'

Mr Collins smiled.

'All right,' he said. 'It sounds as if you've got everything covered. Crack on with that last feature, make up any hours that you've missed, and go to the march. In the meantime, I am going to sit here quietly and write a memo to Lord Overton telling him I am never going on leave again.'

'Good,' I said, springing to my feet. 'Mrs Mahoney worries about you when you're not here. I'll leave you alone now. Thank you for being so nice about it.'

'My pleasure,' he said.

I hesitated for a moment.

'I'm very sorry,' I said. 'About the rotten time you've had.'

As soon as I had walked into his office, I could tell by his face that his old army friend had been lost.

'Thank you,' he said, quietly. 'That's very kind.'

I nodded and seeing how sad he looked, quietly made my way out into the corridor.

But as I left, he called out.

'Emmy Lake, there's one caveat to all this. Whatever you do, don't you dare miss my brother's wedding.'

CHAPTER 26

All Aboard

'AND YOU'RE SURE the paper chains aren't too much?'

Five days later, Bunty and I were walking towards our platform at Paddington station. We had a march to go to and then a wedding, but she was having an attack of doubts.

'Not at all,' I said, confidently. 'The whole room looks beautiful. The holly is lovely, we have the biggest bunch of mistletoe I've ever seen in my life, and the paper chains make it a proper Christmas wedding reception.'

'Newspaper though, Em,' said Bunty. 'I'm still not sure.'

'Bunts,' I said. 'When's the last time you saw green and red crepe paper? Even if we had a thousand pounds, we'd have struggled to find any. Anyway, I like the newspaper chains. It's topical. And by the time Roy and Fred have set up the music, and Thelma and Kath have put out the buffet, it will look like a palace. Everyone has been wonderful. I don't know how I'll ever be able to thank you all.'

Bunty looked happy. 'Everyone wanted to,' she said. 'Although I do slightly question Fred's recipe for a punch. It sounds revolting.'

'It does,' I agreed. 'But that's the whole point of punch, isn't it? According to Mrs Croft's Festive Special in "What's In The Hotpot?" we can throw any old thing in there and it will be fine.'

'What if someone chokes? Is this our platform?'

'Father's a doctor. He'll be able to save them. Yes, it is,' I said, looking up at the Departures Board. 'With Daddy, Roy and Fred, Charles's army chums, and Jack if he can get leave, we've almost all the services covered. There isn't much that can go wrong that one of them won't be able to sort out.'

'The upside of war,' said Bunty, shaking her head.

We showed our tickets at the barrier and began to walk down the platform. People who had managed to get time off at Christmas were crowding towards the edge so they could be first on the train. In normal years they would have been laden down with packages and nice-smelling things from London shops. You might even have seen a big ham sitting in the overhead storage nets. Now, though, it wasn't nearly as ostentatious. It was the third Christmas of the war and the shops had had very little to offer. Home-made gifts were saving the day and I wondered how many people at the station carried crocheted and glued-together presents in their cardboard suitcases and hat boxes.

I hadn't thought as far as Christmas. Having scrambled to get everything ready for the wedding, as well as trying to keep up with the plans for the march through daily letters and phone calls to and from Anne, I hadn't had time for anything – even stage-fright – until now. Bunty and I had planned the day as meticulously as we could. We would be back and at the church well before three o'clock. We had to be.

'You've gone quiet,' said Bunty. 'What is it?'

'I can't quite believe that by the end of today I'll be married,' I said, not mentioning any jitters about the timing. 'Here we are on a platform, me with my notebook, you with your camera, and in a few hours' time we'll be in a church. It doesn't feel real. I'm actually marrying Charles.'

Bunty laughed and put her arm through mine.

'It feels real to me,' she said. 'Under this great thick coat, I'm wearing the fanciest dress ever. My best friend made it for me and it's gorgeous.'

'Aren't you freezing?' I asked.

'I've got a woolly on and thick knickers,' she said. 'If only William was here, he'd be mad for me in these.'

She smiled.

'Oh, Bunts,' I said, squeezing her arm.

'I do want you to know, I'm all right,' she said. 'And I'm going to enjoy every minute of today. Even if I am wearing knickers meant for a granny.'

Before I could say anything, a harassed-sounding lady carrying several bags and trailing two children in school uniforms pushed past us in an effort to secure a good spot.

'Father Christmas knows exactly where Aunty Flory lives,' she said crossly. 'He's very clever like that, but you have to remember he's run out of fruit.'

Bunty and I tried not to laugh, especially when the bigger child asked why Father Christmas couldn't have stocked up.

'Here it comes!' shouted the smaller one as he heard the first sound of the train puffing its way into the station. Smoke rose up into the heights of Paddington's enormous domed roof, and Bunty and I stepped aside so that the little family could get in first. Despite the number of people leaving the city, the train had lots of carriages and we were confident we would get seats.

We helped them with their bags and as doors began to slam shut along the train, Bunty climbed in.

'Mind your camera,' I warned as its case threatened

to swing out from her shoulder and bash itself on the side of the train.

'Gosh, yes,' she said, turning around as she was halfway in. Then she stopped, looked down the platform and started waving so frantically she almost fell out. 'WE'RE OVER HERE,' she shouted. 'IN THIS ONE.'

I turned round to see what was causing the fuss.

There, tearing down the platform, in his army greatcoat and cap, was my lunatic of a fiancé.

'Nothing to do with me,' said Bunty, still waving.

As people hauled up the last of their bags into the carriages and the remaining doors were closed, I stayed on the platform, holding ours open as wide as it would go.

'WAIT! PLEASE, WAIT FOR HIM,' I yelled at the guard, who was looking at his fob watch and coming towards us in a predatory way. 'WE'RE GETTING MARRIED,' I shouted for extra weight.

'We're nearly a minute over,' said the guard, who clearly wasn't a romantic.

Charles was now at the next-door carriage, red-faced but keeping up a very impressive sprint.

'EM,' he shouted as he ran. 'KEEP THE DOOR OPEN.'

'I'm getting out,' declared Bunty.

'Bernard, Larry, don't move,' said the lady with the children, as she got off the train as well. 'THEY CAN'T GO WITHOUT ME,' she bellowed at the poor guard. 'How exciting,' she said, to Bunty. 'Love's young dream.'

'Darling!' gasped Charles, as he finally made it and hurled his arms round me, kissing me passionately and then, less romantically, declaring he had given himself a stitch. 'Thank you,' he panted at the guard.

'ALL ABOARD,' shouted the man.

'Not yet,' said Charles, recovering himself well. 'He's nearly here.'

'WAIT,' came a voice, rather more faintly than everyone else. 'Good grief.'

Mr Collins was running at a decent pace, his hat rammed down onto his head and his coat flapping behind him to reveal a very smart suit.

'Goodness,' said the lady.

'His brother,' said Bunty, filling her in. 'Half-brother really. He's a lot older,' she added, politely lowering her voice.

The guard was very nearly at the end of his tether. 'ALL ABOARD,' he shouted unnecessarily loudly.

'YOU CAN DO IT, SIR!' shouted either Bernard or Larry who were both hanging out of the door.

Mr Collins finally staggered up to us, breathing heavily. 'You're very kind,' he managed, speaking to the guard. 'So sorry. Shall we? Ladies first.'

Bernard and Larry's mother nodded prettily and chivvied the boys back into the carriage as the guard blew his whistle and more or less pushed the rest of us in.

'Not that it isn't utterly lovely to see you,' I began, feeling rather thrilled and turning to Charles as we all took our seats, 'but what on earth are you both doing here?'

Charles put his arm around me.

'It's not that I don't trust you to get back on time,' he said. 'It's just that I thought you might need a little assistance should anything go wrong. You know, if you have to steal a car or something to get back.'

Bernard and Larry's eyes nearly popped out of their heads.

'I can steal my own car,' I said, in mock-indignation.

'Yes, but you don't actually drive,' said Charles. 'Yet. I know. Are you all right, Guy?'

'I'm too old for this,' said his brother, getting his breath back and looking as if he was enjoying himself. 'May have burst a lung. I've brought a spare camera,' he said, turning to Bunty. 'I thought it might be useful if you run out of film.'

He handed it to her, and Bunty gave a squeak.

'I say, it's a Rangefinder,' she said. 'That's heaps nicer than mine.'

'Not at all,' said Mr Collins. 'Have a look and see what you think.'

As Bunty and Mr Collins began to talk about photography, Charles turned to me and smiled.

'I'm so pleased you're here,' I said, quietly.

'Are you sure?' said Charles. 'I did um and ahh over it. That's why we nearly missed the train. I know you don't need me with you, darling, but I just thought if something did go wrong, or held you up, I'd rather be with you missing the wedding, than us being apart.' He patted his breast pocket, gently. 'I have the ring with me, but as far as I'm concerned, I don't care. After today, we're married, legally or not.'

'Me too,' I said. 'Although it's supposed to be awfully bad luck seeing each other before the ceremony.'

Charles pulled a dramatic, mock-horrified face, and I laughed.

'You do know I'm on a serious journalistic assignment, don't you?' I said.

'Absolutely,' replied Charles. 'That's why I'm proud of you.' He dropped his voice. 'You've got a dreadful boss, though.'

'I heard that,' said his brother.

'So did we,' said Bernard and Larry. 'Miss, might you show us your camera, please?'

As Bunty began to show the boys how to look through

the viewfinder, I sat back happily and leaned into Charles. He was right that Bunty and I were more than capable of going to the march and getting to the wedding in time, but I was delighted he had come to show his support.

Now my thoughts turned to Anne Oliver and the Chandlers women.

There was so much riding on this morning, and it most definitely wasn't without risk. I was pleased to bring two more people who would be on their side. I just hoped other people outside the town hall would feel the same way.

While Betty and the others had made extra efforts to keep this morning's march secret, we all knew that there was a good chance Mr Terry would have found out. I had no idea what he was likely to do if that happened, but I would put money on the fact he would not play fair.

All we could do now was get there and see.

CHAPTER 27

I Want to Tell You About My Husband

WE WERE LUCKY. The train stopped once in a siding for twenty minutes, but we passed the time with a spirited game of 'I went to the Shop and I bought . . .' which ended in an unsurprising dead heat between Bernard and Larry, and showed that thinking about vegetables alphabetically could take one's mind off nearly anything.

Wishing each other a happy Christmas and thanking the boys' mother for her kind wishes for the wedding, the four of us got off the train, and as we had decided during the journey, immediately split up. Bunty as photographer stuck with me so that we could be members of the press, and Charles and Mr Collins would pretend to be bystanders and give the women a cheer if it looked as if they needed it.

We were to stay within eyesight in case anything funny happened, and together or not, we all *had* to be on the twenty past eleven train back to Paddington.

Sharing a carriage with the family on the train had meant the mood had been light, with chatter and games suitable for eight-year-olds, but as soon as our journey was over, it felt entirely different. I was back on Mr Terry's ground.

I didn't know what to expect, but any giddiness around Charles racing into view earlier quickly disappeared. There was nothing giddy about what Anne and the others were doing. For all the plans to have the children wear flowers, and pretend it was a parade, the point remained entirely serious. Someone had to begin to listen.

Charles and Guy followed Bunty and me at a distance, not looking out of place as several soldiers also got off, as did a smart-looking naval officer.

Bunts and I walked almost in silence up to the market square to position ourselves very close to the start of the march. We planned to follow it down to the town hall, keeping our distance. My only worry was that if Ruby saw us, anonymity would go straight out the door. It would be hard to appear like a reporter if I was being a human carousel for my small friend.

Anne had been right in her prediction about the town being busy. On a bright winter morning, even if there was little to be bought in the shops, it hadn't stopped people coming to browse. Women with baskets looked determined, while older couples walked more slowly, but on just as much of a mission. There were uniforms everywhere and a definite sense that Christmas was on the way.

'Hurry up, Nan,' said a brisk young Wren to a cheery-looking lady. 'I've only got forty-eight hours and I'm halfway through that.'

The fruit and veg stall was doing a brisk trade, and a queue wound its way out of the butcher's as clusters of women chatted together or watched their children run around in the square. As was the fact everywhere, there was little in the windows. The days of endless fat plucked turkeys hung up in rows had temporarily gone. I overheard someone saying there was chicken and through force of habit I nearly checked my bag for my ration book.

The Christmas tree though hadn't let anyone down. A healthy fir at least twelve feet high had been erected in the square and decorated with dozens of different widths of red ribbons. A small sign had been put up beside it, thanking members of the public for their donations and saying that when the tree came down after Christmas, the ribbons would be washed and sold to go towards the town's War Bonds fund. A small child was trying unsuccessfully to untie one at the back.

To my concern, a Salvation Army band were playing carols close to the tree. A corporal was rattling a tin, again for the war effort, and wishing people a happy Christmas whether they put anything in it or not.

I frowned. None of us had thought of this. The band could well drown out the women, or worse, the women would look as if they were trying to take attention away from the Sally Army who were trying to raise funds.

There was nothing we could do about it now.

'I didn't think about the band,' said Bunty, noticing me watching.

'They'll be here soon,' I said, checking my watch yet again. My stomach was jumping all over the place with butterflies. I wondered how Anne and Betty and the others must be feeling.

'Do you think Mr Terry will come?' whispered Bunty.

'No. I think he'll stay well away,' I said. 'But I bet he'll send people from the factory to see which women are here.'

'And sack them?'

'If he can. But this isn't a protest, it's a patriotic "Help Us in the War Effort" parade.'

'Good point,' said Bunty. 'I'll get the camera out. Guy explained twice how to use it, so I hope I'll be OK.' She took the very up to date camera out of its leather case and had a practice, sizing up shots and playing with the aperture. 'There's Charles,' she said, surreptitiously. 'By the newsagent.'

I glanced to my right and saw Charles lost in a newspaper as any serviceman would be. Searching the square, I could see Mr Collins looking in the taped-up window of a ladies' clothes shop, for all the world a baffled husband plucking up courage to go in and buy something for his wife.

On current performance, they would both make very good spies.

The Salvation Army had just got to the descant in 'Hark the Herald Angels Sing' and I wished I could have enjoyed it, as they were playing quite beautifully. As they came to the end and several people clapped, I was delighted to see the musicians putting down their instruments as their leader told them to have a break for some tea.

'That's good,' I whispered to Bunty. 'Come on, Anne.' I stamped my feet on the ground and jigged around a little, not through cold, but anticipation.

'Hold on,' said Bunty. 'What's that? Is it singing?'

We looked at each other as a group of female voices grew louder. It *was* singing.

Then we saw them. Rounding the market square corner and marching down the side by the shops.

Anne and Betty, Maeve, Violet and Irene, together with what must have been over twenty other women.

Some of them were pushing prams, some holding the hands of warmly wrapped-up children, and almost all of them carrying signs. And every single one was wearing something floral.

With much of it in red, white and blue, from their brightly coloured scarves to home-made rosette-style brooches and little flags on sticks stuck to the prams, for all the world it really was a parade.

To the tune of 'My Old Man Said Follow the Van' they were singing the most patriotic song you might ever hear.

'My old man
Said, "Love, do all you can,"
To help the war work effort every day.
So, off I went and signed up to be a worker,
Proud to help our boys, cos us girls are never shirkers.
Now we say to you daughters, you mothers and
supporters
Of our boys who fight so we are free,
Please all sign up and join us, but we also beg, please
help us
Cos us factory mums with kids need nurseries.'

It was inspired. As their voices rang out across the
square, for all the colour and spectacle it made on a
Saturday morning in a small town, you could see that to
a woman, the marchers were serious.

They may have been singing, and wearing pretty
scarves, but their signs and placards were clear.

Anne had tied one to Tony's pram that read, 'MY
MUMMY WANTS TO HELP WIN THE WAR'. Maeve
and her girls had used chalk to write on blackout cards,
'NURSERIES FOR KIDS, WAR WORK FOR
MOTHERS', while another pram sported a sign saying,
'HELP MUMMY HELP OUR DADDY'. Two women I
didn't recognise held pieces of cardboard that read, 'WE
NEED NURSERIES TO HELP WIN THE WAR'.

Irene walked next to Anne. She was without Sheila and
Enid who were staying with Anne's mum as it was far too
soon for them to be involved in a public show. Betty was
on Irene's other side, placard in one hand and holding
Irene's hand with the other. Irene's sign simply said, 'WAR
WIDOWS NEED NURSERIES'.

And at the front of them all, holding tightly onto Anne's
coat, marched Ruby, wearing a cardboard crown covered

in scrunched-up pieces of newspaper that had been painted in different colours. She wonkily carried her own little sign which she must have written herself. It was one great big, lovely scribble.

They all looked so spectacular, it was all I could do not to jump up and down and cheer, but keeping incognito for now, I ducked behind two women who had stopped to watch. Bunty hid behind the camera, trying to get the best angles, her walking stick under one arm for now, with Bunts choosing her shot carefully so as not to waste precious film.

When the song came to an end, the women began to chant.

'TO WIN THE WAR, WE'RE ASKING, PLEASE,
HELP US GET OUR NURSERIES.'

It was impossible to ignore them, and the Christmas shoppers began to stop and watch, some with amusement, others with interest.

'Look at his little face,' said a woman near me, pointing at Baby Tony in his pram. 'Isn't he a cherub?'

'That looks like your Edna,' said someone else in surprise.

'Give a woman the flaming vote,' muttered an elderly man, who then stomped away in the opposite direction.

The marchers started singing again as they continued walking around the square, and more people began to watch. I thought I saw Mrs Noakes from Chandlers at one point but couldn't be sure. There was no sign of Mr Terry or Mr Rice.

When they came round the second time, to stop outside the town hall, Ruby started to wave at the growing crowd while trotting along on her little stubby legs and gamely managing to keep up. She was hard to resist, and several people waved back, which only encouraged her more, until she was waving so furiously that her paper crown was halfway over her face.

Just as Anne bent down to fix it, Bunty stepped forward and took a photograph. It was enough to catch Anne's eye and before I slipped back into the growing crowd, I was able to give her a huge smile. Now she knew we were here. Having sorted out Ruby's crown and with a quick beam of recognition, Anne nudged Betty, who then broke into a smile as well.

Now, as the march came to a stop, they passed the Salvation Army band who were watching, as curious as anyone. A contingent of the women broke ranks to put pennies in the collecting tins. It was a gesture that could not go unmissed.

At the town hall, the women stopped singing, and gathered into a group. Several people clapped although they kept their distance, waiting to see what would happen next. Betty, who was now at the edge of the marchers, was both unsurprised and ready when the fruit and veg man nipped over and handed her two wooden crates. I guessed she had charmed him into it before the start of the march.

It would have been easy to stand back and enjoy watching my friends, but as I knew the plan was for them to now speak to the crowd, my nervousness returned. There was no doubt that Mr Terry would have sent people, I just didn't know who, or where they would be. I began to search the crowd, looking for men I thought might fit the bill. Anyone in uniform could be ruled out of course, and that cut things down significantly. I kept looking.

The first candidate fitted the bill.

It was Mr Rice.

I put my head down and swiftly about-turned. He was standing with a pleasant-looking woman in a brown hat, and they could have been any middle-aged couple out for the Saturday shop. But he was watching Anne and the others intently.

Just near him were two taller, younger men, in civilian dress. I perhaps wouldn't have picked them out, but one appeared to be searching the crowd as much as I was and the other had his hands in his pockets and was making a show of whistling and not being interested in the march. As bad acting went, it was a winner. I watched him closely. I couldn't be sure, but I thought he might have been one of the foremen I'd seen at work on my first visit to Chandlers.

I moved back towards Anne. She was wearing the same black coat that she had on when we first met, and I hoped she'd layered up underneath. As well as her floral scarf, she was wearing a Royal Navy silver sweetheart brooch. She had a megaphone in her hand and looked apprehensive, but as I watched, she said something to Irene and then climbed up onto one of the crates.

I took out my notebook.

The women stopped their chant and broke into applause for Anne, who cleared her throat and took a deep breath.

'Good morning, ladies and gentlemen,' she said. Then she cleared her throat again. 'My name is Mrs Anne Oliver and I am a war worker.'

The other women clapped again. A soldier nearby shouted, 'Good girl,' and his friend joined in with a, 'Well done, love. Good on you.'

Anne gave them a shy smile and continued. 'I am a war worker and a mother. I have two small children.' She glanced down at Ruby, who was with Violet, and trying on her scarf. 'I want to tell you about their father, my husband. His name was Corporal Anthony Oliver, and he was killed at Dunkirk.'

CHAPTER 28

Demonstrations Are Not Allowed

AS SOON AS Anne said that, she looked at Ruby to assure herself that her daughter was far too interested in the pretty scarf to be listening.

Now that someone was speaking, the crowd had moved closer. When Anne mentioned Anthony, people murmured their sympathies. 'God bless him,' said one.

'This country needs women workers,' continued Anne. 'All of us who you see today work for the war effort.'

I stopped scribbling in shorthand for a moment and looked at Mr Rice. He was going the same purple colour as when we had first met.

'But we can't and won't tell you what we do, or where we do it.'

The soldiers nodded. More people clapped. One of them was Charles who had got rid of the newspaper and was now standing just by the side of the crowd. Guy had also moved closer and was now casually listening to Anne speak.

'All we want you to know is that we want to work for our boys. We urge any girl or woman of working age to join in so that we can support them and get this war won.'

More applause.

'But we have a problem, which is why we are here today. You may know we work shifts and weekends and all hours. We don't mind that if it gets the job done. But our little'ns, our children who are with us today, need looking after. We know Mr Churchill's Government is setting up special nurseries for war workers. But we don't have them yet, even though we need them badly. The fact is, we need them NOW.'

All the women clapped and cheered, and there was a smattering of applause from the crowd.

'I know some of you may think that mothers should be at home, looking after the children, and that we won't be conscripted so we don't have to work. But we are here to tell you that we want to work, and many of us need to work. Especially if we are on our own.'

As Anne continued to reiterate that all the women wanted was nurseries for the children, you could see the crowd's interest grow. When she said that many war widows needed to work, there were nods from other women, including several in middle age. This was not their first war.

Not everyone was impressed. The two men with Mr Rice moved to the front of the crowd and I noticed that Mr Adams had arrived and was talking to an official-looking man who was listening and pointing at things. They looked ready to make some sort of a move.

It was time to put anonymity aside. I slipped through the crowd, excusing myself and inching to the front.

Anne had finished speaking and now Irene stepped up beside her. Anne gave her the megaphone and whispered something to her. Irene, ashen-faced, nodded and then swallowed hard. She was gripping a hankie in her hand. Anne put her arm around her.

Irene began to speak. She was hesitant and looked close to tears. The crowd waited.

'I'm Mrs Irene Barker,' she said, almost in a whisper. 'I was a war worker, but I lost my job because I couldn't find anyone to look after my girls when I was at work.'

Then she looked at Anne, shook her head and nearly in tears, handed her the megaphone and got down off the crate. Betty and one of the other women went to her immediately. I heard Betty say, 'Well done, Rene. You did it. You did him proud.'

Anne started to speak again. A large crowd had now gathered.

'All Mrs Barker wants is to be able to work,' she said. 'That's all. It has taken great courage for her to be here today.' She looked over at Irene. 'Last week she was informed that her husband, Able Seaman Douglas Barker, had given his life for his country.'

Now a very audible murmur of sympathy went through the crowd.

The official-looking man with Mr Adams chose his timing badly.

'I say,' he said loudly. 'I am here on behalf of the council. You ladies are blocking a public thoroughfare and must disperse.'

It was a crass interruption.

'Shame,' said someone behind me.

'They're not doing any harm,' said a young man.

'Demonstrations are not allowed,' said the official.

'Yes, they are,' I said, stepping in front of him. 'This isn't Berlin. And anyway, this is a recruitment parade.'

'Stuff Berlin,' yelled one of the soldiers.

I took my notepad out of my pocket and flipped it open.

'Press,' I said, loudly. 'Good morning. May I take your name? I want to make sure I spell it correctly. Are you an official representative? Our readers will want to know what you have against women who want to do war work. I'm not clear why you want to stand in their way?'

'We just want nurseries so we can work and keep our children safe,' shouted Maeve.

'TO WIN THE WAR, WE'RE ASKING, PLEASE, HELP US GET OUR NURSERIES,' some of the others began to chant.

Mr Rice leaned towards the official. He looked disappointed rather than angry. 'We've seen this one before,' he said, gesturing at me. 'She's from a magazine.'

'YOU MUST DISPERSE,' shouted the official.

'NO,' yelled Betty through the megaphone. 'Not until someone helps us.'

The foreman, who I had recognised from Chandlers, began to move towards her. 'You stupid woman,' he said. 'You won't have any jobs after this.'

'Shut up, Lesley,' called a woman from the crowd. 'Stop showing off.'

Lesley turned round, told her in no uncertain terms to go away, and took a step towards Betty.

Betty didn't move, but Charles did. 'Easy there,' he said, calmly moving between her and the foreman. 'There's no need for that.'

Lesley told Charles where to stick it. Mr Rice told Lesley to calm down. The two soldiers and a very large young sailor walked over and stood by Charles.

Bunty took a photograph and then limped backwards, leaning heavily on her stick.

'Come on, now,' said Charles, ignoring the fact Lesley had just been unutterably rude. 'Let the women finish what they have to say.'

Charles looked unruffled, whereas I'd have been tempted to give Lesley what for. Out of the corner of my eye I noticed that Guy had moved to just a couple of yards away, near Mr Adams. He was taking notes as he watched.

'Can anyone account for this man?' I said, pointing at Lesley and looking at Mr Rice. 'He's frightening the children.'

It wasn't entirely true as Maeve and Violet and two of the other women had sensibly taken the smallest children off to the look at the Christmas tree. But that wasn't the point.

'May I have all your names?' I added, brandishing my pencil. 'I'm writing a piece for the national press.'

The official hesitated, but Mr Adams was less worried.

'Really?' he said sarcastically, now nothing like the chummy type I had first met at the lunchtime concert. 'I thought you wrote about frocks.'

'And I thought you were busy trying to suck up to Tommy Trinder,' I replied. 'But yes, actually, I am writing a piece. Of course, if you'd rather I didn't, perhaps you might like to speak with Mrs Oliver instead.'

Mr Adams looked put out. 'You seem to have forgotten the conversation at your last visit,' he said. 'Lots of people in various places will be very interested to hear about this little stunt.'

'Do you mean how the Government's women workers are treated?' I asked.

Anne and Betty were now at my side. There was a loud click as Bunty took another picture.

Some of the crowd had moved away, but there was still a decent number left, and they started to join in.

'GIVE THEM A NURSERY!' someone shouted.

'WHO ARE YOU, ANYWAY?' called out someone else. Mr Adams didn't like that at all.

'STOP PICKING ON THEM,' cried a woman with a young girl in a school uniform.

'Ah, good, the police,' said Mr Adams, as if he was the head of Scotland Yard and had an officer in tow at all times. 'Now we'll sort it.'

The local constable was a mild-looking man, but with an authoritative air.

'Who's in charge here?' he asked.

The men all kept quiet.

'I am, sir,' said Anne. 'Of the parade anyway. Mrs Oliver. Thirty-two Wilton Street.'

'We're here for war workers,' said Betty.

'Mr Simms,' said the officer, recognising the official, without obvious pleasure. 'Is this anything to do with your department?'

'Certainly not,' said Mr Simms.

'If you're from the council then it is,' said Betty. 'We've been writing to you for weeks.'

'We're only asking for a nursery,' said Anne to the policeman. 'But we've been told it has to be done jointly by local authorities and factory managers. They won't even meet with us. No one seems to want to know.'

'And the Ministries of Health and Labour have to say yes before anything happens,' I added. 'These women just want to be able to work.'

Mr Simms began to protest, launching into an un-intelligible garble of reasons and sounding just like a politician.

Behind him, and very quickly joined by the others, two of the women began singing again.

'So, off I went and signed up to be a worker . . .'

'Can I suggest you all sit down and talk in a civilised manner?' said the policeman. 'I'll give you until after Christmas. I'll take some names and addresses, if you don't mind. No, sir, please stay where you are,' he said, raising his voice as Mr Adams tried to sneak away. To his credit, Mr Rice had stayed put, although admittedly he was slightly hiding behind Mr Simms.

'I'm afraid they've already given me the sack,' said Anne politely. 'And probably will to all the others after this.'

'Very festive,' said the officer, drily. 'Who's the Scrooge?'

299

When no one admitted anything, he started taking down names.

At that moment, one of the younger members of the march, who had become bored with all the standing around, broke ranks from the others and strode over to the policeman.

'Hello,' she said, confidently, but not rudely. 'What's your name?'

The policeman stopped writing. 'Constable Pickering,' he said.

'Picky Wing?'

'Pickering.'

'I can't say that. What are you doing?'

'I'm writing down names,' said Constable Picky Wing, patiently.

'Can you write mine? It's Ruby. With a Ruh,' said Ruby, trying to stand on her toes to see inside his notebook.

'I'm so sorry, Constable,' said Anne. 'This is my daughter. I'm teaching her her letters.'

'Aa, buh, cuh,' said Ruby to the policeman.

'That'll do, Ruby,' said Anne. 'We can do that at home.'

'Your mother's right,' said the constable. 'That's enough for now.'

Ruby looked at him with bewilderment. Giving up was not in her nature.

'Come and stand quietly, please, Ruby,' said Anne, holding out her hand. 'The grown-ups are talking.'

Ruby dutifully took Anne's hand and leant into her coat, looking around as Anne stroked her hair protectively. Now that Constable Pickering was here, the belligerent Lesley had calmed himself down, and the atmosphere was less fraught. Nevertheless, Betty quietly moved nearer Anne and so did I. If tempers flared, we could get Ruby away.

As I had already been identified by Mr Rice, there was

no need for me to pretend that I didn't have an interest in the marchers. I crouched down.

'Hello, Monster,' I whispered.

'Aunty Emmy!' cried Ruby, hurling her arms round my neck. 'Spin me round?'

'In a minute, I promise,' I said, continuing to whisper. Although Constable Pickering had been very nice to her, I wasn't sure how far his patience would stretch if I turned into a merry-go-round. 'We have to be quiet while the grown-ups are talking.'

I stayed crouched down and put my finger to my lips as if it was the best secret plan ever.

Ruby nodded, her eyes wide, then she crouched down too and squashed her chubby finger to her face.

'Now then,' said the constable to Mr Adams. 'Your name please, sir.'

'Actually, Constable,' said Adams, 'I was the person who alerted your station to the possibility of trouble taking place here today.'

'Then you'll be very happy to give me your details, won't you, sir?' said Constable Pickering, who didn't seem impressed at meeting a snitch.

He took down Mr Adams' name and address, and then looked behind Mr Simms to speak to Mr Rice.

'If you could step forward, sir, and give me your name, please,' he said.

As Mr Rice did as he was asked and the constable licked the end of his pencil ready to write down his name, out of nowhere there was an ear-splitting scream.

It was Ruby.

Anne bent down to see what on earth was the matter, but Ruby, who was absolutely beside herself, jumped up and started pulling on the constable's jacket, trying to get him away from Mr Rice.

'NO!' she screamed. 'THAT MAN SCARED MY MUMMY.'

Mr Rice looked horrified and took a step back as Ruby burst into huge wails.

'It's all right, my lovely, it's all right,' said Anne, picking her up and holding her tightly. 'It's just Mr Rice from Mummy's work. He didn't scare me, I promise.'

But Ruby continued to cry.

Constable Pickering looked at her and then back to Mr Rice. His expression had changed to one of distinct disapproval.

'Don't you move,' he said to Mr Rice.

Anne swayed from side to side, trying to calm Ruby down. In between enormous gulps and with her flowery crown all askew, Ruby buried her head into Anne's shoulder. 'He. Made. You. Cry. My Mummy,' she sobbed.

'Oh, Ruby,' said Anne. 'Come on, baby, let's see if we can find Tony. I'm sorry. Constable,' she said. 'I shouldn't have brought her. She's only four.'

Constable Pickering, who already had all of Anne's details, nodded, now looking more interested in Mr Rice.

'Thank you,' said Anne as Ruby continued to cry. 'Don't forget, you're going to be a bridesmaid like a big girl today, aren't you? And you're wearing your crown so it's a happy day isn't it?'

Ruby hiccupped and managed to gasp a brave little, 'Yes.'

Then, just as she began to walk away, Anne stopped and turned to Constable Pickering.

'Constable, it's not Mr Rice's fault,' she said as she hugged Ruby. 'I was tearful when he told me I'd lost my job, and it upset her. She just got a bit of a shock seeing him, that's all. She really will be fine.'

Then she carried Ruby away.

'All right, everyone, time to go,' said Constable

Pickering as he shut his police notebook. He motioned to Mr Rice.

'Just so you know, Mrs Oliver just did you a very great favour,' he said. 'Now, I suggest you try talking to these ladies rather than making their children cry. By the New Year. I'll be checking.'

Then he turned to the crowd. 'That's it, you lot, go and do your shopping before everything runs out. Nice singing,' he added to Irene and the others. 'How about limiting it to carols for the rest of the day? Thank you, ladies, I think you've made your point and suggest you all go now. It is nearly Christmas after all.'

Then he gave a slight nod and with no intention of letting us try to carry on, slowly and very deliberately walked away.

'Well done, girls,' called one of the soldiers. 'You keep it up. We're right behind you.'

There was a small round of applause as the crowd started to disperse, and quite a few people went up to the women to speak with them.

Mr Rice and Mr Adams were in no mood to stay around. Constable Pickering was right. The women had made their point. It was time to go.

The rest of us followed Anne over to Tony's pram, where Ruby was still clinging to her, but had stopped crying and was now sucking her thumb and rather enjoying being carried and not having to be a big girl at all.

'Are you all right?' I said to Anne.

She nodded, looking overwhelmed.

'Are you sure? I'm so sorry Ruby got scared. Poor old sausage,' I said, as Ruby looked up and did another hiccup.

'I'm not a sausage,' she managed, sounding a lot more like herself.

'I see,' I said. 'Then what are you?'

'I'm a bridesmaid,' said Ruby, now beginning to perk up.

'Hooray!' I said. 'I tell you what. Do you want to meet the boy I'm going to marry?'

Ruby nodded.

'I do too,' said Anne. 'I must admit I did try to spot him before Constable Pickering arrived.'

Ruby was now well on her way back to her usual self, and Baby Tony and the other children were all accounted for and so full of ration-defying treats from various onlookers that the greatest threat to any of them was the possibility of being ill. Now, the women were able to take a step back and contemplate what they had done.

The Patriotic Parade had been a success. Finally, the women had started to be heard.

'Congratulations,' I said as Maeve and Violet joined us. 'You did it. Chandlers are going to have to at least talk to some of you now.'

'And give Anne and Irene back their jobs,' said Betty, with feeling.

It was a very good point.

'I don't know if they'll do that,' said Anne. 'But goodness me, hasn't almost everyone been nice? People really listened, didn't they?'

She looked more than relieved, and as everyone now began chatting, I introduced Charles, and then Bunty and I met the other women who had been marching. It gave me the perfect opportunity to ask them some questions. With Anne's speech noted down in its entirety, I was soon happy I had enough information to write my article.

Spotting Guy now chatting to Bunty, I put away my pencil and went over.

'Do you know, I thought you might join in at one point,' I said to him.

'You didn't need me,' he replied. 'You were doing perfectly well. Those instincts of yours are really very good. You knew when to stand back and watch, and when to get involved on behalf of your friends. Well done.'

It was high praise indeed from him.

'Thank you,' I said.

'Not at all. Now, this is all very nice, but what time did you say we had to leave?'

I looked at my wristwatch for the first time since the start of the march. It was ten past eleven. We had ten minutes to catch our train home.

'Oh, my word,' I cried. 'We have to go! Bunts, you and Guy start walking. I'll get Charles. Anne,' I called to her over a small crowd of her friends. 'We have to go. Are you sure you're all right? You *are* going to come to the wedding, aren't you?'

'Of course we are,' she said, rushing over. 'I have to talk to all the girls, but I promise that Ruby and Tony and I will be on the very next train. I've stuffed all our things in Tony's pram. He probably can't feel his feet.'

'And you know where to go?' I said anxiously.

'St Gabriel's Church if I can, and I have the address of the house if we're too late. Look, here's your fiancé, now GO!'

Charles had extricated himself from the many introductions and now he grabbed my hand.

'See you later!' he said to Anne. 'Terrifically well done today. I can't tell you how impressive you all were.'

Anne smiled broadly. 'Thank you, now can you just please leave?!'

The two of us started running. Bunty and Guy were already moving at a good speed. We now had eight minutes to get to the train.

'Let's hope it will be late,' said Charles as we ran. Then he slammed on the brakes.

'What is it?' I said, stopping too and looking at him in alarm.

'We're going to get married,' he said, his eyes absolutely shining.

Then he pulled me into his chest, gave me the most enormous kiss, and took hold of my hand again.

'Ready?' he said, as I was now laughing with delight. 'No time for laughing – RUN!'

CHAPTER 29

A Nice Idea to Split Up

WE REALLY HAD cut it fine, but as the four of us hurried towards the platform, we could see the train sitting there with a few stragglers still getting on.

'I must say,' said Charles as we slowed down, 'now that we're on our way, it does feel a bit odd being together as if we're just going on the morning train to the office or something. Not that I don't want to be with you, darling, but it's not quite the traditional pre-wedding set-up, if you know what I mean?'

I was less concerned. 'I don't mind,' I said. 'At one point this morning I thought we'd all end up getting arrested so it'll be a relief just to sit down in a carriage rather than a cell.'

'I'm with Charles on this one,' said Guy as we showed our return tickets to the collector at the gate. 'It's not quite cricket on the old wedding etiquette front.'

'There's nothing much we can do about that,' said Bunty. She had been on her feet all morning, not to mention having to quick march for the train, and she was leaning quite heavily on her stick.

'Yes, we can,' said Guy. 'Now we're safely here, it might be a nice idea if we split up. Ladies, may I suggest you get into a carriage here, while my brother and I move along to one nearer the front. Charles, you come with me. Best Man's orders.'

'That sounds nice,' said Bunty, gratefully.

'Excellent,' said Guy. 'When we get to Paddington, Charles can get in a taxi and I will check that you ladies are safely in one as well and as long as there isn't a hoo-hah about the timing, you two,' he fixed Charles and me with a stare, 'won't be seeing each other again until Emmy gets to the church. Everyone agree?'

I thought it a lovely idea. 'Perfect,' I said, opening the carriage door. 'Go on, Bunts, you get in first.'

Bunty happily did as she was told. 'See you there!' she called before plonking herself down on the seat.

'Come along, Charles,' ordered Guy, 'before the guard blows the whistle.'

He began to stride along the platform towards the smoke and steam from the engine.

'Be right there,' called Charles. He turned to me. 'We've got a few seconds. The guard's helping an old chap with his bag. Can I get my last ever kiss with a girl who isn't my wife?'

'As long as it jolly well is,' I said, quite happy to oblige.

'Hurry up, you two,' called Bunty who had dramatically put her hand over her eyes in order not to watch. 'Don't muck things up at this stage.'

'Go on then, Emmeline Lake,' said Charles, more or less lifting me into the train, 'or Guy will have a fit. Goodbye, darling. Bye, Bunty. See you at the church!'

He slammed the door behind me, blew a kiss and as we heard the guard's whistle shriek, sprinted off before it was too late.

I sat down opposite Bunty in the carriage, letting out a loud sigh. 'Bunts, we made it,' I said.

'What a relief,' said Bunty, looking much like I felt.

We heard the guard blow his whistle for the final time.

'Made it,' I said. 'Now we can relax.'

The train didn't move. I could hear it hissing and huffing, but nothing happened.

Bunts and I looked at each other.

I jumped up, rammed the window down and stuck my head out, Bunty by my side almost as fast.

Shrouded in billows of smoke and steam, and already picking up speed as we watched, the front half of the train was easing itself out of the station.

'NO!' I shrieked, fumbling to open the door, although it was entirely too late to make any difference.

Nevertheless, I leaped out. Bunty followed closely behind.

We were the only people on the platform.

'Why didn't the guard say?' I wailed. 'How could he let us get on the wrong end of the train?'

'I don't think he saw us,' said Bunty. 'He was helping the elderly chap. It'll be all right,' she added, not sounding terrifically sure. 'We can get the next one. Or Charles and Guy will get off when they realise and wait for us at the next station. If we go straight to the church rather than home first, I'm sure you'll make it.'

I looked at her.

'All perfectly fine,' she finished, her voice trailing off.

'No, Bunts,' I said, failing to join in. 'I really don't think that it is.'

I put my hands on my hips and continued to stare up the platform, as if the engine driver would somehow miraculously reverse back to get us.

'The ticket man will know,' said Bunts, who was doing a good job at attempting to be calm in the face of complete disaster.

'How did Guy and Charles not notice?' I said. 'They must have walked right past where they'd uncoupled the carriages.'

'To be fair, Charles was running,' said Bunty, which was accurate but unhelpful.

I tried to pull myself together. 'Right. Let's think about this. The ticket collector. Good idea. Come on.'

Bunty was ahead of the game on this point and had already started heading back to the platform gate.

'Excuse me,' she said. 'We've been left behind. We didn't realise the train was splitting in two.'

'Oh dear,' said the man. 'Whoops a daisy.'

Bunty saw the look on my face. 'Leave it to me,' she said, laying a hand on my arm. 'Yes,' she continued. 'Bit of a hiccup. Do you know if the next London train is on time? It's just we have to get there rather urgently.'

'Well, now,' said the collector. 'There is a war on.'

Bunty's grip on me tightened.

'Mmm,' she managed. 'Yes, we know that. Perhaps you can tell us if another engine is coming for these carriages?'

'It is,' said the collector.

'There we are!' said Bunty.

'But it'll be taking them into the sidings.'

'For heaven's sake,' I muttered.

'I see,' said Bunty, showing remarkable patience. 'Do you have any idea when we can expect the next train *to London*?'

'The thing is,' I interrupted, now unable to keep quiet any longer, 'I'm supposed to be . . . well that is, I *am* getting married at three o'clock. And we really do have to be on the train.'

The ticket collector chewed his lip. 'You might be all right,' he said. 'Then again.'

'Isn't the next train at a quarter to twelve?' said Bunty. 'Em, that would still be fine as long as it doesn't get stuck somewhere.'

'That one's been cancelled,' said the man. 'But there's another at a quarter to one. Probably.'

'That's just too late,' I said. I was beginning to panic. 'Oh, Bunts, I shouldn't have done this. What was I thinking?'

'Let's go back into town,' said Bunty, having given up on the enigmatic ticket collector. 'How long would it take by car, do you think? If we could find one? That had petrol.'

I wished Charles hadn't made the joke about me stealing a car. Currently it was feeling like a viable option.

'It might be your best bet,' said the ticket collector. 'The lines are right up the spout again today.'

'Come on, Em,' said Bunty. 'It's worth a go. Anne may know someone. And we need to warn her about the trains, anyway.'

I nodded. 'Is your leg up to it? You've hardly sat down.'

'I'm fine,' said Bunty, looking determined.

I didn't believe her for a moment, but I knew her well enough to know not to push further.

We made our way back out of the station and started walking steadily back to the market square.

'You're right,' I said, putting my arm through hers and trying to be positive. 'Anne will know someone. But honestly, Bunts, why did I insist on risking this?'

'Why did I let you?' she answered. 'Because you made a promise. I'd have done exactly the same, and I bet you Charles would have too if it was his army pals. So would Guy.'

'I just can't miss the wedding,' I said, feeling sick at the thought. I couldn't bear the thought of Charles going away if we weren't married.

'You won't miss it,' said Bunty. 'We won't let you. And he will come back, Em. I know that's what you're thinking. You and Charles are not me and Bill. You are not Anne and Anthony.'

She stopped in the middle of the street.

311

'Your story *will* have a happy ending,' she insisted. 'It *will*. Now, let's find a way to get to London.'

Determined and calm, my best friend had known exactly what I was thinking. She gave me a quick smile. 'All right?' she asked.

I took a deep breath. 'Yes,' I said. 'Thank you. For a moment I went a bit defeatist there.'

'Not to worry,' said Bunts, cheerfully.

'It won't happen again,' I said as we started walking more briskly.

'I should hope not. List D: Transport To Church,' she said. 'Working on it, but a bit of an oversight, currently. I can only apologise.'

'I don't know,' I said. 'Look over there.'

Down the road, driving towards us at a pace, was a van. It was familiar yet could have been completely anonymous apart from the person hanging out of the passenger window.

Noreen Noakes was waving at us like mad, while holding tightly onto a now very happy Ruby Oliver. Wilf Noakes slammed on the brakes and they came to a halt right where Bunty and I were standing.

Bunty, who didn't know either of them from Adam, looked at me in bewilderment. I was no help at all as I just stood there with my mouth open wondering what on earth was going on.

Sitting next to Noreen and looking similarly deranged as she waved was Anne, with Baby Tony on her lap.

Wilf turned off the engine as Noreen threw open the door and hurriedly put Ruby onto the seat next to her mum.

'Hello,' said Noreen, climbing out. 'Wilf says the trains are all messed up. He's supposed to be picking up some supplies, but he doesn't think they'll be here for hours. We're giving Anne a lift to a wedding.'

'Where's Charles?' called Anne, leaning over and clinging on to Ruby who was trying to get free.

'They're on the train,' I said. 'Long story. We hope they're carrying on to Paddington.'

'Ladies,' shouted Wilf, 'you can chat later. If we're going to get you to London in time, you really do need to get in the van.'

'Come on,' said Noreen. 'Do you mind a bit of a bumpy ride?'

She walked round to the back of the van and opened the door.

'If one of you wants to get in the front, I don't mind coming in here with the other,' she said. 'Anne volunteered, but Wilf says the children really should sit in the front.'

'Me first,' I said, ignoring her and climbing in.

'I've no idea what's happening,' Bunty said to Noreen as she climbed in after me, 'but if this is your van, I can't let you sit in the back.'

'Oh, it's not ours,' said Noreen. 'It's Chandlers',' she whispered.

'Of course,' said Bunts, calmly. 'Now we're stealing a van.'

A loud thumping came from the front.

'In you go,' said Noreen. 'Can you see all right? Wilf says there should be some sacks to sit on. He'll try not to bounce you around. Mind the pram. It is tied down. Right, I'm shutting the door.'

As Noreen slammed and locked the door, which in terms of safety was something of a relief, Bunty and I sat ourselves down between several large boxes and realised there was a small open hatch between us and the cab. It let in light and as I shuffled forward, I could see the back of Anne's head.

Wrapping my fingers tightly around the sides as it gave me something to hang on to, I peered through to see Noreen scramble back in.

'Right,' yelled Wilf. 'Hold on in the back. We're off.'

With that he switched on the engine and the van roared off down the road.

'WHEEEEE,' shrieked Ruby.

'Everyone all right?' shouted Wilf.

'Yes, thanks,' I yelled back.

Then a less raucous and terribly polite voice joined in. 'I don't wish to be rude,' called Bunty. 'But we haven't formally met. I'm Emmy's friend, Bunty, and I just wondered if someone could please tell me what is actually going on?'

CHAPTER 30

I've Got a Bride in the Back of the Van

UNSURPRISINGLY, WILF WASN'T supposed to use the Chandlers van for his own personal needs. When he had arrived at the station for a pickup, however, and been told about the trains going haywire, he had decided to see if he could find Noreen to give her a lift home from the shops. So it *was* her I had seen in the crowd.

Anne and Noreen took it in turns to tell us the whole story through the little rectangular window, with frequent interruptions from Ruby and Wilf.

'Noreen was talking to Betty and me,' said Anne.

'AND ME,' said Ruby.

'When Wilf came up,' continued Anne. 'We were about to leave for the station, but then Wilf said about the trains.'

'And then Anne said, "I hope Emmy and Charles made the last one," ' said Noreen.

'And I said, "They'll be stuck if they've not," ' said Wilf.

'And that's when we realised Ruby and Tony and I *were* stuck,' said Anne.

'So, Wilf said, "Well, I'm not having that," ' said Noreen.

'I did,' said Wilf. 'Not when there's a very grown-up bridesmaid to get to the ball.'

'ME,' shouted Ruby, if clarification was required.

'So, we thought we'd drive via the station, just in case

anything had gone wrong for you,' said Noreen. 'Good job, as well.'

'Are you really going to take us all the way to London?' I asked. 'What about the petrol?'

'Bit of luck, filled her up yesterday,' said Wilf. 'And as we haven't met, Miss Tavistock, may I say I've never done anything like this before in my life. Well, apart from the last time I met your friend Emmy, that is.'

'She's led him astray,' said Noreen.

'Gosh, I hope not,' I said. 'Wilf, are you sure about all this? Aren't you taking a very big risk?'

The van rattled around a corner, and Bunty and I hung on for grim death.

'You probably can't see it,' said Wilf, 'but there's a box in the back with an address in Chelsea. I'm supposed to be delivering it on Monday. I reckon if anything goes wrong, I'll just say I got hold of the wrong end of the stick and thought I was supposed to take it today.'

I saw Anne shake her head. 'Can we guess who it's from?' she said.

Wilf laughed. 'Our Mr Terry,' he sang.

It wasn't only Betty and Vi who knew what seemed to be the factory's favourite song.

'He does this sort of thing all the time,' said Wilf. 'I could tell you stories about him that would make your hair curl.'

'Wilf,' warned Noreen.

'All right, love,' he said. 'Don't worry. Aye, aye, what's this?'

Wilf slowed the van down and muttered something under his breath.

'Nothing to worry about,' he said, loudly. 'It's just traffic. That's the A4 for you. When do we need to be there? Three? Loads of time.'

Bunty and I glanced at each other. With hardly anyone driving these days, there was no real reason for Traffic.

'How far is it to Pimlico from here?' I asked through the hatch.

'About forty miles,' said Wilf. 'It won't take us more than two hours. If we get a clear road, the wagon can do over thirty-five an hour if I put my foot down, and it's only twelve o'clock now.'

We were moving at nearly a crawl.

'Anyone fancy a sing-song?' he asked.

'Tony's done a smell again,' said Ruby.

'I'm so sorry,' said Anne.

'Well done, Tony, my lad,' said Wilf. 'Anyone else want to drive? I wouldn't mind sitting in the back for a bit.'

The van had now come to a complete halt.

'Nothing to worry about,' said Wilf, but I saw him glance sideways towards Noreen.

Twenty long minutes later, Anne had taught us all the words to the parade version of 'My Old Man Said Follow The Van' and we had also sung it in its original form, which had included Ruby bellowing, 'We dillied and dallied,' at the top of her voice completely out of time with everyone else.

I wondered if anyone had noticed the irony. We weren't so much dillying as not moving anywhere at all.

'I'll get out,' said Wilf. 'See what's up.'

It was a tree. It wasn't so much up as down, which was the whole problem.

'You have to laugh,' I said, pluckily. 'If it isn't the Germans, it's Mother Nature.'

Nobody laughed.

There was nothing to do but wait. For another half an hour. Wilf let Bunty and me out of the back of the van so we could stretch our legs. Anne gave Tony an emergency change and Ruby insisted she didn't want to go to the lavatory behind a bush, which made Anne very nervous indeed.

While it was good to be out in the fresh air, Bunty and I were becoming increasingly jumpy about making a quick move once the tree had been cleared, so everyone got back in again and made a rather more feeble attempt at singing. With time ticking, no one's heart was in it anymore.

At just before one o'clock, when I really was beginning to worry, a policeman walked up to the van.

'Not long now, sir,' he said to Wilf. 'We've got a tractor out and we'll be squeezing people through soon. Are you in a hurry? Ah no, I see it's a family trip.'

Ruby said hello and asked him what his name was.

'Actually, we are up against it, Constable,' said Wilf. 'This might sound a bit strange, but I've got a bride in the back of the van.'

I couldn't see the policeman, but his silence was enough.

'Hello,' I shouted. 'That's me. We're trying to get to London, but the trains are messed up.'

If I pressed my ear right up to the hatch I could hear.

'Well I never,' came a voice. 'Don't worry, miss.'

'There's a bridesmaid with her as well,' said Wilf, as if it was the most natural thing in the world.

'I'm a bridesmaid,' said Ruby. 'I've got a new frock.'

'Should I join in?' whispered Bunty. 'It's just he sounds rather surprised as it is.'

'Shall we get out?' I shouted, just in case the constable though Wilf was a maniac transporting a van load of women to a harem somewhere.

'We've got to be in London by three,' said Wilf. 'I have to admit, it's getting tight.'

'I'm a bridesmaid, too,' said Ruby.

Anne told her to hush. 'She's never been one before,' she said. 'I'm afraid she's rather excited.'

'I can see that,' said the constable. 'Well, we can't have you missing out. Can you start up your vehicle, please, sir. Take it slowly, but you can follow me on the other side of the road. There should be enough room for you.'

Wilf inched the van out of the queue and crawled along as he was told.

'What's happening?' called Bunty.

'He's waving at another copper,' reported Wilf. 'I think they're letting us to the front of the queue.'

I felt a wave of hope. If only Charles was still on the train and on his way to the church, then we'd be in with a chance.

Good as his word, the policeman had sent us to the front of the short queue and and somehow Wilf just about managed to get the van through.

'Right, ladies,' called Wilf. 'Hang on to the children and anything else you can find. Let's see how fast this old thing can go.'

*

The old van could go very fast, it turned out. Wilf put his foot down and we hurtled off to London, with Bunty and me bouncing around like ping-pong balls in the back.

At bang on three o'clock we arrived outside St Gabriel's Church.

There had been no time to go to the house for me to get changed, but Mother and I had agreed that if Bunty and I weren't back by a quarter to three, she and Father were to go to the church with my wedding things and wait for us there.

Wilf brought the van to a juddering halt and everyone scrambled out.

Even though Noreen said she couldn't come into a church in her old shopping clothes, let alone Wilf in his overalls, I had insisted that after everything they had done, they must be at the wedding.

'I'll just find somewhere to park up,' he called. 'Then we'll nip in.'

Mother and Father and my brother Jack stood outside the church, transfixed, as Bunty and I emerged, with Bunty already unbuttoning her coat.

'I'm not even going to ask,' said my mother. 'There's no time. Now take off your things and let's get you into this dress.'

'Is Charles here?' I asked, not moving.

'Of course,' said Mother. 'Jack, go and tell him all is well. The poor boy must be having kittens. And can you tell Reverend Lovell we'll be two minutes. The bride's prerogative. No, there's no time to go into the vestry. Alfred, Bunty, you stand in front of Emmy so no one can see. Hello,' she added, 'you must be Anne. So nice to meet you. Could you just stand there, please. That's right. Emmy will have to get dressed here.'

My brother disappeared into the church as, rather like a small child on a beach changing out of a wet bathing suit, I wriggled out of my woolly and my mother slipped the dress over my head.

Despite the fact I was getting changed in a church porch, the parachute silk felt lovely when I put it on, and Mother did up the buttons on the back. The long sleeves had come up a treat, and I smiled as it turned out I would be wearing my usual common or garden winter vest, rather than the much-maligned silk one, underneath.

Rather than wearing a veil, I had made a tiny headpiece with ribbon flowers on the top as it wasn't on the ration and also went very nicely with the dress. It hid my van-bounced untidy hair and Bunty swore blind no one would know where we'd been.

'The bruises haven't even begun to show yet,' she grinned.

To top it all off, I had a small bouquet of berries and greenery that Mother had picked from the garden and brought up on the train in a box.

After Bunty helped me pin my favourite pearl brooch to the dress, I stood back to see if I met with everyone's approval.

'Oh, darling,' cried Mother. 'It's perfect.'

'Oh, Em,' said Bunty.

'That's *very* nice,' said Father. 'Well done. Jolly good indeed.'

They were all beaming from ear to ear.

Father gave me a kiss as Mother hugged Bunty and told everyone we had plenty of time.

The church door opened and Jack poked his head around it.

'Are you ready?' he asked. 'Dear old Charles is about to take to the hip flask if not. I say,' he added, looking at me, 'that parachute looks good. And Bunts, you're the bee's knees in that frock. Can we have a picture taken so I can show off to the chaps?'

Bunty, who had known Jack since he was three, said yes of course. Then, after my mother had given me one last hug and denied that she had tears in her eyes, Jack offered her his arm and escorted her into the church.

As Anne straightened Ruby's crown for the twentieth time, I looked at Bunty and Father. Bunty had stepped back, but Father took both our hands.

'I want you to know that I am inordinately proud of you girls.' He smiled and turned to me. 'Now then,' he said, 'are you ready?'

I nodded.

As Mrs Peyton began playing the organ, Father and I walked up the red and white marble aisle. Either side was a blur of people I knew and if the church was cold, which I supposed it must be, I didn't feel a thing. I held on to Father's arm and looked forward.

Now I really did feel like a bride.

Even my fancy wedding shoes were surprisingly comfortable. This, I realised, was because I was still wearing my sensible stout shoes from the march.

Charles was there at the end of the aisle with Guy and Reverend Lovell. I felt a rush of excitement. He was looking steadfastly ahead as one should, but when Father whispered, 'Good luck,' and took his seat next to Mother in the front pew, Charles finally turned round and gazed at me for a moment.

'Hello, darling,' he said. 'You took your time.'

'You should see what I've got on my feet,' I said.

Charles looked down and smothered a laugh.

As Reverend Lovell cleared his throat and asked us if we were ready to begin, we both nodded.

'Emmeline Lake,' whispered Charles. 'You're the most beautiful girl in the world.'

CHAPTER 31

The Best Wedding Present Ever

THE CEREMONY WAS perfect, with readings by Guy and Jack, and carols rather than hymns, which made it even cheerier. When Charles and I left the church, all the boys in uniform, including Jack, Roy and Fred from the fire station, and several of Charles's friends who had been able to come, formed a guard of honour for us.

Mr Brand, who had come with Mrs Mahoney and Mr and Mrs Newton, had volunteered to take the 'official' photographs outside the church. I wondered if I would look as overwhelmed in the pictures as I felt. When he had finished, and with the light already beginning to fade and the blackout due, almost the entire congregation became what was my second parade of the day. With Charles and me at the head, and to cheers from neighbours as we went, we all walked together back to the house.

Kath and Thelma had rushed ahead to make final preparations, and now as 'Captain and Mrs Mayhew' we welcomed everyone inside.

The drawing room had been transformed. It looked like Christmas Day for the biggest family, which in a way, it was. The fire was now roaring, thanks to wood donated by Bunty's granny. Swathes of holly, ivy and mistletoe decked this hall, and Bunty's paper chains worked perfectly, almost as a little nod to those of us who worked at the magazine. Down one side of the room, the dining and kitchen tables had been put together and covered with rarely used tablecloths which we had found in the linen cupboards and laboriously washed and ironed. On top was the best feast I had seen since the war started. Small miracles had been worked with the donations from our friends. Large plates with rice and meat moulds sat next to fish savouries and cheese puffs, which smelt so nice that it was worth not having eaten an ounce of cheese since I had got engaged. There were even some salmon patties and the tiniest pies with little dabs of mincemeat. Guy had been true to his word and the day before the wedding, an assortment of bottles had been delivered, which Roy and Fred had made into the delicious if rather potent punch.

In the middle of it all sat our wedding cake, a two-tier affair with one large cake and quite a small one on top. The big one was covered in lace, and on the small one was a little church with a bride and groom. I was fully aware that the large layer was cardboard and white paper for show, but it didn't matter. It looked lovely, and we would be able to cut the little cake, which was very, very real.

I looked for Kath and Thelma to thank them for everything they had done, and to make sure they would now enjoy the party with everyone else. They were still busy running up and down from the kitchen, helped now by young Hester, who was being as good as her word and shyly handing out drinks from a tray.

Although we were surrounded by our family and friends, Charles and I had shared a few precious minutes together as we walked arm in arm from the church. Now as everyone showered us with good wishes and love, and I introduced my husband (how peculiar that sounded) to people he didn't know and he introduced me to some of his army friends, we were almost taken from each other again.

Knowing we were unlikely to have more than the remainder of his seventy-two hours' leave together before Charles was posted, part of me wanted to sneak him away from the hubbub. It felt as if each minute apart was too long. But as I watched everyone shaking his hand, slapping him on the back or raising their glasses of Roy's eye-watering punch, I was happy to share for now. When Charles went away, they would all have a little part of him, even just a moment or two that we could remember or they could tell me about for the first time. It sounded nonsensical, but if I gave other people time with him now, they could give more of him back to me while he was gone.

With so many people packed in, the drawing room was beautifully warm, and I certainly didn't need my sensible and not entirely attractive winter vest. I excused myself and slipped upstairs to my room.

On the landing I saw Bunty coming out of hers.

'I've just had a look at my hair,' she said. 'It was all over the place.'

'You look lovely,' I said. 'Jack was right. The bee's knees.'

'I must get that picture with him,' she grinned. 'That will put the cat amongst the pigeons at work.'

Bunts sat down on the stairs. 'Are you having a lovely time?' she asked.

'It feels like a dream,' I said, sitting beside her. 'This morning seems about a year ago. I've just been trying to work out whether I want every single person to have met Charles, or if I want to hide him away and have him all to myself.'

Bunty smiled.

325

'Are you all right, Bunts?' I asked. 'I saw you limping at the march this morning.'

'I'd just done a bit much, I think,' she said. 'It is getting better all the time, Em. Sometimes I don't need my stick almost at all. It's slow, but I'm getting there.'

'That's the best news,' I said, relieved. Then I hesitated. 'How was this afternoon?' I asked, softly.

I knew she'd understand what I meant.

'It was lovely,' she said. 'Honestly. I didn't know how I might feel in the church, and I was thinking of Bill of course. I knew I would, and it does hurt. Loads, actually. I suppose it always will, but not because of you and Charles. I am so happy for you, Em. I wish Charles wasn't going away so soon, but I'm so very pleased you're married.'

'Me too.' It was colder upstairs, and I shivered a bit. 'I've never loved anyone like this, Bunts. It's almost frightening. I'm so proud of him, but I'm scared as anything he won't come back.'

If anyone would understand it was my best friend.

'Just love him,' she said. 'Whatever happens, if you love someone and know you're loved back, you will always have that.' She paused and then added, 'To be honest, it's not even the tiniest bit as good as when they're actually alive, but you know, you have to try.'

My goodness, she was brave.

She smiled and gave me a shove with her shoulder. 'Am I helping?'

I shoved her back. Mucking about was better than being sad. 'Not in the least,' I said.

'He will come back,' said Bunty. 'I made him promise.'

We sat together for a moment until we heard footsteps coming up the stairs.

'I might have known,' said Charles, cheerfully. 'Tell me you're not hatching a plan.'

'Absolutely not,' I said.

'Thank goodness. Now, people have asked when we are planning to do the first dance,' he said. 'I think everyone's dying to join in.'

'Then we must dance!' I said grandly.

Charles escorted Bunty and me downstairs, where we were met by Anne and Baby Tony, together with Ruby, still wearing her crown.

'What does a bridesmaid do now?' she asked, after I'd picked her up but explained there wasn't quite enough room for swinging her round.

'Well, you get to stay up as late as you want, dance with anyone you like, and eat cheese puffs until they've all gone.'

For the first time since I had met her, Ruby was speechless.

'We'll show you where the cheese puffs are,' I said. 'And then Charles and I will do a dance and then everyone gets to join in. Does that sound good?'

Ruby nodded very seriously. I handed her to Charles, who immediately turned her upside down and carried her, now shrieking with excitement, into the drawing room.

'I'm so glad you're here,' I said to Anne. 'Your room's ready when you want it.'

'We wouldn't have missed this for the world,' said Anne. 'But I'd better go and keep an eye on the monster over those cheese puffs.'

'I'll take you in,' said Bunty. 'And send Charles back out to you as you're supposed to make a grand entrance.'

I stayed in the hallway as I heard my brother ushering people around.

Charles smiled as he came back out. 'Would you care to dance, Mrs Mayhew?'

'Thank you,' I said. 'I very much would.'

We walked into the room arm in arm as Jack announced us.

'Ladies and gentlemen, please welcome the bride and groom, Captain and Mrs Charles Mayhew, who will now take to the floor for the first dance.'

As Roy put on the music, we started to dance. There wasn't enough room to charge around doing a quickstep or anything too showy, but I didn't care. Everyone who meant anything to me was there, particularly the chap who was holding me far tighter than the dance technically required. When the song came to an end and to a rousing cheer, we called for everyone to join in.

As several other couples, including Guy and a very nimble Mrs Mahoney, took to an easy foxtrot, Charles gently pulled me to one side.

'You do know that I intend to dance with you exclusively until we leave this party?' he said.

'I should hope so,' I replied. 'Although I have promised one with Father and then Roy.'

'Quite right too. And actually, there is just one person I have a commitment with, if that's all right with you?'

'Of course,' I said. 'Please do.'

My mother was dancing elegantly with my father, and I looked on, expecting Charles to cut in. Instead, he walked over to Bunty, who was standing by the side watching. She hadn't danced since the night Bill died in the explosion. It was one of the many things that we had all found so awful, because everyone knew it was one of Bunty's favourite things. But although she was getting better, she had shown no interest in trying to dance. She once told me it was partly because of her injury, and partly because she couldn't imagine being happy enough.

I found myself tense, wondering if I should go over and stop Charles. It was well-meaning of him, but he didn't understand.

But when he asked her, Bunty smiled, looked over to me and mouthed, 'May I?'

I nodded my head, uncertainly. 'Of course,' I said.

Bunty put her stick to one side and taking Charles's hand, walked onto the floor. Then, with Charles helping her keep her balance, they began to dance. Slowly and carefully, but as I held my breath, Bunty was dancing.

I saw Charles ask her if she was OK and she nodded in reply, her face a study of concentration but with the widest smile.

Somehow and without fuss, the other couples gave them room, not leaving them on their own as a spectacle, but making sure no one would bump into them.

I looked over at Bunty's granny, who was sitting regally by the fire. She was watching with tears in her eyes.

I felt my brother arrive by my side. He put his arm around my shoulder.

'She's been practising,' he said quietly. 'Secretly, in case she couldn't do it.'

'It's wonderful,' I whispered. 'I didn't know if she would do this again.'

'I was going to help,' said Jack, 'but I'm never around, so she drafted in Charles for a test run. Which I under-stand you very nearly ruined.'

The night when I came home and they had the music on. They must have been rehearsing.

'We're getting her back, Em,' said Jack. 'After everything she's been through, we're getting her back.'

As the song came to an end, Charles thanked Bunty for the dance, and they walked over to Jack and me.

Jack quietly went to get Bunty's stick in case she needed it. I just looked at her, unable to find any words.

'Was that all right?' she said.

'It was perfect,' I said.

After I finished hugging her, we were both in tears and Jack was back, saying that he must have got dust from the fire in his eye.

'Shall we get a drink, Bunts?' he asked. 'Then, if I promise not to tread on your feet, perhaps we could give it a go?'

As Bunty and Jack went to try out the punch, I put my arms around Charles and looked up into his eyes. There was so much more I had to learn about him.

'Thank you,' I said. 'For the best wedding present in the world.'

CHAPTER 32

Woman's Friend

THREE DAYS LATER, Charles returned to his unit and by Boxing Day was on his way overseas. Our time together had been glorious, although after he'd gone, I did occasionally check my left hand to see if I really was wearing a wedding ring. I was newly married but without a husband, and now in exactly the same boat as thousands of other girls. I decided to look at it as a badge of honour.

We spent our honeymoon in a quiet little hotel in Surrey. It was far enough from London to feel like a trip away, and close enough to where Charles was stationed so that we could leave it to the very last minute to say goodbye.

Every single moment of our stay was a joy.

Parting, on the other hand, was awful. I wasn't keen on goodbyes at the best of times, but this was the absolute worst.

Charles and I went to the railway station together so as not to spoil the lovely memories of the hotel. I also hoped that putting on a brave face might be slightly easier in public. I wasn't going to let either Charles or myself down by crying, but that was easier said than done.

Charles's train was the first to arrive, adding insult to injury by being on time.

'Here we are then,' I said, heartily, even though my chest felt as if someone was standing on it.

'Right you are,' said Charles, equally vigorously. Then he broke ranks on the chipper front. 'Damn it,' he said, under his breath.

I had been doing quite well until that. Now I couldn't trust myself to speak.

For our last moments together as the train came into the station, we held onto each other as hard as we could.

'I love you, my darling,' said Charles. 'More than anything else in the world. Never forget that, will you?'

I pulled back to look at him.

'I love you, too,' I said. 'Always.'

Then he was gone.

I waved until after the train was out of sight and then I still stood in the middle of the platform staring at the empty track, until I felt a hand on my arm.

'Well done, you,' said a well-dressed lady in a long blue coat. 'It's hell, isn't it?'

A horrid great tear ran down my cheek. I hastily wiped it away.

'I promised myself I wouldn't cry,' I said, as another tear threatened to jump ship as well.

'You didn't,' she said, 'you did tremendously well, and that's the picture he'll remember while he's away; your smile and how lovely you are. Now, if you're waiting for the London train, shall we sit in the ladies' waiting room? It's awfully chilly today.'

The lady's name was Mrs Ives. I would remember her kindness for a very long time. She chatted to me and asked questions, and told me it was quite all right not to try to be Boadicea all the time as it was impossible to keep up. Sometimes you just had to give in to the odd watery day.

'You should have seen me in the first war when my husband went off to the Front,' she said. 'I didn't know what to do with myself. But saying goodbye is the worst part, I always think.' She patted my arm. 'He's now a tetchy old major who's been in a terrible mood ever since war broke out as he can't go and fight. I'm expecting a medal for having to put up with him.'

You could tell that Mrs Ives loved the old Major to bits.

When our train arrived, we talked all the way to London, and as we parted and wished each other good luck, it was as if a friend, rather than a stranger, had popped up at exactly the moment I needed them.

On Christmas Day, Hong Kong fell to the Japanese. Even the British newspapers found it hard to make anything positive of it, and while Charles hadn't told me where he was being posted, it was a very gloomy start to the New Year.

My answer to the gloom was to write to him every day and throw myself back into my work.

After the march for nurseries, there had been a small flurry of activity. The pictorial magazine kept to its word and printed a piece on 'Nurseries for Women Workers' and included the photograph Bunty had taken of Anne bending down to adjust Ruby's crown. Bunts had captured the moment when Anne was caring for her little girl while still pushing Tony in his pram. You could clearly see the sign saying, 'MY MUMMY WANTS TO HELP WIN THE WAR'. It couldn't have been better.

Although Chandlers hadn't been named, Anne's local *Gazette* had picked up on the story, using another photograph by Bunty and causing a momentary stir. Several members of the public at the march guessed which factory the women were from and said they were going to write to the person in charge to say they sided with the women. It was a step in the right direction.

Mr Adams, the Public Relations Manager, was no fool.

333

Just a handful of female workers had managed to get themselves in the papers, and a policeman had ordered the man from the council to meet with them. Mr Adams had also seen the response of the crowd. Sacking patriotic women war workers at Christmas would not be a good move.

Anne phoned on Boxing Day to tell me that Chandlers had offered her her old job back.

'Well done,' I said, feeling surprised. 'What did you say?'

'I asked them for a decent reference and to take the sacking off my record,' said Anne. 'I don't want to go back just to see Mr Rice have a seizure every time I clock in. And more to the point, nothing has changed. Mum would still struggle with the children and I'd be back in the same position.'

It was a brave stand, especially as Anne was now out of work, and I admired her resolve. Since the march she sounded just like when we first met, if not stronger. No one was going to mess her around now.

'It helps that Betty's moved in,' she said. 'She's going to pay a little bit of rent and depending on her shifts she'll pitch in with the children while I'm looking for a job. She's sharing my room, so we'll be a bit squashed and Ruby will drive her crackers, but Betty hates her landlady and says she'll stay at least until I'm back on my feet. And she's pushing the union at Chandlers to let women join. We're not giving in.'

Not everything, however, was a fairy tale. Irene had had to move back to her mother's in the West Midlands. They didn't like each other one little bit, but on a widow's pension and struggling to find work, Irene hadn't a choice. Everyone felt dreadful about it, but there was nothing they could do. 'There are thousands of girls in the same spot,' said Anne. 'It's an absolute disgrace.'

'I'm writing to our MP again,' Bunty promised. 'He's becoming the worst pen-pal ever as he never manages to write back.'

Bunty was on good form all round. Two weeks into January, the weather seemed to think it would be funny to give everyone another challenge by becoming terribly cold and snowing heavily. Bunts and I spent as much time as possible in the kitchen as it was warm, and when we went outside, thick boots and several layers were in order. We happily re-lived the wedding and the party, especially remembering the food, and just when we thought we'd run out of things to talk about, Thelma or Fred or Roy would call round and we'd start all over again. Roy now called Bunty 'Ginger Rogers' and joked that he was holding a grudge as she had danced with Charles and Jack, but not him. Bunty called his bluff by turning on the wireless and asking him for a turn around the kitchen. He was delighted to oblige.

At *Woman's Friend*, now that the factory series had finished, I had been researching other areas of war work to cover. The Ministry's recruitment campaign was still in full swing and we were keen not to be a flash in the pan. In between spending more time than ever on trains, trying to get access to obscure training grounds for the WAAF, or to interview new recruits to the Women's Land Army in a field in the back of beyond, "Yours Cheerfully" was taking up most of my time. Every week, the number of letters seemed to double. I couldn't write replies fast enough and the leaflets we printed were gone as soon as they came in. Circulation was up so Mrs Mahoney was kept busy managing production, and I was more than happy to look after the readers' letters almost entirely on my own.

On a very dark Wednesday afternoon, Kath and I were

putting on our coats and woolly hats, ready to take on the snow and leave for the day. I'd had a letter from Anne that morning, which had been jam-packed with news.

'Apparently,' I said as Kath adjusted her new tam-o'-shanter to try to cover her ears, 'Betty says the local authority reckon it will take them two months to contact the Ministry of Health just to ask if they will have a meeting about getting Chandlers a nursery. Two months. For a meeting!'

'How is Anne?' asked Kath.

'She's doing well,' I said. 'She's got an interview for a job working as the Women's Officer at the Labour Exchange. Nine to five hours and everything.'

'Good for her,' said Kath. 'I'm so glad it's gone well.'

'So am I,' I said. 'Even if getting anything done is like pulling teeth.'

I tutted crossly as Mr Collins came in.

'What takes two months?' he asked.

'The Ministries and local authorities,' I said, crossly. 'Anne's not getting anywhere very fast. And we've had three letters to "Yours Cheerfully" in the last week from women who say they've read about the Government Nurseries, but no one has a clue how to get one. I'm still trying to work out what to say in reply.'

'Can I show you something?' said Mr Collins. 'Sorry, I know it's the end of the day, but I've just seen it myself.'

'Yes of course,' I said, realising my vehemence was no way to speak to one's boss, new brother-in-law or not.

He turned to Kath.

'I'll only keep Emmy a minute,' he said, 'unless you're in a rush to get home.'

'Not at all, I'll wait,' said Kath. 'We're going to the cinema.'

336

'Very nice,' said Mr Collins as I followed him into his office, where his desk was covered in a large mock-up of a page for the magazine.

'I've been working on something and want to know what you think,' he said. 'I thought it could go on page three instead of the usual rather dull welcome from me. I think Mr Brand has made it look very nice. Go ahead, have a look.'

He stood back as I bent over the desk to look more closely.

There, under a large heading, "Woman's Friend to Friend", was a new page full of letters. At the top of the page it said, 'Government Nurseries – We Ask What's The Hold Up?'

I looked at him in surprise.

'I've used letters we already had from readers,' Mr Collins explained. 'If we do this page, topics could range from anything – from the nurseries issue to tips on darning socks. Seriously. A real mix of things, but the Editor's letter will highlight any significant issues we think are causing the most concern. This first one just explains the page.'

I began to read his piece.

Welcome to our new page, which we're calling "Woman's Friend to Friend". This is *your* page – it belongs entirely to you, our readers. It's here for you to get things off your chest – talk about what's bothering you or share your favourite helpful ideas.

Why the change?

I would like to tell you that the other day a wise friend of mine, a young woman not afraid of making a stand, said to me that as well as doing one's bit, she felt it terrifically important to stick together and stand up for each other, now more than ever.

I must say I agree. We're in this together and while none of us want moaners, that doesn't mean we have to take everything sitting down! We want to share your thoughts and questions on how we can make things better for each other, both while we are at war, and on that wonderful day we know is coming, when the world is free again.

We at *Woman's Friend* know that you are all working your socks off to help the war effort and make sure we win the war, so we want you to have your say about the things that matter the most to you.

I very much hope you like our, or rather, your new page, "Woman's Friend to Friend". Please feel free to write in and let me know what you think.

Yours,

The Editor

I could hardly believe what I had read.

Woman's Friend was joining the call for Government Nurseries, and asking our readers to air their views in the magazine!

'If you think it hits the right note, I plan to run this in the next issue,' Mr Collins said, calmly. 'I think it could go down quite well. As you've been saying all along, it's about time we started sticking up for the readers.'

It was the most splendid news.

'I don't know what to say,' I said. 'Thank you.'

Mr Collins smiled.

'It was your idea,' he replied. 'I just took some time to get there. Bit slow. It's my age. Far too old. Oh, and I have this for you.' He handed me an envelope. 'You can open it now, if you like.'

Dear Mrs Mayhew

  It is with pleasure that I confirm your promotion, with immediate effect, to Readers and Advice Editor for <u>Woman's</u> <u>Friend</u> magazine. Your duties will include full responsibility for the page "Yours Cheerfully" together with reader interest based features and articles . . .

For the second time in a matter of minutes, I gaped at my boss.

'It's a new role,' he said. 'But I assure you it is real, not a made-up one this time. I must say, Emmy, I'm as pleased as punch.'

'Seriously?' I said, still at a loss.

'Seriously,' he confirmed. 'And before you ask, no it isn't nepotism. You thoroughly deserve it. Are you going to say anything?'

Now he was smiling broadly.

'Thank you, again,' I managed. I very much wanted to give him a hug, although even with my head spinning, I realised this was entirely inappropriate in a work setting. It was still early days on the boss/brother-in-law front, and a tricky one to navigate around. 'And by the way, you're not old,' I said. 'You can't be, not if we're related.'

'Ha!' said Mr Collins. 'Sometimes I feel it. I'm going to go home in a minute and have a quiet sit-down.'

'That sounds awful,' I said. 'We should be celebrating. Come with us, to the cinema. We're meeting Bunty and having an early dinner first.' I looked at my wristwatch. It was a quarter past five. 'As my brother-in-law,' I said. 'Not Mr Collins. It's after work hours now.'

Navigational concerns, solved in one blow.

'That's very kind, Emmy,' he said. 'But I'm sure you won't want me . . .'

'*A very wise friend of mine said it's terrifically important to stick together,*' I quoted back at him. 'That doesn't come with an age limit.'

Before he could say anything else, I went to the door.

'Kath,' I called. 'Would it be just too horrible if we took my husband's grumpy old brother with us tonight?'

'I don't know any grumpy old brothers,' she shouted back. 'Only occasionally grumpy, really quite young ones. I wouldn't mind at all if *they* came along.'

Mr Collins, or now that it was after five o'clock, Guy, looked at a loss, but quite pleased at the same time.

'If you're absolutely sure,' he said.

I nodded. Of course I was. I paused for a moment.

'You do know Charles told me I have to look after you, don't you?' I said.

Guy nodded. 'I thought he might. And you do know he said the same thing to me about you? And about Bunty. And then a really quite extensive list of what turned out to be nearly everyone I'd met at your wedding.'

We both laughed. My darling boy.

'Well then, you're lumbered,' I said. 'There'll be no shaking us off now, even if you want to.'

'I wouldn't dream of trying,' he answered.

'Good,' I said, 'then that's agreed. Now, would you mind if we get going? I am told that Humphrey Bogart waits for no man, and as I think you're probably going to get used to, neither do Bunty or Kath!'

Feeling more cheerful than I had done for weeks, I carefully tucked the letter away and began to do up my coat.

Charles knew, of course, that we would all look after each other while he was away.

'I have complete faith that everyone will be fine,' he'd said, 'despite the fact I am entirely aware you won't be able to resist the odd challenge, should it crop up.'

I smiled and thought of my notebook, which as ever, was crammed with jotted down thoughts.

'About the new job,' I said to his brother. 'If you have a spare minute tomorrow, I'm awfully keen to tell you some of my ideas.'

Acknowledgements

I am hugely indebted to the late Joan Ketteman, who shared with me her early memories as a child in the factory where her mother worked. While the women, children and factory in *Yours Cheerfully* are all entirely fictional, Joan was the inspiration for the storyline and set me on my way to writing about working mothers during the war. I do hope she would be pleased with how Anne and her friends take on Mr Terry in this novel.

I would also like to thank Beryl Uren, Olive Newland and Jean Williams for answering my questions and bringing to life the experiences of girls and young women during the war. Thank you, Beryl, for letting me take over your sitting room! If I have managed to give the young women in this story spirit, it is because of women like you, Olive, Jean and Joan.

While researching this novel, wartime women's and news magazines have been invaluable, together with contemporaneous books: *Women in War Factories* (1943) by Amabel Williams-Ellis, *What of the Women: A Study of Women in Wartime* (1941) by Elaine Burton, *British Women at War* (1941) by M. D. Cox and *They Made Invasion Possible* (1944) by Peggy Scott are all fascinating if you can track them down. I also treasure a copy of *Workshop Sense: A Book Written for Munitions Workers and Other Entrants into Productive Industry* (1941) by W. A. J. Chapman. On the opening page it has a hand-drawn pencil sketch of what looks like a piece of machinery, and I often wonder who this little book belonged to.

I highly recommend *War's Forgotten Women* (2011) by Maureen Shaw & Helen D. Millgate, which opened my eyes to the reality faced by thousands of war widows, and *Women Workers in the Second World War: Production and Patriarchy in Conflict* (1984) by Penny Summerfield, which was hugely helpful in terms of understanding the hurdles women faced and their battles in tackling them.

Thank you to Edward Flint at the Royal Military Academy Sandhurst for his generous time and advice about the Royal Artillery, and for discussing Charles Mayhew's career as if he was a real person. Special thanks to Major General Karl

Ford for introducing me, despite my track record in asking him ridiculous questions!

If there are any errors in this book, it goes without saying they are entirely mine.

Thank you to my agent Jo Unwin, who is quite simply wonderful and without whom I would be hopeless. Thank you to Milly Reilly and Donna Greaves for all your support. JULA really is a dream agency.

Thank you to everyone at Picador and Pan Macmillan, especially Jeremy Trevathan and Philip Gwyn Jones, Katie Bowden, Hope Ndaba and all in Marketing, Emma Bravo, Charlotte Williams, Jade Tolley, Katie Tooke, Becky Lloyd, Nicholas Blake and Christine Jones, Emily Bromfield and all in the UK Sales Team. Very special thanks to my editor, Gillian Fitzgerald-Kelly, for her enormous patience and support, and to Camilla Elworthy for being the legend everyone said she was and the best fun on literary road trips even when I do drop sandwich all over the rental car.

Thank you to Francesca Main, who gave Emmy, Bunty, Mr Collins and me our chance in the first place, and who set this book on its journey and told me it would work!

Thank you to Deborah Schneider of Gelfman Schneider, the coolest, calmest person in stormy weather, and to Nan Graham and everyone at Scribner especially Ashley Gillam, Abigail Novak, Jason Chappell and Jaya Miceli. Very special thanks to my editor Kara Watson for her support, clarity and tireless championing of Emmy and Bunty from the very start.

Thank you to Jake Smith-Bosanquet, Alexander Cochran, Kate Burton, Matilda Ayris and everyone at C&W for sending my characters on so many travels around the world. I would also like to thank all my international publishers and in particular, the incredible translators who wrestle my words into other languages. How you manage with all the 1940s phrases will always amaze me.

The most enormous thank you to all the booksellers, librarians, book bloggers and reviewers who have cheered on, supported and spread the word about Emmy and Bunts. I know you all have an absolutely bonkers number of books to support and I can't thank you enough for everything you do.

Massive thanks and love to my family as ever – and thank goodness for Skype! One day when quarantines end, we will all be together again and then we will talk and laugh until our sides ache.

Thank you to *all* my friends. As it says at the very start of this book – this one is for you. Special thanks to Katie Fforde, Jo Thomas and Penny Parkes for being the most supportive writerly friends ever! And to Gail Cheetham, Rachel Fieldwick, Mary Ford, Brin Greenman, Nicki Pettitt, Sue Thearle and Janice Withey for when the road got a little bumpy for a time.

Finally, my huge thanks to the readers, especially for your kind words through tweets, posts, letters and emails. I know sequels are always a bit of a risk, so thank you for coming with me on this new adventure. I really hope you've enjoyed it.

I am very pleased to include the full UK team here.

Credits

Publisher, Pan Macmillan Adult Books   Jeremy Trevathan

Publisher, Picador   Philip Gwyn Jones

Commissioning Editor   Gillian Fitzgerald-Kelly

Finance Director, Pan Macmillan   Lara Borlenghi

Finance Director, Adult Publishing   Jo Mower

Head of Contracts   Clare Miller

Contracts Assistant   Senel Enver

Audio Publishing Director   Rebecca Lloyd

Audio Publishing Executive   Molly Robinson

Associate Publisher   Sophie Brewer

Managing Editor   Laura Carr

Editorial Manager   Nicholas Blake

Art and Design Director   James Annal

Jacket Designer   Katie Tooke

Jacket Illustrator   Emily Sutton

Interior Illustrations, with grateful credit to Elliot Jaffar

Studio Manager   Lloyd Jones

Head of Adult Production   Simon Rhodes

Senior Production Controller   Giacomo Russo

Production Controller   Bryony Croft

Text Design Manager   Lindsay Nash

Digital and Communications Director, Pan Macmillan   Sara Lloyd

Communications Director, Picador   Emma Bravo

Publicity Director   Camilla Elworthy

Head of Marketing   Katie Bowden

Audience Development Manager   Andy Joannou

Digital Publishing Senior Executive   Alex Ellis

Senior Brand Manager   Charlotte Williams

Senior Brand Executive   Jade Tolley

The UK Sales Team

Senior Trade Marketing Manager   Ruth Brooks

Trade Marketing Designer   Katie Bradburn

Sales and Marketing Executive   Alexandra Payne

International Director   Jonathan Atkins

Head of International Sales, Picador   Emily Scorer

Sales Director   Leanne Williams

Marketing and Communications Director   Lee Dibble

Senior Metadata and Content Manager   Eleanor Jones

Metadata Executive   Marisa Davies

Operations Manager   Kerry Pretty

Operations Administrator   Josh Craig

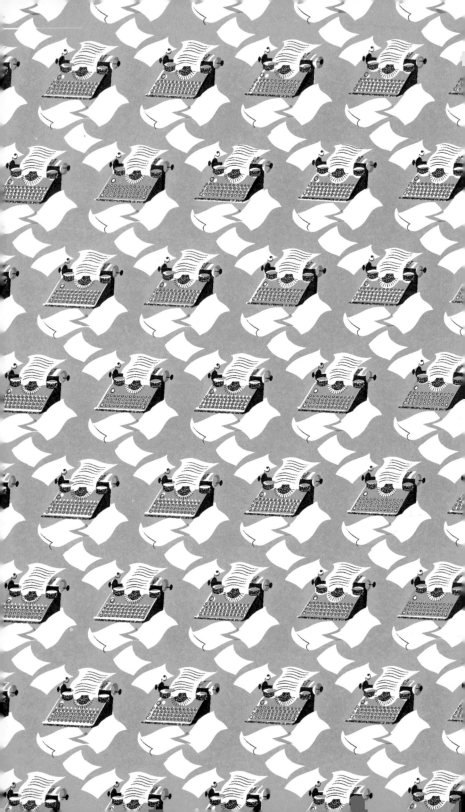